W9-CPO-784

Sweet Return

Anna Jeffrey

A SIGNET ECLIPSE BOOK

SIGNET ECLIPSE
Published by New American Library, a division of
Penguin Group (USA) Inc., 375 Hudson Street,
New York, New York 10014, USA
Penguin Group (Canada), 90 Eglinton Avenue East, Suite 700, Toronto,
Ontario M4P 2Y3, Canada (a division of Pearson Penguin Canada Inc.)
Penguin Books Ltd., 80 Strand, London WC2R 0RL, England
Penguin Ireland, 25 St. Stephen's Green, Dublin 2,
Ireland (a division of Penguin Books Ltd.)
Penguin Group (Australia), 250 Camberwell Road, Camberwell, Victoria 3124,
Australia (a division of Pearson Australia Group Pty. Ltd.)
Penguin Books India Pvt. Ltd., 11 Community Centre, Panchsheel Park,
New Delhi - 110 017, India
Penguin Group (NZ), 67 Apollo Drive, Rosedale, North Shore 0632,
New Zealand (a division of Pearson New Zealand Ltd.)
Penguin Books (South Africa) (Pty.) Ltd., 24 Sturdee Avenue,
Rosebank, Johannesburg 2196, South Africa

Penguin Books Ltd., Registered Offices:
80 Strand, London WC2R 0RL, England

First published by Signet Eclipse, an imprint of New American Library,
a division of Penguin Group (USA) Inc.

First Printing, December 2007
10 9 8 7 6 5 4 3 2 1

As always, this is for my biggest fans—my husband, George, and my daughter, Adrienne

ACKNOWLEDGMENTS

A special thanks to my neighbor, a retired oilman, for advising me on oil well drilling. Though I grew up in the West Texas oil patch, I've been away from it for many years and he helped refresh my memory.

Thanks also to hardworking, egg-laying hens everywhere. We really do take those birds for granted.

Chapter 1

The headlights of Joanna Walsh's pickup cast two wide fans of gold over a highway so dark it looked like black water. She had met only two cars since leaving the city limits of Hatlow, Texas. She saw just one other vestige of civilization. It showed in the form of occasional narrow columns of white lights from distant drilling rigs spearing the black sky like javelins.

Still half an hour from Lubbock, she pressed the accelerator more firmly—eighty, eighty-five, ninety . . .

Beside her, swallowed up by an old brown barn coat, Clova Cherry, her friend of thirteen years, huddled in the passenger seat. "I asked 'em if he's gonna make it," she said, "but they didn't give me no answer. I don't know what I'll do if he don't make it."

The "he" was Clova's twenty-nine-year-old son, Lane. Joanna heard the quaver in the older woman's voice, heard the fear, not just for Lane's well-being, but for her very future.

The phone call from Lubbock Memorial Hospital had come to Clova an hour earlier. Life Flight had choppered Lane to the hospital after EMTs pulled him from his pickup truck, which was found overturned in a ditch beside the highway that ran between Hatlow and Lovington, New Mexico. Clova, in turn, had awakened Joanna from a sound sleep and asked that she drive her the seventy-five miles from Hatlow to Lubbock. As one of the few friends Clova had, Joanna wouldn't have dreamed of saying no.

"He'll make it," Joanna said with confidence she didn't feel. She knew of too many times Hatlow citizens had been killed on the desolate Wacker County highways. Too often, the isolation of the locale and the monotony of an unremarkable, arrow-straight highway made drivers assume exceeding the speed limit was safe. On that thought, Joanna lifted her right foot and dropped her speed back to eighty. "Maybe he's just got a few broken bones."

"I'm prayin' for that. God knows he's had 'em before."

True enough, Joanna thought. Tonight's wreck wasn't Lane Cherry's first or even his second. Whatever his injuries were, they weren't his first, either. From his vehicular mishaps to his years of bronc and bull riding in rodeos, he boasted a host of trophy scars and pinned bones.

Clova said nothing else and Joanna was glad. At eighty miles an hour, she had to concentrate on not wrecking her own pickup.

At last they reached the outskirts of Lubbock. She well knew the location of Lubbock Memorial. Every Hatlow citizen who suffered serious injury or illness sooner or later found him- or herself at the regional medical facility. She made her way there over empty streets. With the exception of a few college kids, Lubbock citizens weren't out cruising at this hour.

Once they were in front of the reception desk inside the hospital's expansive modern entry, an aide hustled them to the basement, into a chilled, poorly lit waiting room outside the surgery suite. A nurse reported that Lane had been in surgery an hour and assured them someone would speak to them soon.

Joanna and Clova were the only people present in

the stark waiting room. Clova wilted onto the edge of the seat of a beige armchair, the worry in her brown eyes almost palpable. She didn't look well in general. Her skin had a pallor and dark crescents showed under her eyes. She had teetered on the verge of breaking down for most of the trip from Hatlow.

"Looks like we could be here a while," Joanna said. "There must be a coffee machine or something around here somewhere. I'll get you—"

"Thanks, hon, but I don't need nothin'." Clova broke into a hard, raspy cough. It had been with her for weeks. It sounded like a smoker's cough, but Clova didn't smoke and never had, as far as Joanna knew. Recovered, Clova inhaled a great breath and let it out, her eyes vacant and seemingly focused on nothing. Joanna couldn't guess what she might be thinking.

She sank into an armchair beside her friend, finally acknowledging the chill in the large room. The decor— beige tile floor, square furniture, abstract paintings of multicolored squares hanging on the walls—did nothing to add warmth to what felt like a subzero temperature. As she scanned their surroundings, she thought of how the sharp edges and hard, cold surfaces were so much like Clova Parker Cherry's life.

Joanna began to shiver. She was wearing jeans and a T-shirt. In such a hurry when she threw on her clothes and left her house, she hadn't thought of a jacket or a sweater. She picked up her purse and stood up. "I'm freezing. I'm going to find something hot to drink."

Still wired from driving eighty to ninety miles an hour most of the trip from Hatlow, she had to move around. She hung her purse on her shoulder and walked out of the waiting room into a vacant hallway. A distance up the tiled corridor, she saw a pink neon sign pointing to a snack bar. There she found two pots of coffee simmering on hot plates, but no one manning the cash register. On the Formica pay-out counter sat a cardboard box with a slot in the top and a crude, hand-printed sign requesting the customers use the honor system.

She dug a couple of singles from her purse and stuffed them into the slotted box. She poured coffee into two Styrofoam cups, her weary mind wandering to why she had just raced up a lonely highway in the middle of the night after working a fifteen-hour day. Oh, she knew the answer well enough. Either her mother or her sister, or both, reminded her daily of her penchant for worrying about and taking on someone else's problems at the expense of solving her own. Fretting over a friend's troubles was one of her great weaknesses. With such a reputation to live up to, how could she not be doing exactly what she was doing now?

She carried the two cups to a waist-high counter and sprinkled a packet of Sweet'N Low and poured two packets of artificial cream into one. She didn't really like coffee but could tolerate it if she changed the flavor enough. She desired it tonight because it was hot and she was still bleary-eyed from lack of sleep.

As she stirred the coffee, she began to worry about whether Lane Cherry would come out of this alive or if he might be unable to work for some long period of time, and how either of those outcomes would impact the old Parker ranch. Clova had been struggling to hang on to it ever since Joanna had known her. Lane was more or less the manager. When he was sober and at home, that is.

As she returned to the waiting room with the two cups of coffee, Joanna remembered Clova's other son, who lived in California. His name was Dalton and he was roughly the same age as Joanna's older sister. In high school, Lanita had dated him once or twice. Joanna knew he was a photographer whose work had been published in big, expensive-looking books. She had seen them stacked on the coffee table and the end tables in Clova's living room. But that was the extent of her knowledge about him. As many times as she had visited Clova's home, she had thumbed through those books only rarely.

She handed Clova the cup of hot black coffee. "I brought you some just in case you change your mind."

Clova gave her a wan smile and took the cup. "Thanks, hon."

Joanna seated herself beside the older woman again, resting her elbows on the chair arms and looking at her across her shoulder. "I was just thinking. Lane could be laid up a while. Why don't you call Dalton and tell him you need help. Maybe he could come to the ranch and stay a few days. Or even a few weeks."

Clova drew herself ever deeper into her coat, sniffed and shook her head. "No use talkin' 'bout Dalton. Or tryin' to talk *to* him. He ain't never home. He don't care nothin' 'bout us, anyway, Joanna. And I don't blame him. Back when it mattered, we didn't act like we cared much about him."

Joanna didn't know what she meant by that. Maybe it had something to do with what everyone in Hatlow said about Dalton being mistreated by his stepfather and, indirectly, by his mother. Hatlow was a place where few "secrets" were secret. She refused to believe Clova had ever mistreated anyone, especially one of her children. Later she might ask her about it, but not tonight.

"I know you need to get your cattle to the sale. I think Harvey McAdoo's kid will be home another couple of weeks before he goes back to school. He can probably help you out. I'm sure he wouldn't mind earning a little extra money."

"Lord God, Joanna, I ain't sure I could pay him.

Lane ain't got any hospital insurance, you know. No telling what this bill's gonna cost." She closed her eyes and rubbed a furrowed brow with her fingertips.

At the hopelessness of the woman's situation, Joanna released a sigh and stared at the tan liquid in her own cup. Her head had begun to ache. Her eyes felt hot and gritty, as if she had spent the day in a sandstorm. At this moment, problem solving didn't rate high on her list of priorities. She was worn out.

And dammit, she was freezing to the point of shivering. Didn't anyone know how to turn off the air-conditioning in this place? Cold-enough-to-freeze-fire might be fine in the daytime when the outside temperature climbed to a hundred, but at two a.m., after it had dropped forty degrees, it was cold. She set her coffee on the table beside her chair and rubbed her palms up and down her arms for warmth.

Despite knowing she couldn't add one more chore to her own to-do list, she said, "I can help you with some chores when I come out to tend the hens and gather the eggs."

Somehow she would find the time.

Before more could be said, a woman dressed in blue scrubs bustled in and quickstepped to a desk at the end of the room. A highway patrolman from Texas's Department of Public Safety followed her and waited while she opened drawers, brought out papers and attached them to a clipboard. The two talked in low tones. Joanna strained her ears but could make out only snippets of their conversation. The words that came to her in capital letters were "blood alcohol test." *Oh, hell.*

Joanna had feared Lane was drunk. In recent months, he had spent a lot of his time in that state. She glanced at Clova, who had to have heard the same words but appeared to be unaffected.

Joanna had seen her close her mind to a problem

related to Lane before. Clova Cherry was a tough, strong woman in many ways. Somehow, in the face of punishing obstacles and monumental odds stacked against her, she had held together the cattle ranch she inherited from her family. But Joanna had been acquainted with her long enough to know she wasn't strong emotionally.

They had been friends ever since Joanna returned to Hatlow thirteen years ago to work as a hairdresser and nail tech. Clova was one of the first Hatlow citizens to let Joanna do her hair. Brave on her part, Joanna always thought. Clova's willingness to let a struggling twenty-two-year-old earn twenty dollars for cutting and perming her hair had forged an unwavering loyalty in Joanna.

Back then, Clova's hair had been coal black and hung straight as a string, genetic evidence of her Comanche ancestry. Her daddy had claimed to be related to Quanah Parker, so Clova claimed that, too. Tonight, strands of black and gray hair had come loose from the bun on the back of her head and she looked to be held together by a skeleton as fragile as toothpicks. She was somewhere around fifty-five years old, younger than Joanna's mother, but she looked ten years older. Weathered by winter's blue northers, summer's blazing sun and the hot, dry wind that showed no mercy in its ceaseless sweep of the high plains, Texas Panhandle ranchwomen often looked older than their years.

Since Clova didn't show a reaction to what the nurse and the DPS trooper had said, Joanna didn't mention it. Conversation only added to her fatigue. She leaned back in the chair, propped her neck on its cold steel back and closed her eyes, her thoughts settling on Dalton Parker.

Clova might not want to talk about him, but other people in Hatlow did. In a West Texas town of seven thousand, he was one of the few who had ever climbed to even token celebrity. Joanna hadn't heard much about him of late, but she remembered that in high school he had been a hunky football player. Quarterback, she recalled. Everyone said he was smart. He had a high IQ, had been valedictorian of his class. Most of the girls in school had a crush on him, she among them. Strictly from a distance, though, in her case, because in truth, she had known him only by sight.

Then it dawned on her that with him being in the same grade as Lanita, he must be thirty-eight or so. She opened her eyes and looked at Clova again.

"Dalton's what, nearly forty?"

"He turned thirty-seven back in April."

Hearing the number spoken reminded Joanna that Clova had been a teenager when her oldest son was born. Joanna knew she hadn't finished high school, and was sure that when Clova was a teenager, unmarried pregnant girls didn't stay in school. "When's the last time you called him?"

Clova shook her head. "I don't call him. I used to, but I quit. He's always gone somewhere."

"Then when's the last time he called you?"

"He don't call me, neither. We don't talk much anymore."

"Where's he living now?"

"Los Angeles, far as I know."

Joanna felt renewed compassion at the gap that existed between Clova and her son, but feeling sorry didn't solve the problem at hand, which was the operation of a working cattle ranch with no man around to do a man's work.

Joanna Faye Walsh never let trouble fester. At some point in her life, without consciously knowing it, she formed the notion that it was better to face a crisis head-on and do something about it, even if what you did was wrong. She could thank her mom for that attitude. Alvadean Walsh could not—and had never been able to—deal with so much as a simple problem without turning it into a calamity. Not that Joanna didn't love her mother, but Mom, plain and simple, was a dingbat.

In self-defense, as Joanna had grown up, she had morphed into a person who "fixed things." That trait had seen her through a chaotic childhood. That same trait contributed to the hectic disorder that sometimes existed in her present life. Every day, she fought the compulsion to insert herself into other people's business in some circumstance or other.

"Do you still have Dalton's number?" she asked Clova.

"I got an old number. I don't know if it's any good now."

"Look, give it to me and I'll call him for you. It might be better for a stranger to call him anyway."

Without a word, Clova picked up a stained tooled leather purse from the floor and pawed through it. She came up with a worn address book, the kind you get for free at Christmas from some insurance company that wants your business. It was badly frayed and the loose pages were held together by a red rubber band. With work-worn fingers, Clova slowly removed the binding, found a ragged page and handed it over. "Just take the whole page," she said. "I don't need it anyway."

Joanna looked down at it and saw one phone number. No name. Just a faded number. "I left my cell at home on the charger, but there must be a pay phone around here somewhere. I can call him collect. It's two hours earlier in California."

"Wait, Joanna. Give me back that number. On second thought, I don't want you callin' him."

"Why not?"

Clova looked down at her hands, which were clenched into a tight knot. "I don't want him thinkin' I call him up only when I got problems."

But he's your son. Joanna looked at the number again, doing her best to commit it to memory. "Okay. But I think you should call him." She handed the page back to Clova, who returned it to the tattered address book.

Joanna ran the seven digits through her mind again, knowing Clova wouldn't call him. If Joanna ever saw home again, she vowed, she just might make that call anyway. If she didn't, who would come to Clova's rescue?

Chapter 2

After Lane had been brought out of surgery, barely alive and bandaged and mummified by a plaster cast, a stubble-jawed surgeon met for a few minutes with Clova. Joanna stood in the background and kept her silence, but her weary mind translated the medical jargon into real words she understood: busted spleen, broken ribs, broken collarbone, shattered left leg. Lane was more hurt than either she or his mother had imagined.

"Death" and "crippled" were the next words that floated into Joanna's mind, but the doctor offset her thoughts with a positive prognosis.

Still, a single tear leaked from a corner of Clova's eye and a shard of anger pierced Joanna. Lane Cherry, at times, had been the most irresponsible twenty-nine-year-old man she could think of, with little apparent consideration for how his behavior affected those around him. Because he was younger than her own thirty-five years, Joanna had known him only since he had become an adult. His diligent pursuit of wine, women and song was a common topic of conversation in Joanna's Salon & Supplies, the Hatlow beauty salon/beauty supply/janitorial supply store she owned.

Tonight Lane had broken more than bones; he had broken his mother's heart. Again.

Soon she and Clova were on the road back to Hatlow. They rode in silence for the most part. Clova showed little emotion and Joanna wanted to say nothing to make her feel worse.

They arrived just as the world turned from darkness to predawn's translucence. Joanna dropped Clova off with a brief good-bye and a promise to see her later.

The Parker ranch was located ten miles south of town, but Joanna lived inside the city limits. By the time she reached her own cozy cottage, she had been up three hours short of twenty-four. Her exhausted body felt as if it had just completed a marathon run.

In her garage, while she waited for the door to rumble to a close, she keyed in the number of the beauty salon and left a voice mail message for her mom to pick up when she opened. It was too early to call Mom at home.

Joanna entered the house through the utility room door but didn't turn on a light. On her way to her bedroom, she trudged through the kitchen, then the dining room, skirting furniture made colorless by dawn's filmy light. She plopped her purse on the dining table as she passed it.

With her last ounce of energy she changed into a pair of knit shorts and a holey T-shirt, then climbed into bed, thinking all the while that her life was killing her. Thirty-five was too damned old for this staying-up-all-night shit.

The phone's warble jarred her awake. She popped up on the edge of the mattress and grabbed the receiver, her brain cells and eyesight only half functioning. She grunted a greeting.

"Hey, you, rise and shine." Shari Huddleston, Joanna's best friend. Shari, her husband, Jay, and Joanna had started kindergarten together. Brothers and sisters couldn't know one another any better.

Joanna shoved a hank of hair off her face and managed a harrumph. "What time is it?"

"High noon. Where were you last night? We waited for you."

A frown creased Joanna's brow. She just now remembered she had told Shari she might drop in at Sylvia's Café after work and join her, Jay and Owen Luck for supper. "Crap, Shari, I forgot all about it."

Not entirely a true statement, but Joanna considered it a tactful fib rather than a lie. Owen Luck was a newly divorced accountant who looked after Shari and Jay's business bookkeeping and their taxes. Both he and his ex-wife were long-standing customers in Joanna's Salon & Supplies. And Hatlow was the gossip capital of Texas. Even if Joanna found Owen personally appealing, which she didn't, going out with him wasn't worth losing a customer. She had told them she would meet them in the first place only because Shari had nagged her into it.

"I told Owen you probably got tied up," Shari said. "We tried to call you on your cell, but all we got was voice mail."

Glancing down at her fingers, Joanna toyed with a hangnail, reluctant to reveal last night's whereabouts and fuel a gossip bomb that had probably already exploded. "I didn't have my cell with me. Was Owen mad?"

"A little. He ate and left. Said he was going over to the bars at the state line."

Joanna's mouth flatlined, but she wasn't surprised. Many Hatlow citizens, including Joanna herself, sometimes sought to interrupt the sameness of small-town life in the bars and nightclubs at the New Mexico state line. Not even a beer could be bought legally in Wacker County.

Shari chortled. "He said he wanted to go where he

could find a woman who was more interested in him than in a bunch of damn chickens."

That remark brought a scowl to Joanna's mouth. Everyone in Hatlow, including all of her friends, thought her poultry-and-egg venture was a dive off the deep end. And lately, she had to admit, she had entertained similar thoughts herself. "It's just as well. One thing I do not need is a newly divorced guy crying on my shoulder about his ex-wife and three kids. Besides, Shari, he probably spends all his money on child support."

"Yeah, yeah. At least he can afford the price of supper. So where were you?" Joanna recognized the determination in her friend's voice.

"I hate to tell you. But you've probably already heard about Lane Cherry's wreck. I drove Clova to the hospital in Lubbock."

"My God, Joanna. That must've taken all night. I did hear something about him having a wreck. How bad was he hurt?"

Joanna didn't even ask how Shari had heard. Gossip in Hatlow seemed to move through the ether from out of nowhere. "Pretty bad. Broken bones. Internal injuries. He's out of commission for a good long while."

"Uh-oh. That'll upset Megan Richardson. She's sleeping with him, you know. She's been telling everybody in town what a hot lay he is." Shari giggled. "She says he's hung like a bull. I hope, for her sake, that part of him wasn't damaged."

Joanna's shoulders sagged as she stared at a cheap framed print of a wolf face on her wall. When it came to relationships between men and women, Shari's first thought was always of sex. Probably why she had given birth to four kids. As a girl growing up, Joanna's source of sex education might have been her big sister, but as an adult, it had been and continued to be Shari

Huddleston. "Shari, forgodsakes. He could have died. He could still die. He's in ICU."

"I'm just repeating what Megan said."

"Well, I don't know anything about his bedroom prowess, but if that's all Megan's interested in, she might have to go elsewhere. If Lane makes it through this, I imagine he might not be *laying* for the rest of the year."

The digital clock on Joanna's nightstand whirred and clicked past one o'clock. "And speaking of laying, I've got to get going. I've got to get out to Clova's and check on my hens and gather my eggs."

She pictured Shari rolling her eyes.

"Did he run into another car or what?" Shari asked, persistent in her quest to learn more details.

"Rolled his pickup. Hit a power pole. Or vice versa."

"Where at?"

"On the Lovington highway, just this side of the state line."

"Good God. How weird is that? There aren't that many power poles along that highway."

"I know. I guess one just happened to be standing in the right place."

"I'll bet he was partying at those joints at the state line. It's a wonder he didn't run into Owen Luck. Was he drunk?"

Joanna almost said, *Hell, yes, he was drunk,* but then she remembered that Shari worked for the insurance agency that probably carried Lane's auto insurance policy, if he had one. She suddenly didn't want to be disseminating information to her. "I don't know," she lied. "He was already in surgery when Clova and I got there."

"I hope Clova's okay. That boy's given her a lot of grief."

"He's not a boy. And that's the disgusting part. But, yeah, Clova's okay. She's used to getting bad news about Lane."

"Bless her heart. Now would be a good time for Dalton to come home and help her. It's a crying shame to have two grown sons and neither one of them does a damn thing for her. If my boys grow up to treat me like that, I'll just kill 'em."

"Shari, I've got to get going," Joanna said.

"Wait a minute. Do you want Jay to fix up another date with Owen?"

To Joanna's annoyance, Shari and Jay constantly searched for "a man for Joanna." "No, Shari. I'm not interested."

"Joanna, listen to yourself. I swear to God, you're gonna die an old maid."

"Shari. I've got to go."

After she hung up, Joanna called the beauty salon and told her mom she had returned to the land of the living and that she would be in as soon as she tended the hens.

"You don't have to go out there," Mom said. "I got your message 'bout you bein' up all night. Alicia come in and I sent her out. She didn't get all the eggs, but she filled up the feeders and changed the drinkin' water."

Thank God. Alicia Garza was Joanna's conscientious seventeen-year-old employee who helped her do almost everything. She worked for Joanna's Salon & Supplies part-time and was one of the few people who didn't make fun of Joanna. She was so fascinated by the egg business and the hens, Joanna let her choose names for the new chicks. She didn't have to worry about the teenager doing a poor job.

Joanna showered and shampooed, then dried her hair and dressed in a T-shirt, a pair of Cruel Girl jeans and boots, her attire for every occasion these days. A

few dresses hung in her closet, but she couldn't remember the last time she had worn one. She brushed
on a scant layer of makeup, then spritzed herself with
something that smelled like roses. Since she sold cos-
metics and fragrances at the beauty supply store, she
tried to always wear her products. The mirrored oval
tray that sat on her bathroom counter held so many
bottles of various colognes and perfumes, she didn't
even concern herself with the brand or name. She just
picked one and sprayed it.

She moved on into the kitchen. The sight of her
purse on the dining table brought thoughts of Clova's
oldest son back to her. At the hospital, while she still
remembered his phone number, she had gone into
the ladies' room and written it on a grocery store
receipt she found in her purse. She chewed on her
lower lip, wishing Clova hadn't asked her not to call
Dalton. The compulsion to do it anyway was almost
overwhelming. The woman needed help from somewhere.

You're butting in, her sister would tell her. But was
Lanita going to come to Hatlow, go out to the Parker
ranch and help Clova? No.

*Stickin' your nose in other people's business gets you
in a lotta trouble.* Her mom had said those words to
her just last week. Was Mom going out to the Parker
ranch to help Clova? No.

Still undecided, Joanna veered her thoughts to
something she *could* decide on: food. She peered into
the refrigerator and saw poor pickings—sliced ham
with an expired date on the package, sliced processed
cheese and stale bread. No telling how long the bread
had been there, but it appeared to be free of mold.
She smoothed mayonnaise on a slice, added a squirt
of mustard and folded it over some ham and cheese.
It's fine, she told herself as she filled a glass with ice
cubes and Diet Pepsi.

She carried her lunch to the dining table. The purse that held the California phone number sat there staring back at her like a dare. What would she say to a son who hadn't returned to visit his mother more than a dozen times in twenty years? Without sounding like a hysterical lunatic, how could she convey to him the seriousness of his brother's condition and the gravity of his mother's dilemma?

Through all of her dithering over the phone call, Clova's state of mind, Lane's condition and a million other niggling little worries, the bottom line kept pushing its way toward the forefront of her thoughts. Joanna hadn't wanted to acknowledge it, even to herself, because she hadn't wanted to seem callous. But she couldn't forget that her two hundred hens lived at the Parker ranch and she had mortgaged the very roof over her head to pay for her free-range egg business. Didn't that fact alone make her interest in what happened to the Parker ranch extend beyond caring about Clova and Lane as friends?

She easily convinced herself that it did. On a note of determination, she carried the phone and the yellow legal pad she kept beside it back to the table. While she ate, she made a few notes—"talking points," the sophisticated businesspeople called them.

Clova had told her Dalton traveled a lot. Since Joanna wasn't sure he would even be at home, she decided to abandon talking points and wrote out the voice mail message she would read if necessary.

She finished her sandwich, then dug the receipt from her purse and smoothed out the wrinkles. Maybe Clova would never know she had called him. The decision to butt in made, she summoned her nerve and keyed in the California number. Sure enough, she got voice mail. She left her rehearsed message and her business number, but the machine cut her off before she could leave her complete home number.

* * *

Dalton Parker had no sooner killed his truck engine in his garage and scooted out when Candace Carlisle handed him a note. *Uh-oh.* She never came into the garage except to get into her car.

"A woman from Texas left a personal message on voice mail," Candace said.

A pulse jumped in Dalton's stomach. These days he knew no one in Texas but his family. "Shit," he mumbled under his breath. "Okay, thanks."

He stepped back to his truck bed and lifted out a heavy cardboard box filled with cans of paint and supplies he had just bought at Home Depot. He intended to clean and repaint his office and his studio. He carried the box over and thunked it onto the wooden workbench he had built on one side of the garage.

"Who is she, Dalton?"

He turned and looked closer at Candace's face, saw a shimmer of tears in her blue eyes and made a mental groan. "I don't know. She must be who she says she is. A friend of my mother's."

Candace turned sharply and left the garage, her high-heeled shoes clacking out anger in quick little steps. As Dalton watched her go, he sighed. He still couldn't sort out exactly how she came to be living in his house, but he knew himself well enough to know that in a weak moment he must have invited her. He loved sex. He didn't always love women, but they controlled the thing that he loved. Ergo, Candace Carlisle had moved in.

Inside the house, he went to his office, made dim by a huge bush outside the window, and played back his voice mail messages—his agent in New York, his editor, his insurance agent. Finally he reached one from a voice he had never heard before:

"Mr. Parker, this is Joanna Walsh in Hatlow, Texas. I'm a friend of your mother's. You might

*not remember me, but we knew each other in
school. Sort of. You dated my sister. I'm calling
to let you know your brother was in a bad wreck
early this morning and he's in the ICU in Lubbock Memorial Hospital. His leg was crushed and
the doctors aren't willing to say yet how it's gonna
turn out. Your mom's doing the best she can, but
she could really use some help. She was real sick
this past spring and isn't completely well, and she
can't afford to hire a hand to replace Lane. She
and Lane don't have any health insurance, either.
I'm hoping you can come home to the ranch for
a while. If you want to call me, I have two phone
numbers—806-555 . . ."*

Had she said, *Come home to the ranch*? Dalton
could almost laugh. The Parker ranch hadn't been his
home since his mother married Earl Cherry more than
thirty years ago. It might have been where he had
spent his youth, but it hadn't been his home.

Standing behind his desk, he listened for the second
time to the message. The name Walsh had a familiar
ring, but he couldn't associate a person or an event
with it. And he didn't remember any of the girls he
dated in high school. As for the message itself, it was
only an extension of problems and depressing times
from long ago. Those he did remember, though he
didn't want to.

He plopped into his ergonomic desk chair, his
thoughts settling on his little brother. He recalled
times before when he had heard of Lane's different
accidents and injuries. He had heard of him having
car wrecks before. Dalton only hoped the little bastard
hadn't been driving drunk. A vain hope, he knew,
thinking back on some of his phone conversations with
his mother. Apparently the kid had craved liquor ever
since he was old enough to drink and drive. In that

way, he was like his old man. Come to think of it, a
session with whiskey and a sharp curve in the highway
between Lovington and Hatlow had sent Earl Cherry
to purgatory.

He propped an elbow on his chair arm and rubbed
his eyes with his fingers, family issues pricking at him.
He didn't have time to make a trip to Texas. He
looked across the room to the corner of his office. His
cameras, camera bags and other equipment, as well as
duffel bags and backpacks, still lay in a heap. He had
been home a month, but he hadn't been able to muster the enthusiasm or the energy to even sort them.
All he had done was unpack his dirty clothes.

He was taking a break. And he needed it, he had
to admit. He had shot some priceless photographs during the three-month tour from which he had just returned: a month in Afghanistan, a month in Iraq and
a month in Israel. The book he was putting together
would be the best he had done yet. But the experience
had drained him physically, mentally and emotionally.
And the last leg of it had damn near killed him. A
suicide bomber had detonated himself inside a bus
stopped in front of a café in Haifa where Dalton happened to be eating lunch. His custom of sitting in the
back of the room had saved him that day from what
could have been a fatal result.

As an American photojournalist documenting con-
troversial people, places and events in the Middle
East, his MO had been to go about his business as
inconspicuously as possible. Being beheaded with a
dull knife held even less appeal than being blown to
bits in a café. Through the years, curiosity and a thirst
for adventure had led him into any number of hair-
raising incidents. But the one in Haifa had been
enough of a close call to make him decide to wait a
spell to allow himself to tame the nightmares before
tackling another of the world's hellholes.

He needed to do something simple, he had told himself, and had chosen to paint his office. He did *not* need to make a trip to Texas to visit his family. By any stretch of the imagination, that would be anything but simple.

Chapter 3

Well after noon, Joanna put in an appearance at her downtown shop. She took customers in the beauty salon only one day a week nowadays, and those were her friends and patrons of long standing. She and her mom shared a chair. Joanna did still attend schools to stay up with the latest styling trends and products. Thankfully, she had no difficulty keeping hairdressers to man the other three chairs in the salon.

After greeting everyone, deflecting conversation about Lane Cherry's accident and parrying an attempt by Judy Harrison to arrange an introduction to a newly divorced cousin in Denver City, Joanna finally made it to her office. It was nothing more than a desk tucked behind a half wall in the back of the long room that was the retail store, and it offered no privacy. To keep her mother from snooping, Joanna was cautious with what she left in plain sight or even in desk drawers and had password protected everything on her computer.

She had no sooner sat down than a ping came from the chime mounted on the wall over the plateglass front door, the signal that a customer had entered the store. She stood up, looked over the half wall and saw Bert Marshall, Hatlow's elementary school custodian. "Hi, Bert. Be right with you."

"Hi, Joanna," he said from across the room. "Need

a couple o' gallons of that high-powered disinfectant floor wash."

Joanna's Salon & Supplies was Hatlow's only janitorial supply. For that matter, it was the only one in half a dozen surrounding counties except for Lubbock. After Joanna bought the beauty salon and the building that housed it ten years ago, she had more space than she needed for the salon. She hired a carpenter to build a wall between the salon and what was now the store area and added beauty products and fragrances.

After the construction work was completed, while cleaning up the disorder, she stumbled across another need—this one for easily available janitorial supplies. On a hunch, she converted one entire wall of the beauty supply store to a display of commercial cleaning products and rental cleaning equipment.

Now the janitorial products produced as much income as the beauty supplies. Customers drove from other small towns to the south to keep from driving to Lubbock and dealing with the traffic madness. Most small-town West Texans, used to the wide-open spaces, equated a trip to Lubbock with a trip to hell. If requested to do so, Joanna even provided shipping.

She walked out into the store to talk to Bert, a wiry-haired older gentleman and a Hatlow native. "What needs disinfecting at the elementary school?"

"Oh, nothing different," Bert answered. "Just trying to keep the place clean and wipe out a few germs." He reached into his shirt pocket and produced a purchase order from the Wacker County School District. "Those kids sure do mess things up." He bent over the counter and filled in the blanks on the purchase order forms. "Makes you wonder what they're like at home."

"I know what you mean," Joanna said absently, though she really didn't. She had no children. And at her age, unmarried and too busy to even think about kowtowing to some man, she wasn't likely to have any.

"I heard about Lane Cherry's wreck." Bert shook his gray head.

"Yeah, I suppose everybody has by now."

"That boy's gonna kill hisself one o' these days."

Joanna had heard that comment about Lane for years, but she was unconvinced. He seemed to have nine lives. "I know."

"How's Clova holding up under the strain?"

"Oh, you know Clova. She's the Energizer Bunny. She just keeps going and going."

"Do ya reckon Dalton will come back and help her out?"

All of a sudden, everyone seemed to be interested in what Dalton Parker might do next. "Who knows? Maybe."

"I heard he's over in I-raq taking pictures."

Joanna's expectations plummeted. If he wasn't even in the country, he wouldn't be coming back to Texas to help out his mother anytime soon. *Now what?* she wondered. "Really? I hadn't heard that."

The custodian gathered four plastic gallon jugs and brought them back to the cash register. "Gonna be a hot one today. We'll be lucky if we don't get one o' them barn flatteners tonight."

Joanna glanced through the shop's plate-glass windows and saw an overcast sky. The temperature had already climbed to ninetysomething before she left home. Bert was right. Conditions were coming together for a violent storm in the evening. She needed to get out to Clova's early and pen up the hens.

"How's your egg business doin'?"

"It's okay, Bert. It's doing okay. In fact, I'm out in front of my business plan. I'm hoping to show a profit this year." An exaggeration, but not a total fib. She believed putting a positive spin on things did no harm.

"How're those hens gettin' along with those donkeys?"

Joanna had adopted two rescue donkeys from the Bureau of Land Management in New Mexico, having read that donkeys, while harmless to chickens, would frighten away other predators. "Great," Joanna answered. "They're buds."

Bert gave an old man's *heh-heh-heh.* "I laugh ever' time I think about donkeys and chickens grazin' with the cows on that ranch. Lord, Earl Cherry's prob'ly spinnin' in his grave."

Joanna huffed. "From what I've heard about him, he's lucky if that's the worst that's happening to him."

"Yep. Ol' Earl was cut from a different cloth, that's fer sure. I s'pose when he was livin', he was awful unkind to his family."

As he lugged his purchases toward the front door, she stepped ahead of him, opened the door and held it for him.

"You stay out of the weather, now, you hear?" he said.

"I will," she assured him.

As she completed the paperwork on the sale of supplies to the school, her mother came in from the salon. Mom might work six days a week, but she kept banker's hours. "Taking a break?" Joanna asked her.

"I wish you'd make up your mind just what business you're gonna be in, Joanna. Everybody in the shop was gigglin' 'bout you sellin' disinfectant from the same counter you sell perfume and permanent waves."

Just as Hatlowites made good-natured fun of Joanna's egg business, they made fun of her other businesses, too. She tried to ignore the jeers. Multidimensional, she called herself. She wanted to live in Hatlow, but with the town having almost no job market, she'd had to figure out how to make a living on her own. If she hadn't been able to mold it all together and make it work, she would have had to stay in Lubbock, where she had gone to college for a year and beauty school for another year and worked as a hairdresser and nail tech for a short time. Or she might have had to move to Amarillo, or, God forbid, Fort Worth. She would hate any of those options. "Mom, do you not have any customers this morning?"

"I'm waitin' on Ida Crocker. She's comin' in for a perm."

"Please tell me you asked her to leave Charlie at home."

Charlie was a miniature Yorkie weighing less than four pounds, but he barked louder than a St. Bernard and snarled and snapped at other patrons who came into the beauty shop. He usually left a deposit in some corner or under a station so that someone had to crawl under and clean up his souvenir after Ida left.

"I always ask her, but she does what she wants. I hate to say too much. That dog's all she's got, and I need the business."

"Hm." Joanna returned to her office, unlocked a file cabinet drawer and lifted out a small stack of invoices.

Her mother followed and braced a shoulder against the doorjamb, blocking the doorway. "I heard Lane Cherry's in a bad way. What's Clova gonna do now?"

Good question, Joanna thought, dropping into her desk chair and sorting the invoices on her desktop. "Whatever she has to, Mom. You know Clova."

"Suzy Martinez from the bank said she's in real bad shape. Financially, I mean. She could lose that ranch."

Ah, gossip. The beauty salon was a conduit of unparalleled effectiveness in spreading it. With no fewer than three full-time hairdressers and their patrons present most of the time, every triumph and tragedy that occurred in Hatlow was picked apart and analyzed daily. Only occasionally in a malicious way, Joanna was always quick to point out.

She didn't look up from her sorting task. "Suzy shouldn't be coming to the beauty shop and talking about the bank's customers. That's private information. I just wonder what she tells about *my* business."

"She don't mean no harm. She's just concerned."

"Mom, she has a vicious mouth and it's scary that she has access to everyone in town's financial information. Don't you need to get ready for Ida?"

"Yeah." Mom looked across the store and out the wide display window. "And here she comes now. Carrying Charlie."

"Just try to make sure she hangs on to him," Joanna said in her cranky voice. Suzy, a Farmers Bank employee, talking about Clova's money, or lack of it, in the beauty shop had rankled her and compounded her bad mood. "Even if Charlie was a sweet dog instead of a pest, you know we can't have even a little dog running around the shop. It's unsanitary. He's supposed to be a lap dog, so make him stay on her lap."

"My Lord, Joanna, I don't know where you got such a bee in your bonnet about keeping everything so damn clean. You sure didn't inherit that from me."

No kidding, Joanna thought, glancing up at her mother with an arch look.

Alvadean pushed away from the doorjamb and went out into the beauty supply store. Joanna heard the front door chime, then heard her mother greeting Ida.

Joanna booted up her computer, opened the file she had named EGGS and began to study the records. She did that often. As she perused the record of the baby chicks purchased compared to the hens lost or the ones that had stopped laying, her thoughts traveled back to how she came to own two hundred hens.

She had Clova to thank. Two and a half years ago, at the older friend's urging, Joanna started with fifty pullets. Little by little, despite a constant battle with predators and the missteps of learning how to cull the roosters and retain and manage the hens, the flock of fifty had grown to two hundred.

Why Clova had wanted to see her in the egg business, Joanna didn't know, but she had a suspicion. She thought it might have something to do with the fact that Clova was a lonely person whose two grown kids ignored her. Joanna believed she longed for company. She felt as if Clova looked at her sort of as the daughter she never had and figured the chickens living at her place would ensure that Joanna would be out to the Parker ranch often.

Now Joanna had a variety of hens, a few exotics along with a majority of the more common breeds of layers. She ended up with blue eggs, green eggs, even some she called "khaki" and many brown eggs. The exotic hens didn't lay as well as the more traditional layers, but it was fun to take "Easter eggs" to market. Her customers in Lubbock and Amarillo liked them, too. She collected three dollars per dozen at wholesale or five dollars at retail. Customers didn't seem to balk at the prices. That fact blew Joanna away. A few years back, she wouldn't have believed someone would pay more than forty cents an egg for a dozen free-range eggs. But there it was. Another fad. The American way.

In spite of those numbers, she wasn't making a fortune. The business barely paid its way, and during some months, she had to dip into the funds from the beauty salon or the retail store to pay for something related to the egg business. She fretted day and night over how to make more profit from the eggs. If the business made more money, she could hire someone to work at it full-time and not be so tied down herself. But alas, she knew only too well that a small entrepreneur, if she couldn't afford to hire help, had to be willing to do any and every task required.

Sometimes she felt guilty about using Clova's land rent free, but every time she looked at the egg business's financial records, that guilt slunk into the background. The plain truth was that if she were required to pay rent to Clova or anyone else, the egg business would be in the hole monthly. To free herself of guilt and a constant feeling of obligation, she needed her own little piece of real estate. In West Texas, land was cheap, but now the chance of her finding enough extra money to buy some of it was almost nonexistent.

At one point, Joanna had held the Pollyanna-ish notion that the egg venture might grow into a business she could sell, then invest the proceeds in a retirement fund. She needed a retirement fund, having started to consider that she might be alone and self-supporting until the day she died.

Thinking about the Parker ranch took her mind back to Clova's problems and hearing Bert say that Dalton Parker might be in Iraq. She tried to think of how she could find out whether that was true. She decided to call his California number again.

This time, a woman who sounded like Betty Boop answered the phone. Joanna knew it was none of her business, but she couldn't keep from wondering who the woman might be, because Clova had said he was divorced now. The phone answerer reported that he had gone to run errands, so Joanna repeated the same message she had left on his voice mail earlier and added, "I would really, really like to talk to him."

When Joanna reached the ranch in the late afternoon, she didn't see Clova anywhere outdoors in the places where she usually could be found, but both of the ranch's pickups and the ATV that no one could start were parked in their shed near the barn. Joanna walked over to the house, knocked on the screen door and called out.

Clova came to the door and invited her in. "I was just makin' a sandwich for supper. Come on in and eat with me."

Joanna followed her into the kitchen and Clova proceeded to build a sandwich, complaining about store-bought produce as she stacked tomato slices, then crispy bacon onto two slabs of homemade bread. Yum.

Supper over, Joanna helped her hostess straighten the kitchen, then went to her egg-processing room, which had been an unused, tumbledown outbuilding Clova had let her convert. Joanna used the room to wash and store the eggs until they could be delivered to their respective markets.

She had designed the interior herself. A friend who worked as a mechanic had saved her a few dollars by bringing his steam washer out and steam cleaning the floor and walls. She hired a handyman to insulate the walls and ceiling and hang new wallboard. Then she painted the room herself with a soft blue enamel paint so she could easily wash the surfaces. The room's finish was one of the many expenses that had been covered by the money she had borrowed against her home.

For the most part, she was pleased with the project. She felt a surge of pride every time she walked into the clean, brightly lit blue room. Just like her businesses downtown, she had done the best with what she had to make her egg operation look professional.

She had already put on her work clothes before she left the shop in town, so all she had to do was pull on a pair of canvas gloves. From the utility storage shelves against the back wall, she took wire baskets and a plastic bucket in which to put any broken eggs she might pick up and moseyed out to the nests.

"Evening, ladies," she said to a few hens scratching and pecking near the gate. "Let's go see if you girls have been busy while I've been gone."

Three of them trailed along with her as she gathered eggs. People had told her that chickens, with little-bitty brains, were stupid. They might be, but *her* hens had personalities.

Some of them had become pets. Dulce, an Ameraucauna named by Alicia, was one that had. Alicia had originally named her Pequeño Pollo Dulce, or Sweet Little Chicken, but Joanna talked the teenager into shortening the name to Dulce. The hen would hop up on Joanna's lap, and if Joanna rubbed her head with her finger, Dulce would cluck and sing. Sometimes the little white hen faithfully followed, pecking and clucking, all through the egg gathering.

Joanna usually gathered eggs morning and evening. Frequent emptying of the nests prevented breakage and egg eating by the hens as well as too many egg losses to predators she couldn't keep out—snakes and skunks and bobcats. Because Alicia had collected some of the eggs this morning, the afternoon's gathering would be it for today.

From two hundred chickens, she collected an average of fourteen dozen eggs per day. She lost a few in the washing process and rejected some misshapen ones. Sometimes she set a carton aside for Clova or Mom and a few more to sell to locals who came into the beauty shop to buy them. But she had to admit, she hadn't found many in Hatlow willing to pay five dollars for a dozen eggs.

Today she would end up with roughly twelve dozen to add to the order she was accumulating for the Better Health stores in Lubbock and Amarillo and a couple of restaurants near the college. That number would net about thirty-six bucks for the day, not much profit for the amount of work she did. If she was going to make it big as an egg farmer, she needed to find some superhens that could lay more often than every three days or she had to have more than two hundred producers.

*   *   *

Before Dalton was ready to leave his office, Candace came in. Apparently she had recovered from her snit. "She doesn't sound old," she said.

Funny how they both knew what she meant without her actually saying it. Since his return, she had started to show a possessive streak and insert herself into what he claimed as "his space." He didn't recall her being that pushy before he left.

"No, I guess she doesn't," he replied warily.

"Are you going to call her back?"

He had never discussed his family with Candace. Or with anyone. "I don't know," he answered sharply.

She angled a sultry pout in his direction. "Well, aren't you the big meanie." She came to where he stood and edged between him and his desk, rubbing her belly against his genitals. "Dalty, I don't like women calling you," she said softly.

"Candace, for chrissake, my brother's—"

Her mouth on his halted what he would have said. He let her tongue play with his until things started to progress. Then, his hands resting on the rise of her hips, he pulled back and looked at her. "Baby, I'm hungrier than hell. Where are we on those steaks and that salad?"

She frowned and pushed out her lower lip, then moved away from him, rubbing herself against him like a pet cat as she went. "It's all ready. All you have to do is cook it."

"Great," he said cheerily, hoping to ward off the fight he could see bubbling close to the surface.

He watched her saunter toward the door, moving just slowly enough to let him take a good long look. She knew he would, too. A mane of whorls and swirls in a dozen shades of gold fell to the middle of her back. He let his eyes feast again on the tanned, perfectly heart-shaped ass that was damn near bare thanks to a tiny white bikini. White high-heeled shoes gave it a sexy swing. A white barely there halter top showed off her perfect tan and her full tits. Candace Carlisle's very presence in a room made grown men slobber. She was, inarguably, the best-looking woman he had ever slept with. She wasn't a bad lay, either.

But in too many ways, she was brain-dead.

Exactly when his needs in a woman had transformed from the physical, he couldn't say, but lately a part of him he didn't understand seemed to require more than a raunchy roll in the hay.

Feeling like a chickenshit for his surliness—his screwed-up family wasn't *her* fault—he dropped the phone message on his desk, making a mental note to decide what to do about it later. He headed for his bedroom but stopped off at the bar in the rec room for a sip of Jack Daniel's. He stood for a few seconds and savored the burn all the way down. He had missed having good whiskey on his trip.

He traded his jeans for a swimsuit and followed Candace out to the sunny backyard. He found her setting the table under the fiberglass patio cover. Two thick steaks waited for him on one end of the barbecue grill. He walked over beside Candace, cupped a handful of firm ass cheek and squeezed. She leaned into him, and the scent of coconut sunscreen and hot woman surrounded him.

"How well did she know you in school?" she asked.

He arched his brow rather than voice his irritation. Trying to explain to Candace was too much trouble. He knew from experience that explanation would turn to argument. He replied by covering her mouth with his for another kiss and felt himself getting hard.

When the kiss ended, she looked up at him with hooded eyes, her lips wet and vivid. Her hand came between them and she rubbed him through his swimsuit. "We don't have to eat right now," she said softly.

"Baby, you're something else," he murmured.

A knowing smile tipped the corners of her mouth. She knew she didn't have to do much to give him a hard-on. "So?"

"So. We screwed half the morning."

"But this is afternoon."

"And I need my strength. Let me do some laps, then I'll cook the steaks." He slapped her bottom and said against her ear, "Don't let it get cold. I'm working on a comeback."

He left her and dove into the lap pool that spanned the width of his backyard. God, he had missed this swimming pool those months in the desert.

He swam in a smooth, steady crawl, pacing himself and thinking about Candace and his own restiveness. He had met her last year at a publicity photo gig. Not an assignment he normally hired out for, but the money had been too good to turn down. The shoot ran late and Candace had offered herself as a dinner companion. Then one thing led to another.

When it came to women, a man could do worse than Candace, he reasoned. She wanted to fuck night and day and was game for damn near anything in bed. The fact that most of her beauty was man-made didn't bother him. He had no problem with a woman assisting Mother Nature a little. If a man were particular about that in LA, he could pass up a lot of entertaining stuff.

What did bother him was that in the year he had known her, they had rarely had a conversation about anything other than the movie business. Except for the energy she exerted in the sack, the only other effort he had seen her put forth was to get a part in a movie.

He had recognized early that she was no house-keeper. Though she had only a part-time job and spent a good part of her days off watching TV or doing something to enhance her appearance, he continued to pay someone to clean the house. He had tried to teach her to cook, had tried to teach her to help him with his photographs. Hell, he had even tried—and failed—to teach her to play poker. Damn near everything she knew outside the movie and glamour business was something he had succeeded only with great effort in teaching her.

She was driving him fuckin' crazy.

And he had been back only a month.

After cleaning up the supper dishes, he and Candace smooched on the sofa in the rec room and halfheartedly watched a movie. It was a sexy movie, the love scenes were hot, so before it ended, they were naked on the sofa. They moved into the bedroom and finished there.

Afterward, he switched off the light and lay there, staring into the darkness. He felt empty and dissatisfied and didn't know why. He couldn't put his mother's problems and the Texas ranch where he had grown up out of his mind.

"Are you asleep?" Candace asked him softly.

"Hm."

"Whatcha thinking about?"

"Nothing much."

"Texas?"

"A little."

"We could go see your mom. I've never been to Texas."

He looked at her profile silhouetted against the bedroom's moonlit drapes. He hadn't thought once about taking Candace, or any woman, to meet his mother. Christ, he had taken his former wife to Hatlow only a couple of times.

He didn't reply.

After an extended silence, she said, "Where are we going, Dalton?"

"What do you mean?"

But he knew what she meant. What he didn't know was the answer to her question. Hell, he didn't know where *he* was going, much less "we." But wherever it might be, he was sure he would go alone.

"We've been together almost a year. I haven't, you know, been with anyone else. Even when you were gone."

If that were true, it could be some kind of miracle. Since Candace had moved in, Dalton had been gone almost as much as he had been present. She liked men and sex, and she just wasn't a woman who would go without. Nor would she have to. While overseas, he had sometimes wondered who she might be banging in his bed, but it had been a curiosity rather than a worry. He supposed he would have to care for it to worry him.

He chuckled. "You sure about that?"

"Yes, I am," she said indignantly. A few seconds later, she added, "Well, maybe once or twice. But I didn't bring anyone here."

Thank God for that, he thought.

"I nearly went crazy while you were gone," she said. "You know how horny I get."

He chuckled again. "Baby, you're the horniest woman I've ever known."

He turned on his side, braced his elbow on the mattress and leaned his head on his hand. The profile of her breasts and nipples in silhouette in the moonlight was almost as interesting as seeing her nakedness in the light. He still didn't understand what a woman who looked like her saw in him. Hell, he was getting old. He couldn't fuck all night like he used to. His black hair was peppered with gray. His body bore scars. He now wore glasses for close work, and he was crankier than a sleep-deprived bear.

He trailed a finger from her throat down the middle

of her silky body. She arched her back, covered his hand with hers and placed it between her opened thighs. "I know you thought about this while you were gone," she said huskily.

"Hmm," he said, slipping two fingers into her. Jesus, she was wet and ready again. He took her nipple into his mouth. Then he remembered that she didn't respond well to breast stimulation. She'd had so much plastic surgery, some of the feeling was missing. For some reason, on this particular night, that annoyed him. He let go and flopped over to his back.

"What's wrong?"

"Nothing," he answered.

She turned to him and pressed her breasts against him. "You could have me for good, you know."

Her hand slid down his belly and her nimble fingers began to stroke his soft dick. At the same time she dragged her tongue over his nipples.

Now it was he who wasn't responding, which was both puzzling and a little frightening because he'd had no plastic surgery. "Don't, baby." He moved her hand, cupped the back of her head and brought it to his shoulder. "I think I'm out of juice. Let's just go to sleep."

Seconds later, he heard her sniffle. He suppressed a sigh, fearing that if he released it and she heard, she would interpret it as a desire to "talk about it." He stroked her hair. "C'mon baby. There's no need to cry now. Let's just go to sleep."

He probably should feel a pang of conscience, he told himself, but he couldn't help it because the emotion she wanted from him wasn't there. He hadn't been able to muster an enduring emotional attachment to any female in a long time.

Another part of him, the part that felt used by Candace, stepped up and asked why he should feel guilty. Hell, she had made out okay. When he met her, she was on the verge of being evicted from a thirties-vintage dump in Venice Beach, working part-time in a Starbucks and surviving on tuna fish and crackers. Now she enjoyed rent-free living in a pretty damn nice place, free food and use of his truck and was required to do zip in return for any of it. He even gave her spending money. She earned a little working at the coffee shop near his house, but he never questioned her about the money she earned. He assumed she spent it on herself.

"I thought you'd, you know, miss me . . . while you were gone," she said, her nose stuffy from crying. "I thought . . . when you got back . . . we'd, you know, ma-make things . . . per-permanent."

Another mental sigh. He had never promised her anything, nor asked her to make promises to him. He had learned his lesson about making pledges to women. He had done it once, before God and state. When it ended a few years later, all he had left was less than half of some expensive photography equipment, a mortgaged house badly in need of remodeling and the shirt on his back. Later, after he learned his ex had put his photo equipment up for sale on eBay, he had bid on and rebought what he couldn't afford to replace new. "I've never said that, Candy."

"But you di-didn't say you—you wouldn't. I wa-want to be your wife, Dalton."

"Candy, please. I've already said I'm not interested in getting—"

"You know what you are, Dalton? I'll tell you what you are. You're a self-centered son of a bitch." She flounced out of bed and left the room.

And at that moment, he knew his next destination. He *had* to go to Texas.

Chapter 4

Sunday. A day to work with the hens and do maintenance in the chicken yard. As always, when this was Joanna's purpose, she rose early, donned ragged jeans and old boots and a T-shirt and covered her hair with a ball cap. Through her morning ablution, she drank three cups of coffee heavily laced with cream and Sweet'N Low. She followed up with a breakfast consisting of a high-protein energy bar and a Diet Pepsi, which she consumed as she walked to her pickup.

Most of Hatlow's citizens dressed in their better clothes and went to Sunday school and church. They sang and rejoiced over their blessings, prayed for their families, friends and neighbors, and prayed for the country, and, no matter what else might be happening, they never failed to pray for rain. They followed church with a delicious Sunday dinner.

But not Joanna. True, she had gone to Sunday school and church as a child, and still did on occasion. But when her grandparents passed on, Sunday dinner went with them. Delicious home-cooked meals had never existed in Alvadean Walsh's household. Joanna's mother could barely boil water and, as far as anyone knew, had never been interested in learning to do more.

Sunday was also a day of rest for many in Hatlow. That luxury didn't exist for Joanna, either. She had made the ten-mile trip to the Parker ranch almost every morning just after sunrise, including Sundays, for two and a half years now. Sometimes she could count on Alicia for some relief in the evenings, but at the crack of dawn, not even the loyal Alicia volunteered to drive out to the Parker ranch, tend the hens and gather the eggs. She did it if Joanna asked, but reluctantly.

Joanna had heard the old adage all of her life about the owner of a dairy herd being tied down. Well, she could give testimony from experience that a dairy herd couldn't possibly be any more confining than a flock of egg-laying hens. Nor could a dairy herd be as sensitive. If something upset the hens—and it could be something as simple as a little noise out of the ordinary—they molted. If they got mad at one of their own for some chicken reason, they might peck her to death. If their food and water didn't suit them or if they became traumatized by something, they refused to lay eggs.

Joanna battled bobcats, feral cats, raccoons, weasels and coyotes, and the damn snakes, which could eat a dozen eggs faster than she could chase them off. But worst of all were the hawks. The ever-loving, relentless, ruthless, bastard hawks that liked nothing better than a fat hen for lunch. She had read about all of that before plunging with both feet into a business that provided ideal food for predators, but reality hadn't set in until it touched her.

Beyond those everyday hazards were the bizarre ones—last spring, for instance, when fire ants attacked and murdered a whole batch of baby chicks. More recently, she had even heard that marauding feral hogs might be moving into West Texas. Feral hogs? She had never seen a feral hog.

Listening to the radio, she drove slowly with the windows down, taking in the cool, pleasant temperature and the clear blue sky that always followed a storm. Last night's expected tempest had passed through as a lamb rather than a lion, but it had sprinkled Wacker County's parched earth with moisture and blown away the heat temporarily. The smells of the earth rejuvenated by rain filled the cab of her truck. Even the ever-present west wind seemed to have taken a respite.

On either side of the highway, ripening cotton bolls stood in neatly plowed rows of brown earth that marched straight as a ruler's edge until they disappeared into the distant horizon. Occasionally she passed working pump jacks and she thought of the little surge of new activity in the oil business. Amazing what doubling the price of oil per barrel could do to lift spirits and hope. In West Texas, the price for a barrel of oil was far more important than the cost of a gallon of gasoline.

Soon the windmill in her chicken yard came into view. A few miles later, she came to the beginning of the Parker ranch and the fenced pastures holding grazing cattle with their freeze-dried Lazy P brands. By Texas standards, at roughly seventeen sections, the Lazy P wasn't a big ranch. It wasn't even the biggest ranch in Wacker County. But eleven thousand acres was still a heck of a lot of land to someone who had never owned more than a house on a city lot. Joanna wasn't a jealous-hearted person, but she sometimes wondered how it would feel to own acres and acres of land.

On Sundays Joanna did chores such as making sure the feeders and waterers worked properly, and repairing the fence, roosts and nests. Since becoming an egg farmer, she had become adept with a hammer and saw and tools in general. She couldn't complain about that. Who knew when those skills would come in handy somewhere besides the chicken yard? Since her dad's passing, she hadn't always been able to find some man to do those kinds of chores.

Often, when she arrived at the Parker ranch on Sunday mornings, she found Clova, who was a great cook, starting a big Sunday dinner. Much of the time Clova was the only one around to eat it, but the habit was so ingrained in her from years of cooking for ranch hands that she continued to do it. Joanna was often the beneficiary of the tradition and of Clova's hospitality, and she looked forward to a delicious meal.

Joanna cooked poorly. Since her mother had never spent much time in the kitchen, Joanna and her sister hadn't learned to be cooks in their youth like most young rural women. Thus, Joanna particularly enjoyed the aromas and ambience of Clova's country kitchen. They represented a hominess missing from her life since the passing of her grandparents years back.

This morning, she caught Clova just leaving for the hospital in Lubbock. She was dressed in black Rockies and her new black lace-up Ropers. She had on a red long-sleeve snap-button shirt and heavy turquoise bracelets on each arm. Her long thick hair was held at the crown with a turquoise-inlaid barrette. She looked prettier than Joanna had seen her look in a long time.

After a good-bye, Joanna pulled on her work gloves and proceeded to gather the eggs, with Dulce clucking and scratching and pecking behind her. She gathered eight dozen eggs, finding only two cracked. This unusually large number pleased her immensely since the hens laid fewer eggs in the fall. If she could collect the same number in the evening's gathering, that would mean she would have sixteen dozen eggs for the day. Not a record, but more than she had expected.

On the way back to the egg-processing room, she picked up Dulce and carried her along, talking and making clucking noises at her. Dulce was one of the few hens that would allow herself to be picked up and carried without squawking and making a racket. An Ameraucauna, she wasn't as hysterical by nature as some of the Leghorns were. The white Leghorns might be the best layers, but they had been known to start a riot in the chicken yard.

Leaving the door open, she put the hen on the ground outside to peck for bugs and plants while she worked with the new eggs. Then she stepped into clean coveralls and set about washing the eggs. All alone, working at her chores, she experienced a taste of why Clova was so lonely. Except for the occasional low of a cow, the call of a bird or the noise she made herself, Joanna heard not a sound.

To keep her company, she switched on the old radio that stayed on a shelf above the sink. As she sang along with a Carrie Underwood number, she heard Dulce's clarion call just outside the door. Joanna looked out and saw the hen hopping to the ground from a large clay pot that was filled with a dead plant. Behind her, in the center of the plant, lay a fresh blue egg.

Joanna laughed. "Dulce, you take the cake. You are such a good hen."

Dulce continued to cluck and strut proudly.

Once the eggs had been washed and laid out to dry, she set about cleaning inside her room. Her operation wasn't subject to inspection by the USDA, but that didn't mean she gave cleanliness and sanitation short shrift.

By the time she finished cleaning, the washed eggs had dried. She packed them into tan cardboard cartons decorated with her logo, WALSH'S NATURALS, FARM-FRESH FREE-RANGE EGGS, and put them away in the refrigerator. As she did this, her thoughts drifted to Clova's oldest son again. Because he hadn't called her home number, she had checked her office voice mail this morning to see if he had left a message. Nothing.

Her cell phone chirped and she keyed in to the call. "Lanita's here," her mother said. "Darrell took the kids fishin', so she drove down here to see us."

Joanna's older sister lived up in Lubbock. Her husband was a high school teacher and coach, and Lanita worked as a loan processor for a mortgage broker. She hadn't been to Hatlow in a couple of months. "I'll come over," Joanna said. "Have y'all had lunch?"

"Not yet. We was thinkin' 'bout gettin' some burgers at the Sonic."

Joanna grinned. One thing she could count on was that Mom hadn't gone out of her way to prepare a Sunday dinner for company. "I'm just ready to leave here," Joanna said. "I'll stop by and pick some up."

She took a couple dozen eggs from the cooler to give to her sister, then closed up everything and washed her hands with disinfecting soap. She drove back to town, stopped off at Sonic and bought burgers, French fries and onion rings, then drove to the small ranch-style house of tan brick where she and Lanita had spent the first part of their lives.

Inside, she found Lanita watching one of Mom's John Wayne movies. To her surprise, their mother was ironing a shirt. After saying hello and hugging her sister, Joanna turned to Mom. "You're ironing?"

"I got to have clothes to wear," her mother replied. "Since I ain't got nobody else to do it, I got to, bad as I hate it. I like wearin' cotton. It's still too hot for polyester."

No way did Joanna intend to be conned into doing Mom's ironing. She studied her mother for a few seconds. She couldn't recall a time when she had seen her enjoy any part of housekeeping or cooking. Joanna often wondered just exactly what part of married life Mom *had* enjoyed. "Do you have tea brewed? I didn't buy any."

"I made sweet tea yesterday," her mom answered. "It's in the 'frigerator."

Joanna went to the kitchen, wagging the Sonic sack with her.

"Be sure to wash that chicken crap off your hands," her mother called behind her.

Lanita followed her into the kitchen, giggling. "So how's the egg farm?"

Joanna turned on the water in the stainless steel sink for yet another hand washing. Since becoming a chicken owner, she had become obsessive about it. "It's okay. Not as profitable as I'd like, though. I brought you a couple dozen eggs."

"Oh, thanks." Lanita leaned her backside against the counter edge and crossed her arms. "If you aren't making money, I can't believe you're still doing this, Joanna. What a lot of work."

Joanna grinned, tore off some sheets of paper towel and dried her hands. "Tell me about it."

"Are you dating anyone now?"

Uh-oh. That question usually meant Lanita had someone in mind for Joanna to date. Intending to block her big sister's good intentions, she answered, "I'm through with men."

Lanita made an exaggerated sigh. "I guess you might as well take that attitude. Who would you date in Hatlow, even if you wanted to? What happened to what's his name from Lubbock?"

Joanna began to put away some of the dozens of items strewn over the countertop. "Scott Goodman? He moved to Fort Worth."

"Did you break up with him?"

"You might say that." Scott Goddman, a pharmaceutical salesman from Lubbock, was suave, good-looking and overcritical. Joanna had spent every weekend with him for six months, until she discovered he spent weekdays with someone else who lived in Lubbock.

"I didn't like him dating someone in Lubbock while he was sleeping with me. I'm funny that way."

Lanita sniggered. "It's just as well. He'll never be anything but a salesman. Some new guys have come in to help Darrell coach and—"

"Lanita, does Darrell think it's part of his job description to force his unsuspecting staff to go out with his pitiful sister-in-law? That must be embarrassing."

"That isn't the way it is. They're new in town. They don't know anyone. You should enjoy the opportunity to get out and go somewhere."

"Forget it, Sister. I'm not interested. I've got too much to do to put up with some demanding man. That let's-get-acquainted dance is too much trouble. And I don't even like football."

Lanita heaved another sigh. "My God, Joanna. Have you looked in the mirror lately? You might still look great, but you're thirty-five years old. You're becoming an old maid."

Joanna had heard herself referred as to an old maid so often, she felt as if it were tattooed across her forehead. The label had hurt her feelings when she had first heard it, but she had grown a hard shell and become immune to it.

Lanita was nearly a head shorter than Joanna. She'd had three kids and hadn't lost extra pounds after any one of them. That and a soft office job put her on the pudgy side. Joanna wouldn't hurt *her* feelings by mentioning any of that. But she did stop her task to give her sister an indignant glower. "I like who and what I am just fine, thank you."

She turned to the cupboards, opened a door and found paper plates and large red plastic cups. Most people had some kind of china or pottery serving

dishes in their cupboards, but not Alvadean Walsh.
Joanna pulled down three of the paper plates.

"Let's eat on real dishes," Lanita said. "Me and the
kids eat on paper plates all the time at home."

"Mom decided dishes that have to be washed are
too much trouble," Joanna said.

Lanita frowned. "She's got a dishwasher."

Instead of replying, Joanna reached for three plastic
cups and lined them up on the counter.

For the first time, Lanita looked at the cupboard
contents. "So now she just has paper plates and plastic
cups?" Lanita's voice was laced with puzzlement and
indignation.

"Afraid so. But she does vary the colors and pat-
terns."

Lanita rolled her big green eyes. She and Joanna
both had their daddy's eyes. "This is ridiculous," she
snapped.

Joanna chuckled. "It's her house, Sister. She can do
what she wants."

"I don't care. It's still ridiculous. I suppose we're
going to have to eat with plastic forks, too." She yanked
open the drawer where stainless-steel flatware had always been kept and found nothing but white plastic.

Now Joanna's chuckle evolved into a laugh. She had
grown accustomed to her mother's latest effort to avoid
keeping house. "Hey, you know Mom. You don't live
here, remember? And neither do I. To each his own."

"Where do you suppose she put all of the dishes
we used to have?" Lanita asked.

"I think she packed them up and put them in the
storeroom out back."

"Why didn't she give them to me? Or to you?"

"Well, of all the things I need, Sister, a set of cheap
dishes isn't one of them."

"Well, I could use them. I don't even have a whole
set anymore. The only ones I ever had were what I

got as a wedding present, and the kids have broken half of those."

"I guess you could ask her for them," Joanna said. "It won't hurt *my* feelings. And I think I'd be safe in betting a million she isn't going to use them."

Lanita shook her head, pursing her mouth and not attempting to hide her annoyance. "Oh, not today. I don't want to start something. I see the house is practically sparkling. At least she hasn't give up cleaning the house."

"That isn't entirely true, either. A Mexican woman named Lupe comes in on Saturdays and cleans. So you caught it at its best."

Lanita set the plastic utensils on the counter with a clack. "Mom has a maid?"

"Yep. Every Saturday."

"That really pisses me off," Lanita snapped, her eyes wide with ire. "I don't have a maid myself, and I've got three kids. Why, Darrell and I have been sending her a hundred dollars every month because we thought she was having a hard time."

Joanna knew about the monthly stipend. In some conversation at some point, Mom had let it slip. "Hmm," Joanna said. "I think that's about what the maid costs her."

"I can't believe this. I don't know if I should even tell Darrell. We've kept the kids from doing some things so we could send money down here." With jerky movements, she picked out three sets of plastic forks and knives. "A maid. My God. Our daddy would turn over in his grave."

"Lanita, chill out. It's what she wants to do. I doubt if Daddy would care. I'm sure he didn't marry her for her housekeeping skills. For that matter, I'll bet Darrell wouldn't care, either."

Joanna unwrapped the burgers and fries and onion rings and placed them on the paper plates, squeezed puddles of ketchup onto each plate, then filled the plastic cups with ice.

"Don't pour tea for me," Lanita said when Joanna dragged the pitcher of tea from the refrigerator. "That sweet stuff has too much sugar. And too many calories. I'll just have water and lemon." She crossed to the refrigerator and looked in. "Well, there's no food. I suppose it would be too much to hope she would have a lemon."

"Yep," Joanna said. "Too much. If you don't want sweet tea, looks like your other choice is plain water." Joanna left her sister in front of the refrigerator, dug a cookie sheet from a drawer under the oven and arranged the three servings on it.

"I'm glad I don't live around here anymore," Lanita groused, closing the refrigerator door. She leveled a hard glare at the cookie sheet. "My God. That's not a tray. It's a cookie sheet. You mean she *hasn't* disposed of the cooking utensils?"

"Could happen any day, I suspect." Joanna carried their lunch toward the living room on the cookie sheet. "Set up one of those TV trays for me, okay?"

Lanita complied, unfolding two metal TV trays in front of the sofa and one in front of their mother's chair. Mom didn't eat at the dining table, either. It was covered with assorted beads, baubles and tools for her jewelry-making hobby. Joanna distributed the food and drinks and they settled in to watch the rest of the movie while they ate.

"You usually eat out to Clova's on Sunday," her mother said.

"She's gone to Lubbock Memorial to visit Lane," Joanna replied.

"Humph." Her mother took a bite of her burger. "Looks like he survived after all."

"I heard about his car wreck," Lanita said. "You

know, I barely remember him from when we were kids."

"Well," Mom put in, "he *is* nine years younger than you are, Sister."

"Mom," Joanna said, "Dalton Parker didn't call after I left the shop yesterday, did he?"

"Why would Dalton Parker be calling *you*?" Lanita asked pointedly.

"Because I asked him to. I left him a message about Clova and the ranch."

Mom dabbed a French fry into ketchup. "You might as well forget that, Joanna. He ain't gonna call."

"What is the deal with him? All of a sudden, he's like this phantom out there that everyone's speculating about. Why wouldn't he call and show some concern for his brother and his mother?"

"My God, Joanna," Lanita said. "He probably hates his parents. Don't you remember him when we were kids? How he used to come to school black and blue?"

Joanna thought back but couldn't remember that about him. She couldn't even clearly remember exactly how he looked. "I guess I don't." Then she couldn't keep from giving her big sister an evil grin. "But then, I wasn't close to him like you were."

Lanita ducked the piercing look and dipped a French fry in the mound of ketchup on her plate. "If it was nowadays, the school would have to report parents who treated their kid like Dalton's mother and stepdaddy treated him. And Child Services would take him away from them and put him in some foster home."

"What I remember mostly is that everyone thought he was cute," Joanna said.

"Oh, he was more than cute. He was sooo hot. He filled out a pair of Levi's in *all* the right places, if you know what I mean."

Joanna's wicked thoughts flew to what Shari had told her that Megan Richardson had said about Lane. How could anyone not wonder if that physical characteristic ran in the family?

"Lanita, stop that kind of talk," Mom said, continuing to mop up ketchup with an onion ring.

Joanna suppressed a grin as her memory zoomed back to 1987, when Lanita and Dalton Parker were seniors. Joanna was a sophomore and just starting to learn about boys and sex, mostly from Lanita. Her older sister had been a cheerleader, and Joanna could still see her leaping and cartwheeling in her short pleated skirt, her long blond curls unfurled and bouncing.

"I wonder what he looks like now," Lanita went on, a distant look in her eye and a French fry poised in the air. "Me and every last one of my girlfriends used to practically cream in our jeans when he walked up the hall."

"That's vulgar," Mom said. "Don't be sayin' stuff like that. Why, what if somebody heard you?"

Lanita's full lips flattened. "It's a joke, Mom. Who's going to hear?"

Not liking hearing that someone she liked had been cruel to one of her children, Joanna said, "I can't imagine Clova beating anybody up. She's a gentle person."

"Oh, I don't think she whupped 'im herself," Mom said. "She just didn't do nothin' to stop Earl from it."

"I can't see that happening, either," Joanna said. "She treats Lane like he's gold. You know what she's put up with from him. And she never even raises her voice to him."

"Joanna, you would o' had to know Earl Cherry. That man was ornery as a mad bull. And poor little Dalton, bless his heart. Even when he was a little boy, Earl worked him like he was a grown man. With all that Comanche blood Clova's got runnin' in her veins, you'd o' thought she'd o' found the nerve to stand up for Dalton. But she didn't. Lord, Earl had her cowed so bad, you'd o' thought it was him that inherited that ranch 'stead o' her."

The three of them sat in silence for a few seconds, as if they each needed the extra time to digest Mom's narrative. Then Mom added, "Course, if you'd o' knowed Clova's daddy, you might understand why she was like that. Wilburn Parker was a stern man who lived in another time. When Clova got pregnant, he yanked her out o' school and hid her away and nobody even saw her anymore. She didn't even go to the hospital to have Dalton. He was a big kid and walkin' before she brought him out in public."

Knowing Clova as she did, Joanna could imagine all of that. And it made her heart hurt for Clova, who for all practical purposes had to be viewed as an emotional cripple.

"Dalton was the loneliest boy I ever dated," Lanita said, her legs tucked under her as she studied her fingernails pensively. "Even though I was only eighteen, I could tell he carried a hurt. But it wasn't caused by some girl. It was from something deeper than that. My goodness, he could have had any girl he wanted. We were all the same. We wanted to take care of him." She sent Joanna a mischievous look from beneath her brow. "Well, I might have wanted to do more than that."

Mom frowned and sputtered. "Lanita Marie! I told you not to talk like that in my house!"

"Mom, good grief! Do you think I don't know anything about sex? How do you think I got three kids?"

"That's different. Why, what if Darrell heard you say somethin' like that?"

Joanna turned her head and grinned. Her memory took her back to a conversation she and Lanita had

had one day after Lanita had married and had kids and the two of them were in the kitchen doing dishes and talking. Joanna had asked her if she had fooled around with Dalton in high school. Lanita told her no. She would have, she said, but Dalton believed she was a virgin and he wouldn't. Joanna had always thought that odd, and the conversation stuck in her memory for some reason. She couldn't decide whom it said the most about, her sister or Dalton Parker.

Mom dredged another onion ring through ketchup and popped the whole thing in her mouth. "Ever'body said Earl was mean to Dalton 'cause Dalton wasn't his, but I say Earl was just mean, period."

"Well, who *is* Dalton's father?" Joanna asked, curious now.

"Nobody's ever known," Mom answered. "Best-kept secret in Hatlow. Some said it was a college boy from up at Tech. Others said it was Mason Jergens. But if it was, Clova's daddy never done nothin' about it. Prob'ly 'cause Mason was married."

"I don't believe that," Lanita said. "Mason Jergens is uglier than a frog and he was back then, too. Dalton didn't look anything like him."

"Lane *is* Earl's kid," Mom went on as if Lanita hadn't spoken, "but Earl was mean to him, too. I 'member onc't when Earl went to the high school drunker'n a dog and dragged Lane out of a classroom, kickin' him and beatin' on him all the way to his truck. The principal called the sheriff, but nothin' ever come of it. Earl wasn't afraid o' no sheriff."

"Dalton had a chance at football scholarships," Lanita said, "but when the scouts tried to talk to his mama and daddy, they practically slammed the door in their faces."

Of all the tales Joanna routinely heard, she hadn't heard this one. "So Dalton did what?"

"Why, he joined the army. Well, it was the marines,

really. I guess there's a difference. He left the day after graduation. I suppose nobody knows much of what's gone on with him since." Lanita shook her head. "It's a shame. Earl and Clova ought to be ashamed."

"Let's change the subject," Joanna said.

Lanita and their mother went on to yakking and bickering over other topics. As the afternoon waned, Lanita declared she had to get back to Lubbock and cook supper, putting heavy emphasis on the word "cook." To Joanna's amusement, if their mother noticed the dig, she didn't acknowledge it.

After Lanita left, Joanna, too, said her good-byes and started back to the Parker ranch for the evening's egg gathering, her thoughts heavy with the notion of her friend Clova Cherry abusing her children.

Chapter 5

At the Parker ranch, Joanna met Clova just as she was sliding out of her dusty pickup in front of the garage. Joanna parked her own pickup behind Clova's and climbed out, eager to hear a report on Lane's condition. "Hi. How's everything in Lubbock?"

Clova shook her head. "It don't look good, hon. Lane's in real bad shape. They still got him in that ICU place. I don't know what to think o' that leg. They got it screwed together with nuts and bolts. I just wonder if he's gonna end up crippled." She closed her pickup door quietly, a woman resigned to accept what fate had handed her.

"Don't believe the worst. It takes a few days before they can tell what's what."

Clova looked off in a distant stare. "If he lives through this, I 'magine they're gonna charge him with drunk drivin'."

Joanna couldn't guess what memories that possibility aroused, given the talk in Hatlow about Clova's deceased husband. "Really?"

Clova nodded. "This ain't his first time, you know. I got to get him a lawyer. Can't afford to have him in jail. If it was our sheriff that was handlin' it, I wouldn't be so worried, but it's the DPS. Them state cops ain't gonna look the other way."

"I know," Joanna said, trying to appear sympathetic. But in truth, in her opinion, if Lane really had been drunk enough to hit a power pole and roll his pickup into the ditch, he had no business behind the wheel. Only blind luck had kept him from colliding with another vehicle. "Look, are you up to walking with me to gather the eggs?"

"I'll walk a little piece with you."

Joanna ambled toward the egg-washing room with Clova close behind, her hands stuffed into the pockets of her jeans.

"Up to the hospital," Clova said, "I had to meet with a woman in the bookkeepin' department. When I told her Lane didn't have no insurance, she got testy with me about payin' the bill, and I said, 'What're you gonna do, kick him out on the sidewalk?' " Clova gave a humorless chuckle. "You'd think bill collectors would take Sunday off."

"How did you resolve it?" Joanna asked, knowing the last thing the Lazy P could afford was an expensive hospital bill.

"I told her I'd pay 'em when we sell the yearlin's."

Joanna's brow arched and she blinked. Depending on how much Lane's bill was, that could leave Clova without funds to get through the winter.

The older woman went into a coughing spasm but soon regained her voice. "Hon, I ain't got nothin' cooked today."

Joanna smiled at her. "I didn't come to eat, Clova. I came to gather the eggs, do my chores and see how things are. If there's Sunday dinner when I come out, it's a bonus."

"They told me they'd take my credit card." Clova laughed. This time, she did find something genuinely humorous in the statement. "Can you believe that?"

Sometimes talking to Clova wrenched at Joanna's heart. The woman wasn't so old in years, but she was a throwback to another time. In Clova's world, if you needed to borrow money, you went to the local bank

and did business with someone you knew and who
knew you. You didn't charge a debt owed on an account with an obscure financier, the whereabouts of
which you didn't know. Joanna found a laugh, too,
though the circumstances weren't funny. "We live in
a credit card world," she said, opening the door to
her egg-washing room.

Clova remained outside. With the space used by the
three-tub stainless-steel sink, the egg-washing equipment, the large commercial refrigerator and the utility
shelving, the area left was barely large enough for
two people.

"Well, I ain't got a credit card," Clova said defi-
antly. "And I ain't never had one. And I don't want
one. Lane used to have some. The bastards charged
him twenty-five percent interest. Lord God. I liked to
never got 'em all paid for. Now he don't have none.
And I say that's just fine. Whoever heard of a bank
chargin' poor people twenty-five percent interest?"

Joanna zipped up the coveralls she had lifted from
the tiny closet beside the refrigerator. "I know it's an
outrageous fee, but no one forced Lane to run up his
credit card bills, Clova. He did that on his own. Why
would you pay his debts like that?"

" 'Cause I pay all the bills that come to this ranch.
Lane lives here, and he's part o' the operation. He
don't get much in the way o' wages. Besides that, I've
always felt a little bit sorry for him 'cause he ain't got
no judgment about him. He ain't like Dalton always
was. Dalton knew the right thing even when he was
a boy."

Pulling on a pair of clean cotton gloves, Joanna
stepped outside. "Ready?"

Side by side, they sauntered toward the chicken
yard, with Clova continuing to talk. "Lane's more like
his daddy. He gets to drinkin' and thinkin' he's a big
shot, and the next thing you know, he's spent money

he ain't got. When I found out about them cards, I cut 'em up. If I hadn't o' stopped him, he could o' got the ranch in trouble. His credit's so bad now, he couldn't get a card if he wanted to. It's a relief."

Hearing of Clova's proactive approach to Lane's irresponsible spending was a surprise. Joanna had rarely seen her oppose her youngest son. "I've got an idea," she said. "When I get these eggs gathered up and washed, why don't we go to town and eat at Sylvia's? I'll buy you supper."

Clova chuckled, bringing deep creases to the corners of her eyes. "Hon, you don't have to buy me supper. I ain't that broke yet."

Joanna smiled. "I know. But look at all the times I've eaten Sunday dinner out here. If I tried to pay you back by cooking you a meal, you might not survive it. But I can buy you a steak."

"I guess we could do that. I still got on my good clothes and all."

They walked across the gravel driveway to the chicken yard. At the gate, they stepped over the two electric fence wires that surrounded the chicken yard and headed toward the first nest. Clova had let Joanna stretch the electrified wires around the area where the chickens lived. The wire didn't carry a strong current, but it was strong enough to keep the chickens in and most small, four-legged predators out. Touching it would give a human an unforgettable zap. Unfortunately, the damn bobcats had figured how to avoid the charged fence, and electric wires near the ground did nothing to prevent an eagle or a hawk from having dinner on Joanna.

"I've been thinkin', Joanna," Clova said. She began to help pick eggs from the nests. "You know this part here where you've got your chickens? It's part of a section o' land we've always called the peanut farm."

Joanna did know that. Peanuts had never grown

here in her lifetime, but sometime in the past, they must have. It was a square section of land, with a mile of highway frontage and very few mesquite trees. The small pasture where her hens presently lived used a tiny corner of it. "Uh-huh."

"I've been thinkin' 'bout going in to town to see Clyde and havin' him draw up a deed to that section. I was thinkin' 'bout just givin' it to you, Joanna."

Joanna's heart skipped a beat. She couldn't stop a nervous twitter. "You can't do that, Clova. You need the grazing. And your boys would die. It's their inheritance. And I wouldn't take it, anyway. It's one of the best spots on your place. Why, it's got a windmill on it."

Clova stopped, put her hand on Joanna's forearm and looked up, her dark eyes soft with sincerity. "I'm serious. This last sick spell I had started me to thinkin'. I'm gettin' old. I could catch somethin' and pass away."

Her mind reeling, Joanna picked three eggs from a nest and frowned at seeing that one was cracked. "Clova, listen to me. In the first place, you're not old. And in the second, I won't take land from you for free. It's more than enough you're letting me use it without paying. Why would you want to give it to me when you have two sons to leave it to?"

"Them boys ain't never done for me what you have. Dalton don't even come around 'cept ever' two or three years. And I can't depend on Lane for nothin'. He's got his daddy's weakness. Whatever he inherits, he's gonna drink up. I don't know what'll happen to the place after I'm gone, but my grandpa and my daddy would stand at the Pearly Gates and shut me out if they saw I didn't do my best to take care of the land and keep this place all together. My great-granddaddy had a hard time gettin' to own it, bein' Indian and all. And he had a even harder time a-keepin' it. It meant ever'thin' to him."

She looked across her shoulder at Joanna and smiled, the light of affection in her eyes. "But I don't guess the elders would get upset at me givin' a little piece of it to somebody that's been good to me."

A fullness rising in her chest, Joanna focused her gaze on her egg basket. She might break into tears if she kept looking Clova in the face. "I haven't been especially good to you, Clova. I haven't done any more for you than I would have for anyone I call a friend."

Indeed, it wasn't in Joanna to expect a gift in return for favors done for a friend, but a selfish part of her dared to acknowledge that six hundred forty acres would be enough land for expanding her egg business and even keeping a cow or two. "Tell you what. Maybe you could figure out what it's worth and I could buy it. Or I could buy just a few acres from you. I don't need all six hundred and forty acres. You could let me pay it out over time."

"That ain't what I wanna do. I feel like it's my fault you got all these worthless chickens and the struggle to sell these damn eggs. If I hadn't o' talked you into it, you wouldn't be doin' it. I feel bad that now you got that mortgage on your house and all. If somethin' happened to me, I know them boys wouldn't let you keep these chickens or these donkeys here. They'd prob'ly run you clear off."

"Look, Clova. I'm not your responsibility, okay? I made a conscious decision to take out the mortgage on the house, and I was stone-cold sober when I did it. Let's both think about it some more."

"I'm done thinkin'. I thought all the way home from Lubbock. Practic'ly gave m'self a headache. This last little trick of Lane's has did it for me."

"Clova, listen. Before you do anything hasty, I want you to know I called Dalton. He wasn't at home, but I left a message on his voice mail. I asked him to come for a visit. He hasn't called back yet, but I'm hoping he will. If he decides to come home for a few days to help out, maybe we can talk to him about it. Sort of see how he'd feel about your giving away land he expects to inherit."

"Inheritin' ain't a automatic right, Joanna. Just 'cause him and Lane are next in line don't mean they get it. Both of 'em need to show respect for it and do somethin' to earn it. Like I did."

Joanna's heart would hardly hold the emotion that swelled. Her dad had never earned much; he had driven a bread delivery truck for a Lubbock bakery until the day he became too ill to continue. He had left Mom a home and a small amount of insurance money, but she still held a job to make ends meet. Love and affection were all he'd had to leave his daughters. Everything Joanna owned she had earned from hard work. No one had ever given her so fine a gift as acres of land.

"I still think we should both think about it some more," she told Clova.

Together they completed the egg-washing and storing process, then Joanna drove them into Hatlow to Sylvia's Café. Sylvia herself was cooking, so they feasted on her special recipe of pot roast with fresh carrots, potatoes and onions and her homemade sourdough bread. Years back, Sylvia's husband had worked as a chuckwagon cook at a legendary West Texas ranch, and he had brought his recipes to Sylvia's Café. He had passed on, but his wife continued to cook in his style.

They avoided discussing why Clova showed no enthusiasm for the possibility of her oldest son returning for a visit after so long. They didn't discuss where

he had been or why. Nor did they speculate on the
consequences if Lane came out of his latest escapade
crippled. Though Joanna was still burdened by the
comments about Clova and Dalton from the day's earlier conversation with her own mother and sister, tonight, with Clova, she talked about the food and
music. They laughed about TV programs as if neither
of them had a thing to worry about.

Later, Joanna lay in her bed in the darkness watching the turn of the ceiling fan's dimly visible blades.
Joanna Faye Walsh, landowner. She could hardly believe it. *Wow*, was all she could think.

Owning land opened doors to all kinds of opportunities. Why, she could sell her house. Then she could
buy a mobile home and put it on the land and maybe
have a free-and-clear roof over her head again. That
way, she could be near the hens and wouldn't have to
make two trips a day to take care of them. She could
even think about going into the broiler business. Didn't
someone tell her just last week that a meal of free-
range chicken sold for forty dollars in the fancy restaurants in Dallas?

With highway frontage, maybe she could put up a
small stand and sell eggs and fresh fruits and vegetables. She would go organic on the fruits and vegetables, too, following the latest hot trend. She envisioned
baskets of plump, golden Parker County peaches and
vivid Texas Rio and Ruby Red grapefruit; stacks of
fragrant, sweet Pecos cantaloupes. And a parade of
people stopping off to buy from her.

She meant it when she said she didn't need six hundred forty acres. She truly did not need so much, and
she wasn't a greedy person.

But how could she take land for free from Clova
or anyone else? It just wasn't right. The land belonged
to the Parker family. With West Texas landowners,
the children inherited. It had always been that way.

In the midst of that maze of thought, she drifted to sleep.

By the end of the week, Joanna had spent so much time at the Parker ranch, she was beginning to feel as if she had become a resident. So that Clova was free to make trips to Lubbock to spend time with Lane and do other chores away from the ranch, Joanna and Alicia had been feeding the Lazy P cattle every day. Alicia was on the Joanna's Salon & Supplies payroll. What task she performed didn't matter so long as it was something the teenager was willing to do.

A few times Clova's neighbors had pitched in, but their help came in sporadic bursts. Thus, every morning at daylight, Joanna had put on her most ragged jeans, her most worn boots and a long-sleeve shirt, picked up Alicia and driven to the Parker ranch. After taking care of the chickens and the eggs, they heaved bales of hay four stacks high into the bed of the old beat-up ranch truck. Then they bumped and crept across the pastures, pushing the dusty, scratchy bales off the bed's tailgate, with the cattle bellowing and following behind. They traded off driving. Alicia had never driven a pickup and thought it fun.

Joanna had girded herself for a long haul, but that didn't keep her from collapsing at night, nostrils filled with dust, made worse by the drought, skin and hair caked with sweat and dirt. She went to bed with muscles stiff and aching and rose before daylight in the same state. In just a week's time, she had lost five pounds. In the past, when Lane wasn't around for whatever reason, Clova herself had somehow done this work alone every day, rain or shine. No wonder she was thin as a reed. No wonder she looked so worn.

Alicia loved the cattle. She had begun to recognize them individually and was now giving them long Spanish names, all of which included the Spanish word *"dulce."*

Joanna was fascinated by how quickly she, herself, learned to pick an individual white-faced cow from a sea of white-faced cows that basically all looked alike. Like her hens, the cattle had personalities.

This morning, she found herself alone at the ranch doing chores of her own in the chicken yard. The back neighbor, the elderly August Hulsey, had called and reported a fence being down and Lazy P cattle roaming into his pasture. Clova and Alicia had taken the work pickup to do the feeding and at the same time investigate and possibly work on the downed fence.

Compared to taking care of the cattle, tending the hens felt like a walk in a park. Joanna was exhausted. For all of her good intentions, she wondered just how long this could go on. But she couldn't throw in the towel. Clova was a friend. If Joanna didn't help her without expecting pay, she could think of few who would.

Chapter 6

Dalton Parker shoved on his sunglasses and left the Lubbock airport in a rented car the size of a roller skate. He hated cars. Had never owned one. He lumbered around LA in a seven-year-old three-quarter-ton Chevy pickup truck with a camper canopy mounted on the bed.

He had spent the week putting his life in good enough order to be able to leave LA. As it was, his agent and his editor were worried about him meeting his deadline on the new book. He had assured them he was almost finished.

He had been forced to leave his house in the care of Candace, though they had mutually agreed their affair was over. Once she clearly understood that a wedding ring wasn't in their future, she had been eager to move on to more promising pastures. Since she was homeless for the time being, he had made a deal with her to stay in the house in exchange for looking after it. But for all he knew, in his absence, she might set the place afire.

He bitched and swore at the traffic all the way to Lubbock Memorial Hospital. He didn't recall heavy traffic being a problem in Lubbock before he left this part of the country, but then, except for a few short visits, he had been away nearly twenty years.

At the hospital, when he told a receptionist why he came, she summoned a nurse's aide, who whisked him to the far end of a long hallway, her shoes squeaking in quick rhythm against the shiny tile floor. At the ICU, a nurse with a military bearing, if he had ever seen one, brusquely asked his name and checked to see whether it was on some list. To his astonishment, it was, and he wondered who had put it there. Who had been so certain he would show up?

Inside the brightly lit ICU, Dalton realized he hadn't prepared himself for how severely injured his little brother was. Seeing the kid's pale face, the sunken eyes, his broken body bandaged and hooked up to monster machines by a web of tubes, Dalton was reminded of the horrors he had photographed and left behind on the other side of the world. His pulse rate quickened.

Lane was semiconscious and recognized him. When Dalton touched his hand, Lane attempted to grip his finger. Memories flew into Dalton's mind. In a way, he had been like a father to Lane. Earl Cherry had been drunk all of his only child's life and paid him little attention. As a little boy, eight years younger than Dalton and afraid of his shadow, Lane had looked up to his big brother as if he were a hero.

As Dalton remembered that Lane had always wanted to hold his hand, a lump sprang to his throat. He took his little brother's weak hand, gently squeezed and continued to hold it. "Hey, buddy," he said quietly, "they don't make those power poles out of rubber, you know."

An expression Dalton took to be a smile passed through Lane's drugged brown eyes, but words didn't follow.

Only minutes later, a nurse came to Dalton's side and urged him away. Reluctantly he left the bedside, unable to take his eyes off his brother as he went. He stopped at the nurses' station. "What's going on with him? Is he gonna be okay?"

"He's doing well, considering," the nurse answered. "His doctor's already been here today, but he'll be back tomorrow morning. You can discuss it with him."

Dalton looked around at the array of machines and monitors stuffed in every nook and cranny of the large room.

The nurse smiled as if she sensed his trepidation. "Don't let all of this worry you. It looks scary, but it's really life-saving equipment."

"I know." And he did know. He had seen and photographed wilder-looking technical stuff and more of it at the Camp Ramadi hospital in Iraq. The battlefield itself hadn't shaken him nearly as deeply as what he had witnessed in those brightly lit operating rooms. "How long will he be in here?" he asked her.

"That's for his doctor to say."

"Who is he? And where is he?"

"Dr. Naran. As I said, he'll be back tomorrow morning."

"What time? I'll be here."

"Try to come around ten," she said.

He left the hospital with his emotions in turmoil. He felt light-headed. His heart was beating a tattoo. He had presumed he knew what to expect when he reached Texas, but he had been wrong.

He had navigated out of the Lubbock city limits and hit the highway south before his insides began to settle. At least Lane wasn't dead. A week had passed since the accident. Dalton thought of the words he had heard often in Iraq: "the golden hour," the precious span of time that immediately followed a potentially mortal injury. If a soldier could survive the golden hour, he had a chance. If Lane had been able to stay alive a week, surely he would recover.

Hatlow was an hour and a half from Lubbock. Dalton hadn't eaten a meal all day, and the coffee and pretzels they served on the plane were long gone. He stopped off at a convenience store and bought a Coke and a rubber sandwich, then continued on his way, munching as he drove.

A sense of home and history washed over him, reminding him that his Comanche ancestors had ruled, roamed and hunted this part of Texas for hundreds of years. In their time, this plain had been covered by wild grass and a sea of buffalo, and his great-great-grandfather's people had hunted for survival, lived off the land and defended their way of life against encroachment.

His genetic connection might be far removed from the fierce warriors of long ago, but he still took pride in knowing he was a part of something greater than himself. In all of his life, lacking a cohesive family, he had clung to his Native American heritage. Until the Marine Corps, his ancestry was the only thing he had ever felt he belonged to.

Bringing his thoughts more down to earth, he observed that, just as they had in his childhood, endless fields of cotton stretched to the horizon on either side of the highway. He had no trouble seeing through an imaginary camera lens the bolls bursting with white fluff, clinging to thigh-high stalks against a backdrop of a brilliant blue sky. *Fall.* The best time of year in West Texas. Cotton harvest was just around the corner.

His mind drifted to the Parker ranch. Since hearing of his mother's troubles last Saturday—and at the end of the day, his mother's troubles were the ranch's troubles—he had been considering what obligation he had to help bail her out with his own money. She had never asked and had never discussed the ranch's financial situation with him. He wasn't filthy rich, but he had done well enough. He could afford to help her a little if she needed it.

Thinking of money took his mind to his younger brother again. He could already see that if the kid really had no hospitalization insurance, as the phone message had said, somebody was going to be called on to pay his hospital bill, which could climb to six digits in a hurry.

Soon Dalton began to see pump jacks seesawing against the sky, sucking crude oil from the bowels of the earth. He recalled that in his youth, Parker land had been under a drilling lease constantly, though only one oil well had ever been sunk. The production from the well was never developed, and his family never became oil rich.

He spotted a new drilling rig not far off the highway, its tower thrusting in a straight line toward the sky. The last time he had passed this way, most of the existing wells were static and no drilling rigs existed. But why wouldn't drilling activity be starting up again? Jesus, with the price of a barrel of oil more than doubling, wildcatters and big oil producers should be turning cartwheels and falling all over themselves to get moving again.

Oil. Black gold. Dalton could almost smell it in the air, and it smelled like money. From his experience and observations in the world, he had concluded that most of the world's great wealth came from two commodities: crude oil and narcotic drugs. And it was a toss-up which was the greater source of most of the world's problems.

Reaching a familiar crossroad, he made a right turn, as he had done a thousand times in the past. Now the fenced Parker ranch lay on either side of him and white-faced cattle marked with a Lazy P brand leisurely grazed. The sight salved his soul in a way nothing else ever had. He had traveled all over the world but had never found a place that touched him this deeply.

He had left it behind when he wasn't much more than a boy because blind hatred for his mother's husband had overridden every other emotion in his life.

He had rarely come back even to visit for the same reason. On his few return trips, his stays had been marred by the rebirth of his antipathy for Cherry's very presence.

But his stepfather had been dead for ten years. Why hadn't Dalton returned and tried to revive some kind of relationship with his mother? He didn't know the answer. He supposed he simply got used to having no ties or feeling of obligation to family. And at the deepest level, a part of him resented his mother. In his youth when he was at his most vulnerable, she hadn't defended him against Earl Cherry.

The house shimmered in the distance, and he could see the silhouette of the windmill nearby. A sense of elation filled his chest. Soon he would reach the twenty-acre pasture where new calves or heifers that might have trouble delivering had always been kept. He could hardly wait to see what animals were penned in the small pasture. He had always loved the cattle. A baby calf with its fresh black or russet coat, curly-haired white face and white eyelashes was his favorite animal. Once when his granddad had tried to give him a puppy, he had opted for a calf.

Arriving at the corner of the pasture he saw . . .

Chickens?

He slammed on the brakes, pulled to the shoulder and stared into the pasture. He had never seen so goddamn many chickens all in one place. He couldn't even count them all.

And *chicken houses*.

And *jackasses*.

His mother was raising chickens and jackasses?

The Lazy P was a cattle ranch. Had she lost her friggin' mind?

Walking toward the ranch house's front door, Joanna saw a gallon jar of tea bags and water sitting in

the sun on the stone pathway that led from the driveway to the rickety wooden porch. The tea had brewed,
so she took it into the cavernous kitchen to pour it
into glass pitchers like Clova always did.

As she poured, she heard tires on the gravel driveway. She wiped her hands on her apron and walked
to the front door to look through the old wooden
screen door's haze.

A white car had parked in the driveway at the end
of the stone path, and a man was climbing out. He
closed the door with a clack that resounded in the
morning's stillness. He stood a moment and planted
his hands on his hips, looking around. He had on sunglasses and a white T-shirt with an unidentifiable logo
on the chest. The tail fell loosely over faded jeans.

He lifted his hand and adjusted the sunglasses. Even
from thirty feet away, Joanna could see his tanned
biceps knot against the shirt's short sleeves. He seemed
to dwarf the midsize Ford, but not because he was
such a huge man. There was something else about
him. And just like that, she knew who he was. And
in that same millisecond of recognition, she also knew
he was trouble. Her stomach dropped like a rock.
"Oh, hell."

He started up the limestone pathway toward the
porch with a get-out-of-my-way swagger. His face might
not be clearly visible, but the shape of his body—square
shoulders and slim hips—couldn't be mistaken. A
schoolgirl giddiness skittered around inside her. She
didn't even try to resist letting her starved eyes feast
on his total maleness.

Though she was wearing her worst clothing, she was
glad she hadn't been out to feed the cattle this morning, glad he wouldn't see her dripping with sweat and
covered with hay dirt and cow manure. In fact, for
some reason this morning, she had taken extra pains
with her makeup, and she was glad of that, too.

Still wiping her hands on her apron, she slipped
through the screen door onto the plank porch. Feeling
strangely insecure and trembly, she didn't say anything.

He didn't, either. His sunglasses were the mirrored
aviator type, so she couldn't see his eyes. He peeled them
off, hung them in the neck of his T-shirt, planted his
hands on his hips again and looked up at her with the
most intense eyes she had ever seen on a man. They
were the color of strong coffee, like Clova's eyes. They
seemed to touch her everywhere at the same time,
from her face to her feet, jolting her at a keenly vis-
ceral level. Hearing him accurately quote her bra size
wouldn't even surprise her.

Months, even years, had passed since she had seen
that lean and hungry look in a man, a look that had
always stirred her blood and sent her skulking to a
dark corner to give herself a constructive lecture on
men. As clear as the blue in the sky, she saw it today
in Dalton Parker. She might not be an expert when it
came to the human male, but that mysterious allure
that shimmered off Dalton Parker in waves charged
through her system like a raging river.

"You the one who called?" he asked.

His speech was sharp and clipped. Her ear detected
no sign of a Texas twang. At the same time, his voice
was deep and soft, with an almost smoky rasp. The
sound zoomed straight to the same deeply buried part
of her that her first glimpse of him had gone.

A gentle breeze sent strands of hair across her face.
Grateful for the distraction, she reached up and tried
to tuck them back into place, forcing herself to look
him in the eye and fighting for a smile. "You must
be Dalton."

Two wooden steps led from the porch down to the
stone path. For the first time ever, she looked down
to make sure she didn't miss one of them as she

stepped down to where he stood. She stuck out her right hand and he took it.

"I'm Joanna Walsh." She pumped their hands up and down, still looking into his face, not daring to let her gaze drop to where her aberrant thoughts had taken her. "I was a sophomore when you were a senior. When I was in school I went by my whole name, which is Joanna Faye, after my grandmother. But I shortened it because . . . Well, for obvious reasons. I remember you, though. I used to go to the football games with my big sister, Lanita, and see you playing. You might—"

"Yeah, you're right." He freed his hand from hers and continued to look around. "I don't remember."

"Oh. Well, you've been gone a long time." *Shut-up,* she told herself and drew a breath.

"Where's my mom?" he asked.

"Uh, one of the neighbors called about a break in the fence. She's gone to feed and to check on it."

"Which one?"

"Excuse me?"

"Which neighbor?"

"Oh. Uh, Hulsey. August Hulsey. Do you know him?"

"Not anymore."

"Oh. Of course you used to know him." She lifted her open palms and let them fall. "I mean, he's been around here forever. He's old now."

It was eleven o'clock on a Friday morning in September in the Texas Panhandle. The sun was already a ball of fire in a blue sky dotted with mushrooming white thunderheads, and the temperature was over ninety. "It's hot," she said. "There's some fresh sun tea. Would you like some?"

"Yeah."

She stepped back up onto the porch and reached

for the screen door handle. As she pulled, the old
wooden door stuck. She jerked and it came loose with
a pop. The edge whacked her right between the eyes,
knocking her head backward and causing a shot of
pain that almost blinded her.

He was suddenly standing behind her, his thick arm
to the right of her face, holding the door open. His
scent, woodsy and masculine, surrounded her. "You
hurt?"

"Uh, no. I'm fine. Sorry. It needs work done on it.
The porch has shifted and . . . well, anyway." She
shrugged and walked on into the house. The spot just
above the bridge of her nose throbbed with every
quick pulse beat, but she resisted rubbing it.

The Parker ranch house had been built before
homes had entries, so the front door opened into the
living room. He stopped just inside and looked around,
no doubt reacquainting himself.

"Uh, that tea's in the kitchen." She wound her way
through the dining room into the kitchen. He followed.

She grabbed a bowl from the cupboard, pulled a
plastic ice tray from the refrigerator and began to twist
it and break out ice cubes into the bowl. "Uh, your
mom doesn't use the ice maker. The well water isn't
fit to drink, as you may remember. It corrodes plumbing so bad, Clova has to battle it all the time. The
cistern got a crack in it last year and quit holding
water. She buys drinking water in town now."

He continued to look at her intently as she prattled
like a twit. Under his scrutiny, just preparing a glass of
iced tea seemed like a Herculean task, but she finally
succeeded and handed it to him. He took it and sipped,
then looked down into the brown liquid for a few
seconds. He looked back at her. "Got any sugar?"

"Sugar? Oh, yes. Certainly." She could have sworn
she had put sugar in that tea. She strode across the

kitchen as if it were her own, lifted a china sugar bowl from the cupboard and a spoon from a drawer and handed both to him.

He sauntered into the dining room carrying his tea and the sugar bowl. He took a seat at the round oak dining table, dumped three heaping teaspoons of sugar into the tea and stirred. When he caught her staring, he said, as if she had asked, "I got used to the way they drink tea overseas."

She nodded and sank to a chair adjacent to his. Now, with him no more than three feet away, she let herself take in his square jaw, the dark shadow of his beard, the defined cleft of his upper lip that perfectly fit against a full, square lower lip. She stopped herself; she never stared at men's mouths. "I see. Where, um, would 'overseas' be?"

"The Middle East." He nodded toward the glass she had poured for herself. She wasn't even conscious she had brought it from the kitchen. "Aren't you drinking?" he asked.

"Yes. Yes, I am." She picked up her glass and sipped. "I take mine straight," she added with a silly giggle. Her forehead throbbed like hell and she could feel the sting of broken skin. No doubt a bruise would greet her in the mirror tomorrow.

He picked up his glass and she watched as he drank deeply, his throat muscles working rhythmically. The temperature in the old house was probably eighty, but she felt an urge to shiver.

The glass had made a ring of condensation on the table. The round table, an antique, had been refinished recently and Clova was careful about marring it. Joanna grabbed a paper napkin from a holder in the middle of the table and swiped away the moisture.

He gave the tabletop, then her, a look. "Do you live here or something?"

"Uh, no. I'm just . . ." She stopped. How could she

come up with a short explanation for why she was in someone else's house making herself at home. Whatever explanation she concocted, she suspected this guy wouldn't believe her. "I live in town. It's like I said in the phone message I left you. I'm a friend helping out."

His forearms, tanned, with ropey veins standing out against defined muscle, came to rest on the tabletop. "Then you must know when my mother started raising chickens."

Chapter 7

"Oh." Joanna sat up straighter and blinked. "Well, uh, those are mine. I'm in the egg business. You know, free-range eggs?"

"Are you kidding?"

The words came at her sharp as knives. "No. I'm not. It's—it's part of the organic food craze that's going around these days. What it means is the hens aren't kept penned up. They live freely and feed on bugs and grass and stuff, like they used to in the old days. I still have to feed them some, but—"

"I know about free-range eggs. You'd have to sell a helluva a lot of eggs to make that worthwhile. So you're what, leasing land from Mom for that?"

She almost told him that she used the land for free, but the tone of his question and a gut instinct stilled her tongue. Clova's statement of a few days ago flew into her consciousness. *If somethin' happened to me, I know them boys wouldn't let you keep these chickens or these donkeys here. They'd prob'ly run you clear off.*

Dammit, she didn't want to have this conversation with him without his mother's presence. And she certainly didn't want to end up in a confrontation with a friend's son whom she didn't even know. Wounded by his antagonistic tone, she stammered, "Uh, well, um, not really. We've kind of got a deal we both like. It's, um, hard to explain."

"I'm beginning to see that. And those jackasses are part of this egg business?"

"Actually, they're supposed to keep predators away." His mouth didn't smirk, but she could see the disdain in his eyes. As quick as lightning, that look turned her anxiety into irritation, if not downright anger. She had done nothing wrong. Why should she feel so intimidated by him? After all, he was the one who had ignored his family. "They *do* keep the predators away," she added more firmly.

"That's hard to believe. Your message said my mother's sick. What's wrong with her?"

"I can't imagine that you don't know, but she had walking pneumonia back in the spring. It really got a grip on her and she hasn't been able to stop working long enough to get well. She's better, but still not a hundred percent. She waited too long to go to the doctor."

He said not one word, just looked at her, picked up his glass and finished off his tea.

She abandoned hope of congenial conversation. "Did you drive here, uh, Dalton? I can call you Dalton, right? Or would you prefer Mr. Parker?"

"You can call me Dalton."

Ass! She held her tongue, but her eyes bugged.

He turned his attention to the dining room's picture window and the view of the fenced pasture where the hens lived. In the sun-brightened area, they were strutting and clucking and scratching the ground for bugs.

Gray, life-size plastic owls perched on posts at strategic locations. Her two donkeys grazed beside the short flagpole from which thin, silky Asian flags fluttered and flicked pointed ends in the breeze, all of it her effort to protect the hens from flying predators. She didn't have to be told that a source even more fatal than a chicken hawk suddenly jeopardized her business. She had no idea whether Clova would resist if her oldest son insisted the hens be removed.

She cleared her throat. "So, um, did you drive all the way from California?"

"Flew to Lubbock. That piece of shit in the driveway's a rental." He got to his feet. "There's usually a work truck around here. Where is it?"

"Your mom took it. To feed the cows and check on the downed fence. Her dually's parked in the shed, but she doesn't usually drive it out into the pasture. There's an ATV, but it isn't working."

He mumbled a cussword.

She made up her mind to try again. Miss Congeniality. "Look, my truck's here. Your mom's all the way at the back of the south pasture. I—I could—I'd be glad to drive you down there. There really isn't a road, but my truck's got four-wheel drive."

His head turned her way and he stared at her. "I know where Hulsey's place is." Then a smirk tipped up a corner of his mouth. "But, yeah, you can take me down there. Let's go." He walked to the coat tree in the corner, helped himself to a bill cap and walked out, letting the screen door slam behind him.

Asshole! She sat at the table a few more seconds, collecting herself. She had met all kinds of people in her various enterprises, but she couldn't recall ever meeting someone she wanted to throttle at the same time she imagined jumping his bones. On a deep breath, she got to her feet, picked up the two glasses and took them to the kitchen, then followed him outside.

She found him standing on the porch, staring across the driveway at her hens. Without looking at her, he lifted the cap, pushed his fingers through thick, but short, graying hair, then shoved the cap down on his head. "Just exactly how many chickens have you got here?"

She hesitated, debating whether she should fib

about the number. Horse sense told her not to. "At this moment? Two hundred. Sometimes a few more, sometimes less."

He turned his head her way. The look that came at her was a cross between anger and incredulity. "Two hundred? Goddamn . . . chickens?"

Oh, dear God. She did a mental eye roll. "Look, Mr. Parker—"

"I said you can call me Dalton."

She mustered a glare of her own. "I think I prefer Mr. Parker."

He shrugged a shoulder. "Suit yourself. Let's go see about that fence." He left the porch in a long stride, trekked toward her Chevy pickup and climbed in on the passenger side as if the vehicle were his.

Now Joanna was so put off she didn't know if she could even drive, but she trailed after him and hoisted herself into the cab. She cranked the engine and away they went.

They soon reached the road that led to the south pasture. It was nothing more than two parallel tire tracks that traveled over grassy humps and bumps and through sandy gullies and arroyos. She set her jaw. Her pickup was her only vehicle, and she kept it clean and shiny. Though it was a four-wheel-drive pickup, she didn't drive it on rough terrain or through bushes. Unfortunately, it was too late to unvolunteer for this ride. Shifting into four-wheel drive, she steeled herself to ignore what the sagebrush branches and mesquite tree thorns would do to her paint job, not to mention that she could end up with mesquite thorns in all four tires.

At five miles per hour, the five-mile trip took almost that long—an hour.

He didn't say much, just looked all around, sometimes sticking his head out the window as if that allowed him to see more clearly. As they passed a cluster of grazing cattle, every one of them looked up and stared at them with curiosity, which, Joanna had learned since spending so much time with the Lazy P herd, was the nature of cattle.

"Cows don't look too bad," he said, more to himself than to her. "I assume they're all pregnant. Looks like Mom's still got the same crosses."

Joanna wasn't an expert on cattle and didn't know if they were pregnant. She didn't comment, though she did know that most of the Lazy P cattle were a crossbreed of Hereford and Black Angus. At this time of year, with sleek black or russet bodies and snow-white faces, they looked fat and round and healthy. Maybe they *were* pregnant.

After long minutes of a dearth of conversation, he finally said, "Pasture's in piss-poor shape."

No arguing that point. Joanna wasn't an expert on rangeland, either, but she didn't have to be to see the wide patches of bare sandy dirt where grass had once grown, and talk of the lengthy drought was common all over the county. "We've had a drought for several years running. And Clova thinks the pasture's been overgrazed."

"If it's overgrazed, why didn't she sell off some stock or move 'em to another pasture?"

Inside, Joanna winced. Any answer she gave to his question could be classified only as tattling. She couldn't remember when she had ever been so uptight. Having not eaten since early morning, her stomach began to cramp. "It wasn't . . . uh, well, it wasn't totally under her control."

"Why the hell not? She still owns the place, doesn't she?"

"Well, yes, but . . ." Joanna stopped herself. How Clova ran the Parker ranch *really* was none of her business.

"What's the 'but'?"

She drew in a breath. "Lane's supposed to be taking care of the cows, but he's gone a lot and he's—"

"Forget it. I know what he's been doing. Or not doing. He's too much like his old man."

"Mr. Parker, I'm not anxious to criticize Lane. You need to discuss this with your mother." Aggravation spiked within her again, and she found the nerve to say, "*You* haven't been around here, either, you know."

"Touché," he said, drilling her with those penetrating eyes, his irritation so sentient it almost had a life of its own. "What's your name again?" he asked.

Damn him. She refused to believe he didn't remember her name. She had left it on his voice mail and she had just told him again in the front yard. "Joanna."

He returned to staring out the window and said nothing else. She would give an arm to know what was stewing inside his head. Soon they drove up on the old blue ranch truck. A few yards away, they saw Alicia and Clova surrounded by curious cattle and struggling with a wire stretcher. They had succeeded in closing the hole in the fence.

Clova must have recognized her son immediately because she dropped her tools. She started toward them in a walk that soon became a run. Dalton opened the door and slid to the ground just in time to wrap his arms around his mother. Clova broke into sobs of joy against his chest and they stood there in an embrace inside the shade of the pickup door.

"It's okay, Mom," he said softly against her hair, patting her back. "I'm here now."

"You should o' tol' somebody you's comin'," Clova said on a hitch of breath. "I ain't got nothin' cooked or anything."

"Shh-shh," he told her softly.

The obvious affection between them didn't mesh with the gossip Joanna had heard from her mother and sister last Sunday or with the impression he had made on her in the last hour and a half. He might be an overbearing bastard, but something about him made her know that somehow he would fix everything. And he might even save the Parker ranch. From what she could see, Clova felt that way, too. Joanna looked away and wiped a tear of her own.

With Clova's love for her oldest son so obviously desperate and long-suffering, Joanna found their reunion painful to watch. It touched her in an unexpected way. If Clova loved him so much, why and how had she gone so long without contact with him?

Taking Alicia into her pickup, Joanna left mother and son at the broken fence. Once on the road back to town, fatigue that had been accumulating for a week fell on her like a boulder. The energy she had left to devote to Clova's dysfunctional family waned. All she could think of was a long, peaceful nap.

"You've done a good job this week, kiddo," she told Alicia. "Above and beyond the call, I'd say."

"You have the sore head," Alicia said, pointing to her own forehead.

Joanna didn't have the will to discuss it or explain it in detail. She gingerly touched the injury between her eyes and chuckled. "Would you believe I ran into a door?"

"Oh," the teenager said, her eyes wide with puzzlement.

"Listen, Alicia, don't come to the store tomorrow, okay? Stay home and rest."

"But who will do the work?"

Responsible Alicia. Seventeen going on thirty. Joanna dreaded the day she would have to do without her. "I'll ask Mom to fill in," Joanna answered.

"Poor Clova," the teenager said, her eyes downcast. "She such a nice lady. I don' mind helping her."

"I know. Listen, when you do come in on Monday,

pick out a bottle of your favorite fragrance, okay? I'm delivering the eggs, so I won't be there. Just leave me a note which one you chose. So I can take it off of inventory."

Alicia's face broke into a big grin. "Okay. *Sí*. I will take Angel. Pablo will be so happy. He like for me to smell good."

Joanna drove home thinking about Alicia and her boyfriend. Opposite from Alicia, Pablo Sanchez was a worthless kid who was probably in Alicia's pants, which didn't bode well for Joanna's favorite teenager's future. For an instant she wondered if she should say something to Alicia, but she quickly put that thought out of her mind. She simply had to stop involving herself in other people's lives.

At home, she shoved a Lean Cuisine frozen dinner in the microwave without even looking to see what she would be eating, then sorted her laundry and stuffed a few items into the washer. Dinner turned out to be low-fat lasagna. She ate, then changed into her sleeping clothes and crawled into bed. She didn't intend to merely nap. She intended to sink into unconsciousness. Mom and the three girls who worked in the beauty salon had done without her all week. They could do without her one more day.

She snuggled into her pillow with Clova's son on her mind. Meeting him might have left her baser urges unsettled, but that didn't keep her from drifting into a deep sleep.

She awoke a few hours later remembering all that she had to do. She had told Shari and Jay she would meet them at the football game tonight. Their oldest son was a player.

With Dalton now present to help Clova, Joanna could use tomorrow and Sunday to pack the cartons of eggs she had accumulated into cases and prepare them for delivery to her customers in Lubbock and

Amarillo on Monday. Then she could wallow in a pay-day. She could eat lunch at Tia Maria's or Pasta House, and she might even drop into a mall and shop.

But before she could do any of that, she had to return to the Parker ranch for this evening's egg gathering, risking another confrontation with Dalton. It was crazy how she had hoped so avidly for him to show up. Now she could hardly wait for him to leave.

But she had an insane side that sometimes raised its irrational head, and it seemed to have more fantastical ideas.

She made her way to the bathroom. There the vanity mirror confirmed her worst fear. A dark bruise the size of a half dollar showed between her eyebrows and on up her forehead. A small red line where the skin had been broken by the blow from the screen door's edge looked like an inch-long stripe. "Shit," she muttered.

She washed her face, wincing and frowning as her washcloth touched the injured area. Afterward, she dabbed antibiotic cream onto the broken skin. Following that, she smoothed a cream she sold in her retail store under her eyes. Formulated by a company with a French name, it claimed to reduce puffiness and dark circles, and it cost more than she would ever have paid if she hadn't been able to buy it at wholesale. Being single and with myriad skincare products available to her, she had no intention of looking any older than she had to.

Back in her bedroom, remembering Dalton Parker's eyes, which looked as if they could penetrate cement and how they had scanned her body, she rummaged through her dresser for a shirt. The *right* shirt. She found it at the bottom of a drawer, testimony to how much time had passed since she had been inspired to try to impress some guy. The shirt was a bright blue

cotton and Spandex tank she usually wore with her
tightest Cruel Girl jeans and her crystal-studded belt
when she went dancing in the cowboy nightclubs over
at the state line. Free of adornment, the top was cut
low enough to be fun, and it hugged her torso like
a glove. She always received compliments, even wolf
whistles, when she wore it.

She slid it over her head, then stood in front of the
mirror, assessing herself. Though Dalton Parker was
a couple of years older than she, a man as sexy as he
was probably had his choice of women a lot younger
than thirty-five.

Thirty-five. A landmark age. So what? Her body
didn't look so bad. She turned in front of the mirror,
happy to note she still had a firm, flat tummy. At least
she was getting some benefit from heaving all those
sacks of feed for the hens. Her boobs weren't huge,
but they didn't sag and she had cleavage, facts that
made Shari envious. Of course, Shari had nursed all
four of her kids, so it really wasn't a fair contest.

She pulled on jeans and made another appraisal in
the mirror. Then she stopped herself. "What are you
doing?" she whispered to her reflection. Dalton Parker was a rude jerk. And he had already shown his
dislike for her. But even if he *liked* her, it wouldn't
matter. He probably had a parade of Valley Girls
chasing him, not to mention the woman who answered
his phone as if she lived at his house. He would definitely go for the tanned and blond type. Joanna
yanked off the tank top and replaced it with a work
shirt, grumbling and cussing.

Once at the Parker ranch, she saw that the ranch's
work truck hadn't returned, so Clova and Dalton must
still be working on the fence. Thank God for that, a
part of her said, but the wicked part that had been
dancing with glee since his arrival this morning was

disappointed. "Face it, Joanna," she mumbled. "You just want another opportunity to try to get his attention. And why would you want that from a bastard?"

She went about her business, gathering eggs and listening to Dulce cluck and scratch along beside her. As she started for the egg-processing room to wash and refrigerate the eggs, she lifted Dulce out of the fenced area to come with her. Forcing herself to not even look at the ranch house, she made her way to her own little space.

She was taking the last batch of eggs from the washer and laying them out on clean towels to drain when she heard a motor she recognized. The ranch's work truck. She concentrated on the task at hand as first one door, then the other slammed with a metallic clap. Soon she heard footsteps on the gravel driveway, and she was sure they weren't Clova's. Her whole body stiffened.

Dalton stepped up on the small concrete slab just outside the door, almost trampling Dulce. The hen squawked and flapped and flew off in a commotion of noise and feathers. "Oh, shit," Joanna cried. She dropped everything and shoved past Dalton to the outside, where Dulce was squawking and hopping around a few feet away. She threw a glare at Dalton over her shoulder. "Dammit, you scared her!"

Darting left and right, she finally caught up with the hen, scooped her up with both hands and looked back at the egg-washing room. Dalton was standing in the doorway, watching her, his shoulder leaning against the doorjamb, his hands stuffed into his jeans pockets. His T-shirt was covered with dirt and his cap had been shoved to the back of his head.

Careless, thoughtless jerk. He could have hurt her favorite hen.

Sending him another withering glare, she marched across the driveway to the pasture where Dulce lived, turned her loose inside the fence and returned to the processing room.

"Hey, I'm sorry," he said, turning sideways as she squeezed past him through the doorway. "I'm not used to dodging chickens when I walk."

Mentally swearing, she stripped off her latex gloves and her coveralls and dug clean ones out of the closet, resisting the urge to slam the closet door. She still had to pack the washed eggs into cartons, so she shook a clean jumpsuit free of its folds.

"You're changing clothes?" His gaze leveled on her face.

She was sure he was looking at the bruise between her eyes. "I don't handle the eggs with the same gloves and clothes after I've handled the chickens," she groused, looking up at him as she stepped into fresh blue coveralls.

She saw amusement in his expression. She also felt his gaze roaming over her, head to toe. What she interpreted in that was less easily defined.

"I don't blame you," he said. "Chickens are filthy fuckers."

Inside, she winced. This was Hatlow. She rarely heard men use the *F* word in female company. She glared at him again as she zipped up her coveralls. "Do you eat eggs, Mr. Parker?"

"Yep. Over easy. Preferably with bacon. Preferably served up by a hot woman who knows how to cook."

"Do tell. Well, that wouldn't be me." She snapped on a new pair of purple latex gloves.

He braced a shoulder against the doorjamb again, watching her unhook the egg washer from the faucet. "Oh, I don't know. Before you put that sack on, what I saw looked pretty hot."

Hot? She didn't often hear men in Hatlow openly and unabashedly call a woman "hot," either. She wished to God she could feel insulted, but that insane part of her she had already debated in front of her bathroom mirror at home felt a tiny thrill at his words. "The cooking part was what I referred to. I raise hens and sell eggs. I do not *cook* eggs."

He tilted his head back and laughed, and she wondered whether she saw a teasing glint in his eyes. He craned his neck, poking his head inside her room and looking around, but he didn't come in. "When I was a young buck, this was a workshop. Mom told me you fixed it up."

Joanna would have loved being a fly on the wall during the talk between him and Clova. She couldn't keep from worrying over the consequences if Clova told him she had offered to give Joanna land. "It was covered with dirt and grease. I almost never got it cleaned up."

"Must have cost you a bundle."

Oh, not much. Just my house and practically every spare dime I could get my hands on. "Did you get the fence fixed?"

"Temporarily. Doing it right is more than a day's work. It's been neglected too long. That whole south line needs to be rebuilt."

"There are a couple of fence-building crews around here. I'm sure Clova has their names and phone numbers."

"I'm gonna do it myself. Save Mom some money. I think I still remember how to fix a fence."

"That would be nice. Where's Clova now?"

"She went in to do laundry. I tried to get her to rest, but she wouldn't."

"Well, that's your mom. She works all the time. I don't know how she does it."

"She sent me over here to tell you to come over to the house for supper when you finish. She's frying steak."

"I'm going to the football game with friends."

"Oh, yeah. Friday night football. I remember those days."

"I should think you would. When you lived here, you were the Friday night hero."

"Hero's a relative term, babe." He came inside, walked to her drain counter and picked up a blue egg. "Do you dye these or what?"

Her egg-washing room was barely large enough for herself and a person as small as Clova or Alicia. Dalton Parker filled the room. His chest was only inches from her shoulder, and his manly scent surrounded her. Pheromones. She had read about that weird chemical in perfume ads. Her jaw tightened, but she schooled her face into what she hoped was a normal, unruffled expression and looked up at him. "The Ameraucana hens lay them that way."

"The what?"

"Ameraucana. They're descended from a South American breed called Araucanas. Most of the time they lay blue and green eggs. I think Dulce, the hen you almost stomped, is a purer strain of Ameraucana. Most of her eggs are turquoise. They're pretty."

"Huh," he said, holding the egg with his fingertips as he turned it over and studied it. He carefully placed it back on the towel. "Does being blue make some kind of difference?"

"Some people think the colored eggs are more nutritious, but I don't know if there's any science to back that up."

"Tell me something." He cocked his head and gave her a squint-eyed look. "How'd you con my mother into letting you do this?"

Chapter 8

Anger swept through Joanna like a range fire. She gasped. "Do what?"

He made a broad gesture around the room with his arm. "My mom's a cowman. Has been since the day she was born. So was her pa, her grandpa, her great-grandpa and her great-great. No fuckin' way would she turn this place over to a bunch of nasty goddamn chickens. I nearly wrecked that piece-of-shit rental when I drove up and saw them this morning."

"I beg your pardon," she said firmly, working not to snarl. "I didn't *con* her into anything. She volunteered. The egg business was her idea. And the chickens are hens. Premium hybrid egg layers that have cost me a lot of money."

He didn't say anything, just continued to glare at her with heated eyes and a scowling mouth. No doubt he thought she was lying about the egg business being Clova's idea. "Not that you'd know, Mr. Parker, but your mother is a lonely woman. She—"

"What I *know*, Miz Walsh"—he came closer, invading her space and leaning into her, his face no farther than a foot from hers—"is that no self-respecting cattle grower willingly turns a working cattle ranch into a goddamn chicken yard without a little outside persuasion."

She could stand his arrogance no longer. She stepped back, looking him in the eye and stabbing the

air with her finger. "Since you seem to know everything about something you haven't been near in years,
I guess you'd be shocked to hear that your mother
wanted me and my hens out here because she likes
our company."

"Is that a fact."

"It sure is. Lane isn't here half the time, and she
doesn't hear from you." Joanna stopped herself. *Good
grief, I am almost yelling.* She dropped her hand to
her hip and lowered her voice. "If you were so concerned about what she might be doing in your lengthy
absence, perhaps you should have come home. Or at
the very least, made a phone call and pretended you
cared what happens to her and to this place."

Tears burned her eyes. Anger did that to her, but
she willed them away. "What's it been since you were
last here, three or four years?" She paused, shooting
daggers at him with her eyes, then turned back to her
eggs. "Now. If you'll excuse me, *sir*, I'd like to finish
up so I can leave."

His brow arched and he tucked back his chin. "Sir,
huh? Very good, Miz Walsh. Damn few people call
me sir."

"I don't wonder," she snapped, scowling up at him.

As they held each other's hot glares, a cell phone
warbled. He looked down, picked the device off his
belt and glanced at it. He flipped it open, checked the
screen and stuck it to his ear, his demeanor changing.
He smiled into the phone. "Hey, babe. It's me."

Betty Boop, Joanna thought.

"Flight was fine, darlin'. . . . No, but I've been helping Mom with some fencing. I'm sore all over. I need
one of your, ah, rubdowns." He gave a low, lascivious
chuckle, then waited. "That's okay. I'll call him
Monday. . . . Aww, you're a sweetheart, honey. I miss
you, too, baby."

Joanna rolled her eyes.

The phone still plastered against his ear, he stepped out of the room and out of earshot.

"Good riddance," she grumbled. Maybe Betty Boop wanted him to come home so she could give him that rubdown. And maybe he would go.

Joanna put away her equipment, then packed the eggs into cartons. She slid them into the refrigerator, tossed her latex gloves into the trash and peeled off her cap and jumpsuit. She gathered up the two used jumpsuits to take home with her so she could send them out to be laundered with the towels from the beauty salon.

When she stepped outside, her tormentor was leaning his backside against her pickup door, arms crossed over his chest, one ankle crossed over the other. "Looks like your truck got scratched going through the brush this morning."

She glowered at the long marks and scratches on her beautiful burgundy red pickup. "Yeah, it does, doesn't it?"

"Look, I didn't come out here to yank your chain."

"Really? Then why did you do it?" She reached past him for the door latch, her arm brushing his. Startled by the touch, she shot a look at him across her shoulder.

His gaze held hers as he stepped aside. "I don't know. Must be the chickens. I can't figure out what's gone on with my mom. I'm not usually such a horse's ass. And Mom's gonna be pissed off if I don't bring you over to the house for supper."

She turned her attention to opening the door and shoved her jumpsuits onto the passenger seat. "Clova knows I go to the football game on Friday nights. My best friend's kid plays."

She climbed behind the wheel and shut the door. When she turned the key in the ignition, loud country-western music blasted into the pickup cab and she jumped. She turned it down and buzzed down the window. "Just so you'll know, I come out here twice a day, every day. If I can't make it, I send my teenage employee, Alicia. She was the one out at the fence today helping your mother. You can rag on me and I can take it, but I really would appreciate it if you don't attack her. She—"

"I don't attack people," he growled.

"What would you call that ambush this morning? And this evening? I'll be amazed if Dulce doesn't go into a molt."

Hot tears flew to her eyes. Not only was she angry, she couldn't bear the thought of her Dulce losing her feathers and being cannibalized by the other hens.

"What the hell's that?"

"Never mind."

"Goddammit, I didn't mean to make you cry," he snapped.

Detecting no sincere contrition, she wiped her nose with the back of her hand. "I'm not crying. The hens are harmless and—"

"Lady, chickens aren't harmless. I was in Israel when they slaughtered thousands of the filthy damn things because of that goddamn bird flu. The same thing in Turkey and in Greece. So they aren't *harmless*."

Bird flu. Crap. Joanna worried about it every day, read every word she could find. "As I started to say, my hens are harmless and so am I. I'm clean and I try to keep a tight rein on my little operation so it isn't any more intrusive than necessary. But all of that's beside the point. I've got your message." She revved the engine, pressed the brake and yanked the transmission into reverse. "I don't know how long you're planning on being here, but maybe you'll feel better when I come out if you stay away from me and my hens."

He didn't answer right away, just stared at her with unreadable eyes hiding behind black eyelashes that most women would kill for. "That's fair," he said at last.

"Be sure to tell your mom I'm going to the ballgame. She'll understand."

"Okay. Fine."

Joanna buzzed up her window and backed up in an arc, keeping her eyes trained on him in her side mirror. He continued to stand there on the driveway, watching her. "Asshole," she muttered.

When she reached the highway, she glanced at the dash clock. By the time she got home and changed clothes, she would be late to the ball game. Nothing new about that. She arrived late everywhere she went, not deliberately, but she never seemed to have enough time to do everything that needed doing.

She worried all the way home. Clova's offer of a parcel of land now seemed as nonexistent as if it hadn't been spoken. Now that Dalton had come, she could see there was every possibility that in the very near future, her hens would have nowhere to live.

Headed for a bleacher seat, Joanna squeezed past several football fans decked out in black and gold, Hatlow High School's colors. Though the daytime temperature had been hot, the night air nipped at her cheeks. She was glad she had changed into a warm pullover sweater—one with black and gold stripes, of course. She dropped to the seat Shari had saved for her, relieved to sit down at last.

Beneath tall banks of brilliant lights, the Hatlow High School band, neatly uniformed in black with white trim, was marching up the field, playing a lively march as it maintained precision formation. The crowd cheered and whistled. Hatlow was as proud of its band as it was of its winning football team.

Shari looked at her watch. "You're late."

Joanna had missed the first half of the game and the band performance of the opposing team. She craned to see the scoreboard. "Sorry. Who's winning?"

"Our boys are ahead. Cody's doing good."

Cody was Shari and Jay Huddleston's seventeen-year-old son, the oldest of their four boys. He was a hard-bodied high school jock glaringly suffering from testosterone overload. Joanna had been present the day he was born.

Shari finally looked Joanna's way. "Oh, my God. What happened to your head?"

Joanna had tried to cover the bruise between her eyes with concealer, then foundation. Apparently that hadn't worked. She gave an audible sigh. "I ran into Clova's screen door."

"Ouch. Is that what kept you so long?"

Jay, sitting to Shari's left, peered around his wife. "Yeah, Joanna, where you been? A fox get in the henhouse?" He yuck-yucked at his own joke.

Jay had been a high school hunk himself. He had grown into a man who still made women go silly and giggly when he was around. His brown hair had turned silver at the temples, but his blue eyes continued to twinkle with mischief, as they always had.

Shari had thickened around the middle, but Jay was still lean and trim, with broad shoulders that filled out a subdued button-down and a cute butt that filled out a pair of tight Wranglers. Though he and Shari needled each other incessantly, everyone knew they were as much in love today as they had been at eighteen. In the early years of their marriage, Shari had seemingly been pregnant constantly. Back then, the common joke in Hatlow was that with Shari sharing a bed every night with a stud like Jay, no wonder she was pregnant all the time.

In many ways, Joanna envied Shari and her rowdy

family of males, envied the way Jay looked at his wife as if there were no other woman in the world and the possessive posturing he sometimes displayed. If a man had ever looked or felt the same way about Joanna, she didn't know it.

Now she leaned forward and replied to Jay across Shari. "I'll have you know, Jay Huddleston, if I stopped bringing you eggs, you'd miss them."

He laughed again. "How is that possible? Do I look like a man that can tell the difference between a forty-cent egg and one that costs a nickel? So who took a swing at you?"

"She ran into a door," Shari told him.

He guffawed. "What were you drinking?"

"I got delayed," Joanna said to Shari, ignoring the teasing. "Clova's son showed up."

Shari drew a quick breath. "Dalton? You are shitting me."

Jay peered around his wife again. "Dalton Parker's back in town?"

"He drove up in a rental car this morning."

"Wow," Shari said. "That is amazing. Listen, what does he look like?"

"Like a guy. What else?"

"Is he still good-looking? He was so hot when we were in high school."

Joanna's thoughts rushed to her first reaction upon renewing acquaintance with Dalton Parker. *Yep, he's hot.*

"And you're an expert on hot," Jay said, veering a sidelong glance at his wife.

"I married you, didn't I?" She slugged his shoulder with her small fist and let her hand rest there. Joanna had figured out long ago that with Shari and Jay, this sarcastic back-and-forth was nothing more—or less— than foreplay. More than once she had wondered if they jumped into bed the minute they reached home.

"He's still hot to look at," Joanna said. "But he's an absolute and totally arrogant jerk."

"I can't believe that," Jay said. "We played football together, him and me. I always thought he was a good guy. He was a couple of years older and smarter'n all the rest of us, but still a good guy."

"He must have changed," Joanna said. "I'm not sure I'd call him a good guy. And I didn't see anything that made me believe the smart part."

The band left the field and formed up in two columns in the end zone, setting up a great roll of drums. A double row of cheerleaders and pep squad members lined up at the oversize doorway leading from the dressing rooms.

"Here they come, Mama." Jay slapped Shari's knee, then stood up, whistling and clapping his hands.

Seconds later, Hatlow's Mustangs, brightly uniformed in black and gold, ran the gauntlet of supporters to drum rolls and cheers and whistles from the bleachers.

"Joanna," Jay said, looking back at her across his shoulder as he continued to clap to the rhythm of the band music. "I want you to keep an eye on Cody this half. He's doing a damn good job."

Joanna could see the pride and excitement in Jay. Every time she saw that enthusiasm in him, she couldn't keep from remembering the day of Cody's birth. On that day, Jay's expression had been closer to bewilderment than pride. He was eighteen years old, still a few weeks away from high school graduation.

"The one I want you to keep an eye on is that little blond cheerleader with the hair down to her butt," Shari said. "Jay caught Cody and her half naked in the backseat of his pickup last night."

Knowing Cody as she did, Joanna could envision the scene. She remembered Jay being much the same when they were in high school. Joanna gazed harder

at the line of cheerleaders wearing short black skirts
and bright gold sweaters. The subject blonde looked
like a typical high school hottie. "Like father, like
son," she said.

"What's that supposed to mean?" Shari asked.

"Nothing. I just remember how it used to be when
we were kids."

Of Joanna's small circle of close friends in high
school, Shari had been the first to "do it." In high
school in Hatlow, Texas, that had been a big deal. Just
those few years ago, there were no reports of thirteen-
year-olds engaging in sex acts for entertainment. Shari
had shocked all of them by declaring her intention to
"go all the way" with Jay, and the remaining virgins
eagerly awaited her report at the following night's
slumber party. "It was icky and messy and I didn't like
it," Shari said. Obviously her attitude had changed.

"Where were they parked?" Joanna asked.

"Right here under these bleachers," Shari answered,
pointing downward with her thumb. "So he's grounded.
Jay and him are gonna be spending some quality
father-son time every evening until Cody's forty."

"Humph," Joanna said. "I suppose he hasn't figured
out that his mother was six months pregnant when she
and his father got married."

"We don't discuss that."

The teams lined up across the field, facing each other
for the kickoff. Drums rolled and everyone in the stands
stood up, sounding out a collective "ooooohhh" until
the kicker booted the ball. With the game under way
and boosters seated again, the band broke into Hatlow's fight song. The cheerleaders set up a chant and
another hand-clapping routine.

Clapping to the rhythm of the music, Shari leaned
toward Joanna. "Jay and I are celebrating my birthday
Wednesday night. He's taking me to the Rusty Spur
over at the state line."

Oops. Joanna had forgotten Shari's upcoming birthday. What kind of friend was she? "They have a band on a weeknight?"

"No, just the jukebox, but that's okay. You're gonna come with us, right?"

"Oh, damn, Shari. I don't know if I can do it on a weeknight. I get up with the chickens, you know. Literally."

"Joanna, I'll be thirty-six years old. You're my best friend. You've got to be there to witness me going over the hill."

"You're not over the hill 'til you're forty."

Jay piped up. "When you live in a house with four half-grown boys, you're over the hill at thirty-five. Believe me. C'mon, Joanna. Go with us. Some horny dude might be lurking in the Spur. When was the last time you got a little?"

"Jay!" Shari punched his arm. "That's none of your business."

"I'll go on one condition," Joanna said. "I have to get home—"

"Get him! Get him! Stop him!" Jay leapt to his feet, yelling and waving his fist. He slapped Shari on the shoulder with a ham-size hand and nearly unseated her. "Did you see that, Mama? Did you see that?"

"Oh, hell, I missed it," Shari said, squinting toward the huddled football players. "Is Cody still on the field?"

Jay gave an exaggerated sigh and clasped the sides of his head with both hands. "God Almighty, Shari. Not anymore. He's an offensive lineman. The other team got the ball."

"Oh." Still, she sprang to her feet and thrust a fist in the air. "Go, Cody!" Then she sat back down and refocused on Joanna. "Anyway, you're gonna come with us, right?"

"I guess so," Joanna replied, already regretting making the commitment. She would prefer to take Shari to lunch, just the two of them, and give her a nice present.

Dalton had forgotten what a fine cook his mother was. She, on the other hand, must have remembered how much he used to love chicken-fried steak with mashed potatoes and cream gravy. These days he rarely ate such fare, but tonight he stuffed himself.

Joanna Walsh would be sorry she didn't stay for supper. He was still annoyed that she hadn't been all that accepting of his apology. He thought he had been gracious.

Mom topped off the meal with hot peach cobbler made from home-canned peaches, and he couldn't resist a serving with some vanilla ice cream.

After they ate, he helped police the kitchen. Mom washed dishes by hand, he noticed, then recalled how the ranch's hard water calcified plumbing. A dishwasher would have stood no chance. He dried the dishes for her, something he had done as a child, stacking them as he dried them on the ancient butcher block that had sat in the middle of the kitchen for as long as he could remember.

He strained for conversation. Communication was hard with a woman he hardly knew anymore. Hell, he had never known her, really. She had been a puzzle to him forever.

Now even her appearance seemed alien. The face of the mother that had always been affixed in his mind didn't show deep creases around her mouth or fans of wrinkles at the corners of her eyes. It struck him as he glimpsed her profile that though she had aged, he could still see the strong resemblance between himself and her—the dark brown eyes and black hair, the prominent facial features, the same olive skin. Anyone could tell they were blood kin.

"I'm glad you went to the hospital and saw Lane," she said. "You always meant a lot to him."

Dalton didn't like being reminded of that. Guilt pinched him that he had made little effort to stay in touch with Lane. He had sent a postcard from here, a snapshot from there, some silly souvenir that had little meaning. "He looks pitiful lying in that hospital bed."

"I'm pretty sure a drunk drivin' charge is comin'. I asked Clyde to find us a lawyer."

Clyde, Clyde, Clyde. Dalton searched his memory. "I must have forgotten who Clyde is."

"Clyde Jordan? Why, Dalton Parker, I can't believe you don't remember him. He's been a friend o' this family since I was a girl. Lord, he was friends with my daddy."

An old guy, Dalton thought. He had probably never known him. "Do you know what Lane's blood alcohol was?"

She shook her head. "I 'magine it was too high. He's been hittin' the bottle hard. He don't seem to be able to help hisself. Too bad he can't go to one o' them fancy clinics like them movie stars go to."

"Yeah, I guess," Dalton said, recalling that a penchant for alcoholism is hereditary. He might not know his father's identity, but he was glad not to be the spawn of Earl Cherry.

The chickens had been stuck in his mind since the moment he saw them and more so after he learned the story of them. He wanted to bring them up, but he didn't want to risk a quarrel so soon after his arrival. The chickens could wait. "So what's going on with the ranch, Mom?" He carefully set a dried bowl on top of another one. "That back fence looked like it hasn't been taken care of in a helluva long time."

"The ranch ain't got no money, Dalton. It's been touch and go for a long time. The drought, cattle prices. Somethin' new I can't do nothin' about comes up ever' day. A lot of the old-timers have sold out." She rearranged the dishes waiting to be dried in the dish drainer. "Sometimes I think I ought to, too, but if I did, I wouldn't get nothin' in my pocket. The bank would get it all. Then I'd be even poorer than I am now."

A red flag unfurled in Dalton's mind. "Farmers Bank downtown? Do you owe them much?"

"They're holdin' paper on ever'thin'."

As Dalton recalled, it wasn't unusual for some part of a rancher's livestock and equipment to be used as collateral for operating loans. "But not the land, right?"

She continued to wash dishes without acknowledging his question.

"Mom. You've mortgaged the land?" He couldn't mask the incredulity in the question. His grandpa, her father, would have said a rancher who mortgaged his land was on his way to doomsday.

She heaved a huge sigh, still not looking at him. " 'Til Lane got hurt, that was my worst trouble." She shook water from her hands, picked up a dish towel and dried them, then walked over to an envelope-filled pocket hanging on the wall. She picked one and brought it back to him. "I wasn't gonna bother you with this, but I guess you might as well know it. I 'magine ever'body in town knows it."

He slung the dish towel over his shoulder and took the envelope. The letter inside warned her that the land taxes hadn't been paid for the past two years and failure to pay them was grounds for foreclosure. A copy of a summary from the county tax assessor was attached. He saw that the ranch had an agriculture tax exemption, but still, two years' worth of taxes on seventeen sections added up. He looked up at her, but her eyes and hands were busy with scrubbing a skillet.

"But you've banked there forever," he said. "They know you. They'll work with you. Just go talk to them."

She stopped her work and finally looked at him, and he saw the angst that was in her heart in her eyes.

"No, Dalton. Things is changed. Some foreigners bought the bank. Ain't even any o' the old people workin' there anymore. They wanted ever'body that worked there to speak Spanish. Most of 'em quit. They didn't wanna speak Spanish."

Puzzled, Dalton's eyes narrowed. "So who owns the bank now?"

"I don't know 'em. It's a bank from Spain."

"Spain? As in Europe? How the hell did a bank in Spain even find Hatlow, Texas?"

"I don't know. They've bought a bunch o' the banks in the little towns around. All I know is they ain't farmer friendly anymore. They want the Mexcun bizness. They's gettin' to be more Mexcuns than Americans around here."

As a resident of Southern California, Dalton well knew the dramatic changes brought by the massive Latino immigration. He had no trouble believing that the bank, seeking the Hispanic business, would require its employees to speak Spanish before it would insist that the Hispanic customers speak English. He made a mental note. Monday morning he would be on Farmers Bank's doorstep. He would get to the bottom of this situation.

"So, Mom, that back pasture looks awful. There's big chunks of bare dirt back there. How many cows are you grazing now?"

"I got a little over four hundred mother cows."

The longer Dalton had been removed from the ranching industry, the farther it had receded in his thoughts, but bits came back to him. He did a simple arithmetic calculation in his head, at the same time considering that raising cattle in the arid environment of West Texas called for deft range management. Four hundred cows plus their calves were too many for the amount of grazing the Parker ranch owned. An even bigger red flag waved in his mind. "That sounds like a lot."

She shrugged. "Lane thought if we added some extra cows, in a couple o' years, we'd get ahead o' the bank. If we could o' got some rain, it might o' worked. When the Good Lord didn't bless us, I thought we could get out of it by buyin' a little extra feed. But since they started makin' gasoline outta all the corn, feed's got so damn high. Besides that, feedin' every day makes a lot o' extra work."

Thoughts tumbled through Dalton's mind. Overgrazing was a disaster irremediable in a short amount of time. In a fuckin' desert, it could take a generation. Hell, it was possible it couldn't be fixed at all. A sharp ache traveled from temple to temple through his brain. By coming back here, what the hell had he stepped into?

His mother finished straightening the kitchen, came over to him and looked into his face. She reached up and laid a hand on his shoulder. "I thank you for comin' home, Dalton. Seein' you makes me happy. You've been gone a long time."

He patted her hand, his mind still on the ranch's problems. "I know, Mom. I've just been . . . well, busy."

"I think I'll turn in." She gave him a weak smile, placing a hand on her back and rubbing. "That fence buildin's hard on an ol' woman."

Dalton watched as she left the kitchen and disappeared into the hallway, the visual from earlier in the afternoon of her and that teenage kid struggling with a wire stretcher vivid in his mind. She was a small woman, probably didn't weigh much over a hundred pounds. She had no business building fence. But what the hell could he do about any of it? He didn't live here anymore.

He turned on the TV and channel surfed a while, then settled on a news channel out of habit. TV news was so much a part of his life, he felt as if he knew the commentators personally. He could even predict what some of them would say next. World events dictated his daily plan. A part of him was trained to wonder if there was somewhere in the world he needed to be. Somewhere besides Texas.

Chapter 9

Joanna, Shari and Jay left the Hatlow High School stadium soon after ten o'clock. Hatlow's Mustangs had won, a fact that had Jay overjoyed. As far as Joanna knew, Jay and Shari, having gotten married so young, had rarely been out of Wacker County. Their son's participation in high school football was the most exciting thing in Jay's life. For that matter, most of Hatlow was the same.

"Joanna," Jay said as the three of them walked to the parking lot, "what ever happened to that Scott dude you were hanging out with?"

She gave an unladylike snort. "He was the last straw. Thanks to him, I gave up on men."

"I told you that," Shari said to her husband.

"I must've forgot," Jay said.

"You never listen to a word I say, Jay Huddleston."

"Shari, you say so damn many words, my ears can't sort 'em all out. Listen," he said to Joanna, "when you see ol' Dalton again, tell him to come by my shop and I'll give him a beer or a cup of coffee. I can't remember the last time I saw that guy."

"If I ever talk to him again, I'll be sure to tell him," Joanna grumbled.

The thought of seeing Dalton again held zero appeal. In fact, she would like to figure out a way to avoid him until he departed for California.

* * *

At eleven Dalton decided to turn in. It was early for him. Back in California, it was only nine o'clock. He went to bed in the room where he had slept in his youth. Faded floral wallpaper, filmy white curtains, a paper window shade.

The smell of dust and disuse surrounded him. If he had to guess, he would say he lay on the same lumpy, sagging mattress on which he had slept the last time he visited several years back, the same one that had been his as a kid. Only now it felt worse. Back when he was a teenager, he had slid a piece of plywood between the mattress and the box spring to make the bed firmer. That was more than twenty years ago. Of course the plywood had been removed.

Hell, he should just get a new bed. In fact, he could easily do that while he was in Lubbock tomorrow.

Working on the fence all afternoon had worn on him, too, but not in a bad way. Most work around the ranch, any ranch, was physically demanding, but he had never minded. Besides liking the cattle, he liked the outdoors, liked the physical exertion.

His thoughts veered to his mother. His feeling for her was a confused mixture of affection and resentment—respect for her role in giving him life, but bitterness because she had chosen Earl Cherry's happiness and welfare over that of either of her sons. And after she had demonstrated so much unflinching loyalty, Cherry hadn't even been faithful to her. The son of a bitch had fucked around with women all over the county and even in Lovington. Dalton had known it even as a kid, had seen women in the truck with Earl. His mother had known, too, but ignored it or made excuses for it. Of the many things about her that Dalton had never understood, number one on the list was her relationship with Cherry.

He was stunned that she had hocked the friggin' land, the bedrock of any ranching operation. It might be too late to do much about that, but he could manage a solution to the tax problem. Monday, he would go to the courthouse and simply write a check. Catching up the taxes would lift some pressure.

He had always believed that someday the ranch would belong to him and Lane, though he, personally, had never longed for it or felt it was owed to him. Still, seeing the chickens was a brutal reminder of how quickly things could change. Hell, even if his mother got out of this financial bind, she could get married again, and as capricious as she had always been with her feelings for her sons, she could give the whole damn place to her new husband.

Dalton had had the latter thought before, which he had used as a reason not to invest his own funds in the place. Even by paying the taxes, he could well be pouring money down a rat hole. He wasn't stingy, but he didn't like wasting money.

So was selling the place the long-term solution? When it came to the nut cutting, he doubted Mom would do it. Generations of Parker ancestors were buried in the old family cemetery a few miles from the house. That had meaning to a family that had endured prejudice and discrimination for all of the years the Parker Comanche ancestors had. Dalton hadn't experienced those offenses himself, but he knew his grandparents had.

He began to sink into the well of sleep, making a plan for tomorrow. Return the rental car, take his mother with him to the hospital, talk to Lane's doctor. From looking at the kid, Dalton suspected he could be laid up for a long time.

Following the hospital visit, he and Mom would pick up some fence-mending supplies and he would find a place to buy a new bed. Then he had to find a Best Buy or somewhere to pick up some computer peripherals. He had brought his laptop and his drivers and

software with him. The quiet nights would be perfect
for choosing and editing the photographs he had shot
overseas. Regardless of what else happened, he couldn't
forget he had promised his editor he would have no
problem meeting his deadline on his next book of
photographs.

Two hours later, he was wide awake, lying in a pool
of sweat, his heart pounding in his ears. The nightmare, a horror filled with chaos, Technicolor images
of rubble and blood and scattered body parts, did that
to him. He heard the human screams and wails, the
screeching sirens. He smelled the stench of cordite
lingering in the air.

He sat up, swinging his feet to the floor, mentally
and emotionally fighting his way back to the reality of
being in a safe place. The dream didn't come every
night, but once it had awakened him, he usually remained sleepless and strung out for an hour or two
or even a whole night. He rubbed his eyes and sat
there a few minutes, waiting for his heartbeat to slow.
Finally, he looked at his watch, which he could read
in the dark. Midnight in LA.

The clean smell of the dewy rangeland and the
steady saw of crickets drifted in through two tall open
windows. He didn't sleep with the windows open in
his Los Angeles house. He didn't dare. But in this
house, the open windows were a necessity. Built some
years before 1900, the house had no ducted air-
conditioning system. As a kid, Dalton had scarcely
noticed. When temperatures rose to sweltering in late
summer and early fall, his mother and Earl put swamp
coolers in a couple of the windows. They turned them
on only during the hottest part of the day.

No question in Dalton's mind, his rugged youth had
conditioned him to survive in the desert. Growing up,
he had spent his days outdoors, too tired by night to
let the temperature affect him. Endurance was a men-

tal thing anyway. He had learned that much in the
Marine Corps and from the GIs in Iraq. Even with
the temperature at 130 degrees, those kids slogged
around the desert covered by pounds of clothing, carrying pounds of equipment.

The open windows and the cooler outside temperature didn't keep the room from being stuffy. He rose,
pulled on his shirt and jeans and slid his feet into his
boots. He stole from the room, through the house and
out onto the front porch, stuffing his hands into his
jeans pockets against the cool of the night.

A three-quarter moon and a billion stars in a velvet
sky stained the landscape silver. The long white caliche driveway stretched ahead of him like a pale ribbon
leading to the highway. Far out on the horizon several
columns of the bright white lights of oil derricks shimmered like skinny Christmas trees against the black
sky.

Nothing stirred. From a great distance he heard the
call of a whippoorwill. The familiar sound brought
back his childhood for a flicker of memory, but to this
day, as familiar as the sound was to his ear, as far as
he knew, he had never seen one of those friggin' birds.

From an even greater distance, the shrill bark of
coyotes pierced the night. . . . Coyotes? Hell, yes, coyotes. Why weren't they out there in that nasty damn
chicken yard feasting on those fuckin' chickens?

He stepped off the porch and walked over to the
fenced pasture where the stinking damned things lived.
He could see the silhouettes of at least four coops
made of weathered plywood, and he presumed chickens roosted in all of them. The jackasses stood together beneath a small open shed that looked like a
bunch of junk lumber had been thrown together. To-
bacco road. Shit. How could his mother do this to
the ranch?

If you were so concerned about what she might be

*doing in your lengthy absence, perhaps you should
have come home. Or at the very least, made a phone
call and pretended you cared what happens to her and
to this place.*

Joanna Walsh's words pushed their way into his
head. He couldn't argue with what she had said to
him about his approach to his family, but he hated
being reminded by an outsider that he had given his
mom, his brother or Texas little thought and even
less time.

Who the hell was this Walsh woman, anyway? And
why couldn't he remember her from school? She had
been flitting in and out of his space and his mind all
day. Not because she was his type, for damn sure.
There was something else about her that gnawed at
him.

With shiny brown-red hair and expressive green
eyes, she was sort of pretty in a wholesome way. Not
a knockout like, say, Candace, but her ass did do won-
ders for a pair of tight jeans. Lean and mean, he la-
beled her.

Still, despite the stir her appearance had caused
within him, his cursory opinion was that she might be
too pushy and too damn smart for her own good. Or
for his own good. God save him from smart women.

Then it dawned on him—the thing about her that
bothered him, the thing that kept bringing her back
into his mind, other than her friggin' chickens. She
seemed not to like him. Women rarely failed to like
him. More females than he could manage had always
been easy to coax into bed. The Walsh woman, on the
other hand, seemed to want to escape from him, a
fact that only made him more curious about her.

He strolled up the caliche driveway, watching the
drilling rig lights and how the aura they created flick-
ered erratically against the black sky. All at once it
came to him that those distant columns of bright lights

were sending him a message. A memory from his
youth hurtled back. The oil well that had been drilled
on Parker land had been near the house. There had
been trucks and noise and excitement. But he couldn't
recall the well's exact location, and no one had ever
told him why it wasn't developed.

Jesus Christ, the solution to the Parker ranch's financial problems could be right under his feet. *Oil*. In
the great Permian Basin, with oil wells everywhere, in
every direction he looked, and with drilling resurging,
surely to God, somewhere under seventeen sections
of land, a drop or two of crude oil waited to be found.

The next morning, when Joanna arrived at the Parker ranch she found it eerily quiet. Not a soul could
be seen. The rental car was gone from the driveway
and Clova's big green Dodge dually was missing from
its usual spot under the shed. No doubt she had gone
to the hospital in Lubbock to visit Lane, but the rental
car's absence was puzzling. Had Dalton already returned to California?

Thank God. He wasn't doing any good here anyway.

Yet, even as that presumption jelled into certainty
and a sense of relief passed through her, a splinter of
disappointment pricked her. Only now that he was
gone could she dare admit, if only silently, that he was
an extremely attractive man who had awakened urges
she had thought dormant. Why that would happen
with someone she didn't like she couldn't understand.

After processing the eggs, she returned to downtown and her shop, determined to have a productive
day without being distracted by Clova's family.

Typically, Saturdays were busy in both the beauty
salon and the beauty supply business. Having given
Alicia the weekend off, Joanna knew she would be

tied down in her shop all day, so she decided to make
the most of the time. She dove into a thorough cleaning of the retail half of the business, allowed Tammy,
one of the hairdressers, to add some gold highlights
to her auburn hair, and talked to several retailers on
the phone, making arrangements for egg deliveries in
Lubbock and Amarillo on Monday.

At the end of the day, she was tired, but she had
worked herself into an upbeat mood. With Toby Keith
blaring from the radio, she drove out to the Parker
ranch for the evening egg gathering. Once there, she
saw the green dually parked in the driveway, but no
rental car. So the long-distance son really had left. A
tension she had carried inside for a week melted away.

She parked behind the dually, noticing a thick,
round bundle of steel fence posts in the bed, along
with a box of fence staples and other assorted cardboard boxes. Clova must have decided to hire someone to work on the fence. Expecting to find her friend
alone, Joanna rapped on the ranch house's front door
and stepped into the living room at the same time.
"Clova? It's me, Joanna."

She looked across her left shoulder into the dining
room, and there at the dining table sat Dalton. *Damn.*
Where was the rental car?

A laptop computer was open on the table, with assorted cardboard boxes and packing materials strewn
all over the tabletop around it. Joanna almost gasped
her surprise—and frustration.

He looked up and removed a pair of steel-rimmed
glasses. "Mom's in her bedroom. She isn't feeling
well." He raised a longneck bottle of beer, tilted his
head back and chugged a long swig, exposing those
powerful neck muscles working with every swallow.

Joanna swallowed, too, and caught herself staring.
Why did he have to be so damn . . . so damn macho?

Even sitting behind a computer and wearing glasses, he was just . . . just plain damn *macho*! "Oh," she said, recovering.

At the same time, she remembered that back in the spring, Clova had spent four days in the Wacker County Hospital. A burst of concern flared. She took a step toward the older woman's bedroom, then remembered this wasn't her house. "Uh, okay if I go back there?" she asked Dalton.

He leveled a steady look at her, his beer bottle poised midair. Finally, he said, "Sure."

Chapter 10

Joanna crossed the living room to the hallway, feeling his eyes on her back with every step. At Clova's bedroom door, she tapped lightly with her knuckle. Hearing an invitation to come in, she eased the door open, poked her head through the crack and saw Clova, wearing a faded cotton nightgown, crawling into bed. "Clova? Sweetie, Dalton said you aren't feeling good."

She walked on into the room and closed the door behind her, enclosing the two of them in a frilly, feminine sanctuary. She had always been fascinated that Clova's bedroom decor was so different from what anyone who knew her only by sight would imagine. Floral wallpaper, lace curtains and jars and pots of lotions and creams on top of a tall armoire. Joanna had often wondered whether the bedroom represented who Clova really was or perhaps who she longed to be.

"Oh, I ain't sick," the older woman said. "I'm just worn out is all." She proceeded to straighten an obviously old handmade quilt around her legs. "Sit down, sit down." She patted the mattress in an indication for Joanna to take a seat on the edge. "Me and Dalton got outta bed and went up to Lubbock real early and run all over the place gettin' stuff done. Havin' him around keeps me busy."

As if she weren't busy anyway, Joanna thought. "You saw Lane, of course. How is he?"

Clova looked down at her calloused hands and nodded. A tear fell on her thumb.

Doom and gloom. Learning that Dalton hadn't left after all might have been a surprise and a disappointment to Joanna, but not enough to darken her good mood. Seeing Clova again in tears over Lane did the trick. She sighed. "What did they say?"

Clova turned her head and looked toward the window. The yellowed shade was pulled down, so there was nothing to see but it and limp lace curtains. "Dalton chased down that foreign doctor that's takin' care o' Lane. Ever'where you look nowadays, the hospitals are fillin' up with foreigners. I don't know what the world's a-comin' to."

"What did he say?"

Clova's head shook slowly. Her eyes squeezed shut and she pressed a knobby knuckle to her mouth. Joanna plucked a tissue from a box on the bedside table and handed it to her. "Tell me what he said, okay?"

Clova returned her eyes to the drawn window shade. "Lane's gonna be a cripple, Joanna. His left leg's over an inch shorter than it was. I don't know exactly what caused it, but that doctor said it was so messed up, that was the best he could do."

Joanna swallowed the clot of tears that rushed to her own throat. She couldn't imagine the good-looking, happy-go-lucky, always-grinning Lane limping for the rest of his life. Or walking with a cane. Of course the information was no huge surprise. Joanna still remembered what she had heard the surgeon say the night of the accident. She supposed Lane could count himself lucky he still had the leg, even if it was shorter. "Oh, Clova. I'm so sorry."

Clova blew her nose on the tissue. "I don't know how many times I told him about gettin' in that truck and roarin' around the highways drunk. He's lucky, I guess, he hasn't killed hisself."

Or someone else, Joanna thought.

"He would o' been better off joinin' the army like Dalton done. Maybe they could o' straightened him out."

Joanna only nodded, attempting to digest what kind of new problems having a crippled alcoholic around the ranch would generate. "Is he okay otherwise? I mean his other injuries—"

"They're gonna move him out of that intensive care place on Monday." She shrugged and looked down at the tissue wadded into a ball in her hand. "Good thing. No tellin' what that's costin'."

Joanna nodded again. "I suppose he'll be taking physical therapy, right?"

"I don't know. We ain't got any instructions yet. Or a plan, either."

Chaos and confusion seemed to be the norm with Clova, but Joanna mustered a smile. "Look, it's suppertime. Have you eaten?"

"I ain't hungry."

"What if I went into the kitchen and made a pot of soup? It's kind of chilly out. Cool enough for me to turn on the lightbulbs in the chicken coops. Soup sounds good, doesn't it? I know I'm not much of a cook, but I can manage soup."

Clova looked up at her, her cheeks wet with tears. "You're a good woman, Joanna. Havin' you for a friend means a lot to me. I know I'm a burden to you. I don't mean to be, but seems like I got troubles ever' time I turn around these days. Don't bother cookin' no soup for me. Dalton's out there puttin' that machine together. If I get hungry, maybe I can get him to fix me somethin'."

"Nonsense. I don't consider you a burden."

Clova leaned forward, looked closer at Joanna's forehead. "What happened to your head, hon?"

"I ran into something. Look, I'm going to make soup. I'll be done in no time."

Clova sat up and started to move from the bed. "Nope," Joanna said, urging her back under the covers. "I don't need your help. Stay right where you are."

When she walked out of the bedroom into the hall, she crashed headlong into Dalton. His hands came out reflexively and grabbed her shoulders. Shaken by the collision, she stepped back, looking up at him. His hands dropped, but his eyes held hers until she blinked. "Were you eavesdropping?" she asked him.

"I cannot tell a lie."

Arrogant asshole! Jaw clenched, she spun and stalked toward the kitchen. She heard him say behind her, "I'm going to the kitchen, Mom. I'll be back in a minute to see if you need anything."

Joanna was shaking with anger as she picked an onion and a potato from the dry vegetable bin under the counter. In the refrigerator amid multiple bottles of beer, she found carrots, celery and a package of ground meat. She unwrapped the meat and put it in a cast-iron frying pan to sear.

A minute later, Dalton showed up in the kitchen.

Knowing they were out of Clova's hearing, Joanna turned on him. "It isn't necessary for you to spy on me. If you want to know something, just ask me."

Two feet away, in her space, he stood there, his hands on his hips, his dark eyes leveled on hers. "I think I already know what I need to."

"Then why waste your valuable time listening at doors?"

Instead of answering her, his mouth curved into a one-sided smirk, he gave a one-shoulder shrug and sauntered to the refrigerator. He pulled out a longneck and tipped the top in her direction. "I don't suppose you'd want a beer?"

She would have to be stupid not to hear the sarcasm in his tone. He was baiting her and she didn't intend to stand for it. She pulled a knife from its storage slot in the wooden butcher block that sat in the center of the kitchen, placed the onion and whacked off the ends. "No. And don't come in here and heckle me. I'm going to make this pot of soup for your mom, then I'm out of here. I can't leave soon enough."

Thinking of the computer on the dining table, another annoyance surfaced. It had been in the back of her mind since she entered the house and saw the laptop. Clova didn't know the first thing about a computer, so Joanna felt almost certain she hadn't bought it. That meant Dalton had. If he wanted to spend money, this ranch needed many things more than it needed a computer. "I'm wondering why you bought your mother a computer. I'm not aware she can use it."

"I didn't buy her a computer," he said defensively. "That's my laptop I brought with me. Although I'd buy her one if she wanted it." He tilted his head back and swallowed a long swig of beer from the frosty bottle. "What I did buy is a few accessories, like a good monitor and a printer. Not that it's any of your damn business, but I gotta get a little work done while I'm here."

What kind of work? she wondered as she chopped the onion into small pieces. But she refused to give him the satisfaction of asking.

As if she had posed the question, he said, "I've got a deadline on my new book. Looks like I'm not gonna get back home quick as I thought. Somebody's gotta start rebuilding that fence tomorrow. I'm thinking that somebody's me."

That explained the supplies she had seen in the dually's bed. She knew enough about barbed-wire fences to surmise that fence building would be easier with more than one person working at it. "You're going to work on the fence all by yourself?"

"Why not? When I was a kid, I built a million miles of fence without a damn bit of help from anybody. Who's around to help me, anyway?" He raised the bottle and took another long swig.

Joanna forced herself not to watch. "Right," she said peevishly.

Anyone with half a brain knew that working on a barbed-wire fence alone in a remote place could be dangerous. Barbed wire had a mind of its own. She had heard plenty of horror stories, had seen many scratches and gashes, even stitches. But hey, if he thought he was Superman, what difference did it make to her? She wondered whether he was a little drunk. She had seen him down two beers since she came and didn't know how many he'd had before her arrival.

"Exactly what did the doctor say about Lane?" She scraped the chopped onion into a bowl and started peeling the potato. "Clova seems to think he's permanently affected."

"His left leg's screwed up real bad. He lost some bone. He's facing a long road back. But I've seen a helluva lot worse. I've seen plenty of fine kids lose a leg or an arm or both doing something considerably more noble than driving drunk. I hate Lane being hurt, but I have a hard time feeling sorry for him, even if he is my brother."

At least they agreed on that much. "What about his other injuries?"

"He'll be okay eventually. He can live without a spleen. I'm sure they'll tell him his boozing days are over. He was lucky this time."

"I knew it was bad. I was there that night—"

"Why am I not surprised?" His eyes narrowed and

a look of suspicion came at her like a spear. "What did my mom do, adopt you or something?"

Joanna's spine stiffened and she aimed a hard glare right back into his eyes. "And what's that supposed to mean?"

"You seem to be right in the middle of everything that happens around here. That just strikes me as unusual."

Joanna bridled at the implication. "You've already made that point loud and clear. Not that you could possibly understand the situation from thousands of miles away, but Lane's been a mess for quite a while. He's given your mother a lot of trouble and contributed damn little around here lately. Clova's needed a friend, and I happened to be the one present and willing."

He said nothing else with his mouth, but with a withering glare from his X-ray eyes, words were unnecessary. She felt those eyes scrutinize her every move. The meat in the skillet began to sizzle. She walked over to the stove and lowered the flame under the skillet.

He returned to the refrigerator, pulled out another beer and twisted off the cap. "Want me to help you? So you can get out of here sooner, I mean?"

Joanna drew in a deep breath and exhaled, trying to calm herself. Her insides were shaking and she still had carrots to slice. If she didn't calm down, she could cut off a finger. "You can watch the meat. Don't let it burn."

She went back to the cutting board, but from the corner of her eye, she saw him assume a position in front of the stove, beer bottle in one hand, a spatula in the other. She went on slicing carrots, then moved to the celery. When she finished, she dumped the cut-up vegetables, a couple of cans of tomato sauce, some spices and some water into a large pot and carried it to the stove. She came face-to-face with him in the aisle between the butcher block and the stove, and she could feel the uptick in her heartbeat. Their gazes locked for a few seconds before she backed away and set the pot on the burner. "That meat needs to go into this pot. But not the grease."

With skill she hadn't expected to see, he scooped the hamburger out of the pan with the spatula, let it drain for a few seconds, then dropped it into the pot. Between the two of them, they soon had vegetable-beef soup simmering on the stove, and he returned with his bottle of beer to the dining table and the computer.

As the house filled with aromatic smells of spices and tomatoes, she walked to the kitchen doorway, watching him as he deftly hooked devices to the laptop. Despite her confusion of emotions about him, she had to admit she had never seen a man so comfortable with who he was. He might be arrogant and blatant, but he seemed to like himself just fine. "I didn't see the rental car when I drove up."

"Turned it back in. No point paying for that piece o' shit to stay parked in the driveway. I'd rather drive the work truck."

"You're planning on staying a while, then?"

Before he could answer, his cell phone chirped. He flipped it open and placed it to his ear. "Yo. It's me, babe." A big grin came over his face. "How are ya, sweetie? . . . Yeah, I had a couple of beers . . ." He walked out of the dining room and all the way outside, talking as he went.

Joanna's jaw clenched. *Babe*, indeed.

Twenty minutes later, Joanna ladled soup into a crockery bowl, set it and some saltines on a tray and took it in to the bedroom. She found Clova sound asleep.

She carried the tray back to the dining room. Dalton

had come back in. He had pushed the computer and
its parts toward the center of the table and was eating
a bowl of soup. "What's up now?" he asked.

Joanna set the tray down on the table. "Clova's
asleep. She must be feeling really bad. I've never seen
her just go to bed like this."

Dalton looked at her, his spoon poised in the air,
then returned to eating.

Joanna cocked her head and gave him a pointed
scowl. "Aren't you worried about her?"

He put down his spoon and opened his palms.
"What is it you think I should be doing?"

Joanna opened her mouth to scold him but stopped
herself. There wasn't much to be done, by him or
anyone else. Clova probably just needed a good rest.
"I suppose you should keep an eye on her."

"I will." He shrugged. "If she's not okay in the
morning, I'll take her into town to see a doc. If that's
what she wants."

If *he* suggested that Clova see a doctor, she probably would. Satisfied, Joanna picked up the tray. "You
should make her go."

"Soup's good," he said, changing the subject and
making it obvious he didn't want her advice or recom-
mendation. "We did a pretty good job cooking it. Why
don't you have some?"

Joanna gave him a wary glance. He had done another about-face in attitude. What was he up to now?
"I need to get home."

"Oh, yeah. Saturday night. Got a hot date?"

She huffed a laugh. "Only with my Tempur-Pedic
mattress."

The minute the words came out of her mouth, a
tiny lurch zipped through Joanna's middle. She turned
her back and walked into the kitchen carrying the tray.
And wishing she had said yes, she did have a hot date.
In her distraction, she banged the edge of the tray

against the counter, clattering dishes and spilling soup on the linoleum floor. "Shit."

She grabbed some paper towels, dropped to her knees and began mopping up the mess. Fortunately, the soup was no longer hot.

Dalton came up behind her, tore off more paper towels and knelt beside her. His arm and hands touched hers as together they wiped up the soup and heaped the soggy paper towels onto the tray. He made no attempt not to touch her, and every time his skin brushed hers, a new wave of nervousness washed over her.

When they finished, he stood up and placed a hand under her elbow, aiding her getting to her feet. For some weird reason, she felt a new desire to get along with him. "Thanks for helping out," she said.

He gave her a smile that made her knees tremble. "Least I could do for the cook."

Firmly shaking off that weakness, she managed to smile back. "It would be a mistake to call me a cook."

They stood only inches apart. He braced a hand on the counter no more than two feet away, those eyes drilling her, his mouth still tipped into that smile. "How about hot?" he asked in a soft rasp. "Can I call you that?"

And speaking of heat, they were close enough for her to feel his body heat. She could smell his breath, yeasty and warm, and she could see the dark late-day stubble on his jaw. An odd tension traveled through her lower belly. "I wish you wouldn't. I wasn't impressed when you said it last night."

"Why not? Don't like guys, huh?"

The words drove away the seductive moment. "Oh, please," she snapped and moved back a couple of steps.

His eyes widened and he opened his palms. "Hey,

look, what do you expect me to think? Mom says you're not married. Says you don't go out."

Joanna winced inside, wondering just how thoroughly Clova had discussed her with him.

"You don't have any roosters in that flock of chickens," he went on. "Is that symbolic of something? Without a little sex, how do you keep all those hens content?"

She made a tiny sigh of indignation. "The hens don't care about sex."

His brow arched again. "How do you know? Does that blue-egg-laying chicken whisper it in your ear?"

She hesitated a few seconds, stumped for a reply. "I'm sure we'd disagree on what's important to chickens."

She might not know what he was up to, but she knew she shouldn't encourage him. He had a predatory gleam in his eye that, for some damned reason, she found alluring. So alluring, in fact, that if she wasn't careful, he would be sharing her Tempur-Pedic with her faster than she could change the sheets. She turned away, picked up the tray and raked the wet towels into the trash. "You've had too many beers. For your information, roosters cause trouble and try to dominate the flock." *Just like men,* she thought. "They're worthless for egg production."

"Is that a fact? I have to admit, I've never seen chicken sex. Actually, I've never been interested in looking for it, but I know it goes on."

Joanna's stomach lurched again. "Really."

"Yep. Otherwise, there wouldn't be any new chickens. And no eggs. Common sense. It's the same with everything and everybody, darlin'. Even chickens. Takes two to tango."

"And you're an expert."

He grinned. "I know a little about sex, yeah."

Joanna couldn't look into his face. Determined not to react to his goading, she began to stack the soiled dishes. "I don't know you well enough to be discussing sex with you."

"But you do, darlin'. Hell, you've taken over my mother and this whole damn place. I'll bet you know me better than I even think you do. You might even know me better than I know myself."

Enough was enough. She straightened, picked up a dish towel and began to dry her hands. "You know, I've had a long day. I've cooked the soup. Why don't you do the dishes? . . . And I'm not your darling, so don't call me that."

She threw the dish towel onto the counter in a heap and walked out of the kitchen and through the dining room, then the living room, forcing herself to keep a steady step and not look back.

Dalton stood on the front porch watching Joanna Walsh walk to her truck and climb in. Yep, a body like an athlete. Sleek as a gazelle. Nice. Very nice. Imagining those finely toned thighs hugging his hips sent a tightening straight to his lower belly. *Shit.* The beast in his pants had never been able to tell the difference between a smart-ass who was dangerous and an empty-headed bimbo who just liked to screw.

He couldn't keep from wondering, despite what Miss Uptight said about going home to her mattress, what she might really have planned for a Saturday night in a small Texas burg. From what he remembered, a night on the town in Hatlow could be a trip to the Dairy Queen.

He would lay money that she kept herself off-limits, but he had no doubt most of the horny dudes around Hatlow had tried with a woman who owned a body like hers. An image formed in his mind of her and some local yokel humping in a fancy bed. For some reason, he found that perplexing.

Her truck engine fired, her lights came on and just as she had left the kitchen without looking back at him, she drove toward the highway, also without looking back.

Aw, to hell with it, he told himself. While he would like some female company during what looked more and more like an extended stay, even if he wanted to spend the time playing games with Miss Uptight or try to coax her into bed, he couldn't. She was his mother's friend.

Chapter 11

Dalton watched until her truck turned onto the highway and disappeared. Then he walked back into the house, to his mother's bedroom door. He eased the door open, looked in and saw her sleeping. He stood there a few seconds, studying her. She looked frail and small buried beneath an old quilt. He had never thought of her as being a vulnerable person. In truth, he had never known what to think of her. Even now, after all these years, she was an enigma, a wheel within a wheel. He gently closed the door and returned to the dining room.

Cool air from the open windows had chased the day's heat from the house. Fall was like that in West Texas. Hotter than a furnace in the daytime and cold as a desert grave at night. He could hear the steady tick of the old mahogany mantel clock, the mellow sound emphasizing its age and the silence that stole through the house like some friggin' ghost.

Tick . . . tick . . . tick.

The unrelenting sound, an echo from childhood, brought back a thousand memories.

The old timepiece had sat there on the mantel ticking away forever. It had been ticking the night he realized he had become his own man. He was seventeen and had taken the work truck to town to see a girl whose name he no longer remembered. When he returned home, he met his stepfather, drunk and raging, waiting for him in the living room with his belt in hand. The old clock ticked through the fight that ensued.

You got no goddamn right to use that fuckin' truck for anything. I'm gonna whip your ass.

Before the son of a bitch could land a blow with the belt, Dalton doubled him over with a belly punch, then flattened him with a right to the jaw. Then he walked out, climbed back into the truck and returned to town. He had slept in the truck in the city park, and Cherry had carried a facial bruise for weeks.

Through his youth, Dalton had borne the brunt of many of Cherry's fits of violence, but from that night forward, Cherry hadn't hit him again or even threatened him. Until the day Dalton left home for boot camp, a forced and chilly truce prevailed whenever he and the hateful bastard happened to be in the same room.

The old clock had been ticking the night two football scouts from Texas Tech appeared at the door and were turned away by Cherry. Later Dalton came to realize he could have dealt with them himself, but by then he was in the marines and far away from Hatlow. He had liked that better than playing football.

The thing that had been stuck in his craw all these years was that through all of it—the tantrums, the beatings, the meanness—his mother had rarely raised a voice in his defense. For a few years, he spent a lot of his time wondering why, but he never found an answer. He came to believe that she had been glad to see him leave. And he had thought, if that was what she wanted, then that was what she could have.

Tonight, the house had a dark and familiar loneliness about it. Generations of Parkers before him had hunkered within its walls, hoping not to draw attention and risk the small-town society's condemnation or ostracism.

Only his great-grandmother had worn her Comanche relatives proudly. She hadn't worried about what the neighbors might think or say. He remembered her as a skinny, bark-tough woman who feared nothing living or dead except Earl Cherry. Dalton's mind spun back to the night Cherry, in one of his drunken tantrums, had left her shaking and crying after threatening to burn her house to the ground. If his mom had had any balls, she wouldn't have lived with a bullying son of a bitch who had heaped abuse and intimidation on the whole family, especially when he targeted an aged widow who didn't weigh a hundred pounds.

Through Dalton's life, no matter where his thoughts of family had wandered, at some point, they always came back to his animus for Earl Cherry. When he was away from here, it no longer felt important, and he could and did avoid thinking about it. But here in the place where he had spent his most miserable years, on a dark, silent night, memories rose all around him as if to swamp him. He hadn't suffered unease and vulnerability so profoundly in a long time, even in the savagery of the wars he had recorded for history.

This damned old house was haunted, he decided, forcing the blackness from his mind. He sat down at the dining table with his computer and took himself to the place where he was happiest—immersed in his work.

I know a little about sex, yeah.
Something told Joanna he knew more than a little. *Jerk!* She yanked off her clothing and pulled on her knit shorts and T-shirt. *Prick!* At the bathroom sink she scrubbed her face harder than usual with a rough washcloth, carefully avoiding the tender lump between her eyes. *Conceited bastard!* She rubbed her face dry with a hand towel, leaving her cheeks and chin rosy. She threw down her towel, leaned in closer to the mirror and examined the injury to her forehead,

dabbed on more antibiotic cream and applied a Band-Aid to the wound. She studied the fine lines forming at the corners of her eyes. *Crap*. She needed to wear more sunscreen. And a hat.

She generously slathered on antiwrinkle cream, then stamped up the hallway to her bedroom. In her sixty-year-old house, the bathroom wasn't attached to the master bedroom. In truth, her little house had no master bedroom. What it did have was two small bedrooms just alike, with one bathroom between them. But she made no complaint. The house was perfect for her. How much room did a person who spent very few hours at home need?

The best thing about the house wasn't a part of the house at all. The best thing was *in* the house, *in* her bedroom. Almost filling the room was a queen-size Tempur-Pedic bed that had cost her a fortune. With the hours she worked every day, seven days a week, she had reasoned when she bought it, the least she could do was reward herself with an excellent place to lay her weary body at night. Now she flopped back on the bed, spread her arms wide, and with a huge groan of pleasure, closed her eyes.

So just how the hell long would Dalton Parker be here? And how could she avoid running into him?

And she *did* have to avoid him. Good grief, every time she saw him, something weird happened to her insides and he made her so nervous she couldn't function.

And now he had brought up sex, for crying out loud.

Sex. Was the idea of sex responsible for the weird thing that happened to her insides? The word came to her every time she saw him. If there had ever been a time when just seeing a man automatically brought sex to mind, she couldn't recall it.

Well, she had no intention of ever letting something

so perverse escape the confines of her innermost musings. And for a very good reason. For her, sex hadn't been so great. She had never known a fantastic lover like those she read about in romance novels. She doubted such men existed in real life.

Shari was the only woman she knew who appeared to have a fantasy sex life. But different strokes for different folks, Joanna figured. What Shari thought fantastic might be awful for someone else.

She got to her feet, pulled back the covers and slid between them with a great sigh, thinking of her last relationship that had included sex. It had been with Scott Goodman and would have to be classified as spotty at best. Much of the time their encounters had been clumsy. Embarrassing, even. She didn't know if that was her fault or his, but she suspected the problem lay with him.

The experience had been so awkward, so juvenile, she was embarrassed to discuss it even with Shari, with whom she discussed everything that had anything to do with sex. She had been relieved when she learned that Scott was seeing someone else because at that point, she had begun to consider that she could get just as pregnant with a lousy lover as with a great one.

It was all in the past. And just as well. *No* lover was the answer. She had given up.

But as she drifted toward sleep, a filmy image of the swarthy Dalton Parker without his clothes evolved in her mischievous mind.

The next morning, Joanna drove toward the Parker ranch hoping not to run into Dalton. He had spent a good part of the night in her head; she didn't want to be around him the whole of today. Hadn't he said he intended to start work on the fence? That project should cause him to leave early and return late.

Arriving at the ranch, she saw all of the ranch's vehicles in place—the blue beat-up Ford pickup, Clova's newer Dodge Ram dually and the ATV. So Dalton must still be inside the house. Good. She hoped he stayed there.

She went directly to the barn and picked up two slabs of hay to feed the donkeys. She put them by the egg-tending room door as she stepped inside. She donned her cap and gloves and started toward the chicken yard, carrying the hay and her egg baskets and bucket.

She had just put the hay in the donkeys' manger and returned to the gate to pick up her baskets and bucket when Dalton approached. He had on work clothes—faded jeans, a chambray shirt and suede vest and a faded cap. He wore the typical ranch garb so easily, he looked at home in it. The only item that conflicted with his cowboy appearance was his mirrored aviator sunglasses. He came to the fence.

"Watch the hot wire," she warned him and pointed to the low electric fence wires.

He looked down at his feet, and she did, too. He had on well-worn Ropers. She wouldn't have guessed he even owned a pair of Ropers. But of course he was a cowboy. He might no longer be directly involved with ranching, but he had grown up a cowboy.

He looked up. "What, this place is wired?"

"The two bottom wires are hot. To keep out the predators."

"Huh." His sunglasses hid his eyes, but the usually cocky smirk had left his mouth. "I think Mom's got a fever," he said solemnly. "She's feeling pretty bad. Says she can't get her breath. I'm gonna take her into town to the doc. I thought you might go with her."

Joanna had been the one to admit Clova to the hospital back in the spring. Without a word, she set her egg baskets on the ground, peeled off her gloves and stuffed them into her pocket. Then she hurriedly walked to the house and on into Clova's bedroom.

She found Clova still in bed, her eyes bright from fever. Her skin had a pasty pallor. "Hey," Joanna said softly. "Dalton says you've got a fever."

"A little bit," Clova replied. "He called up Russell's answering service and left a message to meet me in his office. I feel like I got the same thing again." She threw back the covers and turned to sit on the edge of the mattress.

Joanna rushed to her. "Let me help you get dressed. You should go on in to the emergency room now and see whatever doctor is there. It's Sunday. Dr. Jones might not get the message for hours. Just stay right there. Let me find you some clothes."

She pulled clean clothing from Clova's closet, glancing toward the doorway, where Dalton stood with his hands on his hips. His sunglasses dangled from one hand and Joanna could see an expression of helplessness and concern on his face. "I think I told you she had pneumonia in the spring," she said. "It's better to be safe than sorry and take her on in to the ER."

A small frown tented his brow and he nodded.

"You could go heat up the pickup while I help her get dressed. It's cool out."

He nodded again and turned away without comment. As Joanna helped Clova to her feet, she heard the front door close.

An hour and a half later, she and Dalton departed acker County Hospital in the dually, having left Clova behind as a patient with respiratory therapy prescribed and tests pending.

He had remained stoic and silent all through the visit to the ER and the doctor's decision to admit Clova to the hospital. Joanna had done most of the talking. When they checked her into the hospital, rather than argue over Clova's lack of insurance, Dalton had signed some kind of document, guaranteeing payment of the bill. Now Joanna wondered just how well-off he was. The cocky arrogance she had seen in him so often had been replaced by a glum face and worry lines.

"Mom never used to get sick," he said, now looking straight ahead, both hands on the steering wheel as he herded the big dually through the town's narrow streets toward the highway.

Joanna stared straight ahead, too, puzzled by his apparent obtuseness. But then, how could he be expected to know what had been going on in Texas? Even if Clova had been in touch with him, Joanna knew she wouldn't have told him the truth of things. Clova was a private person. Joanna knew of her problems herself only because she spent so much time at the ranch.

Joanna had been around Clova daily for more than two years. She had seen the weakening of her health and spirit with every juvenile and dangerous episode Lane brought home and laid on the doorstep like some damn tomcat wagging home a trophy, every new unexpected demand for cash the ranch didn't have. Clova's decline had happened so gradually, Joanna had come to terms with it the same way.

Dalton appeared to be so flummoxed, she felt a need to explain more about his mother. "She's older now, Dalton. And run-down. She's had the ranch to take care of all on her own and doing a man's work the last few years. Not only has Lane not been much help, his shenanigans have kept her in a state of constant worry. His DUIs, his fines, his child-support payments. It's all cost—"

"*What* child support?"

The pickup lurched to a jolting halt. She grabbed the dash to keep her forehead from banging the windshield. She shot a look of outrage at Dalton, but like a black, violent storm, his dark eyes bore down on

her. A few seconds passed before she found words.
"For—for his daughter."

"*What* daughter?"

She sat there stupefied, absorbing the fact that he
didn't know his brother had a child or that he himself
was an uncle. Uncomfortable in the heat of his glare,
she turned to stare out the windshield. "He and Mandy
Ferguson have a little girl. She's almost two. I—I can't
believe you didn't know."

"How the hell would I know? Why the fuck didn't
they get married?"

Stunned at his reaction, Joanna turned back to him.
She had already said too much to stop now. "Because
she doesn't want to live with a drunk," she barked.
"And her family doesn't want her to, either. And no
one blames her or them."

"Jee-zus Christ," he growled, yanking the dually
into gear. "How much are the fuckin' child-support
payments?"

"I think it's eight hundred dollars a month."

"Jesus Christ. That's nearly ten thousand dollars a
year. Who is this woman? Does she work?"

"Of course she works," Joanna snapped. "Her folks
own the Dairy Queen. She works behind the counter."

"Goddammit," he growled.

"She's a nice girl. She and her mother used to be
customers in my shop. She really cared about Lane,
but the way he's been, no one can care about him for
long. He's got this wild streak about him. He's just
too—too . . . well, unpredictable."

"How many DUIs has he got?"

"Why are you grilling *me*?" she said, almost shout-
ing now. "Why don't you ask your mother or your
brother about these things?"

"Because I'm asking the person who seems to know
every fuckin' thing that goes on around here," he almost shouted back.

She drew a calming breath and lifted her chin. "I would really appreciate it if you would spare me the profanity. You're not a marine any longer."

"Just goes to show how much you don't know," he snarled. "Once you're a marine, you're always a marine."

She sent him a fierce glare. "Look, I'm not a prude, but your language is starting to make my ears bleed. I hate the *F* word."

He glared back at her just as fiercely, as if he were stunned that she would dare criticize him.

"I don't know how many DUIs he's got," she said, moving on. "But I won't be surprised if he loses his driver's license this time. I think it only takes three. I think it's possible he could even go to jail. I don't know what Clova will do then."

Dalton's shoulders seemed to sag. He let out a deep breath, like a deflating balloon. Still hanging on to the steering wheel with both hands, he stared straight ahead, slowly shaking his head. "I never thought . . . I don't know what I thought."

Joanna heard a little break in his voice. She couldn't guess what it meant. Nor could she guess Dalton's true feelings for his mother and brother. Or, now, for his niece. She had pegged him for a libertine. A traditional attitude, such as outrage that a man hadn't married the woman with whom he had fathered a child, was the last thing she would have expected. Every encounter with him brought a surprise.

Chapter 12

At the ranch, Dalton parked the dually beside the ranch pickup. "I've got to get these fence posts loaded into the work truck," he said grimly, more to himself than to her. "Got to get started on that fence."

He appeared to be so upset and worried that Joanna's proclivity for worrying about other people rushed to the surface. She felt sorry for him. Last night's sparring match in the kitchen and today's in the dually faded into the background of reality and now seemed silly. "Did you find someone to help you?" she asked.

He shook his head. "I'll manage."

She hesitated a few seconds, suspecting that "manage" was what he had always done. Managed whatever life handed him. Though she hadn't been around him much, she somehow knew he was a man who made the best of the worst circumstances. She knew exactly how he felt. On a different scale and under less calamitous events, she lived her life much the same.

She wondered if he would accept her help. Finally, she knew she had to offer. She would do it for anyone. She looked up at him, shielding her eyes from the morning sun with her hand. "Look, it's not very smart to take on that fence alone. I'll make a deal with you. If you'll help me get my eggs gathered, I'll help you with the fence. I wasn't going to do anything special today, anyway."

He stared down at her, a tic jumping in his square

jaw. "Why would you do that? What do you know about building a fence? Besides, you can get cut up by barbed wire."

"I know teenagers who build fence. If they can do it, I can."

Looking off into the distance, he inflated his cheeks and blew out a loud breath. "Okay. Show me what to do."

"Just wait here. I'll be right back."

She walked over to her egg-washing room, picked up two baskets and two blue plastic buckets and returned with them. She handed him one of each. "Gathering eggs isn't rocket science. You just pick them up and put them in the basket. If you find a cracked or broken one, put it in the blue bucket so I can trash it. If you throw it on the ground or leave it in the nest, the hens will eat it, and that trains them to eat eggs. I don't want them to get into that habit."

"Stupid birds," he muttered, taking the basket and the bucket and looking from one to the other as if each were tainted.

"You don't have to like the hens to gather the eggs, okay?"

They worked in silence. Dulce scratched and clucked along behind them. Every time Dalton turned around, she was underfoot. "Chicken, you pushing your luck," he told the hen after he had almost stepped on her several times and sent her squawking and flapping away. Joanna suppressed a smile. Something told her Dulce was in no danger. Dalton might be arrogant and gruff, but he wasn't mean natured.

When they finished, he handed over his basket filled with eggs and the bucket holding four cracked ones. He walked beside her as she carried them toward her room, his size and close presence making her feel small. "How are you going to get that bundle of fence posts into the ranch truck?" she asked him.

"Well, babe, I'm gonna break it up and load 'em a few at a time. I'm not Superman, you know."

She held back a grin, remembering the thought she'd had yesterday in the kitchen. "I have to wash these eggs. I can do it while you load the posts. I'll hurry so I can help you."

She scrambled into her coveralls, cap and gloves, washed the eight dozen eggs and laid them out to dry. When she went outside, she saw the fence posts already loaded, along with all of the tools and supplies. Dalton was nowhere to be seen. Just then, he came from inside the house carrying a brown paper grocery sack, a denim shirt and a pair of gloves. "I brought some cheese and bread and water for lunch," he said.

"Ugh."

"Hey, don't bitch. I crawled all over a fu— a jungle in Thailand once with little more than that in my pack."

If anyone else had made that statement, she would have been so curious she would have asked for more information, but he wasn't just anyone. Besides, as contentious as he was, if she asked, he might tell her it was none of her damn business. "Whatever," she said. "I don't eat much anyway."

He handed her the shirt and a new pair of leather work gloves. "Maybe these will keep your arms and hands from getting cut up."

He had a point. She was wearing a T-shirt.

Soon they were in the work pickup, creeping across the pasture toward the broken fence, saying little. Finally he said, "Mom told me it was her idea about the chickens. So I guess you weren't lying."

"And of course you thought I was. Of course you thought I befriended a lonely older woman so I could steal your inheritance."

His eyes were hidden by his sunglasses, but a hint of a smile played over his lips. "I'm not worried about a fu— about a damned inheritance. This place doesn't mean shit to me."

At hearing him stop himself at the *F* word a second time, she shot him a quick glance, feeling as if she had won a battle. And at the same time she wondered if it were true that the Lazy P meant nothing to him.

"But it was a helluva shock," he said, "seeing all those goddamn chickens inhabiting the pasture we used to reserve for our prime cows."

She didn't like hearing "goddamn," either, but she satisfied herself with a small victory.

A few more seconds later, he said, "Mom told me you don't pay any rent."

Joanna winced inside, though she had known all along that sooner or later her free use of the land would come up. "Clova gets something out of this," she said, feeling the need for a defense. "The chicken droppings make great fertilizer. She uses it in her garden and—"

"So you're telling me you're paying my mom off in chicken shit?"

"That's ridiculous."

"Tell me something else. All that home-canned food in Mom's pantry. All of that grew in chicken shit?"

"Manure is manure. What's the difference if it comes from horses or cows or chickens? It's all organic."

"You know, in the old days, the cowmen fought wars with the sheepmen who brought in their herds of sheep and squatted on the land. If there had been chicken herds back then, what do you suppose a cowman would've done about that?"

Joanna thought she heard teasing in his tone. She gave him an impish grin. "Probably would have been hard-nosed and narrow-minded. Like you."

He cocked his head and looked at her. "You know, you're pretty when you smile."

She couldn't keep from smiling again. Good Lord,

she couldn't help herself, especially since the compliment sent a little zing right to her center. God help her, she was having fun. She was worse than a silly teenager. "Listen, Hollywood, after all the bad things you've said about my hens, it'll take more than flattery to get on my good side."

This time, one side of his mouth lifted into that knee-weakening half grin. "Then I guess I'll have to think of what that is."

He brought the pickup to an abrupt halt, then eased the truck into a slow roll as they crept over a deep gully. Sometimes she had a hard time understanding how such a landscape could be good for grazing livestock. "You want to know something? I never did figure out why the cattle ranchers hated the sheep so much."

" 'Cause all sheep do is eat and shit."

"That's what all animals do."

"But sheep shit's repulsive to cows. They won't graze where sheep have lived. And sheep chomp the grass down to nothing."

"Is that the truth? Or are you just telling me that?"

"That's the truth."

A new argument came to her and she gave him another grin. "Then I guess you don't have anything to worry about with my hens. Your mom and I have strung chicken droppings all over these pastures and I haven't seen a single cow refuse to eat. But I *have* seen the grass look a whole lot better where we've put it."

His head jerked in her direction. "You set me up for that."

This time she didn't grin; she laughed.

To Dalton's frustration, it was now late morning and the sun had already climbed high and heated the day. He wanted to get most of the fencing done today so he could get into town to go to the bank tomorrow, then to see his old high school friend whose family had been in the oil business.

Knowing the work would go faster with some help had prompted him to accept Joanna's offer, though male assistance would be better. He'd had misgivings about what he could be letting himself in for, but to his surprise, she turned out to be a steady worker and a smart helper. Without being told, she managed to be where he needed her to be all of the time, and she followed his orders without argument. And she had more energy and more physical ability than any woman he knew.

Now it was well past noon. He'd had nothing but coffee all day, and he had driven two dozen posts into the ground with a handheld post driver and strung feet and feet of barbed wire. His energy level had depleted; hunger pangs gnawed at his stomach. "You hungry yet?"

"I don't know." She wiped sweat and dirt off her face with her shirtsleeve.

Dalton felt a shred of guilt. He had pushed her hard.

She looked up at him with a dirty face and a one-eyed squint. "Every time I thought of that gourmet lunch you brought, it sort of squelched my desire for food."

He let the smart-ass quip pass without a comeback. He, too, pulled off his cap and wiped his sweat-drenched face with his shirttail. "Let's stop and eat."

"Okay, you're the boss."

Yeah, right. He wondered if this wiseass woman had ever had a real boss. Again he didn't see the necessity of replying. He walked toward the truck, carrying the post driver. She tagged along beside him, her cap set low over her eyes, the shirt—*his* shirt he had loaned her to wear—hanging to her knees. She looked cute, quickstepping to keep up with his long stride.

"When I was a kid," he said, "I used to drive posts all day long with a sixteen-pound maul. I'd drive the tractor out and stand on the back tire to get leverage."

"No kidding? That must've been killing work. They didn't have that post-driving thingey back then?"

They reached the truck and he clunked the post-driving tool into the bed. "I'm sure they did. But my stepdad, not being a man who intended to do the work himself, didn't have much interest in labor-saving devices. It didn't matter. By the time I learned there was a smarter way to do it, I was already on my way out of town."

"You seem to know a lot about ranching. You've never thought about coming back here and helping your mom?"

He snorted. "Not even when I was hunkered down in a fighting hole with a bunch of unwashed marines taking mortar fire."

He opened the passenger door and dragged out the sack that held the lunch he had thrown together. He pulled a faded bandanna from his back pocket, spread it on the tailgate and laid out the cheese and bread. She gave both the handkerchief and him a dubious look. "It's clean," he told her.

She raised on her tiptoes and scooted her butt onto the tailgate as he lifted bottles of water from the sack. "I brought a surprise," he said and pulled out an apple he had found in the kitchen.

She smiled. "Oh, wow. Imagine that. Dessert."

He paused for a moment, looking into her face as he swallowed her sass. She did have the prettiest smile. Nice kissable lips and perfect white teeth. "I found only one. I'll split it with you."

He dug out his pocketknife and opened it. Holding it between his thumb and finger, he showed it to her. "It's clean, too."

She grinned. "I'll bet. You've probably been using it to gut fish."

"Nope. Never learned to fish. All I do with water is drink it and swim in it." As he sliced the apple into halves, the Adam and Eve story came to him. He handed a half to her. "This is backward, you know. The way the story goes, it's *you* who's supposed to be giving *me* an apple."

Her brow arched, but she took the apple half with a grimy hand and bit into it. He liked that she didn't make a big deal out of having dirty hands. Now he *knew* she had been razzing him about the handkerchief and the pocketknife.

"Since a serpent isn't involved in this scenario," she said, "it probably doesn't matter."

He used the pocketknife to slice off two pieces of cheese and tore off two hunks of the bread with his hand. "You know, I don't have a lot of memories from Hatlow worth keeping, but one thing I do remember was that Mom always baked fresh bread. I'd come home from school and the house would be filled with those cooking smells."

He, too, hiked his butt up onto the tailgate and dug in to the lunch. "You're a good worker, but you must have other things to do. Why did you volunteer to help me?"

She finished off the apple half. "You remember Bart Wilbanks?"

He had shoved most Hatlow citizens so far out of his mind, there was no recalling them. Chewing, he shook his head. "Can't say that I do."

"You must know him. He's an old-timer. His place is out on the canyon."

A vague smattering of memory passed through Dalton's mind. "Yeah? So?"

"Back in the summer, he was working on his fence

all by himself and he got so tangled in new barbed wire he couldn't get loose. He panicked and cut himself all to pieces on the barbs, trying to get free."

"Whoa. How the hell did he do that?"

"You know how it is when you stretch out a strand of new barbed wire off a roll? How it wants to roll itself back up? Somehow he got caught in it. It wrapped all the way around him. He laid out in the sun all tied up and bleeding almost all day before his wife found him. They had to put him in the hospital."

Dalton chuckled, munching on his chunk of bread and savoring the homemade taste. "You made that up, right?" He washed the bread down with a long swig of water.

Joanna tilted her head back and chugalugged a long drink, rivulets of water running from the corners of her mouth down onto her breasts. Dalton couldn't keep from staring. She had good breasts. He had sneaked enough glances at them to determine they weren't phony. She lowered the bottle and wiped her mouth and chin on her shirtsleeve. "True story."

"And did you say Bart's a little on the dim side?"

"I don't know about that. He's smart enough not to go out working on a barbed-wire fence all by himself anymore. That's why I said I'd help you. I didn't want to have to drive out here later and rescue you." She popped her last bite of cheese into her mouth.

He paused, his water bottle poised in the air. He thought he saw a hint of a smirk on her lips as she chewed. She was pulling his leg again. He was sure of it. "Babe, the day will never come when you have to rescue *me*. Now, it might go the other way around, though. I might have to rescue *you*. You might get attacked by some damn horny rooster that just can't stand the thought of all those virgin hens all in one place."

Her mouth flatlined. "I'm not worried. But if you

think there's a danger, maybe I should keep my shotgun handy. It'd make short work of an aggressive rooster."

His eyes widened. A shotgun-wielding woman wasn't his idea of a good time. He had been around any number of armed females in the military. He hadn't been all that comfortable with that, either. "You've got a shotgun?"

"I certainly do. It's a twelve-gauge."

Good God. A twelve-gauge shotgun was an elephant gun, with a kick like a mule. "The hell you say. A twelve-gauge. And you can shoot it and remain standing?"

Her chin lifted as if he had insulted her. "I shoot at the chicken hawks if they come flying over."

A visual came into his mind and he suppressed a laugh. "You ever hit any?"

"As a matter of fact, I do."

He could no longer keep from chuckling. "And where is this cannon?"

"I keep it beside the sink in the egg-washing room."

"At least I've been warned."

"When my dad was alive, he went bird hunting. Sometimes he took my sister and me with him. He taught both of us to shoot."

"Darlin', I don't know what kind of birds your dad hunted, but a twelve-gauge would blow the small birds that live around here to smithereens. You'd be lucky to find a feather, much less end up with meat to eat. Most people use a twelve-gauge to hunt geese or something big."

A frown formed between her brows. "Oh. Well, maybe it isn't a twelve-gauge." She flopped her wrist in dismissal. "Well, whatever it is, it works."

"Don't you ever buy shells for it? You have to know the gauge to buy shells."

"No. I got all of my dad's after he passed on. My

mom and sister didn't want his gun or the shells, either."

"Your dad's gone, huh?"

"He died, oh, ten years ago. He was too young to die. He had cancer."

"How old was too young?"

"Fifty-five. It was hard on all of us, especially my mom."

Remembering that Earl Cherry had been fifty-four at his death, also ten years ago, an unexpected guilt nagged at Dalton. He hadn't returned to Hatlow for the burial. Out of the Marine Corps only a couple of years, he had just started his freelance photography business. He couldn't recall thinking that Cherry's death might have been hard on anybody.

"You said you were in a jungle in Thailand," Joanna said, disrupting his trip through the halls of his memory. "Were you taking pictures?"

He nodded. "Flowers. Rare orchids that grow wild. I was helping a guy. He wanted to show how they look in their natural habitat. He thought it was important to have a pictorial record because smuggling is about to wipe some of them out."

"Really? People smuggle flowers?"

"Yep."

"Huh. I guess there's someone somewhere who'll steal anything." She sat there, her ankles crossed, swinging her feet. "I've never seen a real orchid more than once or twice in my whole life. Why would people smuggle them? If they want them so bad, why don't they just grow them?"

"I'm no flower expert, but according to this guy who was, the nursery-raised flowers don't have the same aura and mystery as the wild ones. Now, me? I thought they all looked alike." He screwed the lid onto his empty bottle and dropped it into the grocery sack. "This guy said avid collectors think growing them is too expensive and time-consuming. Some of the damned things take ten years to bloom."

She finished off her water, too, and handed him the bottle. "You have to know a lot about a lot of different things to do what you do, don't you?"

"Not especially. But if I have time, I usually study up on what I'm gonna shoot. It makes the job a little easier if I'm not totally stupid. Now, combat. I don't have to study that. It's elemental."

"You're working on a new book now?"

"Yep. My last trip to the Middle East."

"It's a book of pictures?"

"Small amount of narrative. I'm not exactly a great writer. But, babe, I'm a damn fantastic photographer."

"Where'd you learn how to take pictures?"

"The Marine Corps. The Marine Corps taught me everything. About everything."

"Clova has all of your books. I've only looked at the one about the mountains. I've always wanted to go to the mountains. Those skiing pictures were so good."

"Hey, thanks. Some of those were for *National Geographic.* I did a piece on extreme skiing." Thinking back on that adventure, he snorted. "I damn near killed myself on that shoot. I don't ski and I don't understand those who do. Especially that wild shit on those steep slopes. It's dangerous as hell."

"It looks to me like you've done a lot of things more dangerous than skiing."

He lifted a shoulder in a shrug. "Matter of perspective, babe. Matter of perspective." He slid off the tailgate and gathered up their lunch leavings. "How about it? You ready to go at it again?"

"Sure am."

She hopped off the tailgate a little too enthusiastically. He suspected she was faking. He also suspected she'd had enough, but unless she cried uncle, he couldn't afford to give her a reprieve. He had to get this fence job finished, get his mom healed up and see a man about an oil well. And now he had to look into the situation with his little brother's bastard child. He couldn't return to LA with a clear conscience without accomplishing all of that.

Beyond that, he didn't know why, but he liked having Joanna Walsh for a work companion, and her help was making the job go faster.

Late afternoon came and the orange sun hung in the west, turning the landscape to a red-gold haze. He declared the fence-building job finished. On the way back to the ranch house, they bumped along in the work truck in silence until she said, "I heard you were in Iraq. There's three people from Hatlow in Iraq. Roy Elkins and Truman Johnson's boys and Bill Morgan's daughter. She's a nurse."

The names meant nothing to Dalton. "Bad place to be. But most of those folks believe in what they're doing. They're more worried about getting screwed over by the politicians over here than about getting killed over there. I want to honor all of them with my book."

"How many wars have you taken pictures of?"

"More than I care to recall. There's a war going on somewhere all the time. Being an objective witness to just how fu— how savage human beings can be is an onerous task for one small man."

He was proud of himself for catching himself on the *F* word. He didn't want to see her ears bleed.

"I can't imagine the kind of life you have," she said, "going all over the world to take pictures. I couldn't even get along living in Lubbock. That's why I'm here."

"I've never regretted the path I took. I'm never bored."

"Then I guess that makes you one of the lucky ones."

Once he had thought that. Lately, he wondered. After his last trip, he felt weary, worn and not enthusiastic to return. "Why? Do *you* have regrets?"

"No. I'm happy where I am. But I know a lot of people who aren't."

They reached the ranch and he brought the work truck to a stop behind the dually.

"Are you going to see your mom?" she asked.

"After I get cleaned up and get something to eat." He slid out of the truck with every joint and muscle protesting. Back in LA, besides swimming every day, he sometimes worked out in a health club, but he couldn't remember the last time he had done so much strenuous work for a sustained period. Just one more reminder that he was getting old and he hadn't taken very good care of himself. Just one more fact that made him wonder if it was time to change directions.

He limped around the front end of the truck and opened the door for Joanna to climb out, but she just sat there. "I don't think I can move," she said.

He offered her his hand. "Come on, Red. You're not gonna quit on me now, are you?"

"Red? Oh, my gosh, am I that sunburned?"

He found the energy to chuckle. "I was talking about your hair."

She looked at him with a thousand-kilowatt smile. He smiled back and took a few seconds and let his eyes feast on her face. She was hot and sweaty and sunburned indeed, and her makeup, whatever she had worn, was gone. She didn't seem to care, and it was just as well. She was pretty without it.

"No one's ever called me Red," she said, then laughed. "Is that better than *babe*?"

Damn, he liked her.

Chapter 13

Dalton stood with his hand extended. She took it and climbed out slowly, letting out a groan when her feet hit the ground. "I've got to gather the eggs." She looked spent, but her face held an expression of resolve as she clapped her cap on her head.

"I'll help you," he said. "It won't take long with the two of us." After she had worked so hard helping him, he could stoop to help her gather eggs one more time.

She nodded. "Thanks. I never turn down help. I'll go get the baskets."

She came out of her little room and led the way to the chicken yard and let them through the gate. They approached the first coop together. "Look," she said, "let's do this like we did this morning. I'll take these on the left and you—"

An ominous sizzle and hiss stopped them.

An adrenaline burst shot through his gut. *Fuck!*

She stopped dead still. "Oh, my God," she whispered and swung a wild-eyed look of horror at him.

There was no mistaking the sound. He scanned a 180 degrees but saw nothing. "Be still." He kept his voice low, not wanting to excite her any more. "I can't see it. Can you?"

"No. I—I think it's on my left. Maybe behind the coop." Her voice held a quaver.

Fuck! He had no weapon of any kind. He knew

there was a good chance the varmint would slither away if left alone and unthreatened. Then again, to be hissing and rattling, it *already* felt threatened. It had probably come for eggs. And if it found food successfully, it would return. He didn't like the idea of either Joanna or his mother facing a rattlesnake. His eyes darted everywhere until he spotted a three-foot-long piece of two-by-four securing the coop's door flap. "That two-by-four on top of the chicken house. Is it nailed down?"

"N-no."

"Don't move a muscle." He stepped gingerly to the right and lifted the two-by-four from the roof. He eased around the back of the coop, coming up on the opposite side. There he saw the snake coiled like a rope at the corner of the shack, its triangular head risen to strike. The damn thing was thick, and it had to be four feet long. He knew two things: It could strike quicker than the blink of an eye and he had to move fast.

He raised the board and struck. *Thwack!*

The rattler twisted and writhed on the ground, its neck broken. He finished it off with the two-by-four and his boot heel.

He glanced in Joanna's direction. She had sunk to her knees, her face covered with her hands. He threw the two-by-four back onto the roof, went to her and squatted beside her. She was shaking all over. "You okay?"

She began to sob in great gulps. "N-no. . . . I'm n-not okay."

He rubbed her back with one hand. "I got him. He can't hurt you now. Everything's all right."

She braced a hand on his knee and stood up, wiping her nose with the heel of her hand. "I have to go home. Right now. I have to go home." She turned and stumbled toward the gate.

"Wait a minute. . . ."

But she didn't stop. She fumbled the gate open and stumbled through but didn't close it. "When you go see your mom, don't tell her about the snake."

He got to his feet and followed her, pausing long enough to latch the gate. He sure didn't want to risk all those friggin' chickens getting out of their pen at sundown.

She was headed on a crooked path toward her truck. He quickstepped behind her. When he reached her she was trying to dig her keys from her jeans pocket, but the tail of his oversize shirt and her trembling prevented it.

"Here," he said, starting to be concerned about her, "let me do that." He shoved his fingers into her jeans pocket, pulled out her keys and handed them to her. "You sure you're okay to drive?" She reached for the door, but he held it closed. "I'm not sure you should be driving—"

"I can drive," she snapped, yanking on the door latch.

"Okay." He lifted his hands in surrender, then pulled the door all the way open and held it for her. She climbed onto the driver's seat and fumbled the keys into the ignition with a shaking hand.

"Don't worry about the eggs," he said, stunned at hearing himself say it. "I'll get 'em for you."

"You don't have to. They can wait." She fired the engine, giving it too much gas. It came to life with a loud roar.

"I said I'll get 'em. And I will." He raised his voice to be heard over the engine noise. "I don't know how to wash 'em, but I'll put 'em in the refrigerator for you."

"Fine. Please. I have to go."

He closed the door and she drove away, leaving him to worry. About her.

*   *   *

Snake! . . . *Rattle*snake! . . . *Shit.*

What the hell was a snake doing slinking around in September? Weren't they all supposed to be asleep by now?

Joanna lay in a bathtub of warm bubbles up to her neck, waiting for the shakes to go away. Her stomach had roiled all the way home, and she had barely made it into the house before it rebelled and she hurled what little she had eaten all day. Her heart continued to pound, and she still felt a buzz all over her body.

She hadn't seen a snake in the chicken yard in a long while. So long, in fact, that she had become complacent about looking out for one. And she had *never* seen a rattlesnake there. In fact, in spite of living in the middle of a rattlesnake haven, she had never seen one up close and personal, *ever*. A rat snake or an ordinary old bullsnake that came to steal eggs didn't scare her. But a rattlesnake terrified her. *Shit.* Reimagining the rattle sent another shiver up her spine.

She couldn't make herself stop thinking about two years ago when Toby Patterson, a local teenager, had been bitten on the hand while picnicking. He didn't die from it, but he came close. Now, more than twenty surgeries in three major hospitals later, he had lost 20 percent of the use of his hand and arm. Gossip said his medical bills had come to a million dollars. Hatlow's churches and citizens still held bake sales, raising money to help his family pay them.

What would she have done if Dalton hadn't been there? No answer to that question came, but the thought of him as her knight in shining armor brought on new and different distress. How illogical was that? One was just as hard to put out of her mind as the other.

Instead of doing any more heavy cogitating, she concentrated on Alan Jackson's mellow voice crooning from the CD player in the bedroom and the haunting lyrics of "Red on a Rose." That endeavor turned out to be a mistake because the song was a haunting ballad about a man's deep love for a woman, something Joanna had never known. How nice would it be to have someone who cared about her all the way to his soul, someone who was strong and would always look out for her, someone who would hold her and tell her she was safe?

New anguish pushed in on her attempt at serenity, and as if it were playing on a movie screen, she saw her future as a lonely old woman who had chosen hard work over the risk of relationships.

Tears welled in her eyes. Her inexplicable attraction to a man as impossible as Dalton Parker and the incident with the rattlesnake only reinforced just how alone she was and the precarious position in which the egg business had put her security. Why couldn't she have been content with the two businesses she already owned that supported her reasonably well? Now the egg business took so much of her time and energy, her other enterprises suffered. And she hadn't been able to put away any more toward her retirement in ages.

Out of control, her thoughts hurtled into even scarier territory and left her pondering what character flaw made her feel unfulfilled and had her constantly reaching for a new success. Was it because she had no family, no husband or children on which to spend her energy? Was that why she often found herself involved with the endless crises in Clova's family? Of course, her history proved that if she hadn't taken Clova's troubles upon herself, she would have found someone else's. When her mother and her friends told her she *had* to stop trying to solve everyone else's problems, they were right.

The song ended. The bathwater had grown tepid.

She forced herself to climb out. A hot bubble bath had not soothed the aches and pains she felt in every cell. Not only had it been dumb for her to volunteer to help a superior physical specimen such as Dalton build a fence, it had been downright stupid to try to keep up with him. She had never seen a human being work so hard and get so much done in so short a time. He was like a damn machine. Helping him had taken all of the physical strength and willpower she possessed.

But no way would she ever let him know it. Her pride wouldn't allow it.

She dried her body, pulled on her shorts and T-shirt and smoothed another layer of antibiotic cream on the injury between her brows and antiwrinkle cream on her face, readying for bed. Tomorrow would be an early day. She wished she could beg off, but she had already made appointments to deliver her product and had already made arrangements for Alicia to gather the coming morning's eggs.

As she snuggled into her bed, a glance at the digital clock on the nightstand told her it wasn't even nine o'clock. Even if she wanted a social life or a relationship with someone, she had no strength for it. On a great sigh, she closed her eyes.

After a fitful night of bad dreams and snarling stomach, she rose even earlier than usual, showered and shampooed her hair and smoothed a strategic layer of concealer on the bruise between her eyes. Then she dressed in khaki Dockers and a royal blue polo and pulled on her new Justin boots. She was starved. Her stomach was in no shape for coffee, so she took an extra few minutes to make a soft scrambled egg. She overcooked it and it felt like Play-Doh in her mouth, but it, a slice of toast and a glass of milk quelled the blistering fire inside her stomach.

Reaching the ranch before daylight, she killed the

headlights as she turned into the long driveway, not wanting to wake Dalton and have him to deal with this morning. The hens would be roosting yet, but she gave the chicken yard a cursory look, then let her eyes and thoughts dwell on the coop behind which the snake had been hiding. Reliving the incident for a few seconds in her mind, she felt a shudder pass over her.

But dammit, she had to forget it. If she didn't, she wouldn't be able to go forward and function. Making a renewed effort to put the incident behind her, she turned her back on the chicken yard and started toward the egg-washing room.

When she opened the refrigerator, she saw four baskets full of eggs. So Dalton really had gathered them. She just now remembered that he said he would. The surprise made a tiny smile crook her lips.

But alas, she didn't put unwashed eggs in the refrigerator. Now the whole interior would have to be washed with disinfectant soap, but no way would she look a gift horse in the mouth by criticizing him. She wrote a note to Alicia telling her to wash the fresh eggs left in the refrigerator along with those she would gather this morning and to wash the inside of the refrigerator before putting the clean eggs inside. Poor kid. She would earn her pay today, but the job had to be done. No way would Joanna risk delivering bacteria-contaminated eggs. She decided she would pick up a special gift for Alicia today in Lubbock or Amarillo.

Since Walsh's Naturals had no refrigeration unit on the pickup and could ill afford to buy one, Joanna used plastic thermal coolers and frozen blue ice blocks to keep the eggs cool during transportation. So far, that method had worked just fine, so long as she wasted no time. She began to load her pickup bed with the coolers filled with cartons of eggs.

*   *   *

Dalton stood in the dark in the dining room, watching Joanna load some kind of boxes into her truck bed. If he were a gentleman, he would go out and help her. But no one had accused him of being a gentleman in years.

She hadn't mentioned yesterday that she would show up here before daylight. Hearing her truck engine and the crunch of the tires on the gravel driveway—and being half awake anyway thinking about Lane and the new addition to the family—he had gotten up to see who might be driving in so early.

Lane wasn't the only one who had been in his head all night. Joanna had been there, too. The fantasy of her naked body had darted in and out of his semiconsciousness, and he felt as if he'd had a hard-on all night. But his thoughts of Joanna were more complicated than those base urges. He kept mulling over her frank honesty, how easy he found her company, her willingness to work at something that had no benefit to her personally. She aroused his emotions in ways he hadn't yet defined, and he couldn't decide if he felt safe being around her this morning.

Or any morning until he figured out just what the hell it was that caused her to pique his interest. Jesus Christ, the only common ground between them was her connection to his mother and the ranch. Seeing the shape she was in when she left last night, he had been concerned about her, sure. But this morning, couldn't he be content with just knowing that she was okay?

"Well, shit," he grumbled in answer to the question. He went back to the bedroom, slipped his feet into his boots and stabbed his arms into a Windbreaker.

Shoving his hands into his jeans pockets against the chill, he walked up to the door of her egg-washing room. "Hey."

She startled, her eyes flew wide and her palm slapped against her chest. "God, you scared me."

"What's going on?"

"Loading up. It's delivery day."

"No shit? You really sell these things, huh?"

"Cut it out. I'm in no mood for teasing. Not that you care, but I've got two new customers."

"How many eggs you hauling out of here?"

"A hundred forty dozen."

Surprised at the number, he whistled. "Overworked chickens, I'd say. PETA's gonna to be after your ass."

A stab from her pretty green eyes came back at him. Not liking the hostile look, he glanced away. "So how'd you do last night, after the snake?"

"Fine," she said.

In a pig's eye, he thought, taking note of the dark circles and puffiness under her eyes. He knew what happened to the body when someone had the shit scared out of him. He had seen plenty of people coming off an adrenaline high and had some experience himself.

"I measured that sumbitch," he said. "Four feet, eight inches. I skinned him. I'm gonna find somebody to make me a fancy hatband."

"Need to show off your trophy, eh? How macho." She tapped her breastbone with her clenched fist and said in a gravelly voice, "Look at me. Big snake killer."

He stared at her a few beats. Damn her, anyway. He was trying to be nice, and here she was being a horse's ass. "You know, I came out here to help you load whatever it is you're loading, but—"

"Okay, look, I'm sorry. I didn't mean to be so short. It's just that I've got a long to-do list today and I'm trying to get organized. I appreciate your help. I appreciate *all* help, believe me."

"Okay," he muttered, still miffed. He scanned the

array of boxes sitting on the ground near the truck bed and realized for the first time that they were thermal coolers. "You deliver eggs in camping coolers?" He couldn't keep incredulity out of his tone.

"Don't criticize. It's what I can afford. They work fine. I just stack them in the back of the pickup. They aren't heavy."

They began to work together lifting the coolers into the truck bed. "So who're you selling all these friggin' eggs to anyway?" In LA, he could think of dozens of places that sold free-range eggs to consumers, but West Texas wasn't LA.

"Health-food markets, mostly. But a couple of restaurants called me last week. They have free-range eggs on their menu. West Texas diners are finally catching up with the rest of the country."

"Humph. I've always figured that organic stuff was bullshit. You want the truth? I doubt if most people can tell the difference."

She gave him an exaggerated gasp as she slid a cooler into the bed. "Have you eaten an egg from your mom's refrigerator since you've been here?"

"Well, sure."

"And you can't tell the difference between what you're eating here and what you get from the grocery store?"

Well, maybe a little. He shook his head. "Nope. Can't say that I can."

"You're impossible." She shoved the last cooler into the truck bed, lifted the tailgate and slammed it, then dusted her palms. "There. All done. Thanks again for your help."

She walked around to the driver's side and climbed into the truck. Left with the choice of standing behind her truck and risking her backing over him, or following her to her door, he followed her to her door.

She closed the door and buzzed down the window.

"Listen, when you go see your mom today, tell her I'll drop by when I get back."

He stuffed his hands in his jeans pockets. "Okay. Who's gonna gather up your eggs this morning?"

"Alicia. Please don't be mean to her."

She fired the engine, obviously eager to leave. And that made him anxious for some damn reason. He raised his voice to be heard above the roar of her truck engine. "I told you before, I'm not mean to people." Without a reply, she put the truck in reverse. That goofy part of himself he didn't understand wanted her to stay. "You coming out here this evening to gather more eggs?"

"Unless I'm dead or disabled, it's what I do. Every day."

"I'm kind of a half-assed cook, being a bachelor and hating restaurants like I do. Mom's got a freezer full of beef. I'd cook up a steak if you wanted to stay and eat. It gets kind of lonesome out here, you know?"

She replied with a long, level look at him with those pretty green eyes, and at that moment, something feral passed between them. He had been given the eye by many women, but this was different. It was like a spark, so sudden and quick, he wondered if he had imagined it. He didn't know what it was, but he did know he wanted nothing more at this moment than for her to come back for supper.

"You might not want to wait," she said. "It could be seven o'clock before I get back."

If that were true, she would be gathering eggs in the dark. And dammit, what if yesterday's rattlesnake had a brother or a sister? "If it starts to get dark and you're not back, I'll get the eggs for you."

She laughed. "Have you gone crazy? Don't tell me you've gotten to like the chickens and the egg business."

Her laugh had a musical quality to it, and he liked that. He also liked the bright smile that went with it. Especially so early in the morning. Any woman that cheerful before daylight had to have a strong constitution.

"I'll see you tonight," he said, stepping back from the truck, feeling a little unsettled by his own unexpected emotion.

"Right." She backed the truck in an arc. When she stopped to change gears, he approached the door again. She buzzed down the window. "Be careful," he said. "I don't know what Mom would do if you ended up like Lane."

"I'm always careful. I'm a good driver."

He watched her drive away and continued to watch until she made a right turn onto the highway. Then he headed for the house. For no reason, he found himself whistling.

Dalton occupied *all* of Joanna's brain as she drove toward town. Unshaven and rumpled, he had looked as if he had just crawled out of bed. And of course, he had. That thought traveled straight to the place within her that had been dormant for a very long time. *Forget it,* she told herself. *He's got someone, and he's only in town temporarily.*

He had been a different man, helping her load up her eggs and teasing her. Then inviting her to eat supper with him. He was nothing if not a puzzle.

It gets kind of lonesome out here, you know?

So he gets lonesome, she thought smugly. Just like everyone else. He was human.

She reached the city limits and passed through town on her way to the Lubbock highway. Hatlow hadn't yet come alive. She saw activity only at Betty Lou's Coffee Cup. There, pickups and cars belonging to the usual coffee and breakfast crowd filled the parking lot.

Betty Lou's was the hub of the local small-business community. Every morning, the group traded gossip and transacted business in the country café atmosphere.

Among the vehicles, she saw Jay Huddleston's big red dually pickup with its white magnetic sign on the doors that said HUDDLESTON WELL SERVICING. Shari would be at home rousing the Huddleston brood and getting them ready for school.

Hatlow hadn't changed much from its bland appearance of Joanna's high school days. If anything, it had become more run-down. Featureless two- and three-story buildings of indeterminate age lined both sides of the main street. Square brick boxes with windows. She couldn't remember when one of them had last received a facelift. The oil bust of the eighties had almost wiped out the town. No one had money for something so frivolous as renovations.

She passed her own white brick building and its pink sign that said JOANNA'S SALON & SUPPLIES, its windows lit and showing off a colorful display of new hair-care products from Redken. As she always did when she saw the business on a quiet morning, she made a silent prayer of thanksgiving that it was still standing. She didn't expect it not to be, but she still felt grateful. Thank God she had organized the salon and the retail store so well they almost ran themselves, because it seemed that she paid less and less attention to them these days.

Speeding along the highway toward Lubbock, her mind wandered again to her rescuer, Dalton Parker. *Be careful.* She was touched that he made the effort to caution her, as if he would care if she had an accident.

She thought of the old proverb from somewhere that said if someone saved your life, they were responsible for you forever. Or something like that. She didn't believe her life had been in danger yesterday, not really. But confronted by a rattlesnake, who knew what would happen? She was just glad he had been there. She had faced challenges, but she had never had to do something so violent as whack a rattlesnake. Firing her shotgun at chicken hawks was different.

She thought of the fence-building project and what her mother had said about Dalton that Sunday following Lane's accident: *Even when he was a little boy, Earl worked him like he was a grown man.*

Every muscle and sinew in Joanna's body could confirm that the man had learned how to work.

Different comments she had heard said about Dalton during the past two weeks came back. Her sister's words: *I could tell he carried a hurt. But it wasn't caused by some girl.*

She thought of what Clova had said that night in the hospital when they waited together to learn Lane's fate: *He don't care nothin' 'bout us, anyway, Joanna. And I don't blame him. Back when it mattered, we didn't act like we cared much about him.*

Now she was more curious than ever to know what Clova had meant. What Joanna had seen of Dalton was inconsistent with the behavior of a man who cared nothing about his mother or brother.

She had not spent all of her adult life in a service business without learning a little about human nature and behavior. It dawned on her now that she might have Dalton Parker figured out. Growing up, he'd had no one. The very person who should have supported him, his mother, had failed him somehow, and he had been hurt profoundly. Joanna believed he had a good heart, but he feared getting hurt again. He had grown a hard edge in self-defense. She had always assumed that Clova adored Dalton, so how had she managed to cut him so deeply? Her own heart softened even more toward both son and mother.

Stop it, her good sense told her. *He's the one person whose problems you don't need to take on.*

Still, Joanna couldn't stop thinking about him. She couldn't imagine growing up in a home where parents were cruel to their children. Her father had been a kind and gentle man. And he had been a patient man to have put up with Alvadean Walsh's eccentricities without quarrel. Clova and her triangular relationship with her deceased husband and her children was becoming a bigger curiosity all the time.

Indeed, Joanna might have Dalton Parker figured out. But now, with a flurry of such unfamiliar emotions, she was no longer sure she understood Joanna Walsh.

Chapter 14

Dalton started his Monday at the Wacker County Courthouse, writing a check that paid the taxes on the Parker ranch. When he had called his business manager in LA last night to arrange for the money to be transferred into his checking account, the guy had given him a stern lecture about paying taxes on real estate he didn't own. But at the moment, Dalton saw no other choice.

From there he crossed the street to Hatlow Farmers Bank. A plaque beside the front door marked it as a Texas historical building. The bank had been founded in the nineteenth century and the hundred-year-old red limestone building had obviously been maintained to reflect its American Victorian-era history. Dalton delivered a copy of the receipt from the tax assessor's office showing the taxes paid current on the Parker ranch. The Hispanic employee who took it couldn't have cared less about a ranch that was as much a Texas historical landmark as the bank. Ironic, he thought.

Leaving the courthouse square and driving along Hatlow's main street, he saw the aftermath of a collapsed economy. What had once been a thriving Norman Rockwell-ish small town, supported by oil and agriculture, was now a dilapidating shell of buildings and stores with boarded-up windows and locked doors. Mom had told him the landscape was the same all

over West Texas. Depressing to see the site of his
youth in decay.

Before Dalton graduated from high school in 1987,
the price of oil had already plummeted. Small oil op-
erators had already started to disappear from the Hatlow business scene. Though he had witnessed the
ruinous event at its genesis, he could see that the impact of the economic crash hadn't fully manifested itself until after his departure.

But more than depressed oil prices affected Hatlow,
according to his mother. Cotton farming had changed.
Many farmers found it easier and more profitable to let
their fields lie fallow in return for government checks.
Ranching had fared only slightly better than farming,
but most of the cattle operations were still hanging on.
The American public could do without American cotton, but they did love their American beef.

Oh, well, he told himself. At least no one had to
fear a sniper hidden behind one of the darkened
second-floor windows. No suicide bombers would be
showing up in the grocery store or the schoolhouse.
Not yet.

He soon came to a flower shop located on the outskirts of downtown in a Hatlow version of a strip mall.
He ordered a bouquet to be delivered to his mother,
folded the receipt for the taxes into a small square
and inserted it into a gift card to be attached to the
bouquet. He requested that the flowers be delivered
today.

When he left the flower shop, he carried a pink
four-foot-tall teddy bear wearing a white lacy bow
around its neck. It was left over from Valentine's Day,
the shop owner had told him. He still pondered the
fact that his mother hadn't said a damn word about
Lane being the father of a small daughter.

These days, the thought of kids, any kids, brought to
the front of his mind the hundreds of pathetic small faces

he had photographed in the poverty-ridden parts of the world. They all had the same mournful expressions—grim little mouths and haunted eyes too old for their years. A little girl lucky enough to be born in the USA should know that her family included two sides.

Dalton might not dwell on the past, he might not be a sterling example of family togetherness, but that didn't mean he had given up on the ideal of family unity. He hadn't forgotten the pain of growing up in a fractured home. Besides that, the Parker clan already had one living bastard. It didn't need another.

He positioned the teddy bear on the passenger seat. As he climbed into the truck and headed for the edge of town. he could think of no time when a pink teddy bear had been his passenger, or for that matter, when he had bought a stuffed toy of any size or color. He had picked it up purely on impulse.

A visit to the Dairy Queen wasn't on his agenda for today, but he had the teddy bear and he had to get rid of it.

At the Dairy Queen order counter, a tall brown-haired girl in a pink smock took his order for a burger and fries, trying to be inconspicuous in staring at him and the giant teddy bear crammed under his left arm. She probably thought he was a nut. She called his order in to the kitchen, then turned back to him. "That'll be six dollars and four cents."

"I'm looking for Mandy Ferguson," he said, juggling the teddy bear while digging into his jeans pocket for money.

She smiled and her whole face lit up. "Oh. I'm Mandy."

She looked fresh and pretty, with long, shining brown hair and the unsullied face of someone no older than twenty-five. He made a mental sigh of relief. At least she wasn't underage.

"Would you like for me to hold that bear for you?" she asked.

"Would you mind?" He handed her the bear. It was wider than she was. "I'm Dalton Parker," he said, pulling a ten from his money clip and dropping it on the counter.

As a glimmer of recognition passed through her eyes, a blush stained her cheeks. "Has something happened to Lane?"

"No, nothing new. I just want to talk to you a minute if you've got time."

She handed the bear back to him, opened the cash register drawer and gave him change. "You're Lane's big brother, aren't you?"

"I am."

"What do you want?"

"To talk. Can we find a private place to sit down?"

"I guess so." She turned and asked a heavyset woman standing at the soft ice cream machine—and obviously eavesdropping—to watch the counter for her. The woman leveled a cold glare at him and Mandy both. Mandy ignored her and rounded the end of the counter. She led the way to a small square table in the back corner of the dining room.

"I wanted to meet you," Dalton said, setting the bear in a chair. With its fat arms protruding rigidly from its sides, it filled the straight-backed chair and looked as if it was waiting to be picked up and hugged. He took a seat across the table from the girl. The teddy bear stared at both of them with big black button eyes and a smiling snout. "I just found out you and Lane have a little girl."

She dropped her gaze to her hands. They looked red and chapped.

"It's okay," Dalton said. "I mean, I'm not here to pass judgment or anything. I heard that you don't want any part of my brother, but you know how talk

is. You never can tell how much of it's true. If that's
how you feel, I'd like to hear it from you directly."

Her head shook slowly. She looked back up at him,
a troubled expression showing in her eyes. "I can't
afford Lane."

Dalton chuckled, hoping to put her at ease. "That
might be true of all of us. But that doesn't tell me
much. Did he not want your little girl or what?"

"Why don't you ask him?"

"I intend to. Tomorrow, when I see him again."

Her head shook again and she looked out the large
picture window beside them. At what, Dalton couldn't
tell. There wasn't much to see in the arid landscape,
not even bushes or trees.

"I would've stuck with him if he'd tried just a little
bit. But after I got pregnant, my mom and dad wanted
to be sure the baby had a good home. They wanted
me to break it off with him. I live at their house and
they give me a job, so . . ." She shrugged and returned
her gaze to her hands.

Dalton glanced toward the woman at the soft ice
cream machine. Given the evil eye she was casting in
his direction, he wondered if she could be this girl's
mother. "You said, 'tried just a little bit.' What did
you want him to do that he wasn't doing?"

"I didn't ask him for much. I just wanted him to be
sober. I thought we could make it if he would just
be sober."

The girl's face might be unblemished, but her eyes
appeared to be nursing a great pain. Her wish was no
different from what any other woman, or mother,
would wish, Dalton supposed. "I see," he said, trying
to hide his unease. He was lousy at conversations like
this. He had a rocky record with women, but at least
a surprise pregnancy wasn't part of it.

The heavyset woman brought a brown sack stained
with grease and handed it to him, along with another

pointed glare. He kept quiet, sliding the hamburger out of the sack and stalling by fiddling with salt and pepper until she returned to her spot behind the counter. "If I said I think things could be different when Lane comes out of the hospital, would it make any difference to you?"

Mandy gave a hint of a smile. "I don't know. I'm pretty easy when it comes to Lane. I always was. At least, that's what my dad says. That was part of the problem. Lane could talk me into just about anything." Her shoulders lifted in a great sigh. "But my mom and dad . . . I just don't know."

"I know he pays child support, but—"

"He wanted to," she said, straightening into a defensive posture. "I didn't make him."

"I'm not questioning that, Mandy. If he has a daughter, he should take care of her. Before he had the wreck, did he see her?"

"Not much. When she was first born, he came around a lot, but most of the time, if my dad was at home . . . well, Daddy always ran him off."

Dalton nodded, chewing on a bite of his hamburger and studying her. Hell, she cared about Lane. Anybody could see it. But did she have the courage of her feelings? Could or would she defy her parents? "Yours is the only kid in our family. I think it would mean a lot to my mom to have a relationship with her granddaughter."

Dalton had no idea whether his last statement was true. Mom had never worn her emotions on her sleeve. "It could also mean a new life for my brother. He's gonna get out of ICU this week. Maybe as early as tomorrow. I'd be happy to take you up to visit him if you want to."

She looked down at her hands again. "I don't know. My mom and dad—"

"You're old enough to make your own decision

about it. I mean, we're talking about your daughter's father and nothing more than a hospital visit."

She looked out the window again. "Someone told me he's going to be crippled."

"That's what the docs are saying, but it's too early to know for sure. Having the support of people who care about him will help him."

"I don't know. I'd have to think about it." She glanced toward the heavyset woman who was now standing at the end of the order counter and openly watching them. Pushing back her chair, Mandy started to rise. "I need to get back."

Dalton got to his feet, too. "I know. I didn't mean to keep you. This bear's a present for your daughter. From her uncle."

The wide smile lit up her face again. "Really? Oh, my gosh. It's twice as big as she is, but she'll just love it."

"Okay if I just leave her sitting there?"

"Yessir. I'll put it in my car in a minute. It's so cute."

He returned her smile. "It is cute. And you don't have to call me sir. What'd you say your daughter's name is?"

She was still smiling. "It's Malaney. Kind of a cross between Lane's name and mine. Lane and I made it up together."

Dalton was touched by her youthful sentimentality. He couldn't imagine his little brother making up a name for a baby or as the father of a child, but if he'd had a hand in choosing the kid's name, he must have had some kind of meaningful relationship with this girl. He took out his wallet and wrote his mother's phone number on the back of his business card, though he would lay money that Mandy knew it. "Just give me a call if you want to go visit my brother. Call any time."

He left the Dairy Queen feeling like the wise older brother. And it felt pretty damn good.

A mile on up the road, he came to his main destination, Huddleston Well Servicing. As he pulled to a stop in front of a flat-roofed metal building, he scanned the surrounding caliche-covered parking area. His high school friend Jay Huddleston had worked here in the family business as a teenager. Today, Dalton saw no trucks parked, so that meant Huddleston's crews must be out working.

When Dalton and Jay were teenagers, the company had owned three pulling units that provided maintenance service for existing oil wells. Dalton hadn't heard or hadn't been interested in knowing what had happened to Huddleston Well Servicing after he left Hatlow. His focus had been on his own survival.

Inside the well-servicing company's office, he met a receptionist at work in stark gray surroundings devoid of luxuries. On a metal table behind her metal desk sat the only decoration—a tiny blue pot with phony daisies perched beside a gold-framed picture of her, a man and two kids. She showed him into her boss's office.

A grinning Jay Huddleston, his right hand extended, came from behind a huge metal desk that looked to be military surplus. "Dalton Parker, you hardheaded devil. Come on in here."

Dalton shook hands with his old high school friend, noticing he had aged well. Except for silver hair and creases around the mouth, he didn't look much different from their school days. Dalton hadn't seen him since then, when they had played football together on Hatlow's winning team. Dalton had been the quarterback and Huddleston had been an end. An image of Jay suited up and catching a pass flashed from the far recesses of Dalton's memory. As Dalton recalled, Jay could outrun the wind.

"Joanna gave you my message, huh?" Jay said.

"Message?"

"I told her to tell you to come by. Beer? Coffee? It's a little early for me for beer, but—"

"It's too early for me, too. A cup of coffee will do."

Jay yelled to the receptionist to bring a cup of coffee. Then his attention returned to Dalton. "Hey, man, you look good. Haven't changed a bit." His expression turned solemn. "Listen, that was too damn bad about Lane. How's he doing now?"

"Coming along."

Jay shook his head, his thick, dark brows pinching together. "That Lovington highway's a son of a bitch. But since the DUI laws got tougher, it's not as bad as it used to be. It used to get a lot of 'em."

"Yep. It sure as hell got Earl Cherry," Dalton replied, revisiting in his mind the irony of Cherry's only son nearly killing himself on the same long, lonesome highway in the middle of the night.

"It damn sure did. I forgot about that."

"So you followed your dad into the well-servicing business?" Dalton said. "I never knew."

"Man, I didn't have much choice." Jay gave a good-natured chuckle. "With Shari pregnant, me only eighteen years old and bills to be paid, I had to do something to make a living. I was lucky my dad took pity on me."

"Looks like it worked out okay for you."

"So far, so good. We got four pulling units and four crews now, and they're all working. We had some lean years through the bust, but Dad was able to hang on 'til the price of oil started to climb back up a little. A lot of the competition didn't make it. Me and Dad worked it together for a long time. Then he decided to quit a few years ago and I took over. It's great having things picking up. People are drilling again, and that means more work for us."

"Guess a few dollars more on a barrel of oil is good for everybody, huh?"

"You know how it is, buddy. The more cake, the more crumbs."

The receptionist came in delivering a steaming cup of black coffee and handed it to Dalton. "Thanks," he said.

"Have a seat, Dalton." Jay moved to his chair behind his desk. Dalton sank to a steel armchair in front of the desk and sipped his coffee.

"I think about you real often, Dalton. Every time somebody brings up that game with Denver City your senior year, I can still see you running the length of the whole damn field for the winning touchdown. Do you remember that?"

"Sure," Dalton said, recalling it only in dim snatches. Having trekked through many foreign countries where mere survival was the gut-wrenching daily goal and having lived in Los Angeles for many years, where the aim was frequently the same, if in a different way, Dalton no longer related to how wrapped up West Texans were in high school football.

"My oldest boy's a football player," Jay said. "He's working for me when he ain't practicing or playing. He's a damn fine ballplayer, Dalton. You oughtta see him. Got some colleges sniffing around, so I might not be able to keep him. Even the army's after him. Anyway, me and Shari are real proud of him."

Dalton nodded, accepting that some things in this part of the world might never change. Years had passed since the last time he had spent an afternoon or an evening watching football, though during his years in Hatlow, the game and the team had been one of the few parts of life he enjoyed. He no longer considered himself a team player, and he didn't do much for outside entertainment.

"You oughtta come around and meet him. I tell him

all the time about when you and me played together. I
still got that picture somebody made of us in our uniforms that day down in Denver City."

"No shit?" Dalton grinned, but now he wanted to
get to the point of why he came.

As if Jay had read what was going on in Dalton's
head, he said, "What can I do for you, Dalton? Something tells me you didn't come to see me just for old
time's sake."

Guilt poked Dalton. Even when he had visited Hatlow the few times in the past, he had made no attempt
to look up high school friends. "I've got some questions about well drilling," he said.

"Ask away. What I can't tell you, I guarantee my
dad can."

Dalton braced his elbows on the chair arms and
leaned forward, holding his coffee cup. "I meant to
discuss this with my mother, but she took ill before I
got the chance. When I was just a kid, someone drilled
a well on our place. I remember all the activity, but I
never knew who did the work. And I can't remember
the location."

Jay shook his head. "Man, I wouldn't know about
that. I would've been a kid, too. As for where it was,
if it was a dry hole, the operator probably plugged it
and abandoned the lease. If your mom can remember
roughly where it was, you might find it with a metal
detector. Something should still be in the ground."

"Where can I get reliable information? I'd like to
talk to whoever did the drilling if he's still around."

"I guess you'd start with the Railroad Commission.
They're the king-shit in the oil business in Texas. See
what kind of records they've got. A lot of the time,
they don't have much, especially from that long ago."

Dalton already knew that much. Just this morning
before going to the courthouse, he'd had a lengthy
phone conversation with the Texas Railroad Commis-

sion and learned that the well had been drilled in 1977, the year of Lane's birth. Dalton was eight years old. No wonder he recalled few of the details about the oil well.

"Or you could ask my dad," Jay was saying. "He knows damn near every oil well that's been drilled in Wacker County like it's a personal friend."

"How can I reach him?"

Jay laughed. "You could step out the back door here and yell at him. He lives in that trailer house behind the workshop. Let me get him over here."

Jay got to his feet and walked out of the office, his boot heels clunking against the gray tile floor. Dalton heard the scrunch of a metal door opening, heard Jay call out to his dad. In a few beats, Jay returned and took his seat behind the desk again. "He'll be over here in a minute."

While they waited for Jim Huddleston, Dalton thought of how comfortable and at home he felt in Jay's company. Other than his buddies in the Marine Corps, he hadn't had close male friends. But in high school, Jay had been the best. It didn't feel as if nearly twenty years lay between them. "So your son must be seventeen or eighteen now."

"Seventeen. He's a good kid, but he's got the whole household tore up right now."

"How's that?"

"I guess he's a horny little fart. I caught him in an embarrassing way with one of the cheerleaders. Shari nearly had a cow. Now we've got one of those hard-learning sessions going on. My wife's scared he'll do something stupid and screw up the rest of his life. You remember Shari, don't you?"

Dalton had no memory of the girls he himself had known and dated at eighteen, much less the girl Jay married. With most of his existence back then having been unpleasant, he had made a diligent effort to forget all of it. His philosophy of continuing to forge ahead had been formed at an early age. That was all that had enabled him to live through growing up amid the unfathomable relationship between his mother and her husband. What he did recall with clarity was that at that time he had recognized a turning point and made some adult decisions.

"Cody won't talk about it to his mother," Jay was saying, "but he and I are hashing it out."

Dalton chuckled at Jay's remarks, then sipped his coffee.

"Me and Shari got four boys," Jay went on. "They're all pistols. They're all athletes except the youngest. I think he's gonna be a musician."

Dalton didn't miss seeing Jay Huddleston's pride in his children. He couldn't imagine himself with kids, but it wasn't an altogether unpleasant thought. He could damn sure do a better job at parenting than his own parents had done. From out of nowhere, he wondered how Lane felt about having a child.

Soon Jim Huddleston came into the office. Dalton rose as Jay introduced them. "I remember you," the slender older man said, extending his right hand.

Dalton took his hand. "Yes, sir?"

"You were the best quarterback Hatlow's ever had. Where'd you disappear to, son?"

Dalton smiled at another reference to high school football and released the man's hand. "Here and there. I left here for the military."

"Dalton wants to know about a well that was drilled on his folks' place, Dad," Jay said.

"Oh, yes. Lemme see." Frowning, he looked down at the floor. "Seventy-seven or seventy-eight, I believe it was. As I recall, it was oversold."

"Oversold?" Dalton asked, unfamiliar with oil industry jargon.

"That's when an operator sells more shares to investors than a well's production will support," Jay put in. "If the well turns out to be a producer, the operator's got his tit in a wringer. He wouldn't dare complete it. If the investors found out what he done, they might have his hide. Or the SEC might come calling. So to save his neck, the operator just tells everybody it was a dry hole, plugs it and takes his profit from overselling."

"Is that better than getting the oil?" Dalton asked, knowing it was a naive question.

Jay's dad's head shook. "Lord, no. A man could make more money off the well production, but at that point, it's too late. Poor ol' boy's got hisself backed into a corner. That kind of stuff used to happen pretty often when there was a lot of drilling around here."

Dalton hid his amazement that investors could be so easily fleeced. The woman he had spoken to at the Texas Railroad Commission had mentioned none of this. "That isn't legal, right?"

Jay and his dad both laughed.

"Hell, no, it ain't legal," the older man said. "But most of the time, nobody never knew nothing about it, least of all a landowner or the folks who put up the money for the well. You can't see down in the ground, you see, so all they got to go on is the operator's word. They didn't used to have all the science they got now. Back in those days, most of those high-rollers willing to invest in a wildcat oil well knew it was a high-risk deal from the git-go. Hell, they were primed to swallow a dry-hole story."

Now that he thought about it, maybe Dalton wasn't surprised. Though he knew little about the oil business, he knew enough about life to know that where there was as much money floating around anywhere as there was in the oil industry, creative crooks abounded. "So does anyone know what happened on my mom's place? I mean, if it was a dry hole, that's one thing, but if it wasn't and there was fraud—"

"I think the operator who drilled it is dead now," Jim Huddleston said, "so I guess it don't hurt to talk about him. He come from down at Odessa. As I recall, it was a pretty good well. What is it you're wanting, Dalton?"

"I want someone to drill on Mom's place. Christ, with the price of oil now, there must be some new activity. I'm trying to get a feel for the possibility of finding oil."

"Oh, there's new activity, to be sure. Reentering some old wells that were plugged, drilling some new ones. They've got all kinds of new techniques now for detecting and getting that crude out of the ground."

"I know a dependable man down in Denver City, Dalton," Jay said. "I don't know what he's up to, far as digging new wells goes. I heard he stacked his rig last year, but—"

"Stacked his rig?" Another term with which Dalton was unfamiliar.

"Quit drilling. He might've retired. But I can put you in touch with him." Jay glanced at his watch. "He might be in his shop today. I don't know if you remember, but it's just twenty-two miles down to Denver City." He walked behind his desk, opened his center drawer and pulled out a business card. He handed it across the desk. "Skeeter Vance is the guy's name. Good man. And honest. Tell him I told you to call him."

Dalton took the card and looked at the name. "I could get down there today. Hey, thanks."

"Glad to help you out. How long you gonna stay in Hatlow?"

"Mom's got pneumonia, so it looks like I'm gonna be around a little longer than I first thought."

"Damn, that's too bad. I knew she was sick back in the spring. Hope she gets okay. I was going to say, if you're looking for some social life, some of us are getting together over at the state line Wednesday night for Shari's birthday. Remember the Rusty Spur?"

"A little. I was never there much, but I—"

"Come on over and have a beer with us. Shari's gonna be thirty-six. I don't know if we're celebrating or mourning, but a bunch of us are gonna be there."

"I'll give it some thought," Dalton said, glancing at his watch. He said good-bye and started for Denver City and a conversation that could alter the future of the Lazy P.

Chapter 15

While he drove to Denver City, Dalton chewed on the information he had picked up from the Huddlestons about oil wells. His mother and Cherry had been screwed over by some slick oilman? And never known the difference? If Earl Cherry had been the only victim, Dalton might have found that humorous, but thinking about some asshole ripping off his mother was another story.

He soon came to Denver City. The town had been larger than Hatlow in his youth, but now it appeared to be just one more crumbling West Texas oil and farming town that had lost 50 percent of its population and 95 percent of its life.

He had no trouble locating Skeeter Vance's shop. It was right on the highway. Vance was a jolly, square-built man a foot shorter than Dalton and maybe ten years older. A fringe of white hair poked out around the edges of a cap showing a SKEETER'S DRILLING logo. The man had freckles, blond eyelashes and no-color eyes, which made Dalton think he had been a redhead in his youth. He had a strong handshake and Dalton liked him at once. He usually did like a man who wasn't afraid to shake hands.

"Jay Huddleston told me to come see you," Dalton told him.

"He called me a little bit ago. Said you want a well dug."

"I'm thinking about it. On my mom's place up in Hatlow."

Vance lifted off his cap and scratched his head. "I've stacked my rigs, but if Jay sends somebody to me, I usually try to oblige. Let's go on in my office and you can tell me what's on your mind."

Dalton followed him into an office that looked to be a converted mobile home. The office was clean and well kept, nothing like Dalton had expected to see. That, too, spoke well of Vance.

"Sit down, sit down," Vance said. "Want a cup of coffee?"

"No, thanks." When Vance moved to his desk chair, Dalton seated himself in front of the desk. "Look, I need to get back up to Hatlow before night comes. I'll get right to the point." Dalton explained the old oil well and what Jim Huddleston had told him had probably happened to it.

"How old's the hole?" Vance asked.

"Thirty years."

"Oo-whee," Vance said, "I'm not fond of entering a well that old. Here's what can happen. First off, even if you find it, if it was a crooked deal, you don't know what they might've throwed down that hole when they abandoned it. If I got down there with my equipment and ran into junk, we could lose the hole. Worse yet, I could lose my equipment. That could cost you and me both a ton of money. Forty, fifty thousand dollars. For nothing."

"What if you drilled a new well alongside it?" Dalton asked. "Can you do that? If there was oil in one place, shouldn't there be some nearby? I don't want to spend a bunch of money on geologists and scientists."

"You're paying for this hole?"

"It's my nickel," Dalton answered. "If I decide to do it, that is."

"Sure, you can go alongside it. Just move over a hundred feet or so."

"And you might or might not hit oil."

Vance broke into a chuckle, his face showing a huge grin. "Well, son, that's the nature of wildcattin' for oil. It's a high-stakes gamble if there ever was one."

"I figured that out. Today I'm mostly collecting information." He still had to discuss the venture with his business manager and his mother.

"Then why don't you just tell me how much hole you might be thinkin' about."

Dalton harked back to his conversation with the Texas Railroad Commission in which he had learned the depth of the old well was 4,732 feet. "I don't know. Let's say not over five thousand feet."

"Good round number. Don't even have to get out my calculator. I can do that for about a hundred and twenty thousand."

Uncertain if he was ready for this kind of expenditure, Dalton assumed his best poker face. "No shit?"

The driller leaned forward, his eyes wide and questioning. "Too much?"

"I don't know. Sounds like a lot. I'd have to think about it. How do you usually get paid?"

"I'm easy to get along with. Half up front, the rest when we either plug a dry hole or start runnin' pipe in a producin' well. Now, if we don't go five thousand . . . Say we go thirty-five hundred. It'll cost you less. But 'til we dig that hole, we just don't know. How deep did you say that old well was?"

Dalton pulled the piece of notepaper where he had jotted the old well depth from his shirt pocket. "Four thousand seven hundred thirty-two feet."

Vance looked down at the floor, either thinking or playing a cat-and-mouse game. Dalton couldn't tell which. "Well. . . . I could drill it m'self. Save a little not hirin' a tool pusher and a driller. If I went thataway, I could do it for a hundred."

Dalton would definitely have to discuss this with his business manager. If oil wasn't found, was he ready to kiss a hundred thousand dollars good-bye? And if that happened, how would his own future be affected? Suddenly he had new and wary respect for those who speculated on oil wells. "How much land do you need?"

"For a well that depth? We oughtta make do with an acre."

Dalton nodded. "No problem. I'd need to get a lease in place and find the old oil well."

"You don't own the land?"

"It belongs to my mother. It's rangeland."

"She own the minerals?"

"The land and the mineral rights have been in our family for more than a hundred years."

Vance grinned again. "Old-timers around here, eh?"

"Wilburn Parker was my granddad. My mother's his daughter."

"Oh, yeah. I heard of him. Then if you and your mama get along, things oughtta go real smooth."

"If I gave you the go-ahead, when could you start?"

"Well, you'd need to get a survey and a drillin' permit. You'd need to get me about five hundred feet of twelve-inch casing. You need to build us a road and a pad—"

"I can't do any of that. I don't live here. I need a turnkey deal."

"I know people to do that work, yes sir. But son, if it's gonna be your oil well, *you've* got to be the one to get the drillin' permit."

"That makes sense," Dalton said. "I think I know roughly where the old well is. A fence and a couple

of small structures might have to be moved, probably
a new gate installed."

"Got livestock, huh? You don't need to worry, son.
We do our best not to leave a mess. And we don't
never harm cattle. They can graze all around us."

"It isn't cattle." Dalton hesitated, feeling silly over
what he had to say next. "It's chickens."

"Chickens."

Vance gave him a look devoid of expression. Dalton
could almost see the gears grinding behind the man's
eyes as he tried to figure out just exactly what Dalton meant.

"Two hundred chickens and two donkeys."

"Hunh," Vance said, still blank faced.

Dalton suspected that the driller, in his career, had
never encountered chickens as an obstacle. But Dalton
had no intention of embarking on an explanation of
free-range chickens and eggs.

"Well, son, we can take care of it, whatever it is.
We work with folks all the time. I can get a fence
moved and rebuilt for three to five hundred dollars.
It'll just take a day or two."

"Fine," Dalton said.

Vance reached for a pad of paper. "Tell me your
name again and how somebody gets ahold of you."

"Dalton Parker." He cited his mother's phone number and his cell phone number.

Vance wrote the information on the pad, then
looked up grinning. "Got it. Just let me know when
you wanna do business and I'll send you a contract."

"Fine. You can fax it to me on my mom's phone
number."

Dalton left Vance's office in a quandary. A hundred
thousand dollars was a shitload of money. The idea
of risking so much on a hole in the ground incited an
unexpected anxiety within him. When he discussed the

venture with his business manager, a disciplined man whose gambling instincts were restricted to the stock market, the guy might have a heart attack.

Dalton wasn't worried about his mother failing to approve, but he had questions about how such a venture would affect Joanna's operation. If he decided to go through with it, he would have to discuss it with her. He hated the damn chickens, but after yesterday, he respected Joanna enough not to want to harm her.

As Joanna motored toward Hatlow from Lubbock, her body felt as if it weighed five hundred pounds. Working so hard yesterday, followed by a confrontation with a rattlesnake and getting little sleep, had left her mind and body numb. Added to that was the blistering sun. Today, it had been not only oppressive but relentless. Typical of September.

She had climbed in and out of the pickup all day and heaved the egg-filled coolers into her customers' locations. To soften asking Alicia to scrub the refrigerator in the egg-washing room, she had trekked through the mall looking for a small gift. She found a delicate gold necklace with a tiny diamond pendant that was perfect for the petite Alicia. Then she had stopped off at a supermarket and bought Clova a potted mum that she could plant in her flower bed after she left the hospital.

All of it had sapped her energy. She coasted along with the air conditioner set on high and the cruise control set on sixty, listening to the radio and thinking. She always used driving time for thinking.

Today she had collected approximately five hundred dollars. From that, she would net less than two hundred. Mental groan. She had to figure out a way to either make the egg business more profitable or quit it.

Being the only egg farmer near enough to personally deliver fresh free-range eggs to the larger city markets, and with the cost of gasoline twice what it used to be, on this trip, she had raised her wholesale price by fifty cents per dozen. Customers had readily accepted her explanation about higher gasoline prices. But adding fifty cents to the price of a carton of eggs was like putting a Band-Aid on a throat slash.

She hated to give up on the egg business. In the first place, she hated to give up on *anything* until she became convinced no other option existed. Second, she respected the chickens as living things that did their best to serve her purpose, and she had grown to love them, even with all of their brainless quirks. Third, a tiny idealistic part of her believed that by providing a natural product, she was doing something beneficial for the people she served and for Earth.

Concluding she could have sold dozens more eggs if she'd had them made her think about Clova's offer of land. Funny how the idea of acquiring more laying hens would have never entered her head as being realistic if Clova hadn't mentioned giving the land to her. Now the idea popped into Joanna's mind often. More land equaled more hens and more eggs, which added up to more income.

She couldn't keep from thinking that if she had that free land with highway frontage, she could be selling eggs at retail instead of wholesale, thus generating more cash. She had almost come to associate the gift of land with being the only way the egg business could survive. Common sense told her different, but sometimes a longing could send a person's thoughts in a wrong direction. She knew about yearning for something just out of reach because she had been doing it her whole life. She hadn't necessarily known what specific thing she wanted, but the yearning never left her.

Thinking of the free land took her mind to Dalton. With Clova ill, Joanna believed Dalton hadn't yet been told of the land offer.

Dalton. Supposedly at home preparing a meal. A meal that she would eat. The visual of a man so masculine fussing around in the kitchen cooking supper was almost ludicrous, and Joanna wondered if he would really do it.

She still couldn't guess what he might be up to by inviting her. Seduction, maybe? Just because he had a girlfriend at home didn't mean he wouldn't bed the chick closest to him. She knew that male behavior well enough. Not only had she experienced it, but the beauty shop was full of talk of it every day.

A sigh involuntarily escaped her lungs. *Whatever,* she thought, annoyed by allowing herself to endlessly cross bridges before she reached them. Why debate the man's motives when she was so tired and hungry she would dine with the devil himself? That is, as long as she didn't have to prepare the meal.

She stopped off at the hospital to visit Clova and deliver the potted mum she had picked up before leaving Lubbock. Before going inside, she called her own mother and reported that she had returned. If she didn't call and say she had safely arrived back in Hatlow, Mom would worry that she'd had an accident on the highway.

Clova's head turned toward her when she entered. "Hi, sweetie," Joanna said softly.

A huge bouquet of yellow roses in a tall clear vase sat on the windowsill in Clova's room. The blooms were as large as baseballs, the color as deep and rich as . . . well, as egg yolks. She walked over and set her small mum beside the yellow roses and both she and Clova laughed at the contrast.

"Thank you, hon. But you shouldn't have spent your money on a flower for me." Clova's voice came in a weak rasp, and her feverish eyes shone like obsidian in her pale face, but in spite of having an oxygen tube in her nose, an IV in her hand and being flat of her back in a hospital bed, she showed a buoyancy Joanna hadn't seen her exhibit in months. No doubt it was because her wandering oldest son had returned, if only temporarily.

"It didn't cost much. You can plant it in your flower bed." Joanna touched one of the rose's blooms. "These are beautiful. Who sent them?"

"Dalton. I can't believe he spent good money on flowers, either. And roses at that."

"Well, you're his mother. I'd spend money on roses for my mom if she were sick. He came to see you today, huh?"

"Joanna, he paid the taxes on the place."

Joanna felt a little leap in her chest. She knew the unpaid taxes had been a threat that lay like a yoke on Clova's narrow shoulders. "Oh, my God. Did he really?"

"I didn't ask him to, but I shore was happy he done it. . . . Joanna, did you tell him about Lane's baby?"

Joanna hated being caught telling something she perhaps shouldn't have. Her stomach made a dip. "Uh, yes, I think I did. Is that a problem?"

"Oh, I guess not. It's just that since Mandy's mama and daddy don't want her havin' nothin' to do with us, I was hopin' Dalton wouldn't find out about all the upset."

"Everyone in town knows, Clova. How could he not find out?"

"He don't see ever'body in town. He don't stay here that long."

Joanna and Clova had discussed the Fergusons' quarrel with Lane before. Fred and Eloise Ferguson called the sheriff every time Lane tried to see his daughter. From the day Mandy, their only child, revealed her pregnancy, they had made no secret of their loathing for Lane Cherry and anyone associated with him. Eloise had even ceased to be a customer of

Joanna's Salon & Supplies. Joanna had never told Clova that being her friend had cost her a customer.

"The way I remember Dalton," Clova said, "if he finds out about Fred tryin' to have Lane arrested, he might think he oughtta do somethin' about it. I don't want him to get trapped into dealin' with that kind o' stuff while he's here. He don't come home that often. This kind o' trouble is just one more reminder how bad things used to be for him when he lived here."

Home? Joanna doubted if the Dalton Parker she had met would refer to Hatlow as "home." As for Fred Ferguson's irrational attitude toward his granddaughter's father, Joanna suspected Dalton was a man who could and would make short order of something so silly.

She couldn't keep from taking Lane's side in that quarrel. Though he sometimes behaved irresponsibly, he had never denied being the father of Mandy's child and had been willing, even eager, to do the right thing. He might straighten up and be a decent father if Fred Ferguson ever gave him a chance.

Beyond that, she wanted to ask Clova just exactly how bad *had* things been for Dalton, from a mother's perspective? She hadn't been able to put out of her mind her own mother's criticism of how Dalton had been raised by his mother and stepfather. But she refrained. A woman in a hospital bed was too ill for anyone to make waves. "So how are you feeling, really?" she asked.

"I still got that deep hurt in my chest, but I guess I'm okay."

"Did Dr. Jones talk to you?"

Clova held up her right hand, into which the IV had been inserted. "Where you think I got this?"

"What is it, antibiotic?"

"I'm leavin' here in a couple o' days, I'll tell ya. I

got too much to do to be layin' up in the bed. I got
to figure out how to get them yearlin's to the sale."

"Did Dr. Jones say you could leave?"

"Naw. That's what *I* said."

"This time, you should stay here until you get
well, Clova."

"I ain't got no more money now than I did back in
the spring, Joanna. Boardin' in a hospital costs. Even
if Dalton did sign that paper when y'all stuck me in
here, I ain't gonna let him or anybody else pay my
doctor bills. It's bad enough he had to pay the taxes."

Joanna did a mental eye roll. She was too tired to
cover the same old ground. She changed the subject
by repeating the various snippets of gossip she had
heard as she went about her egg deliveries, added
some small talk, then said good night. In truth, she
was in a hurry. She still had eggs to gather and supper
to eat, cooked by a sexy, mysterious man.

Chapter 16

Outside, dusk had stained the landscape to mauve, and a creamy three-quarter moon had already popped up on the flat horizon. Good weather was good news for an egg farmer. "Yay. Red sky at night," she mumbled as she climbed into her pickup.

She pulled out of the hospital parking lot, stewing over the fact that it would be completely dark by the time she reached the Parker ranch and she would be gathering the eggs with the help of a flashlight and the moonlight.

Crap.

She had collected eggs after nightfall before without so much as a thought of snakes. But after yesterday, she was certain she would never be able to make a nighttime venture into the chicken yard again without fear. *Crap,* again.

She reached the ranch after seven and parked in front of her egg-processing room. She had thrown old clothes—a pair of jeans, a flannel work shirt and boots—in the pickup when she left home this morning. She carried them inside and stripped out of her dress clothes. Some people might not think of khaki Dockers and a polo shirt as dress clothing, but this was Hatlow, where most of the female population wore jeans and T-shirts.

She was standing in the brilliant white glare of the overhead fluorescent lighting wearing nothing but her

bra and bikini panties when the door opened. She
yelped as Dalton stepped in. "Oh!"

"Hey—"

"Just a minute!" She grabbed up the jeans and
pressed them to her front, her heart hammering.

"Oh, shit!" His eyes flew wide. "I'm sorry." He
stepped backward and slammed the door with a
loud clap.

Though he had been in her egg-washing room before, she hadn't thought of him coming in tonight or
she would have locked the door. Mumbling swear
words under her breath, she hurriedly stepped into
her jeans and pulled on her work shirt. She padded
to the door in bare feet, considering how she should
handle his walking in on her unclothed. *Nonchalant.
Like it never happened*, she finally decided, though she
was well aware that in the few seconds he stood in
the doorway, his eyes had touched all of her.

She opened the door and saw him leaning his backside on her pickup door, his thumbs hooked in his
jeans pockets, his booted feet crossed at the ankles.
Cowboy boots. Then it hit her that this was the mag-
net that drew her to him. Cowboys, *true* cowboys, had
always been her greatest weakness when it came to
men. That particular social group lived close to the
earth. She believed cowboys knew a truth that some
others didn't, and she liked that.

Spotlighted by the golden glow cast from the doorway of the egg-washing room, he looked like the per-
sonification of every temptation she had ever known
all rolled into one brooding package. Sex was the first
word that flew into her mind.

He had on clean clothes—creased and pressed jeans
and a pink, ironed button-down.

Pink?

He hadn't impressed her as the *pink* type or the
ironed-shirt type, either. Scott Goodman was the pink,

ironed-shirt type. Dalton Parker's color type was closer to black. But no question, with his black hair and olive skin, in pink he looked as delicious as cake.

Had he cleaned up and dressed up to have supper with *her*? He must have, because the date had been made this morning when he still needed a shave. A fullness suddenly grew in her chest, and if someone had asked her to explain it, she couldn't.

"Uh, I don't like to go into the chicken yard in my dress clothes," she told him, meeting his gaze and trying not to sound apologetic.

"I already picked up your eggs," he said. "Didn't you see?"

He sounded put out, as if his feelings were hurt. "Oh. Well, I guess I didn't look."

For the first time she glanced at the counter and saw four baskets filled with eggs on the far end. Confusion muddled through her mind, but it wasn't nearly as great as the sense of relief that she wouldn't have to enter the chicken yard in the dark. Wanting to sound appreciative, she said, "Oh, my gosh. Listen, thanks. I don't mind telling you I'm still thinking about that snake."

"I fed those jackasses, too," he said in his clipped way of speaking. "One of them tried to bite me."

His grouchiness no longer struck dread into her. She was now interpreting it as a sort of cynical sense of humor. She thought she saw his eyes crinkle at the corners. He was teasing her again. "Come on, now. Don't falsely accuse my little donkeys. Their names are Joe and Jill. They don't bite."

"Oh, yeah? I never met a jackass that didn't bite." He pushed himself off her pickup door and stood there with his hands jammed against his belt. "I've got the steaks thawed out and ready to cook."

"Listen, I know I got here late. I'll just get these eggs washed and—"

"No hurry. Do what you have to." He turned and strode up the stone pathway toward the front door, obviously perfectly confident that she would follow him rather than just fire up her pickup and drive away. That was another of his traits that lured her. That unabashed self-confidence.

He might have *said* "no hurry," but she had sensed impatience oozing from his every pore. Still unable to believe she was really doing this, she went back to her pile of clothing. She hurriedly put on her dress clothes again, covered them with clean coveralls and finished handling the eggs in record time.

She had left her purse in the pickup, and inside it was a hairbrush. She climbed into the driver's seat and dug it out, along with a tube of Frosted Peach lipstick. Unfortunately, she didn't have a drop of cologne with her. She ran the brush through her shoulder-length do and tried to improve her appearance in front of the visor mirror. In the dim glow from the overhead light, she could scarcely see the mark between her brows, though she was sure the concealer she had applied early this morning had melted away. She let out a breath of resignation. There was nothing she could do about it now.

Before leaving the pickup, she glanced at the brown paper sack of apples sitting on the passenger seat. She had bought them from one of her Lubbock customers for her mom and herself to share. She decided to offer the dozen apples to her host as a gift of appreciation. She doubted he would spend much time in a grocery store, so fresh fruit seemed like a good thing.

Ever the peacemaker, trying to get along, her cantankerous side groused.

"There's nothing wrong with a kind gesture," she mumbled.

She dragged the apples from the pickup and carried them with her, rehearsing as she went something clever to say when she gave them to him. She felt as giddy as a schoolgirl on prom night.

She entered the house without knocking, placed her purse on the dining table and headed for the kitchen with the sack of apples. She was barely inside the door when his scent reached her nose. Soap and water and something outdoorsy. His being all dressed up and looking like a movie star was tantalizing enough, but smelling manly and sexy was almost too much for her starved libido. Especially when *she* looked like a tired old shoe, and felt worse. And she sure wasn't wearing perfume. She tried to identify his fragrance but couldn't. It was ridiculous that she couldn't. She *sold* fragrances, for crying out loud.

He looked up from fussing with the steaks—two big T-bones lying on a large platter. "Hey," he said.

"Hey, yourself," she replied, suddenly self-conscious. She had been in this kitchen countless times, knew where everything in it was stored, but tonight in the sphere of his dominating presence, she felt awkward and out of place. "Uh . . . remember that smart-aleck remark you made to me yesterday about apples?" She set the brown paper sack on the counter. "Here you go. Fresh from the orchards in Washington State. They just got them in at one of the markets I went to in Lubbock. There used to be a dozen, but I ate one on the way home."

He stopped, wiped his hands on a towel and came over. He peered into the sack, then back at her and grinned. Now, he was close enough for her to see his square jaws shining from a fresh shave. He did have the most arresting face. Not pretty, but lean-jawed and rugged. The force of his masculinity came at her like a barrage of pin pricks.

"Apples and snakes," he said. "This might be prophetic." He chuckled in a way that implied intimacy, as if they knew each other well and shared some secret joke.

Redirecting her attention, she saw a bottle of red wine on the counter, the cork already pulled, sitting beside a bowl of salad. The salad looked to be torn lettuce and tomatoes sliced into thin, neat wedges. She could smell potatoes baking in the oven. His being able to cook steaks was to be expected. Every man she had ever known, especially the studly types, thought he could cook meat on a grill, but a crisp, neat salad and baked potatoes surprised her. "Look at all of this," she said. "I thought you were kidding about being a cook."

One side of his mouth tipped into that crooked grin she had first thought was a smirk. "Babe, making a salad and throwing a potato in the oven isn't exactly cooking. You hungry?"

"Yeah, I am. I mostly got along on Diet Pepsi and protein bars today."

"And one of my apples?" He grinned, then added, "That fizzy shit's bad for you, you know. You shouldn't drink too much of it."

And wasn't he bossy? "Hm. I'll try to remember that."

"I've got something for you, too," he said, and left the kitchen.

He came back carrying a manila file folder and handed it to her. Having no clue what could be inside, she opened it cautiously . . . and found an eight-by-ten color photograph of Dulce. It was a stunning shot of the white hen on top of one of the chicken houses, her neck feathers tufted as if she had posed just for Dalton's camera. "Oh. My. Gosh. It's Dulce. What a wonderful picture. How did you ever get her to look like this?"

She looked up at him and could almost see his chest

swelled. He winked. "Photography's my business, remember? Look at the others."

She shuffled through several more photos—another of Dulce, one of Joe and Jill, their heads together and looking like twins staring at the camera; one of a cluster of several of her hens, all in various and striking colors and looking as if they were in a heated gossip session.

"This is so nice of you. I've had these chickens for over two years and I've never taken their pictures."

"I would've fixed them up with mattes, but I didn't have the stuff to do it," he said.

"That's okay." She shuffled through the pictures again. "I'm sure I've got frames somewhere. I can put this one of Dulce on my desk in my office." She looked up at him again and couldn't keep from smiling like a witless fool. "Thank you. Thank you so much." She turned to leave the kitchen. "I'm going to put them with my purse, okay?"

"Sure. I'll make us a drink."

When she returned, a half-gallon jug of Jack Daniel's and a fifth of tequila sat beside the wine. Also, two double-shot glasses, the saltshaker and several limes. *Uh-oh.* "Good grief, are we having a party?"

He picked up the tequila bottle and unscrewed the cap. "You could say that."

"What are we celebrating?"

He leveled a look into her eyes and smiled. "That's up to you."

Was he flirting? In spite of herself, she reacted with a giggle. "Me? I hope you aren't trying to ply me with liquor so—"

"Un-huh. I know what you're gonna say. I never ply. I just think we'd get along better if you weren't so uptight. And if we got along better, who knows what—"

She squared her shoulders and lifted her chin. "I wasn't aware I'm uptight."

He gave another one of those low, intimate chuckles. "See there? What'd I tell you? Darlin', you're the most uptight woman I've been around in a long time."

Who wouldn't be after the way you've behaved? she thought.

He reached up and brushed her hair behind her ear, and his touch sent a tingle all the way to her toes. She stared into his eyes, eyes that no longer seemed so angry, but dark with mystery as much as color. Now she knew what it was about his eyes that hypnotized her. They were intuitive; he could read her mind. Their gazes held, and for a fleeting second, her insides felt as bare as her outside had been in the egg-washing room.

Was he really trying to seduce her? Was that the game they had been playing all along, from the day of his arrival? Maybe it wasn't such a far-fetched notion. Since she had mused over how it would be, maybe he had thought about it, too. A little thrill zipped through her, setting off a drumbeat in her heart. A very long time had passed since she had let herself so much as think about intimacy with a man. "It's my nature to worry."

His face was close enough for her to feel his breath on her lips and breathe in his scent. His fingers cupped her neck and his thumb gently massaged. She closed her eyes and relished the strength in his hand.

"You know, there's a cure for all of that tension," he said, his raspy voice soft and smoky sounding.

She mentally shook herself. *Oh, God.* This was going way too fast. "Huh. What is it, Valium?" She looked up at him and saw that lopsided grin.

"That's not exactly what I had in mind," he said softly.

That funny little ripple squiggled through her belly again. *Devil.* She drew in a deep breath and stepped back, away from his hand. When he was like this, it would be so easy to just go along with whatever game he was playing. But then, as she almost had talked herself into believing that, instantly he ceased to be Don Juan, as if he was offended that she stepped out of his reach.

"I didn't know what you might like to drink," he said. "I didn't have time to drive clear to Kingdom Come to buy booze. I can't believe this county's still dry. This is the twenty-first century, for chrissake. In LA, I buy liquor in the grocery store. On sale."

He picked up the half-full bottle of tequila and looked at the label. "I found all of this in the cupboard. Must be Lane's. Unless she started lately, my mom doesn't drink much."

His last remarks and his touch had left Joanna feeling so unsettled she could scarcely think, but she didn't want to look like an unsophisticated ninny. Rather than confess she didn't drink much, either, she said, "I'll have what you're having."

He poured the two shot glasses full to the brims with tequila, pulled a knife from the knife block, sliced a lime in two and handed half to her. She watched as he licked his thumb knuckle, sprinkled it with salt, then threw back a shot of tequila. He licked the salt off his thumb, and followed with sucking the juice from the lime and a growling noise.

Though she didn't drink tequila unless it was surrounded by a margarita, she knew many, women as well as men, who drank it just as he had demonstrated. She followed suit. The undiluted liquor slid down her throat and hit her empty stomach with a thud. Her whole body involuntarily shuddered. She gasped and grimaced at the kick, slamming the shot glass back onto the counter with a *thunk*. She quickly licked the salt off her knuckle and sucked on a lime half. "Oh, my God," she croaked.

He grinned and picked up the tequila bottle, holding it poised above her shot glass. "The second one will go down easier."

She was certain her eyes were crossed as she blinked away moisture. "Okay." *I guess*.

He poured another shot for her, then one for himself. After she quaffed the second, the alcohol's warmth began to spread through her system and she felt more relaxed than she had in days. In fact, she believed she liked drinking tequila in this fashion better than she had thought she would. But she had to be careful. Two large drinks of tequila were more liquor than she had consumed at one time since New Year's Eve nine months ago.

"That ought to get me through grilling these steaks." He picked up the plate of meat. "Let's go outside."

He stopped off at the refrigerator and pulled out a couple of longnecks. He stuffed one in her hands and gave her a wink. Then he proceeded through the back door.

Holy cow. It couldn't be wise to drink beer on top of tequila. And she sure should be cautious about letting down her guard.

Still, she followed him.

Chapter 17

On the patio, the portable grill usually stored against the wall beside the back door had been rolled out to the middle of the huge limestone-paved square. The CD player that had a home in the kitchen now sat on the windowsill broadcasting Willie Nelson. Plates and silverware had already been placed on the cast-iron, glass-topped table that was tucked just under the patio's partial roof. Joanna was growing more impressed by the minute. Dalton's hosting skills were better than hers.

She spotted a slab of plywood leaning against the wall of the house, a long rattlesnake skin stretched and tacked to it. The skin was at least four feet long and a foot wide. "Is that it?"

"Yep. Big sucker," he answered, fussing with the grill. "If he had struck you, it could've been bad. You want the rattles? I put them on the windowsill." He tilted his head in the direction of the window.

She walked over for a closer look at the cluster of rattles, grateful again that he had been with her for last evening's visit to the chicken yard. A shiver passed up her spine as the sound of the rattle echoed in her ear and a visual came to her of the hateful thing writhing on the ground. It was frightening even after Dalton had whacked it. She swallowed another drink of beer. "I was so upset, I forgot to say thanks for saving me."

"Anytime, babe." She turned and saw him grinning

and holding a steak with a pair of tongs. For the first time she noticed he had near-perfect teeth. Before she could say more, he plopped the steaks onto the grate, generating a smoky sizzle. "How do you like your steak?"

"Um, medium."

As the aroma of charbroiling meat filled the air, her mouth began to water. The lack of real food all day and the alcohol were starting to make her feel loose jointed and ever-more congenial. She sank to a seat at the table and swallowed another swig of beer.

The crickets' serenade had begun with a rhythmic thrum. At the corner of the house, the bare branches of a giant sycamore tree clattered in a westerly breeze. Wind was almost as constant in Hatlow as time itself. In summer the tree's canopy shaded the patio and its leaves rustled softly, and Joanna thought of the summer afternoons and evenings she had sat here in the shade with Clova, drinking iced tea, listening to country music on the radio and talking on into the evening. She wondered how many more times they would do that, if Clova would ever be completely well again, or if by this time next year, Farmers Bank would own the Lazy P. "I went by the hospital and saw your mom."

"And how was Mom this evening?"

"Better, I think. That was nice of you to send her roses. I can't recall her ever receiving roses from anyone."

"No big deal," he replied. "The least a man could do for his mother, right?"

The words came out in a flat tone, devoid of emotion, but she saw a subtle tic in his jaw muscle. She still remembered how confounded he had been yesterday after the ER doctor had told them Clova was too sick not to be admitted to the hospital. Joanna was convinced he cared more than he wanted anyone to know.

She watched his throat muscles as he tipped up the beer bottle and guzzled a long swallow of beer, reminded again of his blatant masculinity. Then she thought of something that, in her own mind, was exceedingly more important than a bouquet of flowers. "And you paid the taxes."

He gave her a look. "Somebody had to."

His critical opinion was glaringly evident in his tone and his expression. To avoid those eyes, she glanced down and picked at the label on the beer bottle, choosing her words carefully. "If you hadn't been willing to do it, I don't know what might have happened. Our bank isn't like it used to be. It really isn't *our* bank anymore. The people who run it don't have much understanding or sympathy for the needs of the people in agriculture."

There. She had revealed she knew of the ranch's deep problems. She waited for a sarcastic comeback.

"I suppose you could say I've got a vested interest," he said instead. "I don't want to see my mother homeless, and Lane's in no shape for an ass-kicking. Of course, the key to avoid being strung up by your thumbs by a bunch of blood-sucking bankers is not to get in hock to them in the first place."

Joanna tilted her head to the side and suppressed a sigh of resignation. From what she saw going on around her every day, it seemed that you couldn't be in the business of farming or ranching without borrowing, at least not in Wacker County. Even if Lane hadn't been off on whatever trip he had been on for the last couple of years, Clova would still have had to get operating funds from somewhere. All of the ranchers and farmers Joanna knew owed money, either to the credit union or to Farmers Bank. Another thought followed that one: And Suzy Martinez made sure she kept the Joanna's Salon & Supplies patrons aware of who and how much every time she came in to have her hair done.

"That's easier said than done," Joanna said. "Maybe you aren't aware of what an iffy business ranching has become nowadays. It's a struggle for even the big operations." She swallowed another drink of beer. "Clova mentioned the cattle sale. Are you going to be around to get the cows to the sale?"

"I don't know. I've been thinking about it." He clamped tongs onto the edge of a steak, lifted it and peeked at the underside. "I haven't been on a horse in a helluva long time, but I guess I could saddle up that gray nag in the pasture and round 'em up and move 'em out." He chuckled at his attempt at levity. He dropped the tongs onto the empty plate and crossed his arms over his chest. His eyes met hers again. "If I don't, are *you* gonna take care of it?"

Her palm automatically flew to her chest. "*Me?* Well, no."

"Guess that settles it, then." He glanced at his watch. "Those potatoes must be ready."

"I'll check," she said, feeling put in her place by the abrupt change of subject. Though she suspected he might like to grab her by the hair and drag her off to his cave, he obviously had no intention of discussing his family or its business with her. So be it.

Inside the kitchen, she removed the potatoes from the oven and wrapped them in foil, then made her way to the bathroom. Returning, she glanced at the large computer monitor on the dining table and saw it filled with small pictures. She walked over to look closer. All of the pictures were obviously from the Middle Eastern desert. She homed in on a vivid photograph of four smiling, brown-eyed, black-haired girls posing for his camera.

"Steaks are ready," he said, coming up behind her

and startling her. He placed his hand on the mouse and enlarged the picture with a click. "Good shot, huh? I captured just what I wanted to in that one. Look at the eyes. Those poor kids are happy." He stared at the picture for a few seconds.

His tone told her something wasn't quite right and made her study the photograph closer. The girls looked to be around ten years old. Gathered shoulder to shoulder and smiling broadly, they were wearing Western-style dresses with white lacy collars and had their hair in neat braids. "They do look happy. And pretty. Where are they, Iraq?"

"Baghdad," he said grimly, his eyes still fixed on the picture. "Everybody involved was pretty happy in that picture, including the army. This was opening day at a school those GIs put together."

Something was definitely wrong, but Joanna couldn't spot it. He clicked off the enlargement and moved the pointer to another small print. "This one I shot about ten minutes later."

He enlarged the photograph and she recognized some parts of the same tan background, but now the four girls in their pretty dresses lay among piles of rubble, other broken bodies and puddles of blood. Joanna's fingers flew to cover her mouth as a breath caught in her throat. "Oh, dear God. Are—are they dead?" She sank to the chair in front of the monitor, unable to take her eyes off the powerful picture.

"I don't know. I heard later one of them might have made it. The Americans tried to save them, of course. I think it was around thirty kids and teachers that bought it that day."

She continued to stare at the picture, shaking her head, Words didn't exist in her safe, American, small-town lexicon for such senseless barbarism. And she was unable to relate to his having been there, having had his wits about him well enough to take pictures of the carnage, and now being able to speak of it so clinically. It dawned on her that he had seen a depth of pain that most ordinary people would never see or understand. No wonder he had such a hard edge.

He must have sensed her incomprehension. "Making a record is what I do, babe," he said quietly, drilling her with another dark gaze. "I'm telling a story. Pictorial accounts of mankind eating its own. This crap goes on every day. And not just in *that* country. Don't you watch the news?"

"Not much," she admitted, still unable to take her eyes off the graphic picture. "I don't have time."

"It's just as well. Most Americans don't get it even when they see it. The American press doesn't get it, either. They've got their own agendas and they do a lousy job of reporting."

"Did you see it . . . it explode?"

He shook his head, moving on to another shot. "I was down the street, about a hundred feet away, loading up my equipment. The blast still knocked me off my feet. I knew what had happened, so I grabbed my camera and ran back."

"Is this going in your book?"

"I don't know yet. I'm inclined to focus on the more positive activities that are taking place over there."

"You mean there are some?"

"Here's one." He clicked through several more photographs until he came to one of a young blond American soldier, doling out candy to a dozen black-haired, dark-eyed boys dressed in bright green and pristine white uniforms. The soldier had a whistle on a lanyard around his neck and a soccer ball tucked under his arm. The boys looked as if they could have been American children, all smiles and excitement over a ball game.

"It's the kids who suffer the worst," Dalton said. "Being helpless, they're easy victims. In all of the backward societies I've seen, and sometimes I feel like I've seen damn near all of them, it's always the kids who have it the toughest. I used to take kids for granted, but traveling in the Third World has changed my perspective on childhood."

Though she had no basis from which to imagine what horrors his eyes had witnessed and the lens of his camera had captured, she began to process all she had heard about his childhood. She looked up at him and held his gaze. "Are you talking about your own childhood?"

"Maybe. When I was a kid, I thought I had it rough. After I left home, and eventually the States, I found out what rough was. There's a lot of sadistic lunatics out there. Some of them are running countries. Compared to them, Earl Cherry was a creampuff."

Without volunteering more, he clicked off the photographs and shut down the computer. "Let's eat. Grab those potatoes and some butter and the wine." He picked up the bowl of salad, bottles of salad dressing and two jelly glasses and started for the back door.

She did as he ordered and followed him, beset by the harsh realization that the chasm between his world experience and hers was as wide as the state of Texas.

To avoid being carried off by flying insects, they sat down with the supper in the lampshine falling through the window from inside the house. He poured a jelly glass half full of red wine and handed it to her. He didn't apologize for the glassware, didn't attempt to explain it away. Just a further reminder of what she had already concluded about him: He couldn't care less what other people thought. Of anything.

"I've been trying to remember you from high school," he said, "but I'm sorry to say I can't."

She almost mentioned her sister Lanita and the fact that she and Dalton had dated, but she stopped herself and remained content to concentrate on her perfectly grilled steak and to sip wine. She didn't drink wine any more often than she drank anything else, but she didn't dislike it. "I was only a sophomore when you were a senior. I wasn't very memorable back then. I didn't get out much. I was one of those boring good girls."

"Past tense? Does that mean you're not anymore?"

"Not what, boring?"

"A good girl."

Only because she rarely met the opportunity not to be. She couldn't keep from laughing. "What I am mostly is a tired girl. I got up at four this morning."

He laughed, too, but she sensed his question hadn't really been a joke. "Long day," he said.

"Delivery days are always long. Lubbock and Amarillo both in one day. It's a trip. It's a considerable distance from Hatlow to anywhere there's a market."

"Tell me about it. What makes you stay here? From what I can see, there's not much going on."

"Oh, I don't know. There's a lot if you look for it."

"What's the population now? When I went to the courthouse today, I drove around a little. Looks like half the buildings are vacant. Some are even boarded up."

"Yeah. Want some cheap real estate? Now we have about seven thousand people, roughly."

"It was twice that when I lived here."

She lifted a shoulder in a shrug. "Hatlow's had some problems. Oil died. A lot of cotton comes from foreign countries now. Kids aren't staying around to take over their parents' farms and ranches like they used to. Once, that was expected, but now . . . ." She shrugged again. "Most of them can't find a good enough reason to do it. They'd rather live in Austin or Fort Worth or even Houston, where they can make more money."

"But you're different. You stay here and fuss around with those chickens and eggs and make a quarter of the money you could make somewhere else. I can see you're a talented businesswoman with a lot of imagination. You've got a lot to offer if you weren't stuck here."

"I'm not stuck. I lived in Lubbock a couple of years. Went to college up at Tech for a year. Went to beauty school for another. I even worked up there for a few months. But I like it here. I'm a small-town girl. I like knowing everyone around me and having everyone know me."

"Having people always looking over your shoulder, nosing into your business?"

"Sometimes that's true, but it's not malicious. I believe in the network. If you stumble and fall, someone will help you get up."

He snorted. "And just how often have you stumbled? You don't strike me as the stumbling type."

Oh, if you only knew. "I might be in the middle of a headlong tumble downhill right this minute."

He cocked his head and grinned. "Yeah?"

He knew she referred to this evening with him. She saw it in those wise eyes. The probing gaze made her uncomfortable. She didn't want to talk about herself, anyway, didn't want to put into words some of her baser musings about her dinner partner. She never talked about herself or her businesses to men. Most of the time they weren't interested. "But whatever happens, I'll survive. Every day's a new day."

He lifted his glass to her. "Now, that's what I'm talking about. Positive thinking." He downed the wine remaining in the glass and poured it half full again.

"What about you?" she said. "Haven't you ever stumbled?"

"More often than I'll ever admit aloud. I've eaten my share of beans. Beans I cooked myself."

Thinking of her own lack of cooking skills, she chuckled. She was having a very good time. "Then you're better off than I am. I've never cooked a pot of beans that was fit to eat."

They laughed together then, as if what was going on between them was casual, ordinary fellowship. But it wasn't. And they both knew it. She had developed a few mind-reading skills herself. Even after so much alcohol had muddled her brain, she still sensed that the intense man who had shown her the pictures on his computer screen, the man who had a hidden compassion for children, was the real Dalton Parker.

"So tell me about what you do," she said. "You've been everywhere, and I've never even been to Dallas."

He began to talk, mesmerizing her with stories of his travels and spellbinding adventures in foreign exotic lands. Many of his stories sounded as exciting and dramatic as fiction. He was the Pied Piper and she was a country mouse.

All at once she noticed that she could almost see two of him. She gave him a narrow-lidded look, trying to erase the ghostlike aura surrounding him. *Damn.* Now she had to figure out how to get home. She didn't dare drive. "Dalton. I, uh, think I should—"

He stopped her with a derisive noise. "You're not gonna drive. The fact is, neither one of us is in great shape."

She braced her hand on the table, prepared to push herself to her feet. "Damn. I never drink this much. I mean, never. Ever."

He raised his palms defensively. "I didn't plan it."

Her eyes squeezed into another squint. "Did I say you did?"

"You almost said it earlier. In the kitchen."

"Oh. I must've forgot that." She got to her feet but had to brace her fingertips on the tabletop to steady herself. "We should get these dishes cleaned up."

He, too, stood up. "Nah. They're not going anywhere."

She pushed her chair out of the way and started for the back door. "I think I should nap on the sofa for a while. Until my head clears a little."

He caught up with her and reached around her for the doorknob, surrounding her with his scent. "You don't have to nap on the sofa. This house is full of beds. Just pick one."

Was that an invitation of some kind? What did he expect her to say? What did she *want* to say? She tried to count in her head the number of beds in the ranch house and came up with five. "Where do *you* sleep?"

"Where I've always slept. In my old room in the back of the house."

"Then I guess I shouldn't pick that one."

He didn't answer. He just kept looking down at her with those chocolate eyes. "Why not?" he finally said, his voice so soft, she wasn't sure she had heard him.

Chapter 18

Time stopped. The radio grew silent. Even Joanna's spinning head took a respite. But her heart stuttered. She looked up into his eyes and saw through the alcohol fog what he wanted from her. Did she want any less from him? Before she could reason through the question, his mouth settled on hers, and nothing could have made her object.

He kissed her sweetly, his palm caressing her jaw, his thumb brushing her cheek as he sipped at her lips. The taste of his mouth, the scent of his breath, the scent of *him* penetrated her psyche like nothing she had known. The very air swirled around her, and it was different from the wooziness in her head.

He gingerly pulled her lower lip between his teeth, paused and looked down at her, the question in his hooded eyes. All she had to do was consent. Or not.

She searched those dark eyes while his ragged breath touched her lips. "Honest," she said, her voice wobbling. "Compared to what I'm sure you're used to, I'm really naive and plain dumb."

"You don't know what I'm used to. No one with lips as sweet as yours could be naive. And you're a long way from dumb." His head bent, his hand cupped her nape and he placed his forehead against hers. "Remember the day I got here? When we were talking out front?"

"I—I think so."

"One of the very first things I thought about that first time I saw you was how kissable your lips looked."

Now, that had to be a line. She might be naive and inexperienced with men, but she wasn't stupid. A little tipsy maybe, but not stupid. "Was that before or after you found out I owned all those hens?"

"Cut it out," he murmured. "Don't ruin this."

He kissed her again, and this time, his tongue swept into her mouth in a way every bit as untamed and carnal as she had suspected him capable of. They played with each other's lips and tongues all the way through the back door and into the dimly lit kitchen. Oh, he was a good kisser. Not even a sane and sober woman would deny him. And at the moment, she was neither.

He walked her backward a few steps, until she felt the sharp counter edge against her backside and his rigid fly against her belly. Caged by his arms braced on the counter, she made no attempt to escape, and they kept kissing and kissing, their breathing growing rougher with every second.

She felt her shirttail being tugged from her waistband. The sensible Goody Two-shoes Hatlow citizen that she was warned her to take control of the situation before it got out of hand, but the woman who hadn't felt a man's touch in too damn long wanted him too much to stop him. Finally, his hand on the bare skin of her back jolted her. She pulled her mouth away from his.

"What is it?" he said.

"This is bad. We don't like each other."

His warm lips brushed beneath her ear, then traveled in a trail down her neck. "We like each other enough."

Now she knew just how far out of it she was because that remark sounded logical. "But you're talking about bed." She tilted her head back and relished his mouth on her throat. "And I'd hate myself in the morning."

"You really think so?" His fingers deftly unhooked her bra, leaving her breasts feeling oddly free.

"No. I don't know."

"I promise, I'll make damn sure you don't hate me."

Oh, this wasn't good. Good Hatlow girls did not do this. "You don't understand. . . . I—I'm really unlucky at—at sex. . . . It's ne—ver worked out that well for me and—"

"You talk too much."

She reached behind herself and pulled his hands away from her bare back and from under her shirt. "Honestly," she choked out, "teenage girls . . . are better at this . . . than I am. Really, don't you think it would be better if I just—just cr-crash on the sofa for a while?"

"If that's what you really want to do," he said, his mouth back at her lips, his hands at the hem of her shirt, easing the front up, "all you have to do is say so."

Her nipples had grown so tight they ached. When the cool air touched them, a shiver passed over her. His warm hand cupped one bare breast. His head moved down and his mouth closed warm and wet around the taut nub of the other. Her breath caught.

His tongue stabbed at her nipple and sensation tore through her secret places. Only a supreme act of will kept her from openly moaning. "It is," she breathed. "I mean, I do."

"You sure?" he whispered against her other breast, his hands lifting her shirt higher.

"No. I mean yes." Now her shirt was pushed up to her neck.

"Yes, what?"

"I'm sure."

"If you're gonna to stop me, do it now. 'Cause I'm losing track of this conversation."

And she was losing her mind. "N-no. I'm—I'm not."

"This is in the way," he said, tugging her knit shirt over her head. Like a robot, she lifted her arms. He peeled it all the way off and dropped it on the floor. Without so much as a peep of protest, she let him remove her bra and drop it to the floor, too.

"Damn," he said and pulled her close. Her bare breasts pressed against his crisp shirt.

"I know," she mumbled and raised her mouth for more kisses. She wrapped her arms around his middle and they kept kissing like savages, all tongues and heat.

He broke away and grasped her hand. "Let's go," he said huskily and strode from the kitchen, dragging her with him. They passed the sofa in the living room as if it weren't there and still, she raised not a protest.

He led her up the hallway to the back bedroom, one of the few rooms in this house she hadn't been inside more than once or twice. The room was dark as a cave, but against the side of her knee, she recognized the edge of a mattress. She dropped to it like a sandbag just as the lamp beside the bed came on and flooded them with low amber light. Instinctively, her arms flew across her bare breasts, her hands gripping her shoulders. She looked up at him. "On second thought, you know, I really should, uh, sleep on the sofa. I'm a lousy sleeper. I snore. And I'm used to having the whole bed."

"Yeah?" He squatted in front of her and pulled off her boots and socks. "I'm tough. I can probably stand it."

He stood up, his fly at her eye level. Her gaze froze on the bulge in the wash-worn denim fabric and reality lunged through the fuzziness that surrounded her. She tried to swallow, but her mouth had gone dry.

He sat down beside her on the bed. She bit down on her lower lip, watching him pry off his own boots and socks. "Dalton, really. We—we shouldn't do this."

"I know."

"What if Clova found out?"

"You think I'm gonna tell my mother?"

"It doesn't . . . it doesn't have any meaning."

He turned toward her, his hand braced behind her on the bed, his face only inches away. His eyes locked on hers. Light as a feather, his finger trailed along the arm that covered her breasts. "What makes you think it doesn't have any meaning? There's damn near nothing that happens that has no meaning."

She gripped her own shoulders tighter. "I don't know. I mean, how could it? I just think—"

"Don't think." He reached for her hands, uncrossed her arms and gazed at her breasts. She closed her eyes and held her breath.

"Your body's all I thought it'd be," he said.

He had been thinking about her body? She opened her eyes and saw him smiling. "Well, I, uh, get a lot of exercise and—"

"Just stop talking"—he clasped her wrists and placed her arms around his neck, and his arms came around her—"and kiss me."

Taking her mouth in another devastating kiss, he eased them backward on the bed as if they were one unit. His knee slipped between hers and all she could manage was a pathetic whimper.

Amid more sensual kissing, she felt her pants zipper slide open, felt his hand slip inside her fly, felt it close over her sex. "Oh, man, you're wet," he whispered, rubbing her slowly through her panties. "And hot."

He sat up and too easily peeled off her Dockers and panties. As his palm came back up the inside of her leg, he leaned and kissed her stomach. "You've got goose bumps," he said.

"Uh, I'm cold."

He chuckled softly. "Thanks a lot."

"I mean, I'm not cold *that* way, but—"

"Shh." He stood up, grasped her arm with one hand and pulled her to her feet. He held her against him as if he thought she might bolt as he pulled back the covers with his free hand. "Scoot in," he ordered.

She obeyed and shuddered as the cold sheets enveloped her. . . .

Oh, my God! This was the worst bed she had ever lain on. She couldn't drink enough liquor to be comfortable on this mattress. Clutching the hem of the sheet under her chin, she said, "What—what kind of ma-mattress is this?"

Unbuttoning his shirt cuffs, he looked down at her. "You're really into mattresses, aren't you?"

She watched him methodically unbuttoning his shirt front, her body heat gradually warming the chilly bed. "We—we spend a third of our lives sleeping. A good place to do it is important."

"It's brand-new. I just bought it Saturday. Compared to what was here before, I thought it felt pretty good." He shrugged out of his shirt, wadded it into a ball and threw it across the room, his tanned shoulders and biceps bunching and rippling with the action.

Seeing him without his shirt instantly diverted her attention from the uncomfortable mattress. Her imagination had already conjured up a picture of him without clothes, but those images were pitifully deficient. He was the most beautiful shirtless man she had ever seen. *Abs.* He had *abs*, for crying out loud. She tried to think if she had ever seen an adult male in real life with abs.

He dug into his pocket, pulled out several condom packets and dropped them onto the bedside table. Seeing them brought another hard swallow, but she lay still and stiff as a corpse. Did he carry those all the time? Or had he bought them today, planning for this to happen? After he fed her enough liquor?

Her eyes followed his hands to his belt. Before she could blink, he had shed his jeans and shorts in one quick motion and his erection filled her line of sight. Like a marble column, it rose from a thatch of curly black hair. It was long and thick, and the tip, engorged with blood to a deep red, looked as luscious as a plum. Muscles deep inside her sex flexed.

She fought to keep her eyes from bulging. Of course she had seen a penis in full arousal before, but not often and not in a really long time. And at the moment, she didn't think she had ever seen one quite so perfect.

As if in your vast experience you're a qualified judge, a sarcastic voice said in her head.

Experienced or not, she knew quality when she saw it.

He opened the covers, slid between them and pulled her against him as if he owned her. And she felt owned, in a way she never had. His arms were so strong, his body so big and solid, and she felt protected and wanted and even, God forbid, loved?

Then his mouth was everywhere, kissing her neck and murmuring sexy, dirty words no man had ever said to her, suckling her breasts again and teasing her nipples with his tongue. His fingers were down there, combing through her pubic hair and stroking her inside her sex, and she was warm and her whole body had become a vessel of an exquisite pleasure. A few beats later, he stopped, stretched over to the bedside table and grabbed a condom, opened the package and reached down under the covers.

He could do this blind?

This is the biggest mistake you've ever made in your life! her Good Girl voice screeched.

He moved over her and somehow, beneath the thick

covers, in spite of her clumsiness, they fumbled their way to joining. In one thrust, he pushed all the way into her. He was big and she wasn't ready. A yelp burst from her throat.

"Shit," he growled. "Did I hurt you?"

She felt everything but pain, including her own pulse steadily beating against his penis. He was so hard. There was so much of him and he was buried so deeply inside her. "N-no."

"I don't want to hurt you," he whispered. "Ever."

Ever? What did that mean?

While she attempted to think about it, he took her mouth in a long kiss, then rose above her, braced his weight on his hands and began to rock with steady, powerful thrusts and maddening friction. She tried to coordinate to the rhythm of his pumping hips, but keeping up with him was impossible, and this was the worst bed she had ever lain on in her life. A cramp gripped her left hip joint and a demanding voice screamed inside her head: *Joanna, he has someone. She calls him all the time on his cell phone. This is just fun and games for him.*

"Come, baby," he gasped as if he were in pain. His chest heaved and his breath bellowed.

But she had too many other things on her mind. "I can't . . . I don't . . . I can't," she managed between panting breaths. But even as she said it, something was beginning to work down there and if she could just shift into the right position or if *he* would just find the right place . . . She squirmed and tried to adjust herself. "Dalton, can—"

"Oh, Jesus, I can't . . ."

His body went rigid, he heaved a great groan, then a deep grunt and collapsed on top of her.

Crap! Was it over?

She lay beneath him, his breath gusting in her ear, staring past the lift and fall of his shoulder at the still blades of the fan attached to the ceiling. *Oh, Joanna, Joanna, Joanna,* her Good Girl voice scolded. *Now you've gone and done it.*

He pushed himself to her side and flopped onto his back, his breath still coming in gasps. "My fault . . . you didn't . . . make it." His head turned toward her, his hair standing in little peaks. "Did you?"

She winced mentally and grabbed for the covers, dragging the quilt to her chin. She cut him a glance from the corner of her eye. "I, uh, I don't think so."

His eyes grew wide and round. "You don't *know?*"

Now she was upset over the whole thing. Hot tears rushed to her eyes. "I told you I wasn't lucky at this."

And she was tired. All she wanted to do was sleep, even if this was the worst damned bed she had ever seen. "I just want to go to sleep."

A growl came from his side of the bed. He sat up and threw back the covers, got to his feet and left the room. To deal with the condom, she presumed. Maybe he wouldn't come back. Maybe he would go to one of the other beds.

Dalton stamped up the hall to the bathroom. Five goddamn bedrooms in this fuckin' house and only one fuckin' bathroom clear at the end of the fuckin' hall. After the low light in the bedroom, the bright light over the sink in the bathroom nearly blinded him. He tossed the rubber, then turned on the tap water. It came out in a weak, cloudy stream. *Shit.* The water in the fuckin' Arabian Desert had been better than the goddamn hard water in West Texas. He waited for the warm water that had to travel all the way from the water heater on the porch off the kitchen, then began to wash himself.

Fuck a running bear. What a freakin' disaster. He felt like a chickenshit. He had gone off like a goddamn teenager. Was that because of his age? Was it the booze? Earlier, something had told him he should have laid off the liquor tonight. He should have listened.

Stone sober, he probably wouldn't have even tried to get Joanna Walsh into bed. All of the sane and sensible reasons he should have kept his dick in his pants crept in, including a decent streak that didn't always raise its head when it came to women. He couldn't keep from thinking that most of the women he fucked knew the score, but Joanna Walsh, he now realized, hadn't even been to the ball game. He glanced up at his reflection in the vanity mirror and saw guilt.

He stared at himself a few beats, then gave up. Hell, it was too late now. He couldn't undo anything. On a sigh, he dried himself with a towel that felt like sandpaper. The hard water did that to towels.

He quickstepped back down the hall, freezing his naked ass off. Entering the bedroom, he saw Joanna buried up to her eyebrows by covers. He slid between the sheets, reached up and clicked off the lamp, plunging the room into stygian darkness. "You want to go to sleep? Tell you what. Let's just do that." With any luck, he could get a couple of hours of shut-eye before daylight.

"It's so dark," she said softly. "Do, uh, you always keep the shades closed?"

Out of habit, he had drawn the shades when he got up this morning. "Are you afraid of the dark?"

"No," she mumbled. "But what if I have to get up?"

"We'll turn on the light."

"Okay." She sighed and gave him her back, her butt pressed against his hip.

In a double bed, such closeness to her body couldn't be avoided. She felt warm and soft and comfortable, one of the things he loved most about sleeping with a woman. He couldn't resist turning to his side, sliding his arm around her midsection and pulling her close. "Go to sleep," he said, molding their bodies together, spoonlike.

In no time he heard her steady breathing. Jesus Christ, had she passed out?

He remembered her words from out on the patio. *What I am mostly is a tired girl. I got up at four this morning.* He didn't doubt either statement. He had seen that she was a dedicated hard worker, willing to hold up her end of a task. A good helpmate and companion.

Whatever.

He, too, closed his eyes and left the world.

Joanna came to semiconsciousness in a pit of darkness. She was naked and freezing. Hissing snakes squirmed and coiled around her ankles, their eyes red as blood. Their black tongues flicked like tiny sharp pitchforks. And she was alone and defenseless. Her own outcry awakened her.

Then, through the dark fog in her brain, gentle hands touched her body. A whispery male voice murmured into her ear, soothing and calming. "Joanna. . . . Hey, it's okay, baby. . . . You're okay. I'm here."

Her eyelids fluttered open for a few seconds. She saw nothing in the darkness, but she recognized the voice. *Dalton*.

She only vaguely remembered all that had happened between them in the previous hours, but in the here and now, even in her muzzy-headed state, she wanted . . . no, *needed* this contact. On a whimper, she turned to the voice and pressed herself against warm, furry flesh. "I'm cold," she said.

"You're uncovered, darlin'." She felt him and the whole bed shift, then as his legs tangled with hers, her chilled shoulders were wrapped in the warmth of thick covers, and strong arms embraced her and held her in a cocoon of heat. And all the while, his soft, raspy voice cooed to her.

He was hard again. And hot. As if it were alive, his erection pushed against her belly. As dark and intimate as the sanctum in which she lay, an arcane craving came over her. No one had made love to her in so long. Giving in to the desire, making no attempt to understand it, she pressed her face into that hot, pungent crevice where his arm joined his shoulder, deeply inhaled his intimate scent undiluted by cologne. And on that primal level, she found what she had forever unwittingly sought, however awkward and stumbling her quest had been. Floating in half sleep, disoriented, she began to stroke with her hand and place openmouth kisses on his chest and nipples.

His hands and body stilled. "Joanna?" His voice came as a husky rumble in the darkness. "You're not still dreaming, are you?"

"No," she mumbled and continued to press her mouth and body to his warm skin.

Whoa! Confusion zigzagged through Dalton's brain. He had already written this night off as a mistake and a royal FUBAR. Hell, she had rejected him. He hadn't even been able to make her come. Now he couldn't believe what was going on. Now she had to be almost sober.

And now she wanted him?

He damn sure wanted her, evidenced by his dick being hard as a crowbar again.

She wanted him. That realization stuck unerasable in his mind and heart. He could find no reason strong enough to make him resist the urges charging through him, not even her friendship with his mother. With no further argument with himself, he burrowed his fingers into her hair and covered her mouth with his.

She kissed back, her tongue probing tentatively, but that was all the encouragement he needed. He drew her tongue into his mouth and it played with his while he skimmed his hands over her firm breasts, brushed her taut nipples with his thumbs, slid his palm down her slender rib cage and over her honed hip. Jesus, her body was fine. And it was all real. A joy for his hands to touch.

Her hands were busy, too. They were all over him—his chest and torso, his butt. They even ventured low on his belly. When they stopped short of where he wanted them, he took charge and molded her fingers around his screaming cock. "Just hold me for a minute," he whispered, his breath ragged in his own ears. And when she did, then followed with trailing her finger up the back side and around the rim, heat and need surged through his veins. He barely kept from pumping within her grip. He couldn't keep from groaning.

Then they were kissing again, wild and desperate, their mouths melded as if they were glued. And their hands were moving again, traveling without discretion, where they would under the thick covers. To gently push her knees apart seemed only natural. When they opened wider with no help from him, that, too, seemed natural. He trailed his fingers up the soft skin of her inner thigh and found paradise, all wet and hot, swollen and waiting. And, thank you, Jesus, unwaxed.

"Push up to me," he whispered against her ear, and she complied. "That's it," he said, sliding two fingers into her.

"Oh . . ."

He recognized a gasp of pleasure when he heard one. Oh, yeah, she liked it. "Good?"

She answered with a little mew.

He dragged her moisture from inside and rubbed her layers in slow, sensuous sweeps, took her breast into his mouth and sucked until her nipple became like a little pebble in his mouth. When she began to whimper his name and clutch at him, he threw back the covers and moved over her. He hung there, kneeling between her thighs, supporting his weight on his hands, able to see her only in silhouette. But he could hear her shuddery breath, feel her soft hands on his ribs and ass. This time, he could last a while. And he intended to. After the disaster of earlier, this was about her, not him. This time, the outcome would be different.

He bent to her mouth, but she came up and met him halfway. "So sweet," he murmured, and meant it. He willed himself to take his time, brushing her cheek, her nose, her eyelids with his lips, then kissing her again and giving her his tongue and taking hers. And all the while her breath came in urgent little pants and whimpers, and he reveled in the sounds of pleasure and need.

He gently urged her back and trailed his mouth and tongue over the slope of her breasts, suckling and teasing. Her whole body responded. Her belly lifted to him and more little sighs and moans filled his ears. "You like that?"

"Yes."

"It gets better."

On a hum, he moved on down, sucking little bits of the supple skin of her midriff into his mouth, lapping her silky belly with his tongue.

Then his mouth was within an inch of his destination. Her musky scent came up to him. Her pubic hair tickled his nose. He blew softly into the silky nest, then pressed his face to it and nuzzled. He breathed in her smell, drifting blindly in a dark, ethereal world of touch and smell. Unadulterated bliss curled through him like smoke.

Her hips shifted, her hands gripped his shoulders. "Dalton, you shouldn't . . ." She tried to scuttle away, but he slid his hands beneath her buttocks, lifted her and pushed his tongue into her slick flesh. She sobbed out and her fingers dug into his shoulders. He draped her leg over his shoulder, gripped her bottom and held her fast while he feasted wildly in a delicious tongue-fuck.

Jesus God, she was sweet. And hot. And eager. And he was turned on like he hadn't been in a helluva long time.

She thrashed and whined like a puppy, sounds that traveled to his core. "Dalton . . . I need—please . . ."

He knew. But he wasn't ready to bring this to its inevitable conclusion. He wanted to hear her scream, and she was almost there. She began to pant and say his name over and over. Her hands grabbed his head and her sweet pussy pushed hard against his face. She was primed. He swept his tongue up and sucked her clit into his mouth.

Crying out, Joanna grabbed the stiles of the cast-iron headboard. She was on fire, poised on the brink of a great flaming abyss. Nothing, *nothing* mattered but this instant and his mouth and the point of contact. Then spasms rushed through her in waves. Sparkles skittered behind her eyes. Sounds she didn't even recognize burst from her throat, but she didn't care. She came and came, until ecstasy turned to agony and tears began to trail past her temples.

Desperation had replaced caution and pride, and a deep place within her hungered for his flesh. Earlier, when he had been inside her, she had wasted the moment. She couldn't let that happen again. She fought her way to a sitting position and reached for him, tears trailing from her eyes. "Dalton . . . Dalton . . . I want you inside me."

Dalton didn't have to be begged. He was so hard his balls were drawn up in his belly. He crawled up her body, guiding his dick with one hand. She was open and ready, and he had no trouble hitting the mark. She clutched his bottom and he shoved into her, joining his flesh with hers and at the same time pushing her knee high and wide. With a deep grunt, he seated himself all the way to the hilt. She gasped. Her arms tightened around him and her free leg tightened around his hip. She came again, her hips bucking, her hot walls grabbing at his cock in powerful contractions. He kissed her fiercely, swallowing the sounds of pleasure that came from her throat.

He tore his mouth from hers and held his breath, clenched his jaw, trying to hold out, but he couldn't. "Oh, Jesus, Joanna." He pumped once, let go, and climax crashed through him like a speeding train. On a great groan he emptied himself of all that he had, including strength. His arms gave way and he crumpled against her body.

Beneath him, her breath continued to hitch. "Oh, God. . . . Oh, God."

He was in no better shape himself, but he moved his weight off of her and fell to her side. "Jesus God . . . that was . . . freakin' fantastic." He pulled her close to him. "Come love me. . . . You can't do that to me . . . then leave me . . . out in the cold."

They lay there, both drenched in sweat, his flaccid penis soft and damp against her belly, their breathing audible in the dark silence. As the chilly temperature cooled their heated bodies, their breathing evened and his strength returned. He caught her thigh and pulled it across his genitals, then tucked her head against his shoulder. "Don't tell me you didn't make it that time. I know damn well you made it."

"I made it," she said softly, and he felt her warm lips against his chest.

She sounded as if she might be crying. He snugged her closer yet and kissed the top of her head. "You okay?"

She sniffled. "I'm all sticky and wet."

Wet? His eyelids popped open. Hell, yes, she was sticky and wet, and so was he. *Fuck!* He hadn't worn a rubber. *Jesus Christ!* He hadn't come inside a woman without a rubber in more years than he could count. "Just a minute," he said, his thoughts racing.

Well, shit, she had to be on the pill. Why wouldn't she insist he use a rubber if she wasn't? He *hoped* she was on the pill, because he had been so damn horny and hot, the possibility of pregnancy hadn't even entered his head. When was the last time *that* happened? He sat up and swung his feet to the floor, stood and switched on the lamp. "Don't move. I'll be right back."

Squinting against the sudden light, Joanna lay there uncovered, his semen slick on her thighs, drying on her belly. The room was cold as ice, but she wasn't. He soon returned with towels and a washcloth and sat down on the edge of the bed. He pushed her legs apart and began to wash her with a warm washcloth.

Embarrassed, she reached for the washcloth. "I can do it."

He moved it out of her reach. "So can I." He gave her a wink. "I always clean up after myself."

He dropped the washcloth on the floor, picked up the towel and dried her. "You're beautiful," he said, then leaned down and kissed her stomach.

He tapped her bottom with his fingers. "Lift up." She braced her heels on the mattress and levered her bottom. "This'll do 'til morning." He arranged the towel over the wet spot underneath her. He covered her up to her chin and kissed her, then walked around the bed and crawled between the covers. Reaching up and switching off the light, he again plunged the room into total blackness. He turned on his side and pulled her against his body. "Shit, it's cold. Keep me warm."

She fit her bottom against his groin, closed her eyes and drifted toward sleep.

"That was pretty damned awesome," he said. "*You're* awesome. I just about lost my mind."

Chapter 19

Joanna awoke buried beneath a mound of warm covers—but lying in the worst bed she had ever known. Her back ached. Her head ached. Something that felt like a towel was caught between her legs.

Towel? Memories from the morning's wee hours flooded her mind. He hadn't used a condom. *Dear God.* She was sure she remembered he had used one the first time. But the second time, she had been so crazy and out of control for a few brief moments, all that had mattered was . . . was . . . was what he was doing with his mouth and . . .

The thought was so damning she couldn't finish it.

His half of the bed was empty, and she wondered when he had gotten up and where he was. She opened her eyes and peeked over the edge of the thick quilt to a dull gold light. Looking toward the two tall windows, she saw that the light came from sunlight filtering through aged openwork curtains and paper roll-up shades. She saw stark and unfamiliar surroundings—bluish floral wallpaper, a vintage chest of drawers made of a red-brown wood, a brown straight-backed chair.

Her khaki Dockers and pink panties lay where Dalton had peeled them off and dropped them in a heap on the linoleum-covered floor. She closed her eyes and groaned. Those Dockers would be a wrinkled mess and she had to walk out of here wearing them. She looked around for her bra and shirt, then remembered she had lost them last night in the kitchen.

Last night.

Dear God. In the light of day, all that had gone on in this bed seemed more like a dream than a reality. Or was it a nightmare? She groaned again as memories of details swarmed into her conscious mind.

That was pretty damned awesome. You're awesome.

As his words swam back, her whole being filled with bliss and she felt a smile cross her lips.

As total awareness asserted itself, she remembered that today was Tuesday. She saw no clock, but judging from the light in the room, it had to be at least eight o'clock. *Oh, hell.* She had to get moving and get to her shop. With the beauty salon being closed on Sundays and Mondays, Tuesdays were always busy days. Her mother would be in early and wondering why she wasn't there.

Joanna listened for activity in the living room or kitchen but heard nothing. She sat up, only to find evermore aches and pains she didn't know she had and a tenderness between her legs. Keeping up with Dalton in bed had been as physically demanding as helping him work on the fence.

If she had eaten ground glass, her stomach couldn't have felt worse. She needed about a dozen aspirin to cure the ache that throbbed behind her eyes. She held out her flattened hand and saw it visibly trembling. Besides that, she needed a shower and a toothbrush in the worst way.

She knew there was only one bathroom, installed many years after the house's original construction date. The tub was stained a rusty red and its smooth enamel finish had been eroded away long ago by the heavily mineralized water. There was a shower, but it was metal and rusted. The showerhead was so corroded from mineral deposit from the water, only a trickle of water came out. She wouldn't shampoo her hair in the ranch's hard well water anyway. A sponge bath in the vanity sink was the only acceptable option.

The bedroom was chilly. The morning sun hadn't had time to warm West Texas. She dragged the quilt from the bed and wrapped it around herself, noticing that the bed was a regular size. No wonder her and Dalton's bodies had been so close all night. There had been no other choice even if they had wanted one.

She opened the door a crack and poked her head through. She saw no one but heard country music coming from the kitchen. Easing out of the bedroom, she padded up the hallway.

She found the bathroom humid and warm. It smelled of cologne. A glance at the shower told her Dalton had used it not long ago. An image came to her of his Greek-god body naked in the shower. Erotic memories zoomed in on her and she closed her eyes and exhaled. Last night he had thought she was awesome, but what would he think this morning? What would Clova think if she knew her friend Joanna had slept with her favorite son? What should Joanna think of herself on a morning after a night of overindulgence in liquor, unbridled passion and uninhibited sex?

On a sigh, she bent to turn on the electric wall heater and her head swam. She grabbed at the wall for balance as the heater blew out a loud roar and instantly began to fill the small room with warmth.

Finally, she dared a glance in the vanity mirror and saw raccoon eyes from yesterday's mascara and whisker burns on her mouth and chin. Her expression looked vacant, her skin sallow, and her hair was a rat's nest. "Oh, hell," she whispered and pressed her fingertips against her mouth. Her fingers smelled like sex.

Dalton's travel bag lay unzipped on the end of the vanity. She picked through it, found toothpaste and brushed her teeth with her finger. Nearly gagging on the bitter, salty taste of the water that came from the tap, she thought of Dalton as a boy and the hardship of growing up in a home where the only running water was so heavy with minerals it was undrinkable and unusable for many purposes. But then, that was the nature of rural living in Wacker County.

She filled the sink with warm water and dropped the quilt to the floor, revealing her own naked body in the mirror. It appeared to be no different from yesterday. No one could tell by looking, thank God, that Dalton Parker's mouth had touched every intimate part of it. "Oh, hell," she muttered again.

She rummaged in the vanity and found a hairbrush. After she had washed herself and improved her appearance as much as possible, she wrapped up in the quilt again and left the bathroom. Before she reached the bedroom, Dalton came into the hallway carrying a coffee mug, a dazzling smile on his face. "Hey, sleepyhead."

Wearing clean jeans and a red long-sleeve T-shirt, he looked scoured, though dark stubble showed on his jaws. He looked so sexy and delectable that just seeing him almost took her breath. When he reached her, he looped one arm around her, pulled her close and kissed her, then offered her a sip of coffee. The scent of his cologne filled her nostrils, the same fragrance as last night and the same one she had smelled in the bathroom.

The thought of putting coffee in her roiling stomach was on a par with swallowing disinfectant. "No, thanks," she said, turning her head away from the mug.

"Not a coffee drinker?" he asked softly but cheerily. He kissed her again.

She pulled the quilt tighter around herself. "My stomach isn't in great shape. How come you twisted my arm last night and made me drink all that stuff?"

He set the mug down on a three-legged table standing against the wall, slid his hands beneath the quilt, wrapped both arms around her and pulled her close to him. "It turned out okay. Look what happened."

She smiled up at him. How could she not when his knowing hands were caressing her bare bottom? "Yeah, just look."

His mouth lowered to hers and they kissed in a long, squishy kiss. He ended it and pecked the tip of her nose. "Know what? You're as awesome in the daylight as you are in the dark."

"You, too," she replied, laughing a little at the relief she felt at hearing him repeat the words.

"Hungry?"

He seemed to be constantly trying to feed her. "I could eat something. Something gentle, that is."

"Want me to help you get dressed?" His thick brows bobbed.

She laughed and snuggled close to his chest. "I'd probably never get my clothes on. We'd end up back in bed."

"Hold that thought. Tonight we'll sleep at your house. I want to try out that fancy mattress you've got. I put your clothes on top of the cedar chest."

She reluctantly pushed away from him and started back to the bedroom. "I need to get my eggs gathered and get out of here."

"Already done," he said. "I put them on the counter in your little room. I've got breakfast all laid out in the kitchen."

She stopped in the bedroom doorway and looked at him. "You gathered the eggs?"

He leaned a shoulder against the doorjamb, his mouth only inches away. "Had to, babe. You were in no shape to do it."

"Dalton, listen, about last night—"

"What about it?" His cheery expression fell and he looked into her eyes intently.

Stymied by the change in his demeanor, she lost the

words she intended to say. She shrugged. "It's just that—"

"Joanna," he said, moving her hair behind her ear, "if you're about to apologize or anything like that, don't. Neither one of us has anything to be sorry for." He captured her chin with his fingers and kissed her long and tenderly.

Those words and his kiss chased away what she had intended to say. It had only been something silly about emotions and feelings and all of that nonsense anyway. When he lifted his lips, she smiled. "I do need to get dressed."

Ten minutes later, she met him in the kitchen and found him standing at the stove arranging strips of bacon in a cast-iron skillet. To put out the fire in her stomach, she helped herself to half a glass of milk from the refrigerator, then walked over to the counter beside him. Four eggs lay on the counter. "You're cooking eggs?"

"Fresh from Walsh's Naturals," he said. "Just laid this morning. How about that?"

She smiled up at him. "Should be good. My hens lay only the best."

He hooked an arm around her shoulder and planted a quick kiss on her temple. "What're you doing today?"

She watched the bacon sizzle and curl in the skillet, loving being attached to his side like another limb. "I take customers in the beauty shop on Tuesdays. How about you?"

"Going by to see Mom, then going to Lubbock. I thought you might be able to go with me."

The invitation was tempting, but she had never allowed anything except illness or an emergency to prevent her from taking care of her oldest and most loyal customers. "I can't. Some of my Tuesday ladies have been coming to me for years. They get upset if I'm not there. Big day in Lubbock?"

"Lane was supposed to get moved out of the ICU yesterday. I need to see what happens next." He turned the bacon with a meat fork, then broke the eggs into a separate skillet. "But I plan to be back before dark."

The bacon grease made a loud pop and they jumped. At the same time, his cell phone chirped from behind them. They both turned and stared at it.

The thing continued to bleat. He didn't move.

It had to be *her*. Otherwise he would answer it. And anyone else would have hung up by now. Like black ink, a feeling Joanna had never known she was capable of spilled into her brain. For the first time in her life, she knew the bitter bile of jealousy. She locked her eyes on his. "You should probably get that."

He gave the phone a scowl and an almost discernible shake of his head. Oh, yes. He did know it was *her*. "I mean it, Dalton. Answer it."

He drew a deep breath. Leaving the stove, he stepped over to the counter across the room, picked up the phone, flipped it open and slapped it against his ear. "Yo. It's me."

Oh, yes, it was the woman in California, and he was uncomfortable talking in her, Joanna's, presence. She blinked away the burn that rushed to her eyes. She waited to hear the "babes," the "darlin's," the "sweeties," tumble from his mouth, but they didn't.

"I've been busy," he said. "Sure. . . . Uh-hunh. . . . Well, yeah . . ."

Dear God. Reality. A cruel messenger. And a reminder that she had never done anything quite so stupid as what she had done last night. How could she have been so . . . so, so *drunk*?

The phone still plastered to his ear, he walked out of the kitchen and on out of the house.

Bastard! Joanna's chin quivered, but she refused to let him see her break down and bawl. Instead, she clenched her jaw, picked up the meat fork and punctured the egg yolks. Puddles of yellow spread through the grease just as a grim little satisfaction spread through her. Then she turned off the burner, grabbed the sack of apples still sitting on the counter and walked out of the kitchen. On her way to the front door, she yanked her purse off the dining table, leaving the file folder of chicken and donkey photographs behind.

Outside, squinting against the brilliant sunshine of early morning, she saw him on the front porch, his back to her, one hand in his pocket, his shoulders scrunched against the morning's cool temperature. To stand out in the cold shivering, he badly wanted a private conversation with Betty Boop.

Joanna strode past him and kept walking until she reached her pickup, parked in front of her egg-processing room. The newly gathered eggs needed washing, but she wasn't up to it.

As she yanked open the pickup's driver's-side door, he hustled up beside her. "Joanna, it's not what you think."

"Yes, it is." She threw her purse and the sack of apples onto the passenger seat. "It's exactly what I think. I've heard you talk to her. I've heard the 'babes' and the 'darlin's' and the 'sweeties.'" She climbed into the pickup and plopped onto the driver's seat.

"Joanna, don't do this. Don't be a horse's ass."

Anger charged through her, heating her face. She stopped and glared at him. "Me a horse's ass? Look in the mirror, buster."

She jerked the door from his grip and slammed it. She did not buzz down the window. She cranked the engine, but he hadn't stepped back. If he didn't, she

would run over his damned feet. She glowered at him
through the window and he finally moved. She backed
up, changed gears and roared toward the highway
without looking back.

She berated herself all the way home. How could
dull, conservative, hardworking Joanna Walsh have allowed herself to get drunk, wind up in bed with Dalton and completely abandon herself and her morals
to his carnal whims? How could she have been so
damn dumb? Hadn't she known from the beginning
that a woman lived with him in his house in California? Joanna had even talked to her the day she left a
message for him. For all she knew, he could be married to her.

By the time Joanna reached the bathroom in her
house, she had stripped. Minutes later, she stood in
the shower letting warm water cascade over her head.
It would serve her right if she drowned.

But soap and water couldn't clean her mind or re-
store her spirit or wash away the humiliation that was
stuck in her chest like a tight knot.

More cold hard facts bombarded her. What if he
had a disease? What if she were pregnant? And if she
was, whose fault was it? Hers, that's who. The very
idea sucked the air from her lungs and every other
thought from her head. The pulse in her temples
pounded harder.

She had to leave the shower when the water became
cool. She shrugged into her favorite robe, a thick pink
chenille that was a size too big for her. She sank into
the chair at her vanity to style her hair and try to put
herself together for the day, but she was perking on
only one cylinder.

More scenes from Dalton's bed began to replay in
her mind. Indeed he had taken her to a place within
herself she hadn't known existed. She could count on

her fingers the number of times she'd had an orgasm with a man, and she had never had several in a night. That pleasure had been so rare, at times she had wondered if something was wrong with her.

Then a new and certain knowledge dawned on her. Today she had a comprehension that she hadn't had yesterday, and she found it almost incredible. She had never quite understood Shari's relationship with Jay, had never related, had thought the two of them silly, had even wondered whether they were perverted. After last night, she got it. Finally. She was thirty-five years old and she finally understood the man-woman thing and the mystery of sex, the riddle that had puzzled her most of her adult life.

Chapter 20

After feeding the gnawing empty feeling in her stomach with another glass of milk, a slice of toast and three aspirins, Joanna dragged into the salon two hours late. Her mother was waiting for her behind the counter in the beauty supply store, scowling from beneath a furrowed brow. "Where have you been? You missed your ten o'clock."

Oh, hell. Evelyn Rogers. "I brought you some apples." Joanna placed the bag of apples she had bought in Lubbock yesterday on the counter, then sailed past her mom, avoiding her accusing eyes. "Was Evelyn mad?"

Sailing past was a poor avoidance tactic. Mom followed her. "A little. But she got better when I told her you was tied up with a problem with them damn chickens. She let me give her a trim."

"Thanks. I'll call her and apologize."

"Where have you been?" her mother asked again. "I tried calling you. I tried your cell phone, too."

Reaching her desk, still ducking her mother's piercing look, Joanna busied herself stowing her purse in a bottom desk drawer, removing her sweater and laying it on top of a file cabinet. "Don't know what happened, Mom. Guess we just didn't make a connection."

Alvadean Walsh might be flighty as a butterfly, but she wasn't one who gave up easily. "Are you sick?"

"I'm probably just tired." Joanna checked her desk for messages. "I went all day yesterday without food."

Mom jammed a fist against her hip, her mouth pursed. "Well, you look awful."

Thanks, Mom.

Her mother's head shook, one-two-three. "I don't know why you don't get rid o' them damn chickens. It's not like you're makin' any money. They ain't worth your health, and they're costin' you business in this beauty shop. Why, if I hadn't o' been here this mornin', Evelyn—"

"Mom, please."

"How far did you have to drive yesterday? Just look at the time and gas you're a-wastin' runnin' up and down the road. With the price gas has gone up to—"

"Mother. It's my time and my gas. Okay?" She placed her hand on Mom's shoulder and captured her eyes with hers. Most of the time, Joanna refrained from hurting her mom's feelings by expressing her own opinions about some of Alvadean's habits and hobbies. Some days, keeping quiet was harder than others. This was one of the hard days.

She saw the rise of reluctant surrender in Mom's eyes. She might nag and wear a cloak of self-righteousness, but Joanna knew that deep down, her mother supported her.

"You've got Shari down on the appointment book," Mom said. "She's due to show up here any minute."

Even as her mother spoke, Joanna heard the front door chime and looked up to see her best pal hurrying in just in time to rescue her from more of Mom's hounding. Time to get on with the day. Joanna met Shari in the salon.

"Are you sick?" Shari asked, dropping into Joanna's hydraulic chair and frowning at her in the mirror.

Joanna wanted to cry. She must look worse than even *she* thought. Indeed she was sick. Sick at heart, sick in the head, sick of men. Again. She wrapped a silver plastic cape around Shari's shoulders. "I don't know. Flu bug maybe. It's that time of year."

"Well, don't get sick now. We're celebrating my birthday tomorrow night."

Joanna huffed a humorless laugh. "I could be dead by then." She picked a sterilized hairbrush from her drawer and began to brush Shari's hair. Heaving a great breath, she directed a long assessment at her best friend in the mirror. "Okay, birthday girl, what are we doing to you today?"

"I found some gray hairs. Do you think I need some color?"

Joanna cocked her head, her mouth twisting as she more closely examined Shari's hair. She had beautiful thick hair the color of coffee. Joanna had created a straight, blunt-cut style that fell just past her nape. It was perfect for a woman who had a houseful of busy kids and a busy husband, and who didn't have time to maintain a fussy hairdo. "I'd leave it alone."

"Okay, then, just trim it and style it. Make me look sexy. For Jay."

Joanna stood back to let her friend rise from the chair. They walked together back to the shampoo room, and Shari seated herself in the chair in front of the sink. "How's Clova?" she asked as Joanna gingerly tilted her head backward into the sink. "I heard she's got pneumonia."

"Yep."

"Bummer. Guess you can't be too good if you're sick enough to be in the hospital."

Joanna nodded, testing the water spray for temperature.

"Dalton came by Jay's shop yesterday."

Shocked, Joanna almost sprayed water on the wall. "When?"

"Yesterday morning."

Instantly Joanna's interest in Shari's conversation perked up. She shuffled back through last night's talk with Dalton, but if he had mentioned visiting Jay Huddleston, it had gone right past her. Unable to believe a man as self-centered as Dalton had any interest in renewing acquaintance with an old school friend for the sake of doing it, she asked, "Whatever for?"

"He was wondering about an oil well that was drilled on the Parker ranch. It was a long time ago. Jay couldn't remember it, but his dad did."

Joanna doused Shari's hair with warm water and shampoo. "Humph. I wonder what that's about."

"You don't know?"

"About an oil well? I might have heard Clova mention it here or there, but no, I don't know." Joanna went about shampooing Shari's hair.

"Jay said Dalton's trying to find somebody to drill on his mom's place."

It dawned on Joanna that in last night's supper conversation they had discussed what Dalton had been doing all over the world in the last fifteen years, but not a word about what he had been doing all day yesterday in Hatlow. Her next thought was about the land Clova had offered to her, and a tiny anxiety came back to niggle at her. "So did he find someone?" Joanna asked cautiously.

"Oh, hell, I don't know. Jay doesn't exactly fill me in on all the details of anything. He said Dalton hasn't changed much except for a little gray hair. But hell, we're all getting gray hair."

"Not me," Joanna replied, thinking about Dalton's hair and the intimate places where it was still coal black.

Finished with the shampoo, Joanna helped her friend to an upright position. Shari looked up at her, her eyes filled with glee. "Virginia Newman said he's still hot. You must see him every day when you go out there to take care of your eggs. What do *you* think?"

Joanna thought back to the Sunday when she and Dalton had taken Clova to the hospital. Virginia had been the admitting clerk. "Nothing much. He's always busy, and so am I."

"But you must be getting acquainted with him a little bit. Practically everyone we know is pea green with envy that you see him every day. Virginia told Sandy Billings he guaranteed Clova's hospital bill. He must be loaded."

"Hm," Joanna replied.

"Don't give me a 'hm.' Virginia said you were there when he signed the paper."

Joanna sighed, thinking of something Dalton *had* said during last night's supper conversation. Indeed everyone in Hatlow did have their noses in everyone's else business. "Yeah, I was there."

"Well, did he guarantee the bill or not? Clova being in the hospital will cost a lot of money. Is he loaded?"

"I suppose he wouldn't have said he'd pay if he couldn't."

And from what Joanna had seen of him, she would bet her last dollar on *that* fact.

They walked back to the chair at Joanna's station. As she snipped away at Shari's ends, her pal's prattle wandered to the new lights at the football stadium and the letter Cody had received from A & M. Her youngest son, Dillon, had to have braces on his teeth. Sometimes a person needed a program to have a conversation with Shari. Today, she seemed even more convoluted than usual.

The hair styling done, Shari stood up with a handheld mirror and did a circular look-see in the big mirror. "It looks great, Joanna. You are so good."

"Thanks," Joanna replied wryly. "I've had a lot of experience."

Shari laid the mirror on the workstation counter and proceeded to write a check for her hairdo. "Let's go

get lunch. I'll buy. I want to show you something. I
need your opinion."

Lunch sounded better now than it would have earlier. Now Joanna's stomach had taken on a different
emptiness. She agreed and they strolled up the street
to Betty Lou's Coffee Cup. As soon as they took
seats in a red vinyl booth, Shari produced a large
white envelope from her purse, pulled out a page
filled with photographs and slid it across the table to
Joanna. "This is what Jay's getting me for my birthday."

Joanna gazed down at six pairs of women's naked
breasts of varying shapes and sizes. Puzzled, she looked
back at Shari. "Boobs? Or six women?"

If Shari got the pitiful joke, she ignored it. Her eyes
glinted with excitement. "Which ones do you like?"

The young waitress came to take their order and
Shari quickly turned the page of photographs face-
down on the tabletop. She ordered a chicken Caesar
salad and iced tea. Joanna ordered the same, plus a
large chocolate milk shake. Today, she doubted her
stomach would appreciate roughage without a cushion.

As soon as the waitress went on her way, Joanna
leaned forward and spoke in a low tone. "You're
going to have a boob job?"

"I've been saying I wanted to for a long time."

Indeed she had, but the remark had always been
offhand and not up for discussion. "Good grief, Shari,
I thought you were kidding. You don't think you're
big enough or what?"

Now Shari leaned forward, her forearms on the
table. "No, no, no, Joanna. It isn't about size. I can
gather them up and fill up a D cup. How much more
would a person want? It's about the way they *look*."
She turned the page of photographs faceup again.

"Oh," Joanna said, realizing that she hadn't seen

Shari naked probably since high school. "What's wrong with the way they look?"

"They're wrecked. Lord, I've nursed four kids, and if you recall, Dillon nursed until after he was a year old. He nearly killed me."

Being a hairdresser for years, besides gossip on almost every person in town, Joanna had heard discussion of women's issues from one end of the spectrum to the other. She mentally acknowledged that she might have heard that nursing sometimes damaged women's breasts, but today, she was too preoccupied with her own damage to even consider a friend's. "I don't know, Shari." She shook her head skeptically. "Isn't it major surgery?"

Shari ignored Joanna's doubt. "They aren't even the same size now. One hangs down farther than the other. They look more like bananas than breasts."

The young waitress returned with glasses of cold tea. Shari sat back and whisked the page of photographs into her lap.

"Damn, Shari, I don't know what to say. And Jay thinks this is a good idea?" Joanna busied herself stirring Sweet'N Low into her tea.

"He doesn't care. They're my boobs. He knows it's what I want. He's only interested in what's below my waist anyway." Laughing, Shari peeled a straw and stuck it into her tea. "I told him I'm gonna get him a board with a knothole in it. Just to see if he notices the difference." She produced the page of photographs again. "So which ones do you like?"

Joanna drew the page of pictures to her side of the table. Knowing Shari, there was no getting out of this. "I don't know." She thoroughly perused each pair of breasts, then pointed at the middle photograph on the left. "Those, I think."

Shari smiled brightly. "I picked those, too. And

those are the ones Jay likes, too." She turned the page back toward herself and studied the picture. "I like those because they look perky. I'm just going for a D cup. I'm short, you know? I don't want to be a freak."

The waitress delivered their salads and Joanna's milk shake. Joanna sucked a large dollop through her straw. "God, that tastes good."

A frown of concern crossed Shari's face. "Your stomach's really upset, huh? You probably caught something in the shop. Take some Pepto-Bismol. That's what I feed the kids when they have an upset stomach."

Joanna sucked up another drink of her milk shake. "When are you planning on doing this, Shari?"

"Before Christmas. We're going on that cruise in February, you know? The Valentine's thing? It's kind of a second honeymoon. That's when I want to show them off. I've bought this sexy bustier thing and guess what else." She scrunched up her shoulders and giggled mischievously.

"Not a clue," Joanna said. She tested a bite of chicken and washed it down with a swallow of tea. Her stomach was starting to feel better.

"I got a pair of matching panties. Crotchless." Shari giggled again.

"Good grief, Shari. Where did you get them?"

"I ordered them from a catalog. I've been thinking about not waiting until Valentine's to show them off, though. I've been thinking about wearing them to Jay's office one day and perching my little ass on his desk, spreading my legs and surprising him. Why, he could go down on me without even taking my panties off. I mean, if we got caught or something. That's happened to us before, you know."

Joanna blinked and sucked up another drink of her milk shake. Through the years, she had been privy to many of the graphic details of Shari and Jay's relationship. She had ceased being shocked or even surprised long ago, but sometimes, knowing the private moments between her two friends made facing Jay difficult. He could never figure out why Joanna sometimes couldn't look him in the eye when he talked about something serious.

"Anyway, I need to get this operation done and get healed up. So I won't be out of commission on that cruise, if you know what I mean."

"Yeah, it would be too bad if something happened to keep you two from having sex."

"Well, it *would*. I'll swear, Joanna, I don't know how you do it. Go without like you do."

Joanna wanted to cry again. She inhaled a deep breath and leaned forward, pushing aside her salad. "Shari, can I ask you something?"

No doubt the body language alerted Shari that something juicy was about to spill. She leaned forward, too, until their foreheads were almost touching. "Is it about sex?"

Joanna laughed in spite of her headache. "Besides raising kids, what else do you know anything about?"

"Ask me. You know you can ask me anything."

"Exactly what days can you get pregnant?"

"Joanna!" Shari's voice came in a stage whisper. "Are you sleeping with somebody?"

"Shh." Joanna looked around the café to see who might have heard her. Fortunately, the lunch crowd had cleared out. "Just tell me. I haven't thought much about it in a long time. I've forgotten practically everything I ever knew about sex education."

"I'm not surprised," Shari said. "You never practice."

Joanna didn't need to be reminded, especially today. She opened her palms and gave her friend a look. "And when have I had time to practice?"

Shari forked another bite of salad, sat back and held

it above her plate, a professorial expression on her face. "Really, it's only about three or four days out of the month. The little soldiers have to be in there swimming around before your egg comes down. It's like they have to be waiting to ambush it. You just count fourteen days from the first day of your last period and figure you should be messing around for three or four days before that. If you're trying to get pregnant, that is."

"Now why would I be *trying* to get pregnant?"

"Oh, no!" Shari's brown eyes grew wide. "It's Alicia, isn't it? I knew she was going to get caught, screwing around with that Pablo kid."

"No! It isn't Alicia. And don't you dare tell people that. And you don't know that she screws around with him."

Shari gave her a flat look. "Joanna. I'm not an idiot. And I'm not blind."

"I don't want you spreading tales about Alicia."

"Then it's you." She pointed a bite of lettuce on the end of her fork straight at Joanna's nose. "Yep, it's you, girlfriend. I can read you like a book. I've known you too long." She leaned across the table and whispered, "You went to Lubbock yesterday. You got back together with Scott Goodman."

A rush of tears burned Joanna's eyes, but she blinked them back. "Dammit, Shari, I'm not ready to discuss it. I just want the answer to a simple question."

A look of concern crossed Shari's face. "Oh, my God. You're upset. Joanna, I'm your best friend. You can tell me about it."

Joanna quickly wiped the moisture from her eyes. "No. I'm not ready to talk about it."

"Okay, don't tell me. But I know it's Scott. I heard he was upset when you broke off with him."

Just go ahead and think that, Joanna thought.

Shari's brow knit into a thoughtful frown and she

rambled on. "At your age, I don't think you have to worry as much. Once you're past thirty, the odds against are real high."

"Shari, get real. I see pregnant women my age every day."

"I'll bet you don't see as many as you think."

"How do you know this?"

"Well . . ." Shari stirred her salad around her plate, then forked a chunk of chicken. "Because Jay and I started trying again a few years ago. We wanted another baby."

"You didn't tell me that."

"We didn't tell anybody. We didn't want people to get all excited. You know that old saying about a watched pot never boiling. I got off the pill and everything. Jay and I did it nearly every night for two months. He even came home at lunch a few times." She leaned forward again, still whispering. "Listen, we did it all kinds of ways. We used to get naked and watch porn movies."

"Porn movies?" Joanna's brow knit into a frown. She had never watched a porn movie, wouldn't know where to get one if she wanted to. "Where did you get porn movies in Hatlow?"

"Jay bought a couple once when he was in Fort Worth."

"Shari, you've got kids."

Shari sat back against the booth, an expression of righteous indignation on her face. "Well, we keep them hidden, Joanna."

Joanna shook her head, frowning. "I don't get it. How does watching porn movies help you get pregnant?"

"Well, stop and think about it. Jay and I've been married going on eighteen years. I've never been with anybody but him. And if he's ever been with anybody but me, he had better never let me find out about it.

We were infants and virgins when we started doing it with each other. Anyway, since we were doing it so often, we thought the movies might add a little spice. Might make it more interesting."

Joanna's head began to pound with a vengeance. The lettuce pieces on her plate seemed to blur into a blob of pastel green. "Hm. They obviously didn't work."

"Actually, they were kind of boring. And kind of disgusting. I mean, the acting is so awful. And it doesn't look real."

"Shari, you're dripping salad dressing on the table."

Shari stuffed her salad bite into her mouth. "Nothing ever happened," she said, undaunted and chewing. "You know, I never have gotten back on the pill. It's been three years and still nothing's ever happened. Dr. Jones says it's just harder after you get older." Another frown creased her brow. "I probably should get back on those pills. With this stuff going on between Cody and that little Nicole, I'm sort of out of the mood for more kids." She speared another forkful of salad. "Just watch. Now, I'll get pregnant."

"Hunh," Joanna said. "Well, all of this is more information than I need to know."

"Joanna, do you realize you're more experienced at sex than I am?"

An unexpected laugh burst from Joanna's throat. "I've never thought about it."

"Well, think about it now. You've been with more than one guy. I'm sure they're all different, aren't they? I mean, they gotta be built different, some big, some little. They gotta act different, don't they?"

Now Joanna really did want to break into tears. One thing she did not need today was a comparative conversation about the few men with whom she'd had sex. It could only remind her of her rotten social life

and her more rotten relationship history. "Take my
word, Shari, variety isn't the answer to anything."

"So who're you sleeping with?"

"Don't nag me. I said I'm not discussing it."

"But you must be worried or you wouldn't have
asked me about getting pregnant. I know you're not
on the pill. Whoever it is, I can't believe you didn't
make him use something."

Me neither. The memory of her own role in what
had happened in Dalton's bed flew back into Joanna's
mind. And so did the same battering emotions that
had almost overwhelmed her earlier in the shower. "It
was, uh, we didn't have anything."

"Wow. And you were that hot? How cool is that?"

"Shari—"

"Can I tell Jay?"

"No! Don't tell anyone. And I mean it. No one. It's
nobody's business, Shari."

"Okay, okay. I won't say a word. But only if you
promise to tell me all about it before you tell anyone else."

Joanna rolled her eyes. She didn't intend to tell one
single person. Her greatest fear was that her mom or
Clova might find out. "I promise. Just don't mention
it. You know how it is around here. I don't want everyone in town to know every intimate detail of my
life. I'm in business here. And most of my customers
are women. I don't want one of them thinking Jezebel
is running the beauty shop. Suzy Martinez would have
a ball telling it everywhere."

Shari sighed. "Yeah, I know what you mean. She
might even go up to Lubbock and talk about it. Or
down to Denver City."

Her demeanor changed abruptly. "Well, I've got to
get home and fix supper for that mob that lives at my
house." She scooted out of the booth, grabbing the

check. "Since I'm feeding them pizza tomorrow night before we go out, I have to fix a decent meal tonight."

Joanna walked with her pal all the way to her pickup in the parking lot beside Joanna's Salon & Supplies. The lunch she had just consumed weighed a hundred pounds in her stomach.

"Now, don't forget," Shari said, climbing behind the wheel. "We'll come by and pick you up around six. Since it's my birthday, I'm going to drink champagne. You might have to be the designated driver." Shari laughed. "I mean, what are friends for? Oh, and I'm wearing my new boots and my fringe jacket."

Joanna had little interest in spending an evening in a honky-tonk and even less in being the designated driver. But a friend was a friend. "Okay," she said ruefully.

Shari started the engine, giving Joanna a long look. "Dammit, Joanna, I'm going to be going crazy, not able to tell Jay you got back with Scott Goodman."

Good, Joanna thought.

Chapter 21

Back in her store, armed with facts from Shari, Joanna marched directly to her desk and calendar. She counted the days as Shari had instructed. If Shari was correct—and Joanna had no reason to doubt her—Dalton's little soldiers had missed their window of opportunity.

A monumental gush of relief flooded Joanna, to the point where she actually felt better than she had all day.

The relief came from believing she had escaped what could have been an onerous result of stupid behavior. But that sentiment conflicted with a sense of loss that had set up a dull, deep ache in her midsection. It was so disappointing that sleeping with Dalton had been nothing more than . . . well, call it what it was—a reckless, meaningless romp with a man she scarcely knew.

What makes you think it doesn't have any meaning? There's damn near nothing that happens that has no meaning.

Not a direct lie, but a lie by implication. From a man who only wanted sex, a man who would soon be leaving town.

Even as that thought passed through her mind, she reminded herself that he wouldn't be leaving tomorrow. He would still be at the ranch for some unknown number of days when she went to tend the hens and gather the eggs. *Crap.*

Unable to imagine how the next meeting with him might go, she chewed on the inside of her cheek. She wasn't up to facing him. Not yet. He was too strong, too aggressive. She couldn't avoid going to the ranch forever, but, she calculated, after a day or two, her pride and ego would be healed enough and her strength restored enough to do combat with him. The passage of time lessened the sting of a lot of prickly things, she had learned. She was nothing if not resilient.

Meanwhile, Joanna intended to enjoy a respite from minding the hens and eggs. When Alicia came in to work, she arranged for the teenager to gather the eggs and feed the hens that evening and twice again tomorrow and to ask her boyfriend to accompany her in case she ran into a varmint.

Dalton stood at the fence that surrounded Joanna's chickens. He no longer hated them quite as badly as he had the first time he saw them.

Still, a more tolerant attitude about the chickens did not prevent his sinking into his worst mood in years. His complicated, but organized, life had suddenly become cluttered with a bunch of emotional crap. Crap like feelings for his little brother, his mother and now Joanna Walsh. Complications he routinely dealt with daily. Clutter was more difficult.

Ah, Joanna. Her angry departure and its cause had troubled him all day. Sometimes events came together in such an ironic way a man couldn't keep from wondering if some damn jokester somewhere was pulling strings and chortling at the result. This was a level of thinking with which he rarely bothered, but Candace calling on this particular morning about the friggin' swimming pool was stunning. Here in Texas, at nine o'clock in the morning, the time in LA had been seven. Candace hadn't been out of bed at seven a.m. since he'd known her.

Now he wasn't sure what to do about Joanna. Wait for her to cool off? That seemed like a good plan. When she was less angry, he could talk to her in a reasonable conversation.

He didn't want her to think him a liar and a selfish asshole. He had to try to make her understand that Candace lived in his house temporarily.

Second, he and Joanna had to finish the more personal conversation of this morning. The phone had interrupted before he had been able to learn if there was a danger she could have gotten pregnant. What the fuck would they do if she did?

They? Hell, there was no *they.*

The question was what would *she* do? More to the point, what the fuck would *he* do?

As far as he knew, he had never even come close to being a father, even when he was married. His ex-wife had been a dedicated career woman. She hadn't wanted kids. And he hadn't to this day considered whether he did. His life was busy, full of excitement and adventure and short notices. Kids wouldn't fit. But he knew one thing for sure—the bastard Dalton Parker would not relish being responsible for bringing another bastard into the world.

He veered to another subject he was wary to bring up with Joanna. Beside him on the ground lay a metal detector he had bought today while in Lubbock. He had used it a short time ago to search for the old oil well.

And he believed he had found it . . . directly under Joe and Jill's shed, damn near in the middle of Joanna's chicken yard. *Fuck.* The chickens would have to go.

He felt guilty about that and he intended to level

with Joanna. That is, if he could ever get back in her good graces. Of course she would be upset. That bothered him, though he wasn't sure why it should. *Jesus Christ*, she had been using the land for free for more than two years. Did she expect such an arrangement to go on forever?

He was also taking heat over the oil-well venture from his business manager in LA. The guy had yelled at him on the phone for thirty minutes, outlining how easily and quickly he could lose a hundred thousand dollars or more in an industry known for its charlatans.

. . . that's the nature of wildcattin' for oil. It's a high-stakes gamble if there ever was one.

Skeeter Vance's words had stuck in Dalton's mind. Even so, Dalton Parker was no stranger to a high-stakes gamble. Up to this point, he had sometimes gambled his very life on nothing more than snapping a picture. When he went into primitive, hostile countries on a photography mission, he knew every time that for one off-the-wall reason or other, he might not survive. Hell, a weird bug bite could kill him even if a bunch of armed combatants who thought they had a cause didn't. He had been willing to take the risk, though as an intelligent man, he had always done everything possible to protect himself.

Compared to what he had already survived, what was risking a little money on a project that had the potential to hugely benefit the ranch and his mother and even himself?

Oilman. Wildcatter. Titles Dalton had never once expected or desired to wear. But what was the alternative? Risk even more by handing his mother the money to save the ranch, then not know how it would be used? He couldn't stay in Hatlow forever and oversee his investment. If Mom and Lane couldn't pull the ranch out of debt and make it work again, his con-

science would never let him demand that she pay the
money back. What assurance would he ever have that
the place—and his money—wouldn't end up in the
hands of the bastards at the Hatlow Farmers Bank?

At least with a drilling venture, he could file legal
documents as the "independent operator" and hope
for the best. And if Vance hit oil, there could be
enough cash to pay the ranch's debts and repay the
drilling costs.

A pragmatic side of him told him he should have
stayed in California and ignored what was going on in
Texas, as he had done for most of his adult life. But
an emotion he couldn't name had overridden practical
sense and he knew he was on the brink of something.
He felt as if he was coming to terms with his very
core. At this moment, that challenge was more com-
pelling than worrying over his checkbook.

In his head, he had made a tentative decision about
the well, but he wouldn't firm up details until he could
talk at greater length to his mother. This morning before going to Lubbock, he had gone by the hospital
and visited her. To his surprise, she was upbeat and
planning on being released tomorrow or the next day.

Beyond all of those issues roiling in his mind,
though his trip to Lubbock had gone well on one level,
it had not gone so well on another.

He had told Lane of meeting Mandy. Lane broke
into tears. Nothing could be resolved with him flat of
his back in a hospital bed in another town, but Lane
admitting his feeling for Mandy and his child was a
start. Dalton resolved to persuade Mandy to accompany him to visit Lane in the hospital. If he weren't
in such a bad mood, he would feel proud of himself
for the Good Samaritan role he was playing in solving
that problem.

The part of the visit that had gone less well was the
meeting he'd had with Lane's doctors and practically

everybody in Lubbock Memorial Hospital. The only people he had missed were the board members. Lane was headed for lengthy rehabilitation. And without a penny's worth of insurance.

Dalton had listened to some damn social worker drone on about how without ownership of a single fuckin' thing, Lane was eligible for some government assistance for his treatment. *Welfare. Jesus.* A member of his family taking welfare. That had *never* happened. But desirable choices didn't abound. The bill Lane had accumulated already could push the teetering ranch over the edge. With the government willing to pick up the tab, Dalton hadn't stepped forward and offered to pay. Yet.

He felt guilty about that, too. But, hell, he wasn't a bottomless pit. He was already committed to paying for his mother's treatment. And who knew how much that would be? Besides that, he had handed the government enough in service and taxes over the years to more than cover Lane's rehabilitation. Selfish? Maybe. But factual.

There were plenty of other places around this damn ranch to spend money, too. He had started to consider a few things he could do to improve the place, like replace the plumbing in the old house. Maybe turn some of the overgrazed areas into crops of some kind. No matter what his business manager said, Dalton couldn't deny the affection he had for the Lazy P and the possessive feeling that had popped up once he had learned it was in trouble.

He had just glanced at his watch, wondering why Joanna hadn't already shown up, when he heard a growling engine slow at the turnoff from the highway. He hadn't noticed her truck making such a noise last night. He waited for it to come into view.

The thing that appeared was a rusted-out old Pontiac, its undercarriage not six inches off the ground.

Inside rode a Hispanic couple. The rolling wreck stopped in front of the egg-washing room and a young woman got out. He recognized her as being Joanna's teenage helper.

"Hola, Señor Cherry," the girl called, waving and smiling broadly, showing bright white teeth.

Dalton winced at being called Mr. Cherry. He walked over to the egg-processing room. "Hi. Let's see, your name's Alicia, right?"

"Sí."

She turned to the scrawny kid with her. He had tattoos from his hairline to his fingertips and assorted metal objects stuck in several places on his face. Dalton had a tattoo himself, an American eagle on his left shoulder. He had done that to mark himself an American patriot. He didn't understand a kid mutilating his body with piercings.

"This is my boyfriend, Pablo. We come to take Joanna's eggs."

"She isn't coming?"

"She feel very bad. I say to her, 'I take the eggs.' And she say, 'Okay.' "

Disappointment settled in Dalton's chest.

Alicia disappeared into the egg-washing room and came out a minute later carrying the baskets and blue buckets, which she handed to the boy as she spoke to him in a stream of Spanish.

"Is she, uh, sick?" Dalton asked.

Alicia nodded, her brow knit with concern. "I thing so. She go home to her big bed."

As Alicia and her boyfriend slipped through the gate into the chicken yard, Dalton watched, chewing on the inside of his lip. "Shit," he mumbled.

At home, Joanna dozed on the sofa and didn't awaken until after dark. She called Alicia and discussed the egg gathering. Then she opened a can of tuna and ate it with crackers while she watched *Law & Order*, hoping the TV crime show would distract her from the disconcerting combination of emotions she had battled all day.

At the end of the show, she switched off the TV, put on her sleeping shorts and T-shirt, wilted into bed and slid into the sleep of the exhausted.

At midnight, Dalton checked the clock in the bottom corner of his computer monitor.

Earlier, in a funky mood after Joanna hadn't come, he had taken his favorite camera out to a remote site—on the Parker ranch those were legion—and shot a couple of the windmills. He loved the windmills. He knew that windmills had been a part of the West Texas landscape long before pumpjacks and oil derricks.

The bust of the eighties had proved that oil derricks could come and go, but Dalton had always known the importance of water in arid West Texas. Even as a kid, he had heard some predict that the day would come when water would become more valuable than oil. Having grown up in and around agriculture, he couldn't argue against the idea. Livestock needed drinking water and crops needed irrigation. The Parker ranch was fortunate to have half a dozen producing water wells and windmills in strategic spots. Somebody at some point back in time had been wise enough to drill them.

And he had shot the sunset. His camera had caught the last long splashes of gold and mauve as the great orange ball sank into the horizon. Sunset had always fascinated him more than sunrise. On one of his computers in LA, he had hundreds of shots of sunsets from all over the world. He had seen the sinking sun when it appeared to be close enough for him to walk over, place his hand on top of it and push it on down, past the horizon. He had edited a picture to where it showed him doing just that. Someday, for one medium or another, he would do a piece on sunsets.

Finally, he'd had to make himself stop playing with his sunset shots. Amusing himself wasn't where his obligation lay. Rapidly approaching was his deadline to turn in a book about his journey through three Middle Eastern countries—his photographic observations and objective commentary. As if a human alive who had grown up in the West could be objective about all that he saw in the Muslim part of the world.

He had sorted and edited those photographs for hours. Many were shots of some of the ruins of some of the oldest civilizations the world knew. Traversing and shooting in the Middle East was like photographing the Bible. He found the pictures disturbing and depressing and at the same time beautiful and haunting, even exhilarating. All of that.

He loved the work, but through it all, Joanna Walsh hovered in his mind, distracting him and hindering his efforts. He had stopped half a dozen times and debated calling her, to the point where he had searched for and found her phone number in Hatlow's thin phone directory and written it down on a notepad beside the phone.

Though he had a hunch a woman as independent as she needed her space, and he was willing to allow her that, the notepad with her phone number lay there like a crouching cougar set to pounce on him. Once he had even picked up the receiver, prepared to punch in her number. But he had stopped himself. He didn't know what to say. He wanted to get it right, and telling her that Candace was just a friend sounded flimsy even to his own ears. He wanted Joanna to think him a better man than he was.

Normally, he didn't worry about what the fairer sex thought of him. Women could either take him as he was or leave him alone. And he sure hadn't often found it necessary to explain a damned thing to most of those he knew. Since his divorce, he hadn't met a woman who made him want to change his attitude, either. His own mother first, his ex-wife second, had taught him just how self-centered women could be.

But he felt he owed something to Joanna. She just wasn't like most of the other women in his world. She was too open and honest. She had no agenda. And that set her apart. It also made her vulnerable to the world's evils. Hell, she needed a keeper and didn't even know it.

There was no need to call her, he had finally decided. Tomorrow morning, she would be back to take care of those friggin' eggs. Then he would talk to her about everything that was on his mind.

The screek of the shifting fan echoing from the windmill in the chicken yard broke the night's silence. In LA, he was never lonely in his house, rarely longed to hear another human voice. Tonight he was amazed at how lonely he felt in this sprawling old ranch house. He removed his glasses, laid them on the dining table and rubbed his eyes with his fingertips.

Annoyed at himself and the situation, and restless, he left his seat at the dining table and strolled outside, letting his thoughts return to windmills. The well that supplied water to the house had an electric pump, but the one in the chicken yard was still powered by wind. He walked across the driveway, unlatched the gate and ambled to the old windmill's wooden tower. He climbed up to the platform, braked the fan and seated himself with his back against the cool holding tank.

Looking out into the far distance, he could see the narrow, low line of Hatlow's lights, shimmering and spitting onto a black backdrop. He could see an occasional pair of headlights on the nearer highway. The view had changed little from when he was a boy.

His mind traveled back to his boyhood and summer nights when he would sneak out of the house and climb this same windmill tower, letting the cool breeze touch his face as he looked out into the dark world. The bird's-eye view of the surrounding vista had given him a sense of freedom like nothing else. Back then he hadn't known the symbolism his innocent childhood activity represented. In many ways, now, as an adult with a camera, he did the same thing.

On those nights, he had spent hours envisioning the day when he would escape the Parker ranch and Hatlow, Texas. And he *had* escaped. He had seen and done much that most men would never see or do. His experiences in unpredictable, sometimes harrowing, sometimes heartrending, circumstances had hardened his hide but in many ways had softened his heart. He had learned that people and societies were too complex for the minds of mortal humans to contemplate. The world's problems were too grave and too complicated for mere human beings to resolve. He had encountered so much of the unreasonable, so much of the unfathomable, that while he'd once had no interest in living a calm, quiet life in a small town like Hatlow, for a while now he had felt growing within him the need for simplicity.

Once he had thought life in Hatlow was complicated. Now he realized just how wrong that notion was.

Chapter 22

Wednesday afternoon came in what seemed like the blink of an eye. Engaged in her egg business for more than two years, trips twice daily to the Parker ranch had become Joanna's routine. Today she was amazed at how productive she had been without the hens and eggs consuming so many hours of her day. There had to be a message there.

She knew it was cowardly to handle her own anxiety over what had happened with Dalton by not facing him, but she had humiliated herself in his presence and she still hadn't built the inner strength she needed to face him and deal with him unemotionally. Not yet.

Beyond that, her heart was in pain. She had become infatuated with him. Knowing he had someone else to whom he would soon return was almost more than she could stand. What was the worst of all, she had known it when she slept with him. A few drinks were no excuse for doing something so dumb.

At least she would have a change of scenery this evening. Dancing was one of her favorite recreations, and she hadn't been out in months. All of a sudden she no longer regretted that she had told Shari she would go with her to celebrate her birthday.

She left the store early, went home and showered and spent a leisurely amount of time styling her hair for the first time in weeks. She decided what to wear in a short time. She didn't own a large selection of going-out clothing, but what she did own was quality stuff purchased in cool shops. She viewed her dress-up clothing sort of like she viewed her mattress. She had earned it.

She dressed in a tan chamois A-line skirt soft to the touch, with perfect drape. Great for dancing. She topped it with a white lacy camisole. She was fussing with her hair again when she heard the Huddleston dually's diesel engine clattering in her driveway.

"Hey, girl, where are you?" Shari's voice, calling from the front of the house. She always came in without knocking.

"I'm in the bathroom," Joanna called back.

"Hey, look at you," Shari said, entering the bathroom and looking her up and down. "Lace with suede. Too cool. Love that camisole. You didn't get *that* at Wal-Mart."

"Up in Lubbock a few months ago. At one of those cute shops out by the college."

"That's what happens when you wear a size seven. You can shop where the college kids shop. Get your boots on. Jay'll be honking the horn."

"Okay, okay." Joanna pulled on her best boots, the ones for which she had paid way too much. She had bought them in Leddy's on an infrequent trip to Fort Worth's North Side. They, too, were cool. Tan ostrich bottoms, with intricate arty stitching on the tops. And leather soles. Dancing boots if any ever had been made.

"I still envy you those boots," Shari said. "They're worth doing without food for."

"As if you'd know," Joanna quipped. Shari did without little. Even through the hard times, Jay had managed to be a good provider.

Joanna covered the camisole with a denim jacket. Daytime temps were still hotter than blazes, but once dark settled, she might be chilly in nothing more than a bare-shouldered camisole. To be stylish, she added a glitzy rhinestone pin to the jacket and her sterling silver Vogt earrings with a crystal teardrop. She had paid too much for them, too, but she adored them.

As Shari watched her hook them into her ears, Joanna couldn't keep from thinking of the differences between her own life and that of her best friend. Shari boasted a box full of "good jewelry" Jay had bought her through the years. He had always come up with something special and expensive for Christmas and special occasions. Joanna, on the other hand, had a box full of beaded odds and ends made by her mother.

Only once had Joanna received a gift of jewelry from a man. A long time ago, an old friend, now married and struggling to pay his bills, had given her a pair of tiny diamond studs. She had promptly lost one of them down the shampoo bowl drain in the beauty salon.

Shari looked at her in the mirror. "You know something, Joanna? I don't think you realize how pretty you are. Just look at you. You're buff, you're tanned, you've got a perfect figure. If I had your height and your body . . ." Shari turned Joanna toward the mirror and together they perused their two reflections side by side. Shari, a good four inches shorter, shook her head, pressing her hands against her sides and stomach. "Look at me. Compared to you, I'm a fat lump."

Joanna laughed. "You aren't fat. You just need to lose a few pounds. You should go on a serious diet before you get your new boobs."

"Forget about me. When those horny single dudes that hang out at the Rusty Spur see you tonight, you'll probably have your pick."

Joanna huffed a sarcastic noise. "I'm really looking for that."

Assessing her reflection, Joanna was satisfied. She didn't dress up and go out often, but she was encouraged to see she could look good, even if she was pushing forty. There was no forgetting that Shari's thirty-sixth birthday meant Joanna's wasn't too far off.

Joanna climbed into the backseat of the Huddlestons' pickup, and they roared toward the New Mexico state line sixty miles to the west.

She sat behind Shari, lost in her thoughts and giving herself a mental pep talk. Going out with Shari and Jay without a male escort was nothing new. Joanna had done it many times, but the tinge of awkwardness was ever present. She hadn't noticed it so much in her twenties, but since she had passed the thirty mark, she thought of it often. She had lived single long enough not to fear or be intimated by going somewhere alone, but now, whenever she went with a couple, she had to battle that out-of-place feeling. Joanna Walsh, the odd woman out. Joanna Walsh, old maid. She repressed a groan.

At the Rusty Spur, as she walked behind her two friends through the wide entryway, that "woman alone" mood threatened to send her back to the pickup. Obviously her emotions were still teetering on the edge. The episode with Dalton had done something to her.

The Rusty Spur drew partiers from all over the Texas Panhandle and eastern New Mexico. Even a few brave hearts all the way from Oklahoma. It was the very definition of a cowboy honky-tonk. It had a rustic interior, including wooden plank walls and exposed bare trusses in a high ceiling. More like a barn than anything else, it was big enough to house a jumbo jet. No one could remember when it had been built, but it had a wooden dance floor worn to a smooth patina from the thousands of boots that had scooted across it to the beat of country-western tunes.

A band usually played on weekends, but tonight, a weeknight, the music came from a loud jukebox piped through an outstanding sound system. George Strait singing "All My Exes Live in Texas" sounded as if

George himself were in the building. Across Shari's shoulder, she saw uncountable couples shuffling around the floor. Everyone danced to George Strait. He was so beloved in Texas, he could probably be governor if he wanted to.

On a silent sigh, Joanna followed her host and hostess into the smoky, crowded room. The Rusty Spur hadn't so much as acknowledged the antismoking movement, much less taken steps toward a smokeless environment.

The seating was, and always had been, long wooden picnic tables with benches one had to climb over to sit down or stand up, either. She had never seen the tables in daylight, but at times when she had been here and bored out of her mind—and there had been some of those times—she had speculated how many layers of paint must cover these old tables. No fewer than twenty, she suspected. But as she had heard Jay say, "With all these drunks spilling beer and booze all over, they gotta have something that'll stand up to a good hosing."

Someone already seated hollered from all the way across the room and waved them over. At least a dozen of Shari's well-wishers from Hatlow were seated at the table. *Crap.* The evening was going to be even worse than Joanna had feared. *Oh, well,* she resolved. At least she knew them all. It would be no worse than a family reunion.

They pushed through the crowd to the table that butted right up to the dance floor. Through the hellos and how-are-yous Jay raised a hand and made a circle with his finger. "Beers all around?" He clumped off toward the bar.

Joanna had just removed her jacket and started to climb onto a spot on the bench seat when she felt a touch on her back. She turned and faced Owen Luck. *Oh, hell.*

"Hi, Jo," he said, a drunken grin on his face. "Feel like dancin'?"

Shari pushed her from behind. "Go dance, Joanna. Show us how it's done."

Joanna let herself be led to the dance floor. Vince Gill was singing something slow and romantic, and to Joanna's dismay, Owen pulled her against him as if he had a right to. Joanna ignored the affront—after all, he was from Hatlow—and tried to follow his steps. Owen was uninteresting company, and he was a worse dancer. All Joanna could think of was how much damage he might be doing to her custom-made boots.

Vince's song ended. They stayed on the dance floor and stumbled through a fast one by Gretchen Wilson. At the end of that, Joanna had had enough. "I'm kind of tired. Let's sit down, okay?"

Owen still wore that same silly grin. "Sure, Jo."

Joanna's teeth clenched. No one who knew her well used that nickname. She hated it. "Owen, I would really, really appreciate it if you'd call me Joanna."

"Oh. Okay. I'm going to get another beer. Want to go with me?"

"No, thanks. But you go ahead." Not wanting him to assume they had suddenly become a couple, Joanna made a beeline back toward her group. When she neared, she saw Jay standing beside the table. His back was to her and he was having an animated conversation with someone, gesturing with his beer bottle and his free hand. She could tell even from a distance that he was talking football. Three steps later, his conversation partner came into clear view. Dalton Parker.

A firestorm roared through Joanna's brain, and riding atop it was the memory of Dalton standing beside his bed stripping off his clothing. *Shit! And double-shit!* She needed a swallow of something liquid and cold in the worst way. She looked around but saw nowhere to hide.

"Joanna, what're you doing?" Shari called.

Joanna steeled herself for what she knew was coming.

As soon as Shari spoke, Jay turned around, exposing Dalton full front. "Hey, Joanna, look who's here."

Look? She couldn't have failed to look on pain of death. Just the sight of him tangled her tongue. He had on one of those new age button-downs with a Navajo zigzag pattern across the chest and tight-fitting Levi's. Yet another image came back of herself sitting half naked on the edge of his bed and staring at his fly. Her eyes locked there again for a few seconds before she was able to force them up to his face.

His intense chocolate eyes nailed her, accusing her of cowardice. He was too smart not to know she hadn't been out to the ranch to tend the hens and eggs because she was avoiding *him*.

"Hey," he said in that devastating raspy voice. His mouth turned up in a long smile.

Her heart had started beating so rapidly, she thought she might faint. All she could choke out was, "Uh, hi." She made a silly wave with her fingers.

"Hey, Parker, you like to dance?" Jay asked, touching Dalton's upper arm with his beer bottle.

"I've been known to trip a fandango or two," Dalton said, his eyes holding her captive.

"Well, there you go. Joanna's the best dancer here."

Dalton came toward her. Before she could figure out how to escape the awkward situation, he had taken charge. His hand was at the small of her back, warm and controlling, and he was guiding her to the dance floor. A part of her that rarely had a chance to surface thrilled at the possessiveness of it.

On the way to claim a space on the dimly lit floor, they passed Owen Luck, who stopped and stared at her, holding two bottles of beer.

"That your date?" Dalton asked, his strong left

hand taking her right wrist in a firm grip and pulling her around to face him.

She slanted a look up at him. "I don't have a date."

When she didn't assume the dance position by placing her left arm around his shoulder, he picked up her hand and placed it for her. Then his right arm encircled her waist and they stepped into an old George Jones "broken heart" two-step.

"Hard to believe," he said.

"What is?"

"That the best dancer here came to a dance hall without a date."

Under his firm lead, they made a turn and Dalton's knee slid between hers, but her skirt, which struck her midcalf, allowed his knee to go only so far. *Thank you, God.* "No one goes on dates anymore."

"They just hook up, right?" he said. "That's what we used to say about dogs in heat."

He expertly steered her into the crowd, his chin against her temple. Even through the scent of his clean and ironed shirt, the masculine smell from Monday night filled her nostrils, traveled to a primal part of her brain and made her even giddier. In perfect time to the beat, he moved with an easy rhythm that she picked up immediately. Big deal. Anyone could two-step.

"Times have changed," she managed to reply.

He two-stepped them to a quieter corner of the dance floor. "You've been busy, huh?"

"I'm always busy."

"Have I missed you when you've been out or have you not been out?"

She leaned back against his arm and looked into his face. "Out where? To get the eggs?" He didn't answer, just kept looking at her and turning them through the steps. "I needed some time off," she felt compelled to say and mentally censured herself for giving him an explanation. "Alicia likes extra money. She and her boyfriend have been taking care of it."

"I know. I helped them. I didn't know if you had told them about the rattlesnake, so I—"

"What?" Was he accusing her of endangering those kids? She tilted her head and cut him a malevolent look. "Pablo says he isn't afraid of snakes."

Dalton chuckled and drew her closer to him. "Calm down. I'm teasing you."

She made a mental harrumph.

He could dance, she now realized. Not in a showy way, but like a man who knew what to do and how to do it. No surprise there, really. She had already figured out he could do anything he wanted to. She let herself loosen up and began to enjoy herself. Dancing with a good partner was fun, and there weren't that many men around who fell into that category.

"I forgot all about this place," he said, " 'til Jay talked me into driving over here."

They were silent for a minute or two as their joined bodies moved smoothly in unison, a warm and heady reminder of just how well they fit together. All she could think of was every one of their intimate parts touching in the Monday night madness.

"Who is that guy?" he asked finally, cocking his head toward the direction where they had passed Owen Luck.

Why would he ask? she wondered. Even if she told him, he wouldn't know him. "He's an accountant in Hatlow. But he isn't a native."

He tilted his head back and laughed. "You mean a stranger moved to Hatlow thinking he could make a living?"

"He married one of the Johnson girls years ago and went to work for her daddy. Mr. Johnson died and now Owen owns the firm. Now he's a Hatlow fixture."

"Ah," Dalton said, leaning back and looking down at her. "So he's married, then."

A statement rather than a question, and it carried a tone that continued to arouse her curiosity. She believed he had no true interest in the state of the Lucks' marriage. Surely he didn't feel the threat of competition.

She disliked gossiping about people who were her customers, but something drove her to explain. "Him and Billie just got a divorce. It's a sticky situation, with Owen owning the firm her daddy started."

"The Hatlow saga continues," Dalton said as George Jones died away.

Vince Gill came on again singing a romantic waltz. Dalton might be able to cowboy dance, but she was sure he wouldn't know how to waltz. "We should sit down," she said, but to her surprise, he picked up the waltz step as aptly as a well-practiced dancer. "You're a good dancer," she told him as they glided and turned in the one-two-three step. "You must go out often."

"Nope. I couldn't find a shit-kicking joint in LA if I was gonna be shot."

"Then where did you learn?"

"Mom used to love to dance. Not that Earl ever took her. But sometimes when the asshole was off on one of his week-long toots, Mom and I would dance."

Joanna couldn't imagine the woman over whom a cloud of unhappiness seemed to constantly hang doing something as lighthearted as dancing. Not once had Clova ever mentioned it. Besides that, she doubted if he had learned to dance so well in the Parker ranch house's living room, and she was reminded of the great difference between his world and hers.

Dalton executed a graceful turn and Joanna could feel her skirt swing out behind her. Waltzing with someone who knew how gave her a sense of being in a fantasy.

The music changed pace. Brooks and Dunn sang out a swinging beat and Dalton segued them into it. He had so much natural rhythm, he didn't miss a step.

"I'm a little rusty at this," he said, reeling her out, then drawing her back and spinning her around his body.

To Joanna, he seemed anything and everything but rusty.

And he belonged to some woman in California who had a voice like Betty Boop's.

At the end of Brooks and Dunn, they were hot and sweaty and a little breathless. The outside temperature might be cool, but that wasn't true of the Rusty Spur's interior. The air-conditioning system was a swamp cooler the size of a boxcar on top of the building. It labored along but did a poor job.

"Want to take a breather outside?" he asked.

The custom at the Rusty Spur was for revelers to walk outside to the front of the building or the parking lot to hang out and cool off or smoke. "Don't tell me you're going to smoke," she said.

"You know I don't smoke. Let's go outside. I want to talk to you about something."

She looked up at him. "Like what? Can't we talk here?"

He nailed her with another one of those uncompromising looks. "Outside," he said. "I'll get us a beer."

She looked away and shrugged. "Okay, I guess. I'll meet you at the door. . . . I guess."

He clasped her chin between his thumb and finger and planted a hard, quick kiss on her lips. "Don't guess. Be there," he said firmly.

Chapter 23

Joanna's cheeks flamed. How dare he kiss her in front of everyone! Then a tiny rebellion flared within her. Who did he think he was, ordering her to wait for him?

He started toward the bar, making his way through the throng of sweaty dancers and drinkers, and she made a furtive scan of the people around her to see if anyone she knew had seen him kiss her. She saw only strangers. *Thank God.*

She debated whether to wait for him at the door as commanded or return to the table with the birthday crowd. She was still in the throes of making the decision when he returned carrying two Coors longnecks.

She didn't want a beer, but she took the bottle he offered her. He opened the plate-glass door for her and they walked out into the cool evening. He caught her upper arm and guided her away from the building, into the parking lot. They strolled along the backside of a long row of vehicles, their boots crunching on the caliche gravel that covered the parking lot.

She crossed her arms against the chilly evening, hanging on to the cold beer bottle with one hand. He tilted his head back and swallowed a swig of beer, then picked up her hand and linked her arm with his, affixing her tightly to his side. "You look pretty in a dress."

Feeling a little burst of pride at the compliment and

one of those silly girly emotions, she picked up a swatch of the chamois skirt and let it drop. "Thanks. I rarely wear one."

"Too bad. I like women to look like women. I'm old-fashioned that way." He tilted up his bottle and drank again.

Joanna had learned enough of him to know he was old-fashioned in many ways, a contradiction to what she had assumed on first meeting him. "What did you want to talk to me about?"

"I want to clear the air, Joanna. About Monday night. It was—"

"A mistake," she said, keeping her eyes straight ahead. Hashing the whole thing to death could only bring her more pain, and she was trying to move on. He might have said he liked her appearance, but she would be foolish to read something other than surface emotion into that. She freed her arm from his. "Don't worry. I'm a big girl. I don't expect anything from you. And you don't have to worry over . . . over what happened." She swallowed a swig from the beer bottle, the cold liquid causing her to shiver.

"Cold?" He looped an arm around her shoulders and drew her closer to his side. "And what is it you think did or didn't happen?"

"We got drunk and we . . . we did something dumb."

"Hot sex we both liked is dumb?"

"That isn't what I mean." *Damn him*. He had to know what she meant. "I'm talking about an . . . an accident."

"Spell that out for me."

She made a little noise, indignant. "You know what I'm talking about. But if you want to hear me say it, I will. Not that you'd worry, but in case you might, I expect my period in a day or two."

"Ah. You don't take the pill."

Not a question. "No, I don't."

He gripped her shoulder and stopped their progress. She looked up at him, though in the poorly lit parking lot, she couldn't clearly see his eyes. "What?"

He turned her to face him. "That wasn't what I came out here to talk about. But since we're on the subject, let's just get it out in the open. You know I'm a catch-cold kid. A bastard."

The statement sounded too harsh, and she winced. "You shouldn't say that about yourself."

"Why not? It's the truth and everybody around here has known it since before I was born."

"No one ever cared about it. You were a local hero. And everyone talks about how much smarter you were, er, *are*, than everyone else."

"Hell, I had to be smarter. And better than everybody at everything." He tilted up his beer bottle and drained it, then gripped her arm again and urged them forward. "I'll tell you something else. To this day, I don't know who my old man is."

Knowing Clova as well as she did, Joanna believed that.

"I don't give a damn anymore," he said, "but when I was a kid, I felt different. I thought back then that if I could just be smart enough and good enough, he, whoever he is, might want to claim me. But that still isn't what I'm getting at."

He stopped again and this time she turned herself to listen to him.

"Bottom line," he said, "and the point I'm making with all this chatter, is I'm the last guy who'd put some little kid on that kind of a downer. I wouldn't do it to a woman, either."

She heard the resolve in his words. Dammit, she believed him. "Dalton. It was wrong for both of us. I know you've got someone waiting for you in California. I knew it Monday night. If I hadn't drunk too much and . . ." A sigh escaped her chest. "I flew off the handle when she called because I was mad and hurt. It reminded me of . . ."

She couldn't finish, couldn't demean herself by putting into words the self-loathing that had been going on inside her head. "I'm mostly mad at myself. I'd like to forget it ever happened, okay? I still have to come out to the ranch and take care of my hens and my eggs, and you haven't left town yet. We both think a lot of your mom, so maybe—"

"You don't know so much. Maybe I don't look at it as a mistake. Or as wrong, either. And that brings me to what I wanted to say when we came out here. I don't usually discuss my private business, Joanna, but I want you to understand that Candace is not my girlfriend."

She grunted. "Don't insult my intelligence. I've heard you take phone calls from her. Are you saying you don't sleep with her?"

"I did. She lived with me a little less than a year. Twice during that time, I was overseas. Two months once and three months this last time."

Joanna forced herself not to try to calculate just how many months out of a year he had been at home and sharing a bed with Candace. Every cell in her body wanted to continue to believe him, but why bother? Taking men at their word hadn't worked out that well for her. And if she did let herself trust him, she might be an even bigger fool than she already had been. He still hadn't explained the *darlin'*s, the *babes*, and the *sweeties*. "I've heard you call her endearing names."

"Darlin', I call all women names. It's a habit. A way to smooth over the rough spots. Sometimes my words come out sounding more abrupt than I mean them to be."

"So what are you telling me? That underneath your crusty self you're a softie?"

"Well . . . yeah."

That, she wouldn't buy.

She forced herself to chuckle. "This is crazy, Dalton. You just want someone to fill your time and your bed while you're here. I'm not that person. Hatlow's full of single women. They might like being called babe and sweetie and darlin'."

"You must think I'm a real shit-heel." He grasped her elbow and they resumed walking along the parking lot.

"I didn't say that."

They had reached the dark green pickup Joanna recognized as Clova's. He propped a boot on the bumper and braced his elbow on his knee, placing his eyes level with hers. "I'm gonna tell you about Candace. Her name's Candace Carlisle. She's a wannabe actress. That and how she looks is all, and I mean *all*, she cares about.

"She continues to stay at my house in LA because if she didn't, she'd be homeless. I couldn't come to Texas for an unknown length of time and leave the house empty. Hell, in LA, somebody might steal it off its foundation. She called me yesterday morning because there's a problem with my swimming pool and she didn't know what to do."

Joanna's skepticism still rode high. She crossed her arms over her chest. "If that's all it was, why was it necessary to go outside so I couldn't hear you talk to her?"

"I don't know why. I don't think about shit like that. It was just a thoughtless reaction. She's broke. She doesn't have a job that amounts to shit. She doesn't have a damned thing. I didn't think it would be right to get into her private problems in front of somebody else. If she meant anything to me in the way you're thinking . . . if I felt any kind of special loyalty to her or to *any* woman, do you think I would've let Monday night take place? I'm not sixteen, you know. I do have a little self-control.''

Unable to come up with a quick rebuttal, she glared at him, though there wasn't enough light for him to see her skeptical expression.

"The whole damn thing in LA—it's got nothing to do with you and me, Joanna.'' He sliced the air with a flattened hand. "Nothing.''

Joanna heard a plea in his raspy voice, but the "whole damn thing in LA'' wasn't that simple. Too many unanswered questions loomed in her mind. "No matter what you say, you're soon going back to California. And to her.''

Now he laughed and straightened. "You're a hard woman, Joanna Walsh. This is Mom's truck and I'm freezing my ass off. Let's sit down inside.''

She drew in a great breath and let out a sigh. *Why not?* She, too, was cold. "Okay.''

He took her beer bottle from her, poured the remaining contents on the ground, then placed it along with his in the dually's bed. She thought of the West Coast influence in his life. Most of the guys she knew in Texas would have thrown the empty bottle into the brush without thought. Another blatant reminder of the difference between his experience and her own.

They walked to the pickup's passenger-side door. He bleeped the door latch and opened the door for her. She started to climb in but missed the step and lurched against him. He caught her and she found herself in his arms, looking into his face only inches away. She ducked her chin.

"Joanna,'' he said softly, "look at me.''

She didn't dare raise her head. She shook her head. Seconds passed.

"Coward," he said.

She shook her head again. "You're right. I'm really bad at games. Things mean things to me. I can't just . . . just have a fling and forget about it. I think I should go back inside."

His knuckle came under her chin and raised it until her face, her mouth, were inches from his. "I told you, you think too much."

His lips brushed hers, then hovered there. She breathed in the scent of his breath. How could she not kiss him back after the intimacy they had shared? She might be afraid of him, she might not trust him entirely, but she loved his kisses. Fool that she was, she touched his lips with hers tentatively, opened her mouth cautiously, but he responded as if she had said *Take me, I'm yours.* His tongue slid into her mouth and his arms came around her. Pressing her tightly against him, he kissed her in a way that felt even more savage than before. Or maybe it seemed so because tonight she was sober.

They broke for air, their breathing audible. "I haven't been able to stop thinking about you," he said. "I can't even get any work done."

Her heart warred with her head. Her body fought for its own needs. They stood without speaking for a few beats until her good sense won the upper hand. "Dalton, see how bad this is for both of us? We need to stop it. Let me go back inside."

"Do you think I can't tell that you like kissing me, Joanna? Listen to me. I didn't plan for this to happen, but I'm not sorry. I haven't met a woman in a long time I wanted to try something with."

And what the hell is "something"? "What am I supposed to say to that?"

"You're supposed to cut out the bullshit and admit you like me. And you liked Monday night as much as I did."

"Okay. I admit it. But so what?"

His mouth came down on hers again. Against her better judgment, she slid her palms over his shoulders until her arms went around his neck and answered him with her kiss. His hands found the hem of her top, slipped underneath and clasped the sides of her breasts. His mouth dragged from hers, over her cheek, down her neck. "You feel so good," he said softly, "And you taste so good." His lips found hers again. His thumbs began stroking her breasts through her bra. Her nipples grew rigid, and that traitorous urgent need for more began crawling around inside her.

He was the one who finally broke away. "God Almighty," he growled.

His hands moved down her sides, over her hips, and at the same time he sank to his knees, pulled her hips forward and buried his face in her skirt just at . . . *Oh, God* . . . "Dalton. Someone could see."

She felt the heat of his breath through her skirt, there on her most intimate place, and memory of his clever mouth and agile tongue heated her blood. Her pulse leaped to a rapid cadence. His hands worked their way beneath the hem of her skirt. They slid up the sides of her thighs, cupped her bottom and gently kneaded. "I do love your ass," he whispered.

Desire threatened to drive her to reckless abandon, but she gained control and glanced around the parking lot to see if anyone was watching them. She felt his fingers in the waistband of her bikini panties, felt the flimsy garment slip off her bottom and renewed heat surged within her. "Dalton . . ."

The panties fell down and caught on her boot tops. She was as trapped as if she were tied with a rope. Panic exploded inside her. Her heart began a tattoo, like a snare drum in a parade. She had never felt so paralyzed, torn between wanting him and not trusting him. And fearing someone might walk up on them. "Dalton. We can't do this. People are all over the place."

He lifted her foot and slid first one leg of the flimsy bikini over her boot, then the other. She grabbed for it but missed. He got to his feet, stuffing the panties into his jeans pocket. "Let's get in the truck," he said huskily.

"Oh, no. *Nada.* We can't do this. Give me back my—"

"Shh, shh. Baby, it's okay. It's dark out here. Nobody can see us. Just get in the truck."

She was so rattled she couldn't think. How could he affect her this way? She hefted herself up onto the running board, believing he would go around to the driver's side. And they would talk. And she would convince him how wrongheaded this was. Instead of walking around, he somehow slid under her and somehow his hands were under her skirt caressing her bare bottom again. "This is crazy," she said, her voice quivering. "We can't do this."

But even as she protested, she was helping him arrange her knees astraddle his lap. She felt her bare genitals open wide, and the very idea sent an explosion of heat to the heart of her sex, and all she could think about was feeling his touch there where she wanted it. She settled onto his lap. He was hard and the rough denim of his starched jeans rasped her tender flesh. Another wave of pure lust shot through her.

"Lift up a little," he whispered on a heavy breath.

Unable to tell him no, she complied. His fingers came between them and began to slowly stroke her. She was so wet, and his thick fingers knew just where to travel. "You're shaking, darlin'," he said softly as he deftly moved his fingers. "Just take it easy."

She closed her eyes and drew a shuddery breath. God, she wanted this. She wanted more of everything that had occurred in his bed Monday night. But most of all, she wanted *him.*

"See?" he whispered. "It's okay. Nobody's watching.... Lift up a little more, sweetheart."

This is worse than teenagers, her Good Girl persona screeched, but she had stopped listening to that side of herself. Though her right knee was trapped between the seat and the console, she braced her hands against his shoulders and somehow rose slightly on her knees.

Just the little extra space allowed two of his fingers to slip into her while his thumb fit perfectly into a place that destroyed all of her will. "Oh," she squeaked.

"Feel good?" he whispered, moving his fingers and thumb. His other hand slid under her top and his fingers found her nipple.

Ohgodohgodohgod. That weird tightening in her belly flared and demanded satisfaction. Her neck bent forward, her eyes squeezed shut. Her deep muscles began to flex against his fingers.

"Good?"

"No," she whimpered.

"Liar."

His fingers worked, and their breathing filled the pickup cab with heavy, humid air. She could come. She was on the edge. Just a few more seconds. She clenched her teeth to hold back the animal noises she now knew he could draw from her.

"Go ahead," he whispered. "Let it happen." His free hand cupped her neck and pulled her toward his mouth.

Just then the crunch of footsteps on gravel came alarmingly near and a couple approached the pickup parked beside them. She sank to Dalton's lap, his fingers still inside her.

"Evening, folks," the stranger said, bleeping his pickup door.

Dalton buzzed down the window. "Evening," he

said in a normal voice, while she sat there shaking worse than a scared rabbit.

"Good jukebox, huh?"

"Yeah. We like it."

"Not as good as the band," the woman said.

The two strangers continued a conversation about the music as they climbed into the pickup on their respective sides. As soon as they backed out, Joanna lunged for the door latch and clumsily freed herself before Dalton could stop her. She scrambled out of the pickup, at the same time adjusting her clothing.

"We shouldn't be doing this," she said, breathless and backing away from the door on shaking knees. "I mean it. I'm *not* doing this."

He didn't try to stop her. He just sat there on the passenger seat, his boot heels hooked on the threshold, his elbows braced on his knees. The overhead light shone on his face, revealing a scowl and eyes boring into her.

When she reached the bumper, she turned, broke into a run and didn't look back to see if he was behind her.

Inside the building's entry, she halted, gasping for breath. Her heart pounded. She was shaking like a wet dog on a cold day. She adjusted her clothing again and straightened her hair. Her cheeks felt warm, her body felt hot.

Oh, crap. Dalton still had her panties, and she was wet and slick between her thighs. When she had regained a modicum of composure a few seconds later, she skirted the far side of the tables and made her way to the ladies' room.

After she had washed and dried herself, she returned to the table and her Hatlow friends, her insides still trembling.

"Where the hell have you been?" Shari asked. "We already sang 'Happy Birthday' and everything."

"Oh, sorry. I didn't know you were ready to sing. I went out for a breath of air. It's hot in here." She glanced furtively over her shoulder to see if Dalton had come back inside, but she saw no sign of him.

She called on deep resources and fortified herself. Somehow she had to endure the remainder of the evening. Several guys, both some she knew and some she didn't, asked her to dance. She had never danced in a public place with any man while not wearing underwear. She felt both terrified and erotic at the same time. Shari kept saying things like, "What's wrong with you?" and "I must be drunk, because you're acting funny."

At convenient opportunities, she strained her sight watching for Dalton, but she didn't see him again. To her dismay, she was disappointed.

Chapter 24

At eleven o'clock, after Shari climbed onto the wooden bench seat at their table and started to accompany the jukebox in a loud voice, Jay announced it was time for his wife to go home. Joanna was so grateful, she volunteered to drive.

"I'm okay to drive," Jay said, grinning and helping Shari into her jacket. "I wasn't about to drink much. I gotta work tomorrow. And I knew Shari was gonna get shit-faced and need taking care of."

Joanna didn't insist. This was the nature of Shari and Jay's relationship. They looked out for each other. She suspected that if today hadn't been Shari's birthday, Jay would have been just as happy to sit at home in his recliner in front of TV, but Shari had had a party in her mind for days.

Outside, Shari flopped into the backseat of Huddleston's Well Servicing pickup, curled into a fetal position and fell sound asleep.

"Sit up front and talk to me," Jay said to Joanna. "It's a lonesome sixty miles from here to Hatlow."

Soon they were on the highway headed east. "Don't know where ol' Dalton disappeared to," Jay said. "I didn't see him leave."

Joanna wondered, too, but didn't comment.

"I enjoyed visiting with him," Jay said. "But he's changed from the way he used to be."

"How?" Joanna asked, interested now in what Jay

had to say about a man who, to Joanna, was an enigma.

"He was always tough, but now he's hard. And kind of edgy. You can't tell what he's thinking."

Indeed. Joanna had been trying to read Dalton's challenging personality from the moment she met him. Monday night's conversation over dinner and the pictures on his computer came back to her. She remembered the grim expression on his face when they had looked at the shots he had made of the bombing victims. "I suppose he's influenced by the places he's been and the things he's done. And he was in the marines."

"It's more than that. Dalton Parker was tough before he ever got to the marines. I'll tell you a story about him that says it all. When I was fifteen, I was the only freshman that made the A team. I was taking all kinds of shit from the upperclassmen, but Dalton always stopped it. He was a starter, and all the other guys listened to him.

"One time in the locker room, we were suitin' up to work out. When Dalton took off his shirt, he had half a dozen big purple marks on his back and arms. I have never had anything wrong with me that looked as sore as his back looked.

"Coach saw him and went over and asked him, 'What happened to you, Dalton?' But Dalton never gave an answer. He just shook his head and stared into his locker and went on with what he was doing. Then Coach said, 'You don't need to suit up today. Just take it easy.' Dalton said, 'No. I'll work out like everybody else.' And that was all there was to it."

Joanna thought of what she had learned of Dalton in her encounters with him. Though he must have been no more than seventeen when Jay was a freshman, Dalton's stoic response was no surprise. A lump

formed in her throat. She had to swallow it to hold
back tears. "Did he work out?"

"Yep. Just like there was nothing wrong. I'll never
forget it. None of us never said nothin' to him and he
never said nothin', neither. But after that, I looked at
him with different eyes. 'Course, the other fellas had
seen it before, and so had Coach. I found out later
Earl had whipped him with a belt, and that wasn't the
first time. I don't know what he done to deserve a
beatin' like that. Knowin' Earl's reputation, prob'ly
not much. After that, I wondered how many times ol'
Dalton come out and played when he was hurt without saying a word about it."

"I've heard my mom say how mean Earl Cherry
was to Dalton and Lane both," Joanna said.

"But there was a difference, Joanna. Daddy says
Earl Cherry's responsible for the mess of a man Lane
grew up to be. And he wasn't talking about bad genes.
Earl's meanness broke Lane. And Lane just folded up
inside hisself and got lost in boozin' and bull bustin'.
One of the reasons he was such a good bull rider was
'cause he just didn't give a shit about nothin'. But
Daddy says Earl never broke Dalton. If anything, it
was the other way around. That's what I mean about
Dalton being tough.

"He could've played college ball," Jay went on.
"Hell, he might've been good enough to've played pro
someday. He had the talent, had the brains, had the
balls. And as for will, I guess you'd have to kill him
to outdo him. It must be that Comanche blood."

Joanna had always discounted those kinds of remarks about the Parker family's "Comanche blood."
How could it be a factor? Dalton, Lane and their
mother's ancestral "blood" was diluted by generations. But she looked across the console, wondering
whether Jay's assessment of Dalton's personality could

be accurate. And if it were, how deeply would a mere woman have to touch him to find his soul? "Why do you think he didn't go ahead and play college ball?"

"I don't know for sure. Everybody talks about it being Earl and Clova's fault, but I think, deep down, Dalton, pure and simple, didn't want to. He wanted to do what he did. That was something I always admired about him, even when we was kids. He always did what he wanted to. It was one of the things that made him different from the rest of us."

They rode a few more miles in dark silence, the dash lights casting the pickup cab in a low glow. Jay hadn't even turned on the radio. "Have you ever whipped your boys?" Joanna asked, though she was certain she would have known if he had.

He snorted. "I've never laid a hand on those boys. And God knows they've needed it a time or two. I just couldn't do it. And if I did, Shari would take after me with a butcher knife."

An anger sprang into Joanna. Why hadn't Clova taken after Dalton's stepfather with a butcher knife?

Jay went on to tell stories from schooldays about football games played and girls dated. Joanna listened, but her mind was on Dalton and what he had said in front of his computer monitor Monday evening: *When I was a kid, I thought I had it rough. After I left home, and eventually the States, I found out what rough was. There's a lot of sadistic lunatics out there. Some of them are running countries. Compared to them, Earl Cherry was a creampuff.*

Though she had barely known Dalton as a teenager, now she, too, recognized the change Jay saw in him.

Jay dropped her off at home at midnight. She washed her face, removed her clothing and slipped into her old pink chenille robe. Then she keyed on the TV to catch tomorrow's weather report, all the while wondering if she could reach Alicia early tomorrow morning and persuade her to be responsible for the eggs one more day. After tonight in the Rusty Spur's parking lot, she would find it more difficult than ever to face Dalton. His very presence turned her into a different person. Lord, when would he go home?

And if he didn't go soon, what was she going to do? She had to take care of her hens and the eggs. She already worried what catastrophe being absent only two days had wrought.

Stress always made her hungry, so she went to the kitchen for ice cream. And that's where she was when her doorbell chimed. Feeling a small drop in her stomach, she glanced at the oven clock. No one came to her house at this hour. She switched off the kitchen light, went to the door, peered through the peephole and saw a man standing on the little square porch. Who else but Dalton. A little dance of joy erupted within her.

He knocked then. She opened the door a crack and peered through. "What is it?"

"Brought you a beer." He held up a six-pack of something.

"I don't want any. It's late. I'm going to bed."

"We need to talk."

"I already fell for that in the parking lot."

"Joanna, c'mon, let me in."

She pressed her forehead to the door's edge as the erotic episode in the front seat of Clova's pickup barged into her mind. It seemed unreal that just a few hours ago, his fingers had been inside her. Lust and her good sense were still waging a battle within her. *Get over it,* she told herself. *Just because you've already slept with him doesn't mean you have to again.* "I'll let you in here only if you promise Monday night or the parking lot won't happen again."

"I said 'talk.' "

Conscious that she was naked beneath her robe, she

retied it tightly, then opened the door and stood back for him to enter.

"Fridge?" he said and held up the six-pack of Coors longnecks. She could see two empty slots in the carton. "You're still drinking? And you're driving?"

"I'm not drunk." He started for the kitchen as if he had been in her house before.

She followed him and clicked on the overhead light, brilliantly lighting the kitchen. She stood with her hip leaning against the counter, her arms crossed over her chest. "I hope you brought back my underwear. Those panties go with a matching bra."

He popped the top on a bottle and offered it to her with a grin. "Souvenir."

"Of what? Nothing memorable happened."

"No?"

He offered the beer to her again, and against her better judgment, she took it. "It's the middle of the night. Why don't you just go home and go to bed?"

He looked around. "So this is your house? Mom said you own it."

"Well, me and a mortgage company."

He stepped to the doorway leading out of the kitchen and looked across the dining room to where her TV was on in the living room. "*Law and Order*, huh? I watch that sometimes."

She lifted a shoulder in a half shrug. "It's a rerun."

He looked back at her for a few seconds, then walked over, took the beer from her hand and set it, along with his, on the counter. "Joanna." He braced a hand on the counter, his eyes homing in on hers. His raspy voice came low and softly. "Something's happening with us. We need to come to terms with it."

"And from your point of view, coming to terms would be what, hopping into bed again?"

"Maybe. That's one way to ease the tension."

She stepped back, putting space between them. "You know what? I can think of a hundred ways to ease tension. If nothing else, there's always a cold shower."

One corner of his mouth tipped into a smile. Or maybe it was a smirk. "Is that what you did when you got home tonight?"

She turned her body away from him, but she couldn't turn her eyes from his. "No."

"It's only a temporary fix anyway. You know, you left me in a helluva shape out there in that parking lot."

This encounter was headed in a direction she dared not go. She closed her eyes and arched her brow. "Dalton, please. Go home."

He stepped in front of her, and from out of nowhere, moisture blurred her sight. Dammit, she was no match for him. A tear escaped one eye and trailed down her cheek.

He placed a knuckle under her chin and lifted it. "Don't cry," he said softly. He wiped her damp cheek with his big rough thumb. "I won't hurt you."

That wasn't true. When she was in his company her brain went to lunch and left her defenseless. He could, and probably would, crush her and leave her as easily as he could crush a paper cup and throw it in the trash.

His hand grasped her arm and drew her to him. Weak-willed dummy that she was, she let herself be drawn. As his mouth moved closer, she looked into his face. "When I said you could come in, you promised you wouldn't do this."

Their gazes held for long seconds. "Tell me to stop and mean it," he said, "and I will. If it's what you really want."

What she really wanted? God help her, what she

wanted was *him*, and she was thrilled he wanted her, if for only a short time. She remained mute, paralyzed, unable to deny him, or herself, anything.

His lips touched hers in the gentlest of sipping kisses. She responded in kind, not minding, even savoring, the yeasty taste of beer. When his lips lifted from hers, slick devil that he was, he tugged at the belt around her waist. It easily came undone, leaving her robe hanging open. They both watched him part the robe. His fingertips brushed her skin and sent a frisson up her spine. His eyes, fierce and dark with desire, locked on the exposed slice of her nude body. Her nipples had grown rigid, a pulse beat in her belly. The tacit urgency that thrummed around them almost sucked the air from the space between them. "See?" he said softly. "You're glad I came by. I wouldn't have if I'd thought you'd turn me away."

She closed her eyes and shook her head. By letting him into her house, she had already acknowledged he had defeated her best intentions. Tears rushed to her eyes again. "Damn you," she said.

His hands slid beneath the robe and she moved against him as if he were a lodestone.

"I want you," he whispered.

His powerful arms wrapped around her in an unyielding embrace. She felt his strength, his solid body, the erection that felt like steel against her bare belly. His mouth covered hers and his hands moved down, his fingers dug into her bottom as his tongue swept deeply into her mouth and rubbed against hers in a sexual rhythm.

She surrendered her last fraction of resistance, hooked a foot around his leg and rubbed herself against his rigid fly. They went at each other like animals, tongues dueling, bodies melded. The room began to spin and she knew she was lost. Desperate for breath, she tore her mouth from his and pushed away, staring into his eyes.

"What?" he said, panting.

"You remember that shotgun in my egg-washing room?" Her voice came out a flutter.

"If there's anything I never forget, it's an armed female."

"God as my witness, Dalton Parker. If you break my heart, I'll shoot you."

"I'll keep that in mind."

She took his hand and led him to her bedroom.

She switched on a bedside lamp and turned back the covers while he jerked through yanking off his boots, sinewy muscles moving in his forearms as he worked. She couldn't imagine that he was nervous, but she saw his strong hands trembling. As he shucked his jeans and shorts, she let her eyes feast on his body in all of its masculine beauty. She loved looking at him, couldn't keep from staring at his erection. The idea that she could arouse him so thoroughly sent her on a rarely felt power trip that made her giddy.

He slid between the covers and looked up at her, waiting. She dropped her robe and started to join him, but he said, "Wait. Let me see you. I haven't gotten to look at you."

She stood there for a few seconds, her eyes closed as she felt his gaze rove over her nakedness. "You're a beautiful woman," he said.

She opened her eyes, he threw open the covers and she crawled in and met him in the center of her queen-size bed. As she pressed herself to him, his finely honed torso felt familiar, as if she had known it many more nights than one.

No words passed between them. What was left to be said? They both knew what they wanted. Without inhibition, she showed him the passion she felt, the pleasure he gave her, sighing and moaning as his hands and fingers tantalized her sensitive places. She touched him, too, cradling his hairy scrotum in her palms, teasing his thick penis with her fingers in ways she had never done before. He groaned and hissed his delight. Fire blazed between them. Need consumed them. When neither of them could stand it any longer, she urged him between her thighs.

"What about a rubber?" he said huskily, kneeling and poised. "I've got—"

"My period's due any day." She reached for him and took him inside her, letting out a great sigh as his hot flesh pushed into her. He seated himself and she felt the shudder that passed over him. For a few beats they didn't move.

"God, Joanna. I feel like this is where I ought to be," he said.

A thrill lifted her heart and she floated in euphoria. "I feel like it's where you ought to be, too."

She wanted more, all, everything. Their eyes locked as they moved together in a slow, silky rhythm. She savored the heat of him up inside her, the soft friction of his flesh moving against hers. Soon smooth became turbulent, breath became ragged and that odd little tickle cried out for relief. She lifted her knees and took every inch of him to her deepest place. He answered her silent plea, his hips pumping hard and fast. She dug her heels into his buttocks and met his powerful thrusts until the need overtook all reason and the demon of pleasure captured her body and soul. She came hard, crying out as her deep muscles contracted and clutched over and over at his penis.

In seconds his body became taut and he pushed hard and ground against her. "Aww, God," he groaned and she felt the wet warmth of his semen.

He lay gasping for air where he had fallen. She held him close, feeling his heart beat against hers. Her chest had never felt so full of emotion. It had to be nothing more than the passion, the ecstasy of the sweet release. It couldn't be true that she loved him.

His warm breath rasped against her ear. "Jesus Christ, Joanna. . . . Eight seconds. . . . They say that's . . . all it takes."

Despite being shaken all the way to her center, she found a tiny laugh. "Does that equate it to a bull ride?"

"You're into rodeos?"

"Who hasn't been to a rodeo?"

"Babe, most of the people in the world haven't been to a rodeo."

"Their loss," she said.

He laughed. "The point I was making, smarty-pants, is it's a damn shame it's so short when it feels so damn good."

"Yeah," she said and hugged him tighter.

For a long while, they lay in each other's arms, his head on her breast, her fingers stroking his hair. "You have curls," she said. "I hadn't noticed them before."

"They don't show up until my hair gets long. I haven't had a haircut lately. Now why do you suppose that is when I know the woman who's probably the best haircutter in town?"

"Clova's hair is so straight. Your dad must have been curly haired."

"I'll never know."

"In the parking lot, you said you don't care that you don't know him. Is that true? Do you really not care?"

"I don't. I don't know what I'd do with the information if I had it. There are a hell of a lot of things I want more."

She scooted down, turned on her side and faced him, their faces only inches apart. "What are they? The things you want more. Deep down, your most secret yearning."

His lips tipped into a smile and he trailed a finger down the side of her face. "You tell me first."

"I don't know. I don't think about that question very often. Security, maybe. I want to be sure I can take care of myself. Everyone keeps reminding me that I'm thirty-five years old and not married."

"You've never wanted to get married?"

"I've never found anyone who I thought could take care of me better than I can take care of myself. I used to think I would eventually. But now I don't know. I'm awfully set in my ways. Maybe I've stopped looking. I've sort of gotten used to being called an old maid."

He chuckled. "That's silly, calling you an old maid. They're all jealous of your independence."

"I'm that, all right. Does it bother you, me being independent?"

"I admire you. You're smart and resourceful and you're doing pretty well in this town that has a lousy economy."

"It's bothered some of the guys I've known."

He grinned. "I'm not some guy. Darlin', I'm your new lover. Now I'll be the first to admit I haven't always hung out with smart women, but that wasn't because I felt threatened by a woman who could think."

She didn't have to ask why he hung out with women he classified as unable to think. She knew. He didn't want the challenge of a partner who might be capable of outmaneuvering him. So in his scheme of things, where did that alpha male thinking put Joanna Walsh? Her feeling for him seemed only to intensify with every encounter, but she knew herself well enough to know that at the end of the day, she would allow him to bulldoze her only so far. "Dalton Parker. You've given yourself away. You're one of those male chauvinist pigs."

He snuggled closer. "Guilty."

Guilty, for sure, she thought. And probably never going to change.

They lay for a few more silent minutes until she realized he hadn't kept his end of the bargain. He hadn't revealed his deepest yearning. "You want to know what else I am?" she said. "I'm also good at people watching. I've been doing it for years. Want me to guess what you want most?"

"Sure. Go ahead."

"I've given it a lot of thought."

"Why would you?"

"Don't you know without me telling you?"

He didn't answer, just stared at her with those beautiful, mysterious eyes.

"I think you're afraid of feeling," she said. "I think the thing you want most is not to get your feelings hurt."

His relaxed smile fell away. "No one wants his feelings hurt."

"But it's more important to you. You're more afraid to risk it than most. I'll bet that if anyone could ever reach you deep down, they'd find a gentle soul whose heart is as fragile as china."

He pulled away from her and sat up. "You were right about this bed. A man could get used to this."

She was right, she thought smugly. "Change the subject if you want to, but that's the real reason you're still single."

He braced a hand on the mattress and looked back at her. "Wrong. The cottage and picket fence routine has never fit my life. I've needed to be able to pick up at a moment's notice and take off for the latest massacre in Butt-fuck, No-Man's-Land. Worrying over who's gonna feed the dog just wouldn't cut it. It's been hard enough worrying about my house and swimming pool."

"If your life's that unscheduled, why do you even own a house?"

"Mostly because I want to. I've had it a long time. It's all I got out of my divorce. And now, the way things are in California, it's worth a lot of money." He reached over to the nightstand and picked up her digital clock. "Christ, it's two thirty. We should get cleaned up and go to sleep. I've got to pick Mom up from the hospital in a few hours."

They left the bed and washed themselves. As she dried, he came behind her, wrapped his arms around her and pulled her against him. "Don't analyze me," he said softly against her neck. "It makes me nervous."

Smiling, she leaned into him, loving the skin-to-skin embrace. She saw their reflection in the mirror, his image tanned to golden all over, hers white as a fish belly except for her arms and neck. His hands caressed her breasts and belly, and something else came to her. "Dalton?" She turned in his embrace, placed her arms around his neck and looked up at him. "You can trust me with your heart, Dalton. I'd never hurt you."

His eyes locked on her face for a long moment. Then he kissed her.

Chapter 25

The next morning, Dalton left Joanna's house before daylight. The happiness he felt bordered on being euphoric, in spite of the conflict raging within him. This was ridiculous, going silly over a woman, especially a woman in Hatlow. His life was in LA. That is, his house, his studio and his stuff were in LA. He had traveled so much in recent years, he was hard-pressed to know where his *life* was.

Even with those realities seated in his mind, all the way from town to the ranch, disquieting questions kept popping up. Questions like, could he fit back into his family? During *this* visit, more so than in the past, he had been reminded how much he loved the ranch and even West Texas. Could he operate from here as easily as from LA? Transportation in and out of this part of the world had once been inconvenient for anyone who wanted to travel beyond the area, but it had improved.

In Hatlow, he wouldn't have to rely on a house sitter when he left town. And if he forgot to lock the front door, he wouldn't worry over everything being there when he returned. He wasn't so attached to his house in LA, but he loved his fantastic pool. Still, the house and the city itself had become a burdensome place to call home.

Finally, the question that had been pushing and shoving to get to the top of the list came at him.

Did he want Joanna Walsh to fit into his future? This morning, he knew only one thing for sure about her. For a reason he couldn't define, she stood out from other women he had known in recent years.

He hated indecision. So when he turned into the ranch's driveway, he stopped whiffling. Though he'd had little sleep, he had a busy day ahead of him. As soon as he brought his mother home from the hospital, they could have that conversation about the wildcatting venture. Foremost in his thoughts, though, was Joanna's chicken operation and the location of the old oil well.

You can trust me with your heart, Dalton. I'd never hurt you.

Her words came back to him as he shaved. Oh, yeah. She would work with him on the oil well. Not only was she a reasonable person, she cared about him. She cared about everybody. No wonder his mother thought so much of her.

He cooked breakfast, grinning like a fool as he broke two eggs from the Walsh's Naturals carton into a frying pan. What a gutsy woman Joanna was to take on a business as fraught with catastrophic possibilities as raising chickens and selling eggs.

He had no sooner finished eating and cleaning up in the kitchen than he heard Joanna's truck out front. His heart lifted in a way it hadn't in a long time. "Wait a minute," he told the unruly organ. "Just cool it."

He met her in her egg-washing room. She looked fresh and pretty, though he knew she had slept no more than he. She came into his arms with a good-morning kiss so tempting, his thoughts traveled to his new mattress in the house. Before things got out of control, he set her away.

"What are you doing out here?" she asked, brightening the whole room with her smile. "Don't tell me you're going to help me gather eggs."

"Snakes seem to like you. One might come to visit."
He gave her a wink and slapped her bottom.

Through the egg-collecting chore, he covered his
dislike for the chickens with sarcastic comments, attempting to be funny. Joanna laughed at his wry jokes,
but he suspected she only humored him. He didn't
care. He liked making her laugh. After they had gathered dozens of eggs, he consented to letting her teach
him how to hook up the egg washer, a task that gave
him another opportunity for cynical wisecracks.

Before going to her shop in town, she offered herself and Alicia as tomorrow's helpers for rounding up
the cattle to be trucked to market in Amarillo. He
could hardly wait. He hadn't been on horseback in
years.

As soon as she left, he drove to town to pick up his
mother. He found her jovial and eagerly waiting to be
released. He had been waiting just as eagerly to discuss the well-drilling venture with her.

As soon as she had settled back into the house, he
made a fresh pot of coffee and invited her to sit down
with him at the dining table. He had printed a generic
land-lease document from a Web site and filled in the
blanks. He picked it up and placed it on the table. "I
think I've got it figured out, Mom," he told her. "A
way to raise the cash the ranch needs and maybe make
life a little easier around here."

As he explained the ins and outs of his idea, to his
delight, she was receptive and enthusiastic. That is,
until he told her where he wanted to place the well.

"But we can't do that," she said. "I promised that
piece o' land to Joanna. I already got Clyde making
a deed."

Wariness crawled through Dalton. "What do you
mean?"

"I tol' Joanna I'm gonna give her that section where
she's got her chickens."

Section? Did she mean *section?* Jesus Christ, a section was 640 acres. "That won't work, Mom." He couldn't keep the sharpness from his reply. "That's where I want to drill the well. You'll have to tell her you're not able to do that."

His mother's dark eyes snapped with anger. "I ain't tellin' her no such thing. She ain't rich. She's got money tied up in those coops and the fencing and her supplies. And in the chickens, too. If you go in there with a bunch of loud equipment and commotion, it'll mess her up."

Hot anger began to inch its way through him, but he kept his emotions in check, still believing the dilemma could be reasoned through. "Mom. We're talking about a few chickens here that don't even belong to you. What's that compared to saving this ranch?"

"And just what's she supposed to do with her chickens? They ain't like cows. You can't just herd 'em around or get 'em all upset. They got feelin's."

Chicken feelings? Bullshit. He leaned forward, holding his mother's gaze. "I don't know what she'll do. That's not the problem I'm dealing with. But chickens or no, you can't just on a whim give away a bunch of land to someone outside the family. This has been Parker land forever."

"It ain't a whim. Joanna *is* family to me. Nobody's ever treated me as good as she has." Her dark eyes began to shimmer with moisture.

She might be on the verge of tears, but her words came at him like a punch. And at the same time, so did the realization that this was what his absence from Hatlow and his failure to maintain a relationship with his mother had wrought.

"And I don't have nothin' else to give her," she added when he didn't reply.

A kaleidoscope of unpleasant childhood memories came at him. *Perhaps not,* he thought bitterly, but she

had somehow managed to find enough money to hire
a lawyer to do something unnecessary. He rose, scraping
his hand through his hair and putting distance between
himself and the woman he had never understood.

He walked over to the dining room window that
overlooked the driveway and the chicken yard. In his
opinion, those friggin' chicken houses looked like piles
of trash. The mismatched feeders and waterers looked
like a cobbled-up hodgepodge. And he didn't even
know a word to express his opinion of the stupid flags
and plastic owls perched around the chicken yard. In
general, the whole area suddenly looked even trashier
and dirtier than before.

Memories tangled in his mind: the hours of love-
making in Joanna's bed; his entire childhood and all
of the times his mother had failed him or had taken
Earl's side against him. "Those chickens live on fewer
than twenty acres. That's a far cry from a section."

His mother sat back in her chair. "If you just got
to do it, drill your well somewheres else. It ain't like
there ain't no more land." The cold defiance in her
voice pierced him.

Dalton's teeth clenched. He couldn't believe she
could be so pigheaded to her own detriment. But as
that thought came to him, so did another one. She
was perfectly capable of cutting her nose off to spite
her face. God knew he had seen her do it a hundred
times.

"No," he said firmly, giving as good as he got from
her. He went back to the table, slid into his chair and
leaned forward, both hands on the table. "Mom. I'm
willing to invest a helluva lot of money to try to save
this goddamn place. Not for myself and not even for
Lane. For *you*. I found that old well with a metal
detector. It's right square underneath that donkey
shack. It'll cost me less and the experts say it's more
of a sure thing to drill alongside it."

She turned her head and looked away. "I wish I'd never told you where that ol' oil well was. I ain't goin' back on what I promised Joanna."

Patience abandoned him like a flock of spooked buzzards. Rage he hadn't felt in years exploded within him. "Look at me, Mom."

Her head slowly turned back to him, her mouth set in a flat line.

"Here's a news flash," he said softly, struggling to keep a civil tone in his voice and holding her eyes with his. "I've taken a pretty good look around here. This place is overstocked, overgrazed and debt heavy. Everything, the barns, the outbuildings, the fences, they're all falling apart from neglect. And you're letting a woman use what was one of our prime pastures to raise a bunch of goddamn stinky chickens without even paying for it. All of the above adds up to gross incompetence."

Her eyes narrowed, but she sat there stoically and took his venom. But, hell, he figured she was conditioned to it. How many times had he seen her cowed and even knocked around by Earl, only to come to the bastard's defense later if somebody condemned him.

"You're out of options," he went on. "Me paying the taxes bought you some time. The government helping to pay Lane's medical bills will save you a few dollars, but the way things are going, you can't keep this place up.

"Lane's coming home in another couple of weeks, but as for work, he's gonna be worthless. In fact, taking care of him will add more work. You're not physically able to do it all, and you can't afford to hire help. Hell, Lane won't even have a goddamn driver's license when the dust all clears here. I don't know the DUI laws in Texas these days, but they might even throw his ass in jail. How're you gonna manage after that?"

He put his fingertips on the edge of the lease and nudged it closer to her. "The ranch and the land have always meant more to you than anything." He paused, letting silence surround them. "Or *anyone*," he added because he felt mean. "I recommend you do yourself and the Parker ranch a favor and sign this lease. Let me try to fix this problem. Because I won't lift a goddamn finger without a legal document that protects my money."

Her lips twisted into a sneer. "Money. If that's all you're interested in—"

"Damn right, that's all I'm interested in. Because you know what? Mine came a little harder earned than some. Too many times it came at the risk of my life."

"Don't throw that up at me. And don't tell me you wanna do this for me. You wanna do it for y'own self. I ain't dumb. I know you're gonna get money out o' this for y'self."

She sat there glaring at him with a look that had been directed at him often in his youth. He no longer feared it. Christ, he had been glared at by machete-toting dictators. "And what's wrong with that?" he said coldly. "I've never asked you for anything, Mother. But I'm asking you now for a little cooperation. God knows, you owe me a little something if, for no other reason, because I'm your son."

She sat there a few beats. Clova the Stoic. "I'll have to think on it," she said.

Dalton tapped his finger on the lease. "Don't take too long. I need to get back to LA. This trip to Hatlow's costing me."

She stood up and walked to her bedroom.

"Goddammit," he growled. He shoved his chair back and stomped outside. He got all the way to the barn before he began to calm and his racing heart began to slow. Inside the dim space of the ramshackle barn, he sank to a hay bale, realizing for the first time since his return that *nothing*, absolutely *nothing*, had changed between him and his mother.

He let a dose of self-pity seep into his thinking. In school, the only period of his life he and his mother had really shared, he won many scholastic awards, but she had rarely been present when he received them. He had been an above-average athlete, but she had never gone to watch a game or a track meet. She had been present at his graduation from high school, but, he had always believed, only because he had informed her he would be leaving home for good the next day. In the Marine Corps, he had climbed in rank in record time, but he hadn't told her and she hadn't asked. In fact, to this day, she didn't even know the branch of the military in which he had served. She thought he had spent eight years in the army.

In the span of a heartbeat, he squelched the unrealistic notion he had entertained that he might actually come back here and make this his base of operation. So he could be around "family." *Family*. That was still a fuckin' joke.

His mother's promise to give Joanna a whole goddamn section of land showed the two women's relationship in a new light. Just how long had Joanna been working on his mother to instill such blind, hardheaded loyalty? Jesus Christ, had his initial impression of Joanna been accurate after all? *Had* she taken advantage of a lonely old woman?

He thought of the special connection he thought he had found with Joanna, which might be the biggest joke of all. Had he fallen into the trap of her Pollyanna notions of the world? Had he been duped by the naive hope of a small-town girl who, by her own admission, had seen nothing of the world? Or had she simply duped him in the same way she had conned his mother? Quite an accomplishment considering that he thought he was beyond being fooled by women.

He walked to the barn door and looked out into the pasture where the horses grazed. His enthusiasm for saddling the gray and rounding up the cattle tomorrow had vanished. Now it became a huge chore he dreaded. Yep, he had to get out of here. Had to get back to the swimming pool he had missed daily.

His cell phone bleated and he plucked it from his belt. "Yo. Hi, Candace."

"Dalton. Guess what." He heard breathless excitement in her voice. "I got a part. I've got to leave here."

"A part?"

"Remember that TV Western I auditioned for a long time ago?"

Dalton searched his mind but had no memory of it. It seemed that she had been auditioning for some damn movie every week. "Not offhand, but—"

"They're shooting in British Columbia," she said excitedly.

"That's good, baby. I'm glad."

"I've got to get up there by next week."

His stomach sank. "Christ, so soon? The house will be vacant."

"I guess that's *your* problem, Dalton. You're the one who said I needed to get a job and start taking care of myself. I stayed here and looked after things like I said I would, but now I want to go."

Dalton rolled his eyes. Yep, he had told her that because it was true. He had no right to detain her. "Look, darlin', I'm about to wind up here. Another week. Can you wait 'til I get back?"

"They said they want me to be there next week. I've already bought my plane ticket."

For a fleeting moment, he wondered where she had

gotten the money for a plane ticket. He had given her a little money for her efforts, but he doubted it was enough to buy a plane ticket to Canada. "Okay, I hear you. I've got a couple of things going on here right now, but I'll call you back tonight and we can talk about it."

"Oh, and Dalton?"

"Yeah, what?

"A real estate agent came by here. She said someone would like to see this house, but I told her it isn't for sale."

"Did she leave a card? What's her phone number?"

"Du-uh. I didn't take her card. I told her the place isn't for sale."

Dalton disconnected and overcame the urge to throw the phone against the barn wall. Candace had gotten a job? *Jesus, Joseph and Mary.* She had actually gotten hired by somebody. And she wanted to leave town. Now he had no choice. He *had* to return to LA.

Mentally making a new plan, he returned to the house. He went to the refrigerator and dragged out a beer. His mother came into the kitchen.

"I thought about it," she said. "I don't un'erstand why you drillin' your well would keep me from givin' Joanna a little piece o' land."

"A section isn't a little piece. A section will graze twenty or so cows. Why would you want to give away a part of the ranch? To her or to anybody? I don't understand it, Mom. You've let her have run of things around here for over two years. And in the second place, it isn't just *my* oil well. As clichéd as it might sound, I'm trying to save the goddamn ranch. And right now, the oil well is about the only idea I've got and about the best I can do."

"I don't wanna talk about it," she said. "I've signed your lease." She handed over the document. "But it ain't keepin' me from givin' Joanna land for her chickens."

He took the document, holding back the sigh of relief he felt over her signing it. "For all I care, you can give her the the whole goddamn place. Except for that land around that old oil well."

He glanced down at the childlike signature. He had forgotten that his mother could barely read and write. Her father, his granddad, had seen no reason for women to be educated.

With the lease in hand, he was free to pursue Plan A. He started for the front door, folding the document and sliding it into his shirt pocket.

"Dalton?"

He stopped at the door without looking back. "Yeah?"

"I only signed that lease for one reason. I signed it 'cause you're my son. If you make a well . . . if the deal turns out and it helps the ranch, that's just a extra blessin'."

For him, the fight was over. He turned and faced her. "Mom—"

"You don't have to tell me I owe you, Dalton. I know it. I know I never did right by you."

"Water over the dam," he said in a lifeless monotone. "I've put it behind me. I don't even hate Earl as much as I used to. I've seen worse."

"I wish I could make you know how it was," she said. He heard sorrow in her voice, saw pain in her eyes. Her hand braced on the dining table and she sank to a chair. "When I was a girl, I didn't have nobody takin' up for me, no brothers or nothin'. Not my mama, either. I 'spect it wasn't that easy for Daddy to find somebody to marry me. But he found Earl. I thought I didn't have no choice. Then after Lane come along, well . . . my future was . . . was what it was."

Dalton's temples began to throb. Two hours' sleep wasn't enough. "What are you telling me? You didn't care about Earl?"

A tear trailed down her cheek. "I mostly felt sorry for him, Dalton. He was weak."

Dalton shook his head and stared at the ceiling, begging for understanding. "But he treated you awful. He treated me and Lane awful. If you knew you were the stronger, why did you put up with it?"

"It was what Daddy expected me to do." She shook her head and wiped her eyes. "I was his wife, Dalton."

Only today, Dalton had begun to consider that the same provincialism that had influenced and plagued all of the previous generations of Parkers was still alive and well in his mother. If he hadn't yet come to a solid conclusion about that, this conversation confirmed it. As tolerance and compassion filtered through him, his heart opened and he saw his mother in a way he hadn't seen her before. He walked over and put a hand on her shoulder.

"When you was a little boy," she said, her eyes downcast, "I used to think you'd be the one that would keep the ranch a-goin' after I'm dead and gone. If you could come back here, maybe things could be different now."

A burn rushed to his eyes and a huff burst from his throat. "I don't know, Mom. I just don't know." He squeezed her shoulder. "But I'll think about it."

She nodded. "That'd be real good if you would."

He squeezed her shoulder again and walked outside without looking back. He was in danger of bawling himself. He crossed the driveway to the chicken yard and stared at the nasty damn things gathered in little clusters, scratching and pecking and clucking in the sun. Two began to peck at another one, squawking and chasing it away from their little group. He thought of women.

That stupid self-pity came back again. Most of the deep pain in his life had been administered by women.

Before negative thoughts could derail him, he pulled himself together, plucked his cell phone from his belt and called Skeeter Vance.

Chapter 26

Though having so little sleep made Joanna feel as if she were functioning in a vacuum, her day had gone better than any in a long while. The sun had shone brightly in a cloudless sky, the temperature had been warm rather than hot and the air almost crackled with the ambience of fall. Her mom had refrained from carping at her about nothing.

She had spent a huge block of time smiling at her memories and humming along with the radio. Only one question loomed at the forefront of thought. Would Dalton tell Clova about them? Would they tell her together? They would have to tell her *something*. How could they continue to see each other if they didn't?

She reached the ranch before sundown, coming to a stop in her usual place in front of her egg-washing room. As she shoved the Silverado into park, Dalton came out of the barn stalking toward her in his usual get-out-of-my-way gait. He had on work clothing, a chambray shirt and jeans and boots. Even from the front seat of her pickup, she could see that his hair curled at his collar. He looked rowdy and sexy and downright delectable. An awareness of his maleness snaked through her and she wondered if the sight of him would always affect her that way. She opened the pickup door and turned to scoot out.

"I'm going back to LA in a few days," he said, his

voice brittle as glass. No hello, no kiss. Her heart began to race.

His face was a thundercloud, his eyes an onyx stone. She still didn't know him well enough to anticipate his moods and behavior, but the bubble of happiness she had enjoyed all day popped. She stayed where her feet hit the ground behind her pickup door and drew a calming breath. "Oh?"

His fists jammed against his belt. "I'm giving you notice. You need to do something with those chickens. I'm putting an oil well down over there." He pointed a finger toward the chicken yard. "It's gonna be just about where that donkey shack is. That fence will be relocated in the next two or three weeks. You've got that much time."

Her mind reeled, leaving her speechless. "Uh . . . well—"

"This ranch is broke. I'm hoping to see enough money to pay it out of debt. I've already hired a drilling contractor. I'm leaving it up to him to get the fence moved where he thinks it should be. I'm going back to LA, and I don't know when I'll be back."

"But—but . . . That—that . . ." Dear God, she was breathless and stammering. She stiffened her spine. "That won't leave much room for my hens."

"Take it up with my mother. She's the one you dealt with in the first place." He looked at his watch. "I've got to go." He gave her his back, stalked toward the old work truck, climbed into it and drove away in a cloud of caliche dust.

She stood there unmoving for long seconds as her thoughts tried to jell. Why had he picked a fight with her? Why hadn't he given her some kind of explanation? Or plainly asked her in a simple conversation to move the chickens?

She had already been a victim of his ire when they

first met. She knew he pulled no punches in a skirmish. She also knew he had learned to fight for survival as a child. He might have the strength of will and character she wanted in a companion and lover, but those traits also meant he viewed every battle as one to win. Tears rushed to her eyes, but she blinked them back and headed for the house.

Inside she found Clova sniffling in the kitchen. She always looked older than her years, but today she looked frail, washed out and ancient. "Clova, what's happened? I hope someone can tell me what's going on."

"It's a long story, Joanna." She shook her head, blew her nose and poured a cup of coffee. "You want some coffee?"

"No." Joanna's mouth had gone dry. She didn't think she could swallow.

Clova carried her cup to the dining table and eased to the seat, looking out the dining room window. "When Dalton was a boy, a wildcatter come in here and leased up our land for drillin'. He said he hit a dry hole, but Earl thought he was lyin'. Earl always said they found oil. Looks like Earl must've been right."

Joanna swallowed finally, her dry throat making a click in her ears. "How did he know?"

"He saw oil circulatin' out on the pits while they was drillin'. But the driller never said nothin' about it. Earl called him a crook and they got into it. The driller abandoned the well and covered it over."

Joanna had lived around the oil industry her whole life. She knew roughly what Clova had said. She also knew a lot of crooked shenanigans took place in the oil business. Still stunned by Dalton's ruthless words, she could find no sympathy for Clova's problems. "Dalton said he's hired someone to put a well where the donkey shed is?"

"Knowin' Dalton, if that's what he said, that's what he means."

At hearing Dalton's statement in Clova's words, Joanna's first reaction was panic. "Is this a new plan? I mean, how long has he been planning this?"

"I don't know. I guess he was waitin' for me to get out o' the hospital to talk to me about it."

Joanna inhaled a great breath. He had seduced her, had made love to her. They had touched each other in the most intimate of ways, but *he* hadn't really been touched at all. He didn't care enough to discuss his plans, even when they affected her. She fought to keep from bursting into sobs. "I just saw him outside. He said soon."

"He's going back to California quick as he can. Some woman out there called him and wants him to come back. He said he's already been here too long."

Candace. The so-called *friend*. "I see."

Clova's eyes came back to hers. "I hate to tell you this, hon, but we're gonna have to figure out somethin' 'bout your chickens. I guess Dalton's plans are gonna mess up your little operation. I had to sign a lease for him, Joanna. He's my son."

The moment of truth Joanna had expected had arrived. While hurt that Clova stood with Dalton against her, she wasn't surprised. As the woman said, Dalton was her son. "Of course you did. I understand. I—I just wish someone would have told me sooner."

"He seems like he's just as hardheaded now as when he was a kid. When he gets his mind set on somethin', there's no changin' it."

Multiple problems began to zoom through Joanna's mind so quickly, she couldn't grab on to even one of them and concentrate on it. But finally her survival instinct, on its own, began to plan. *Time for the hens to go,* it told her. *Figure out where you can sell them.*

Find out where you can get the most money for the used equipment.

"I told him I was gonna give you some land. And I still intend to. You can move your chicken yard a little ways on back behind where it is now."

No fencing. No water. No highway frontage. As tears lumped in her throat, she ducked her chin and shook her head. "That's too far from the windmill, Clova. Getting clean water to the hens would be too hard."

"I guess you could run a pipe—"

She shook her head again. "Even if I had the money for that, doing it doesn't make sense. You know the whole operation is marginal."

"Then maybe we can get Dalton to pay for it. We can get one of those ditch-diggin' machines in here and—"

"No," she managed to choke out without breaking down. She shook her head yet again. If she indeed decided to run a pipe from the windmill to a new chicken yard, she would dig a trench with a spoon before she would ask or expect Dalton Parker to pay for it.

"I feel terrible about it, Joanna."

She cleared her throat and blinked back the wetness in her eyes. "I'm not blaming you, Clova. Listen, I need to think. I'm going back to town, okay?"

"That's fine, hon. I know this makes a bad problem for you. I'm just so sorry."

Joanna looked around for her purse, then noticed it still hanging on her shoulder. She started for the front door but remembered that just this morning, Clova had come home from her stay in the hospital. "Oh. How are you feeling, Clova?"

"I'm all right. Got a sack full o' pills to take. Gotta go back and forth to the hospital to take breathin' treatments. I got to try to take better care o' m'self."

Joanna nodded, but her mind was switching gears. Suddenly all she could think of was getting home and dealing with her own crisis. "I'll, uh, check on you later, okay?"

He'll call and explain, Joanna told herself all the way back to town. She repeated it like a mantra half a dozen times, at the same time gulping down the tears that kept filling her eyes and throat. She had to get control of herself. She couldn't risk bawling like a teenager and running into someone she knew.

He'll call and explain, she told herself again as she closed her garage door and entered her home. Inside, she checked both of her telephones to be sure neither was accidentally off the hook. She changed into sweats, poured a Diet Coke over ice and seated herself in front of the TV.

At last the phone warbled. She sprang to her feet and streaked toward the kitchen phone. On the way, she struck a chair leg with her bare toe and pain shot all the way from her foot to her head. Hobbling, she grabbed up the receiver at the beginning of the fifth warble. "Hello," she barked.

"Joanna?"

Shit. "Hi, Shari. What's up?"

"Did I interrupt something?"

"No, no. I was sort of dozing."

Shari laughed. "I took a nap myself. Now that I'm thirty-six, I think I'm gonna have to give up late nights."

"You must have a terrible hangover."

"Oh, my God. All day, I've felt like somebody hit me with a hammer."

"Hmm, did you go to work today?" Joanna said. She had to be casual and friendly to her best friend, but she hoped this wouldn't be one of Shari's marathon conversations.

"I had to. My boss knew I was going out last night. He would have killed me if I hadn't showed up. Listen, I saw you dancing a lot with Dalton."

A lump knotted in Joanna's throat. "Hm. He was fun to dance with."

"He looks like he'd be fun to do more than that with. He is *so* hot. He was the only guy there not wearing Wranglers, but hey, he looks just fine in Levi's."

"Yeah, well, I didn't notice."

"You two make a good couple. Some of us at the table talked about it. When y'all were out there waltzing? You looked like you'd been dancing together all your lives."

Joanna squeezed her eyes shut, fighting back more tears. "Well, you know I like to waltz."

"All the gals at the table kept envying you."

"Yeah. Listen, Shari, I'm in the middle of some, uh, bookkeeping. Did you need something?"

"You said you were napping. What's going on, Joanna?"

"Nothing," Joanna snapped. "I dozed off, but I've got to get at this bookkeeping."

"Good grief, you don't have to bite my head off. I just wanted to know how it went with him."

Joanna sighed. "I'm sorry, Shari. Too much on my mind, I guess. It didn't go. It was just dancing."

"That's too bad. He's single. You're single. Y'all are about the same age."

A dull ache began to grow in Joanna's chest. "He's on his way back to California."

"I was just thinking. Before he goes home, why don't we get Jay to invite him and let's all go to dinner some night at Sylvia's? It'd really be fun to talk to him. Jay said he's done some really cool stuff."

"I don't want to do that, Shari. I don't have time and I don't enjoy his company that much."

Big sigh coming through the receiver. "Joanna, you beat all. It's just dinner, forgodsake. Nobody wants to marry you off to him. I'd like to hear what he has to say."

"Then why don't you and Jay just invite him over to

your house or something? I've really got to go. I stubbed my toe getting to the phone and it's bleeding."

"Uh-oh. Sorry, girlfriend."

They disconnected and Joanna thought of Clova's phone number. By now, Dalton would surely be at home. Should she call and ask him if he was feeling better? Ask him if she could do something to help him? Ask him if he needed a dry shoulder?

Don't be dumb, her pride told her. *He treated you like something he picked up in the barnyard on the sole of his boot.*

She limped back to her chair, braced her heel on the edge of the seat and studied her injured toe. It was agonizingly painful and already turning purple. "Shit," she muttered wondering if she would be able to wear a shoe. The bruise on her forehead was just now going away.

All at once she remembered, not only had she not gathered the evening's eggs herself, she hadn't made arrangements with Alicia to do it, either. If an ambitious skunk or a weasel found his way into the chicken yard, half the eggs could well be gone by morning. Her shoulders sagged. Lord, she was a mess.

But a part of her brain that had been screaming for attention but been ignored for months now expressed relief that she might soon be out of the egg business.

Dalton leaned back and closed his eyes as the jumbo jet on its way to Los Angeles lifted off the ground. An early-morning flight was the only one he was able to book a seat on. He had gotten little sleep again. Midnight had come and gone before he'd gotten packed and ready to depart. Then his mother had driven him to the airport early.

Now, as he dozed, just like last night for the few hours he had been in bed, Joanna Walsh filled his mind. Last night, after Mom told him she didn't gather

her eggs, he had gathered them for her, all the while berating himself for being a horse's ass. He might have strong emotions about his mother's land gift and Joanna's role in it, but something inside him wouldn't be so despicable as to cost her the evening's eggs.

This morning, now that he had cooled off, he wished he had never met Joanna Walsh, period. What had he been thinking, pushing sex with her?

She was nothing like the women he typically hooked up with, women who required no commitment. She didn't fit that profile on any level. She fell into the category who always got *feelings* mixed up with a good time, who always wanted *relationships*. Women like Joanna were why he usually kept his sexual encounters on the casual side.

He had turned weak with her, let his guard down and violated most of his own rules. Hell, he had even allowed himself to screw without protection. Not that he worried about catching something, but he had shown little regard for the pregnancy possibility, either. *Dumb, dumb, dumb*.

Now that the land deal had been revealed, the survival instinct that had always ruled his life wouldn't allow him to trust her. How could he when she withheld facts from him? She could have told him his mom had promised her land. Why hadn't she? He wouldn't even have known she used the chicken yard for free if his mother hadn't told him.

Besides that, just knowing her and being with her held out a false hope for the future that really had no more place in his life than all that crap about feelings and relationships.

He wasn't a fit partner for any woman, anyway. Christ, he could be on a plane tomorrow headed somewhere for some unknown length of time. No woman had ever understood that or been willing to tolerate it. Recently he might have thought about changing that, but he hadn't thought about it much. Damn sure not enough to actually *do* something about it.

And he wasn't willing to think about it now, either.

He had always gotten his thrills from the excitement and adventure of stepping into the unknown. It had been a mistake to let Joanna inspire him to believe something else might be possible.

Chapter 27

One month later . . .

Dalton sat on the end of a folding lounge chair beside his pool, saying good-bye to the residence he had called home for fifteen years, a tract house that had been built in the sixties. Buyers were at the title company signing closing papers.

He had returned from Texas with no plan to sell the house, but during the years he had owned it, he had occasionally thought of selling it when the time was right. With a real estate agent banging on his door with an offer no man in his right mind would refuse, the time suddenly became right. He had sold the place for a staggering amount of money to buyers who had no interest in the house but loved the pool.

Strangely, he had no regrets. He had been stewing over his future for more than a year. In his chaotic life, owning a house had represented order, but he had never really called Los Angeles "home" in the literal sense. He liked the Southern California climate for sure, and he had taken advantage of and enjoyed the lifestyle of being able to do just damn near anything he wanted to without criticism or judgment. He liked the convenience of flying from the West Coast. Other than all of that, LA had been mostly a place to stash his stuff.

But his urge to move on came from more than restlessness over what corner he would turn next. He wanted something different from anything he had ever desired before. It had taken him a couple of weeks to figure it out, but now he knew. He wanted to return to his roots. He wanted a steady woman to come home to. Finding himself homeless prompted him to make a decision he might have delayed otherwise.

Everything he owned that was worth keeping was in a moving van on its way to a storage facility in Lubbock, Texas. Everything else had been sold or trashed. He had even sold his old truck. He would get something new when he got himself settled, but until then, the Lazy P's ranch truck would work just fine.

He had wrapped up his book and shipped it to his publisher.

By phone, he had helped his mother hire a crew of cowboys who had rounded up the yearlings and shipped them to the sale.

His little brother had returned to the ranch. He was on crutches, but at least he wasn't in a wheelchair as everyone had first feared he would be. The day would come when he would be able to sit a horse again and do a limited day's work. He faced a DUI charge. The deposition was pending, but everyone was hoping for the best.

Mandy Ferguson had gone to visit him and taken their daughter to see him a couple of times in the rehabilitation hospital. Lane believed they could have a future together as a family. Dalton was pleased his meddling had paid off. But that wasn't the best part of Lane's news. Mandy had been working on her parents, and all of them were inching toward a relationship.

Dalton had talked to his mother daily. Her physical and mental health were better. She had sounded overjoyed when he laid out his plans to return to Hatlow for good. Oh, he wasn't giving up photography. He had spent too much time and energy building his reputation in the profession to just throw it to the wind. But he could work from Hatlow with more peace of mind.

Skeeter Vance had already built a road, and a bulldozer was working on a pad for the oil-well site.

Everyone awaited Dalton's return to Hatlow.

The only person he hadn't talked to was Joanna, and he doubted *she* was waiting. If she was, she might have that shotgun loaded.

His mother had told him the chickens had been sold to a pet food outfit, all except for a few Joanna had kept as pets. Hearing that she had gotten rid of them altogether had shocked Dalton. An overwhelming guilt gripped him every time he thought of her doing that. He had figured she would just move the friggin' birds to another place on the ranch.

His mom still had the two donkeys. She liked them. She had decided to keep *them* as pets.

He reached into his pocket and pulled out a tiny velvet box. Inside it was a diamond ring that had cost him more than he would have ever imagined spending on such a thing. He only hoped he didn't have to return it. Bringing it all the way back to a jeweler in Southern California wasn't a trip he would relish. He could have waited to buy a ring in Texas, but he bought it in LA because he needed it for incentive to do what, deep down, he knew he wanted to. Buying it might have been a gamble. But hey, he was a gambling man.

Now that his head had cleared and he had thought through everything that had happened in Texas, he realized that his mother had been the one who was the real manipulator in the relationship between her and Joanna Walsh. Mom had needed and wanted a companion.

Not that you'd know, Mr. Parker, but your mother is a lonely woman.

Joanna had told him, but he had refused to listen. He had never taken the time to consider that his mother was an aging widow in need of friendship. To add to his other guilt, he felt a need to make up with her for ignoring her after Earl Cherry's death.

Of the many words that had passed between him and Joanna Walsh, two sentences stood out in his mind and he had revisited them often in the past month: *You can trust your heart with me, Dalton. I'd never hurt you.*

He believed those words. He believed he and Joanna had a future. But he knew he had hurt her, knew he deserved her loathing after the way he stormed out of Hatlow with no explanation or obvious reason. He had faith she would forgive him. A woman with as much heart as Joanna had wouldn't give up on a hardhead like him.

Joanna sat at her desk studying a catalog of beauty supplies. Her life had calmed so much, it was boring. No trips twice daily to the Parker ranch. No worry about chicken diseases and chicken predators. No daylong trips to Lubbock and Amarillo delivering eggs. Yee-ha. Her monthly gasoline bill had been reduced to double digits.

Closing down the egg business had been costly. She had gotten a pittance from the sale of the hens and had applied every penny of it against the balance she owed on her house. The sad part was that the lump-sum payment had made only a small dent. Little by little, she was getting rid of the egg-processing equipment on eBay. Her mortgage money had gone to buy the equipment, so as she sold those items, that money, too, was being applied to the balance against her house.

All in all, she didn't miss the chickens. Losing the egg business had been painful at first, but she should have gotten out of it before Dalton Parker ever put in an appearance. In reality, he had done her a favor. If he hadn't forced the issue, she might never have faced the losing proposition in which she was engaged or had the nerve to shut it down.

She hadn't forgotten Dalton by any means, but she was ready to move on. He had done something for her she hadn't expected. He had made her feel like a woman again. She had even told Shari and various matchmakers who frequented the beauty salon that she was open to new male acquaintances, something she hadn't done in years. In her limited experience in the battle of the sexes, she had found that one way to wash a man out of her hair was to find another one.

Shari had nagged her unmercifully for an explanation of what had happened between her and Dalton, but Joanna wasn't sure herself. She knew only that though she had spent a scant amount of time with him, she *knew* him. She didn't know where it had come from—perhaps from her long friendship with Clova and listening to her talk about him, perhaps from the gossip that floated around Hatlow like air, perhaps from her own intuition. And knowing him, she felt his pain and she loved him. But that didn't mean she would spend the future pining for him.

She didn't want to talk to Shari, or anyone, about him. The feelings were too private. What she had shared with him might have been brief, but it would go with her to her grave.

The front door chimed and she looked up. With the morning sunlight shining against the front door, she could see only silhouettes of customers entering. Now she saw the outline of a male figure that seemed familiar.

But it couldn't be.

Nope, not possible.

Seconds later, Dalton Parker was standing in her doorway, leaning a shoulder against the doorjamb.

Blood began to swish inside her ears, but she forced herself to keep her composure. "Wh-what are you doing here? I thought you'd left."

"Can we go somewhere and talk?"

"Uh—"

"I've got about a hundred things to say."

It would take at least a hundred, Joanna thought, her heart pounding. He looked beautiful, wearing jeans and boots and a red T-shirt. He had a long round tube tucked under his arm.

"This is my office. I guess you can say what you need to."

He brought the tube from under his arm, his tanned biceps working as he flipped the cap off the end and pulled out a long, rolled document. "I brought you something."

She sat in deafening silence while he unrolled the document and let it hang in front of him. It was a poster that looked to be eighteen by twenty-four inches, an excellent photograph of a shirtless, finely honed male torso lying on its side, covered by fuzzy yellow baby chicks. Chicks all over it as if they were attached—standing on the shoulder, standing on the ribs, two babies nestled in a big hand. She recognized the torso immediately. The American eagle tattoo on the left shoulder gave away the identity. She gave him the squint-eye. "That's you. And those are baby chickens."

"Mom told me you got rid of your chickens. This is fifty to start over with. She said you started with fifty. I figured I'd help you start over."

Her jaw dropped.

"I'll get you more. As many as you want."

She felt her eyes widen, but she closed her mouth. "Dalton, listen—"

"I'll help you build a new place for them. Mom wants to give you that ten acres where she's had her garden. She said you were worried about water. There's water there." He proceeded to roll the document back into a tight roll and slip in back into the tube.

"I brought you something else." His hand shoved into his jeans pocket and came out holding a tiny navy blue velvet box.

Her heart began to flutter and skip beats. He gripped her chair arms and turned her to face him, then sank to one knee, opened the box and thrust it to her. Speechless, she blinked at an incredible ring—a center stone of at least four carats set off by baguettes on either side. She looked up at him and, overwhelmed by emotion, broke into tears.

A wary expression came onto his face. "Are you crying because you're glad? Or mad?"

Shaking her head, she sniffled. "You nearly destroyed me, Dalton. This last month has been—"

"I know. I did it wrong. I had to sort it out in my head, Joanna. I guess I had to get away from here to do it. I know it's a piss-poor excuse, but—"

"Dalton, listen . . ."

"Do you want me to grovel? I'm groveling."

She sniffed. "You owe me groveling, big time."

"I know. I'm a shit-heel. But I'm honest, Joanna. You know I'm honest. And I'll kill every rattlesnake that comes near you. I'll look out for you from now on, Joanna. And I'll be loyal."

She looked at him, blinking, her eyelashes wet with tears. She was sure her mascara was running down her face.

He pried the ring from its slot in the box and picked up her left hand, but it was trembling so badly he had to capture her finger to slip the ring onto it. "My God," he said, looking up at her with rounded eyes. "It fits. That's an omen."

As was typical of him, in a matter of seconds, he had taken control of the situation and refused to allow her to say no. A laugh burst through her tears.

"Oh, Joanna, don't give up on me." He leaned toward her and cupped her jaw with his big palm. As his lips covered her face with kisses, his opposite hand clasped her arm, dragging her out of her chair until she knelt on the floor with him. His arms wrapped all the way around her. "Don't give up on me," he said again, and they kissed and kissed. Finally his mouth pulled away from hers and he was grinning like a monkey. "I know you've figured it out by now. I'm back. For good. I need a place to stay."

"Clova won't let you stay at the ranch?"

She'd had only a couple of conversations with Clova since disposing of the chicken business. She hadn't been able to make herself even ask about Dalton.

"That ranch house isn't really home to me. I'm looking for a place with a good bed."

Her heart was so full, she thought it might explode. Another spate of tears spilled from her eyes as she hugged him with all her might. "I don't know. I might never get over hating you."

"I don't blame you. But I still need a place to stay. I still need a home. Will you take me in for the time being, Joanna? Will you go with me? Just 'til you get over hating me?"

"Go with you where?"

"Into the future. Wherever it goes. I figure we can build a house toward the back of the Lazy P, along the rim of the canyon. I can put a little studio separate from the house where I can work and I can help Mom and Lane take care of things. There's a well back there with good water and we could watch the sun set over the canyon for the rest of our lives."

He was insane. Outrageous. Complicated. Challenging. But he was also exciting and smart and interesting, and she believed in him as she had believed in no other man. There was nothing he couldn't do.

They got to their feet together. Nothing, but nothing, could make her let go of him. She would never let go of him again for as long as she lived. She picked up her purse, smiling through her tears. "I'd follow a man anywhere who promises to save me from snakes."

Applause broke out in the retail store. Joanna hadn't even been aware that everyone in the beauty shop had come out and witnessed Dalton Parker's sweet return.

They left Joanna's Salon & Supplies together. Her heart would scarcely contain the utter joy she felt. There were many blanks that needed filling in, but they had the rest of their lives to do it.

Jay Huddleston's words the night of Shari's birthday party came back to her: *He always did what he wanted to. It was one of the things that made him different from the rest of us.*

She knew this much. Dalton Parker had always been and still was a man who battled life every day to follow his own path. He didn't need a woman in his life. He could go on without Joanna Walsh. But he had come back for her. Not because he had to have her, but because he *wanted* her. And that was the essence of who he was. It was enough.

Her immediate problem now was how to tell him she really didn't want any more chickens.

ALSO AVAILABLE

Rusty Joplin may be back in Salvation,
elected to one of the most powerful
positions in the county, but he isn't about
to let the woman who once cost him
everything get under his skin again.
At least not while there's a cold-blooded
killer on the loose.

**Available wherever books are sold
or at penguin.com**

ALSO AVAILABLE

Though purchasing a remote town in West
Texas on eBay sounds crazy, real-estate
developer Terry Ledger knows a good deal
when he sees it. Now he must curry favor
with the town's unofficial leader, the feisty
Marisa Rutherford, who's fiercely guarding her
hometown—and her recently broken heart.
With different plans for the town's future,
they find themselves agreeing on one thing:
an undeniable attraction.

ALSO AVAILABLE

In this sexy contemporary romance,
the author of *The Love of a Stranger* takes
readers home to a little town in Idaho,
where old flames reignite.

ALSO AVAILABLE FROM ANNA JEFFREY:
THE LOVE OF A COWBOY

**Available wherever books are sold
or at penguin.com**

Penguin Group (USA) Online

What will you be reading tomorrow?

Tom Clancy, Patricia Cornwell, W.E.B. Griffin,
Nora Roberts, William Gibson, Robin Cook,
Brian Jacques, Catherine Coulter, Stephen King,
Dean Koontz, Ken Follett, Clive Cussler,
Eric Jerome Dickey, John Sandford,
Terry McMillan, Sue Monk Kidd, Amy Tan,
John Berendt…

You'll find them all at
penguin.com

*Read excerpts and newsletters,
find tour schedules and reading group guides,
and enter contests.*

Subscribe to Penguin Group (USA) newsletters
and get an exclusive inside look
at exciting new titles and the authors you love
long before everyone else does.

PENGUIN GROUP (USA)
us.penguingroup.com

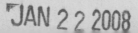